Daughter *of* Sorrow

ABIGAIL SILVER

The Redeeming Grace Trilogy

Book Three

ISBN-13: 978-1-7373558-4-7

Cover art and illustrations by: Abigail Silver

Edited by: Harlow Kelly

Printed in the United States of America

Books in This Series

I.

Child of Awareness

II.
Visions of Fire

III.
Daughter of Sorrow

For More Usuriel Content

For free short stories, character art, and latest updates, visit us at https://abigailsilverstories.wordpress.com/

DEDICATION

This book is for my son, Henry

Thank you for pushing and inspiring me to be a better person every day and reminding me of the joy that is pretend.

Content Advisory

This is a work of fiction intended for mature audiences.

This novel contains mature language and adult situations including sexuality, violence, drug use, self-harm, and child neglect that may be disturbing to some readers.

Reader discretion is advised.

ABIGAIL SILVER

Contents

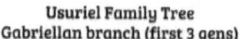

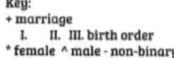

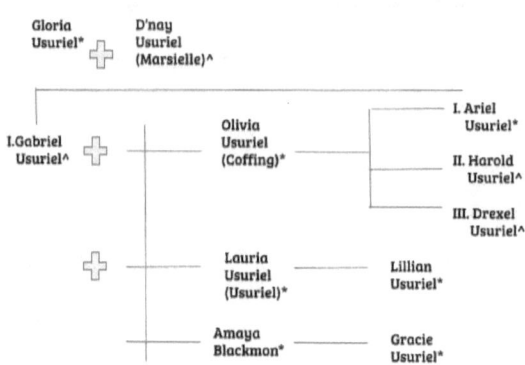

Usuriel Family Tree
Gabriellan branch (first 3 gens)

Key:
+ marriage
I.   II.   III. birth order
* female ^ male - non-binary

Gloria Usuriel* + D'nay Usuriel (Marsielle)^

I.Gabriel Usuriel^ + Olivia Usuriel (Coffing)*
- I. Ariel Usuriel*
- II. Harold Usuriel^
- III. Drexel Usuriel^

+ Lauria Usuriel (Usuriel)* ——— Lillian Usuriel*

Amaya Blackmon* ——— Gracie Usuriel*

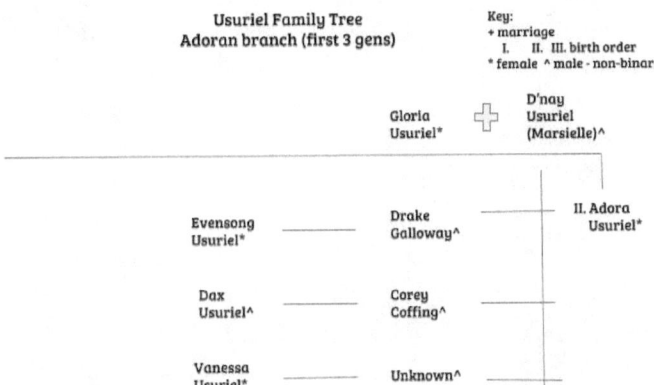

Usuriel Family Tree
Adoran branch (first 3 gens)

Key:
+ marriage
I.   II. III. birth order
* female ^ male - non-binary

Gloria
Usuriel*   +   D'nay
                   Usuriel
                   (Marsielle)^

Evensong   Drake   II. Adora
Usuriel*   Galloway^   Usuriel*

Dax   Corey
Usuriel^   Coffing^

Vanessa   Unknown^
Usuriel*

Prelude

Let me say, before anything else, that I do love my father. Even in our darkest moments, he was still the person who tucked me in as a child. I ran to him when I thought I was losing my mind, and he embraced me without hesitation—blood, tears, and all. No matter what else he is, Gabriel is my dad. I adored him from the moment I saw him walking up the concrete steps to take me away from that dreadful group home.

So how have we ended here: in betrayal and the burning of my whole world?

I want to put it on Vanessa and Evan. It's where Liam wants me to lay the blame, and certainly they have their share. That's not the whole story, though. Our ending would have been different without them, but I wasn't an innocent bystander.

Perhaps my flames are just too strong. I'd like to say they overwhelmed my sense, but that's not completely true. I've never lost control to my fire.

No, I made a choice. In fact, I made it several times, even with my best friends begging me to see reason.

Stupid. So, so stupid.

So what's the real reason we're nearing the edge of the abyss? I don't have one—not one that makes sense, anyway. The best I can do is describe how it happened, and hope that is close enough to the truth.

Chapter 1

Home

I drifted through the familiar rooms of Angelus Quietum. My father's house hadn't changed much in the thirteen years I'd known it. The leather couch, with its plush blankets and spill of comfortable pillows, still beckoned like an old friend. Dad's armchair crouched by the fireplace, facing the flames as it had since James came to stay with us.

A smile tried to lift my trauma-frozen lips at the thought of my blond friend. How many brushed elbows, smoldering glances, and tender words had this room witnessed between us? Enough to break my heart when he chose diplomacy over me.

I hugged myself tightly, a chill in my core. I wandered to the dining room picture window, looking out over Lake Angelus. The broad-winged birds soared over the lake's glittering surface, occasionally dipping close to its water and pulling up a wriggling fish. My father used to watch them for hours when I was a child; back before he took to watching the fire with a bottle at his side.

Maybe things would get better for Gabriel after our conversations the last two days. I tried to hang on to that hope, but my chest felt too heavy to rise with it. The weight of Grayson's death sat in the pit of my stomach like lead.

"Gracie?"

My father entered the room, his dark, wavy hair pulled back in its usual, functional ponytail. Something about him was different, though. Cleaner, perhaps? I narrowed my eyes at Gabriel's finely-chiseled features. He'd shaved this morning; no scruff of dark stubble marred the sharp angle of his jaw. His clothes were pressed, the white folds of his shirt flawless above his customary black slacks. The biggest change, however, was in the way he held himself—head up, back erect, midnight-blue eyes meeting my gaze with a confidence I hadn't seen in years.

"Hi, Dad," I said, finally managing a smile in answer to his.

"Come on." He put an arm around my shoulders and led me towards the kitchen. "Let's make breakfast. I have a list of chores as long as my arm piling up without you around. Feeling up to helping me with a few today?"

"Sure," I agreed, some tension in my shoulders relaxing at the thought of staying busy around the farm.

"How's your neck?" Dad asked while we puttered about the kitchen, scrambling eggs and pouring out cereal and milk.

I fingered the bandage gently. The bite underneath it was hardly sore anymore. The lead in my stomach gained a few kilos at the thought of it healing. Once it faded from my skin, there would be nothing left to show that Grayson had ever existed.

"It's still there," I murmured, setting my bowl on the table. "I didn't hallucinate the whole thing."

"I never said you did." Gabriel stirred the eggs with a spatula.

I sat and took a bite of cereal. I hardly tasted it. "Sometimes it almost seems like a dream."

"Understandable." Dad put a plate of eggs next to my elbow, then sat down with his own helping. "After all, you only met him that night."

"Yeah," I muttered, poking at my bowl. I didn't think I could swallow with my throat this dry.

"Gracie," Dad said gently. "I know I've said this before, but there was no way for you to know your blood might be poisonous. You even warned him about being untasted ahead of time. This really isn't your fault."

I forced a bite of cereal into my mouth to avoid answering. We ate in silence. Before Dad could start up again, I stood and cleared my dishes.

"Grace..." Gabriel came up behind me with his plate.

"No, Dad," I cut him off with a wave of one hand. "We've been over this a dozen times. I know it wasn't my fault, but it feels that way, and nothing we say is going to change that. I don't want to talk about it anymore."

"Okay," Dad agreed, setting his plate into the sink. "Well, then, why don't you tell me about the Overwatch? How have things been going with Vanessa?"

The weight in my stomach sank deeper into my gut. "Seriously? You never want to talk about the OW."

He jabbed a thumb in the direction of the living room. "I finally hung your uniform portrait, didn't I?"

I nodded slowly. He'd objected so hard when I joined the supernatural police force, it was kind of a relief that he was willing to mention my membership in the organization he'd helped found. My last discussion with my cousin, Vanessa, however, made me wish I'd listened to him in the first place.

"Yeah," I allowed. "I guess you did."

"So how is my niece?" he asked, pulling on his fleece jacket and putting a hand to the door plate. I tossed on a ratty old vest that hung by the door before following him to the back deck.

Trying to convince me to kill you, I thought. Aloud, I said, "Her usual one-eyed self."

I shivered. It was chillier out than I expected; the wind must have shifted down from the mountains overnight. I wished I had my father's ability to teleport a hat or scarf to my hand.

"Don't worry," Dad said, "our task today will keep you warm enough. How do you feel about clearing a new riding trail over to the Homestead?"

"Chronurea Valley?" My grandparents lived in the next community over, nestled on the southern bank of Lake Angelus. Since it was the first place the Usuriel family settled, the Family often called it the Homestead. "We've never had a trail out that far."

"I've always valued my privacy." Gabriel strode towards the barn with his characteristic, liquid gait. I matched it easily. "But with Illessia coming, I thought it might be nice for us to have access that doesn't require teleportation. After all, not everyone has that particular skill set."

"I can fly now, you know," I pointed out as we took down the tack and headed towards Aubrie and Charcoal's stalls.

"Yes, I heard." He opened Aubrie's stall and greeted the mare with an apple he plucked from the thin air to his left. "Jillian was the one who came up with that innovative application of pyrokinesis, isn't she?"

"Yeah. Though, she's braver than I am. If I had to use a spark to get my flames going, I'm not sure I'd have the courage to be that far off the ground."

I reached into the vest's pocket for the pouch of sugar cubes I kept there for Charcoal. They were right where I left them on my last visit, and I offered one to my gray stallion. He accepted it with a friendly whicker.

"Well, even if you can travel by air now, there's still your grandfather to think about. And we won't know what Illeesia's powers are until she's six or seven," Gabriel said through the gap window between the two box stalls. "Unless she takes after her sister, of course. We knew Adora was a three-T by the time she was two. But, according to my mother, that was incredibly rare, even for a second-gen."

I froze at his mention of Adora. Growing up, he'd hardly ever said his late sister's name. My prophetic dreams and experiments with time travel had introduced me to my unbalanced, androgynous aunt over the years, but it wasn't until Grayson's death shed light on my psi's temporal connection this week that I admitted as much to my father. Hearing him mention her so freely sent a pang through my chest. I should have told him the truth long ago.

"What was she like?" I asked, settling Charcoal's bit in his mouth and fastening his chin strap. "As a child, I mean. I've dreamed of her death often enough, but I never saw her as a little girl."

Dad's movements paused at my mention of Adora's death. Even though she'd gone off the rails and was obviously a danger to Usuriels and mortals alike, Dad still beat himself up for his role in her execution. He'd never said as much, but I knew it was why he quit the Overwatch.

"She was strange from the beginning," Dad admitted, clearing his throat. "Looking back on it now, I can admit that, though, at the time, we all spun it to make her seem precocious rather than terrifying."

"Terrifying?"

"Well, like I said, her powers came in early." Dad grunted, probably tightening Aubrie's girth. "But your grandmother was able to deal with those for the most part. The scary part was the way she acted. Adora rarely laughed or played like other children, and she understood far more than a toddler should. Like she skipped whole stages of mental development."

"Strange," I agreed. I settled Charcoal's saddle carefully on his back. I knew the stallion hated to have his hair pinched under the blanket.

"At the time, the only other Anori individual I knew well was my mother," Dad said. The door hinge squeaked as he opened it to lead Aubrie out into the hall. "I had no idea that this was unusual behavior for an immortal child, just my parents' word that I hadn't been that way."

"The only one?" I paused in tightening Charcoal's girth and the stallion stomped a foot to bring my attention back to the task. I quickly finished cinching it and grabbed his reins. "I always forget Adora was born on the *Inspiration*. But you were born on Earth. Didn't you meet other immortals before the generation ship left for Cybele?"

"Well, a few of my dad's kind were friendly with us." Gabriel pushed the door to the barn open with an absent telekinetic thought. Bright blue sky and scudding cotton clouds greeted us. I followed him into the warm sunshine. The chill wind had calmed down, and I was comfortable in my vest.

"You mean vampires?"

Dad inclined his head in confirmation, then put his foot into a stirrup and launched himself astride Aubrie's chestnut back. I did the same and perched atop Charcoal in one easy movement. The horses' height difference was just enough that my father and I were eye-to-eye when sitting on their backs. With the gentle nudge of a knee, Gabriel guided the mare towards our southern trail.

"Yes, there was quite a community of them there on Earth. Dad tried to convince a few of them to come along with us, but I think they were afraid of the limited food supply. There's only so many hosts on a tiny ship, floating in the middle of dead space."

I shivered at what the colonists had braved over two hundred years ago to bring us to this world. "I think all of you were incredibly brave to risk it."

Dad gave a little huff of ambivalence. "It was better than staying there, waiting for the other immortals to catch up with us."

I narrowed my eyes at him. This conversation was already miraculous from my tight-lipped father. I didn't want to push so hard that he stopped talking all together, but he'd been so much more relaxed since our conversation after Grayson's death. I might never get a chance to satisfy my burning curiosity again, especially if something knocked him out of this chatty mood.

"Other immortals? You mean like the ones you called demons in the Anori histories?"

"Yeah." His voice was so soft it was hard to hear him above the hoof beats. "Those."

We rode in silence, the trees passing on either side as we penetrated the terraformed forest. Some of the trunks were large enough around that I couldn't have held them in the circle of my arms. I didn't spot any Death's Head fungus at their bases; here and there were patches of Cambria mushrooms Dad was trying to coax to full size. Though they'd been as big as houses when the colonists arrived, few of the Cambria had survived the terraforming efforts. None of these white-and-brown-polka-dotted fungal blooms were taller than my knee.

"Have you seen Grandma Gloria lately?" I asked, trying to re-engage our conversation.

"Oh yes." Gabriel's chuckle reassured me that he hadn't taken offense at my line of questioning. "Taking the whole 'glowing with pregnancy' thing to a new level, as usual."

I joined his quiet laughter at our standard joke. The Usuriel matriarch was the oldest and most powerful individual on the planet. Though it had been a few months since she and Grandpa D'nay announced her pregnancy, it was still hard to wrap my mind around. Teasing about it with Dad made the arrival of the first second-generation Usuriel in over two centuries a little less intimidating.

"I'm glad she's doing well," I said, guiding Charcoal through a blackened area of underbrush. Dad must have done some Death's Head mitigation out here recently.

"This way," Dad called, gesturing to a gap in the trees. I reined in Charcoal to follow Aubrie through the newly cut path. We emerged through the stand of trees and into a large clearing. The left side still had scorch marks from Dad's clearing, but to the right were waving grasses covering a rolling hillside. Two larger trees stood in the center of the field, their branches reaching up to the golden light above.

"Wow, this is beautiful." I dismounted Charcoal and walked towards the closer tree. A collection of birds called each other a warning before taking off from its branches in a flurry of caws and feathers.

Dad smiled and tilted his head back to watch them, one hand shading his eyes. "Come on, let's tether the horses here. They can graze while we keep cutting that way. It should only be half a mile to Mom's walking paths near the lake."

Chapter 2

Grandparents

The next few hours were spent summoning and controlling my fire into creating a clean, easy riding path to Chronurea Valley. Dad's blue fire mingled with my own, equally powerful and controlled on the left side of the path while mine cleared the right. Gabriel pulled a pair of axes from his saddle bag and we took out some of the more stubborn tree stumps with a few strokes. Between the two of us, it was only midday by the time we arrived in a familiar clearing overlooking Lake Angelus.

"That's where she's buried," Gabriel said, pointing with his ax towards a green slope of grass.

"Who?" I blinked at him, caught off guard by his comment. Over the whoosh of flames, we hadn't been able to carry on much of a conversation while we burned the path. His telepathy would have allowed mental communication with anyone else, but my head blind status meant he couldn't read me, let alone send me a message. Despite being born that way, I still found it a frustrating handicap around my telepathic friends and family.

"Adora," Gabriel clarified, wiping sweat from his brow and streaking it with soot. "Dad buried her where she could see the lake and the mountains."

I swallowed hard. Liam would lose his mind when I told him I knew where Adora's final resting place was. He and the rest of Cybele society had been guessing for over sixty years. But on the heels of that excitement came another wave of dread. The weight in my gut twisted.

"I'm sure she would have liked that," I told Dad.

"Nah." There was a spark of mischief in Gabriel's eyes as he regarded his sister's grave. "She would hate how quiet it is here. If Adora had her way, she'd be in the middle of Skykyle or Riland. Somewhere things happen. She was never happy unless she was in the thick of the drama."

"Maybe it's better she's somewhere quiet, then," I muttered, pulling my red curls up off my neck to let the lake breeze cool my sweat-slick skin.

"We should get the horses and bring them up to the house. If we're quick about it, Mom says we can join them for lunch."

I met my father's steady, blue gaze and felt a grin spread across my features. I never thought I'd see him discuss his sister so easily. It almost shook the dread from my shoulders for a moment.

"Okay," I agreed. Dad's soot-streaked hand took mine, then a ripple of his psi surrounded us and the horses' clearing materialized around us in ribbons of psi.

It took much less time to ride the horses down the path we'd cleared than it had to burn it through the woods. Our focus had to be on helping Charcoal and Aubrie navigate the freshly made trail, however, and we didn't talk much.

When we got to the lake overlook, Dad led the way down one hill and up another. As we came over the second rise, the gleaming solar panels of the Usuriel Homestead winked at us in greeting. The massive, white manor with its black shutters and hand-turned banisters was almost as familiar as Angelus Quietum's log cabin.

"Gabriel! Gracie!" Grandma Gloria called from the front porch, her blonde hair gleaming in the midday sun. Normally she would have run to greet us, but today she stayed seated on the glider swing, one hand resting on the swell of her pregnant belly.

"Hi, Mom!" Gabriel shouted, bringing Aubrie close enough to swing her lead rope around a banister. We hadn't bothered to put the bridles and bits back on the horses after their grazing. They were both well-mannered enough to ride with a halter, anyway. "Is Dad around?"

"Oh, he's off getting something this baby simply must have." Grandma rolled her cut-crystal eyes, a fond grin putting the lie to her annoyance. "You'd think we'd never done this before, the way your father's setting up that nursery."

"It has been a while," Dad said, hopping off of Aubrie and climbing the steps to lay a kiss on his mother's cheek.

"Babies haven't changed much in the last few centuries, as far as I know," Grandma Gloria said with a laugh, returning his affection with a kiss of her own. "Oh, you're covered in soot! What have you been up to, you pair of troublemakers?"

"Making a path between our properties," Dad said with a sly twinkle in his eye.

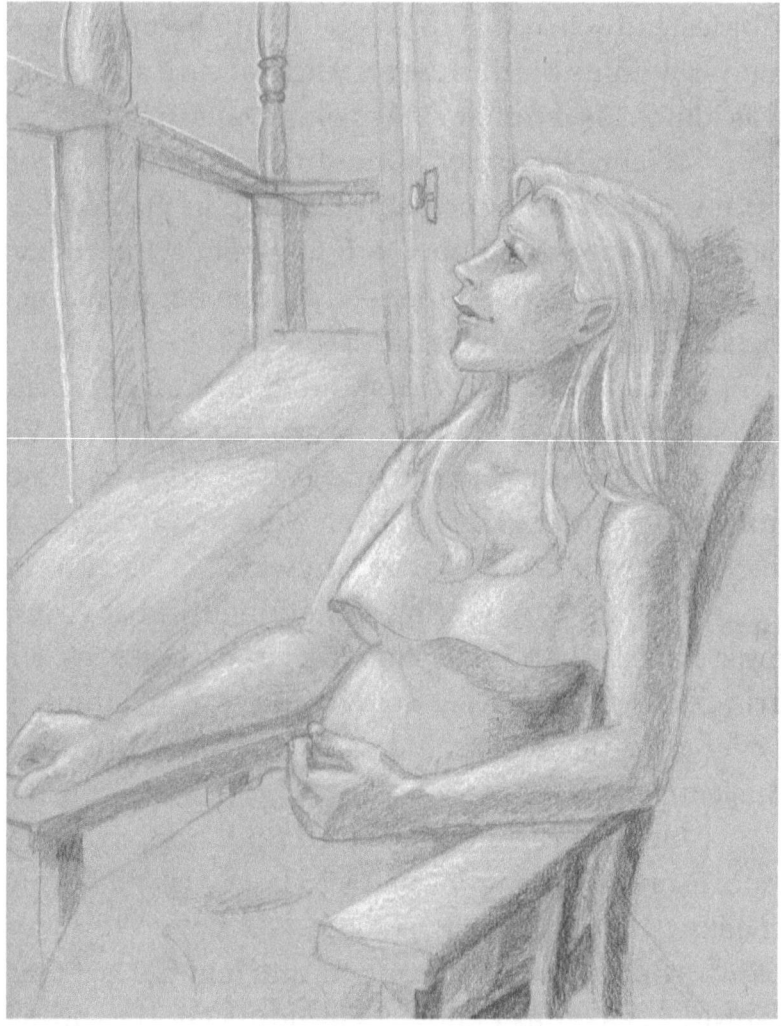

Grandma paused in the middle of giving my freckled cheek its kiss. Then her forever-youthful face split into a grin, and she pressed her lips to my cheek with enthusiasm.

"Oh, Gabe! You finally did it!"

Dad returned his mother's smile. "Just like you've spent the last century begging me to. It'll take some regular traffic to wear it in, but I suspect I'll have it done before my little sister wants to come over to play."

Gloria launched herself into her son's arms, squeezing his neck tightly. When she pulled away, her sky-blue gaze wavered with tears.

"Thank you," she whispered, peering into Gabriel's face.

Dad laid a kiss on her forehead. "You're welcome. Now, mind if we use your shower before lunch?"

***

Once I was damp and clean, I wandered downstairs to my grandparents' sunny kitchen. Grandma was bustling about the flat, glass stove-top with a big pot of soup. Dad sat at the kitchen's island, reading a memory pad and sipping tea.

"There you are, fresh as a daisy!" Grandma Gloria greeted me. Her golden brows knit together, and she tilted her head at my neck. "Did you hurt yourself, dear?"

"What?" I put a hand to the base of my neck. The dull ache sent a sharper pang at my touch. "Oh, that." My cheeks burned.

A knowing expression came over my grandmother's face, her grin curving the sharp Usuriel features into something friendly. "Ah, following in the Family tradition, I see."

"Not... exactly."

I didn't have time to explain further because a whoosh of fresh air from the back door announced the arrival of my grandfather.

"Gabe! Gracie!" D'nay greeted us, his long, dark hair windswept as he balanced half a dozen bags and parcels.

"Whoa, Dad!" Gabriel rushed to help his father with the packages. Standing next to each other, D'nay and Gabriel could almost pass for twins. The subtle differences, like Dad's more hawkish nose and wavier hair, were only obvious if you knew where to look.

"Thanks, kiddo," D'nay said as Gabriel settled two large boxes into his arms. "Will you take those up to the nursery? I'll be right behind you."

"Come on, Gracie," Grandma Gloria chirped, "this soup's about ready. Let's get lunch on the table so when the men come down we can all dig right in."

"Sure." I dutifully brought four bowls over to the stove where she'd summoned a ladle from the air to her left. I knew she'd teleported it from one of the drawers, but the effect was still impressive. I suppressed a sigh of frustration at the accident of genetics that landed me with pyrokinesis instead of telepathy, telekinesis, and teleportation.

Grandpa D'nay and Dad came back into the kitchen, and we sat down for a lunch of soup and salad. My grandparents kept up a steady stream of excited chatter about the baby through the whole meal. They were so happy and adorable, I couldn't bring myself to change the topic to something as morbid as Temporal Mortis.

"Come on, Gracie," Grandpa said, loading his dirty dishes into the dishwasher. "You haven't seen the nursery yet!"

Dad and I exchanged a small smirk before I followed Grandpa D'nay up the plush, carpeted stairs. In the hall, we passed the familiar paintings of Grandma, Grandpa, Dad, and Adora. I glanced at the third one on the left. As usual, it was a landscape of the Homestead at sunset. The first time I came to visit, it had been a wedding portrait of my father and his first wife, Olivia. I'd never seen it since, but Grandma Gloria had been kind enough to tell me who it was beaming next to my father before banishing it to storage. That was the only way I'd identified her ghost for years.

"Right in here," Grandpa said. With a sweeping motion of one arm, he indicated the little bedroom with the slanted ceilings I'd occupied when I came to visit as a child. Pushing the door open, my eyes widened. I hardly recognized the space. A pristine, white crib sat against the left wall, a gray and yellow tapestry of stars and moons hanging above it. A changing station sat atop the low dresser I remembered, though it was now painted white. The name "Ileesia" was spelled out in yellow on that wall. In the right corner was a wooden rocker heaped with pillows and blankets. Rows of tiny outfits filled the closet, each one on its own diminutive hanger, and a brightly painted box overflowed with toys next to the gabled window.

"It's perfect," I said, putting a hand on D'nay's arm.

He pulled me into a hug. "I can't wait for you to meet her. I know you'll be the best of friends."

"Gracie?" Dad called from the stairs. "Come on, the horses need to be fed and watered. And it'll be a cold night if we don't get that firewood stocked up."

I gave Grandpa one last squeeze before returning to the world of chores.

***

Back at Angelus Quietum, I was outside gathering firewood from Dad's stockpile near the barn when psi wind picked up. I glanced over casually as Liam materialized in the yard.

"Gracie!" he exclaimed, blue eyes showing white around the edges. Perhaps having Stella block his attempts at tapping through my implant for the last two days had been a mistake. "Sweet Fate, I've been looking everywhere for you! Are you okay?"

I hefted the load of firewood in my arms a little higher. I hadn't planned to keep the Grayson incident from my OW partner, but suddenly I found that I really didn't want to discuss it. In fact, I was pretty sure I didn't want to talk to Liam about anything at all.

Liam's frown deepened at my lack of response, and he took a step closer to me. I'd forgotten how much taller he was than my father; I suddenly felt very small and vulnerable next to him. I strode purposefully towards the door to the house.

"Obviously, I decided to visit my dad," I called over my shoulder. "Do I have to check in with you every time I leave the dorm now?"

"No, of course not," he replied, irritation clear in his tone. "But you weren't on campus yesterday. I know because I looked everywhere. Then I ran into James at breakfast, and he said the two of you had a fight the night before last. When you still wouldn't answer my tap, I got worried."

It made sense he'd be concerned. In fact, any other day I probably would have been pissed if he hadn't gone looking for me. Today, though, his fear inspired pure fury. I found myself hanging on to my fire by the barest edges of my mental fingernails.

"Worried about what?" I snapped, stomping up the steps of the back porch. "What am I going to do, Liam? Jump off a cliff? I can fly, you know."

Even after I told Liam we couldn't date, I'd never been so nasty or cruel. Today, however, all the negative emotions I'd been trying to deal with since Grayson's death had marked Liam as their new target. It took every ounce of my control not to scream at him.

For his part, Liam's blue eyes looked more puzzled and hurt than angry at my outburst. He trailed me up to the porch and hesitated by the steps.

"Gracie, honestly, I didn't mean to intrude. I just wanted to be sure you were okay," he said, leaning on the handrail. Seventeen generations of mortal marriages had blurred the Usuriel crispness of his features, but there was something about the easy arch of his brow and the full curve of his lips that I found incredibly appealing. I had to look anywhere else. "And that you hadn't done anything... rash."

I frowned at the hand plate by the door, my shoulders falling. "Well, I suppose you're here now so you might as well help me with the firewood," I grumbled, motioning him to follow me.

He bounced up the steps like the giant, eager puppy that he was. Even though he was two years older than me, I found myself thinking he seemed so damn young. Once he got close enough, I dumped the load of firewood into his arms and put my hand on the door plate.

"Come on, Dad will have my hide if I don't let you come in and say hi, anyway. The two of you seemed to get on well enough last time," I said, swinging the door open and marching through it before gesturing to Gabriel as he leaned over the cooling unit, getting out some leftovers for dinner.

"Ah, Liam! Good to see you again," Dad said, giving my OW partner a genuine smile. "Are you staying for dinner?"

"He's just helping me with the firewood," I snapped. "Then he has to get back to the University."

My father raised a dark brow and exchanged a glance with Liam. I suddenly wanted to send them both up in flames. Instead, I stomped over to the arched doorway between the kitchen and living room.

"The fireplace is in here," I hissed through clenched teeth, pointing at the empty grate until Liam dutifully stacked the logs in their rightful place. Once he'd finished,

I crossed my arms tightly across my chest and glared at him. "Thanks for the help. You should probably be going now."

"There's plenty of food," Dad said gently. "You're welcome to sit and have dinner with us, Liam."

"Dad, really!" I stomped a foot. "There's no reason for him to hang about when obviously he has places to be." I turned to Liam. "Thanks for being a big, strong man-thing and hauling the firewood. Now you can be on your way."

"Gracie!" Dad's voice was indignant, but I refused to look at his disapproving expression.

Liam licked his lips nervously, his gaze sliding between Dad and I. "Gracie, you do realize you had a fight with James, not me, right? I know we're not dating, but last time I checked, you were still one of my best friends."

I sighed and put my face in my hands. Through the jumble of emotions, I tried to find a thread of civility. However, it was as elusive as a salamander in the mud and kept slipping through my mental fingers.

"You're a good OW partner," I told him slowly. "But I'm not sure we should be such close friends. You seem to be having a hard time understanding the boundaries of our relationship."

He stared at me, a hurt expression pulling at the corners of his generous mouth. Guilt twisted in my stomach. "Gracie... what happened? What did James say to you?"

I hunched my shoulders and answered the floor. "I don't want to talk about it. Look, you came to see if I was okay." I gestured to myself. "Obviously I'm fine. Mission accomplished. Thanks for the concern. I'll see you at OW training tomorrow."

With a sigh, he turned to Dad. "Nice to see you again, Gabe. Guess I'm not staying." With a shake of his head, he faded from the room in a shower of blue motes.

"Well, that was incredibly rude," Dad rounded on me, his face drawn into a scowl. "Not to mention unkind."

With Liam gone, the anger faded as quickly and inexplicably as it arrived. Deflated, I sat down with very little Family grace in one of the kitchen chairs. "I can't deal with him right now," I moaned, pushing a clump of red curls away from my face.

My father narrowed his eyes. "He's in love with you, you know. The last time we discussed Liam, I thought the problem was a one-way attraction in the other direction. You could certainly do worse."

I hid my face and groaned. "The last man I tried to sleep with is dead because of it," I whispered. "Let me live with that for a little while before you start matchmaking, okay?"

"Ah, I see." Dad helped himself to some leftover pasta salad. "Well, I suppose I can understand that sentiment. I think you might want to explain it to Liam, too, however, before you do permanent damage to that relationship."

"Yeah, well, we'll see," I muttered and began making myself a plate for lunch.

That was the last we discussed of Liam, and I was grateful for it.

Chapter 3

Olivia's Choice

That night, for the first and only time, I dreamed of Olivia.

Her hair was half-gray and half-red curls pulled back in a serviceable braid. The ship suit she wore looked as if it had started out pressed, but over the course of a very long day it had become stained and torn. Her face had aged gracefully in the way that someone well-loved and well-fed often did. Even so, there were little creases and lines about her eyes and mouth that spoke of gathering years. At the moment they were deeply etched; her expression was stressed. I guessed her for somewhere in her early fifties.

"Can you hand me another bandage, Mom?" Ariel asked. I glanced at my half-sister, knowing it was her before I saw her Usuriel features. Ariel was applying some kind of poultice over a very infected wound. Knowing Gloria and Ariel's healing skills, I found it odd that someone in their Med Bay had time to develop an infection.

Dutifully, Olivia dipped one of the bandages she was cutting into the antiseptic-smelling tub of liquid in front of her before handing it to Ariel.

The middle-aged gentleman who owned the leg they were doctoring gave a slight hissing breath as Ariel smoothed another layer of bandage over the top of the wound. His features were extremely mortal, with dull blue eyes and pure gray hair.

"Sorry, Mike," Ariel said, laying a glowing hand against the now-bandaged wound. "But I can't seal this infection in. It would just fester, and could possibly result in blood poisoning. All I can do is bolster your own immune system to fight the infection and give you antimicrobials for you to take orally."

"I appreciate it," Mike said. "And I'm not a Stafford to complain that you can't fix it today. I understand that you're not miracle workers. It already feels a lot better. Thanks for taking the time to see me."

"We couldn't let it go another day," Olivia said, cutting another long length of bandage. "Even if Gloria needed a break, Ariel's getting downright proficient at her shifts down here. I'm sorry we didn't have room for you earlier. It's been a hard week all the way around."

Ariel ducked her head, but I could see a small smile spread across her face at her mother's praise.

"She does a top job, our Ariel does. But these are dangerous times. We're lucky we didn't lose anyone yesterday," Mike said with a shake of his head. "And we're still not out of the wormhole yet, not by a long shot."

Even as he said it, the lights flickered overhead, and the walls seemed to shudder.

"Gabe," Olivia breathed, glancing up at the lights.

"Dad's okay, Mom," Ariel said quickly. "The psi-pilot is pushing his limits, but he's up to it. He's been breaking his own records lately. I don't think he's ever been this strong. He'll see us through, just like he always does."

"I know he's been breaking records," Liv said quietly, turning back to her bandages. "That's why I worry."

Mike shook his head. "He's an old man, Liv. He's been burned enough times to know when he's getting in trouble. Have a little faith."

"Oh, I have faith in my husband," Olivia said pointedly. "It's that sister of his I don't trust. You know I don't like him psi-piloting when she's in the heart ship. She doesn't remember to check on him, and he's too damn stubborn to put his foot down when she's crossing the line."

The ship dropped several meters on its x-axis, its whole frame whining and grinding in protest of the sudden motion. A tray full of medical supplies slid and then crashed off of the counter top.

"A medic! We need a medic!" Voices rose outside the door of the small examining room. Ariel and Olivia rushed to the door, which slid open for them automatically. Even Mike craned his neck from where he was sitting on the bed to see what was going on.

Over their shoulders, I got an impression of several bodies and a lot of blood. There was screaming and crying; several voices raised in pain and panic. The women paused to assess the situation, then gathered themselves to dive into triage.

Just before they could move, however, both of them staggered. The lights flickered one more time before plunging the whole Med Bay into darkness. The soft whir of a generator picked up in the background, and the lights flickered back on. Olivia and Ariel's faces remained pale and stricken.

"Dad," Ariel gasped, holding her mother's gaze.

"I'll take care of him," Olivia said. "You have your hands full here."

"But you're not..."

"I said, I'll take care of him," Olivia snapped. "I don't feel any more echo pain, so I don't think he's too badly injured. Probably just stunned. If I know Mystra and the bridge crew, they'll be too busy salvaging the ship to take care of your father. Teleport me there and then take care of this mess."

Ariel looked reluctant, but the commotion in the main Med Bay was picking up volume again, and one of the nurses was shouting for her.

"Maybe we should wake Grandma?" Ariel said, eyes a little wide.

"If he's seriously hurt when I arrive on the bridge, I will," Olivia reassured her daughter. "Just get me there."

"Right," Ariel nodded too quickly, and I could see that she didn't like the idea but was too used to following her mother's instructions to disobey. She put a hand to her mother's arm, and Olivia disappeared in a flash of blue psi-energy.

I expected to stay with Ariel in the Med Bay, since most of my time warps seemed to rotate heavily around her. However, as things occasionally do in dreams, I found myself suddenly and disorientingly in a new place.

It took me a long moment to recognize the *Inspiration's* bridge. Wires and comm screens had been tossed about randomly. Several injured crew members were being treated by a medic in one corner. A woman with hair that was more white than red barked orders from a platform near the center of the room. Crew members ran back and forth while blue electricity flashed and snapped across exposed circuitry with alarming regularity.

"Liv! Get back!" The older woman who appeared in charge addressed Olivia sharply as she approached the back wall of the bridge.

I turned, as I'd appeared facing away from that wall, and realized that the psi-pilot's interface was currently a sparking ruin. It spilled thick-wired guts across the back half of the bridge. My father's unconscious form was tangled about the center of that disaster of exposed electronics. A larger surge of electricity passed through the wreckage, arching Gabriel's back as it passed over him. Afterwards his eyelids flickered slightly but didn't open.

"Sweet Fate," I breathed, feeling true fear grip my chest. He didn't just look injured; he looked damn near dead.

"Gabe," Olivia called to him, edging closer despite the captain's warning. "Can you hear me?"

He stirred slightly at the sound of her voice, head turning in her direction even half-conscious. "Liv?"

Another spark of electricity flashed to his right, and Olivia darted to the left, skirting several large, exposed circuits.

"Did you hear me, Olivia? You're going to get yourself killed!" the captain said, taking a break from shouting orders at the other scrambling crew members to address the situation behind her. "Where will your children be then? Do you want them to lose both parents tonight?"

"Hopefully my children will be grown, contributing members of this ship," Olivia replied calmly for the state of affairs, I thought. "And they will take my place at my shift when I'm gone. In fact, I'm pretty sure that's where they are right now. Isn't that the point of a generation ship?"

"Liv!" The captain sounded like she wanted to move to stop the historian but was reluctant to leave her post. "Where's Gloria? Shouldn't she handle this?"

"If we call her for every emergency, the woman's going to burn out on us. She's immortal, not invulnerable." Olivia's voice was steady and in control. I got the impression she was used to dealing with authority and wasn't intimidated by it. "Very much like my husband. I'll thank you to take him off the active duty roster for at least a few days after this one." Olivia picked her way over two bent sections of wall that seemed half-melted from the heat of the psi-power that had overloaded my father. "Now, either get over here and help me or stay out of the way, Mystra."

"God, why is it always him," grumbled Mystra, rubbing her forehead as if Gabriel were the source of many a headache. Then, with a last few barked orders, she turned and started towards the ruined psi-pilot.

"Gabe?"

Olivia had reached her husband and was rapidly disentangling him from the wires wrapped around his torso and limbs. She'd pulled a small, foldable ship knife out of one pocket and was neatly cutting any connection that didn't quickly come away at her pulling. With a few strokes, she cleared enough to be able to stand close by his side.

"You with me, sweetheart?" She took a moment to touch his face, and he opened pain-darkened eyes to her before nodding. With a slight sigh of relief, she turned back to cutting him from the wreckage.

"Fate knows what damage you're doing," Mystra complained as she clamored over a broken comm screen.

"Well, I know this thing won't run without a pilot, so that's the part I'm trying to save," Olivia said, not looking up from Gabriel's injured form. He'd roused enough to help her clear away some of the wires, though movement seemed painful for him, and his right arm remained trapped under his own weight. "Alright, sweetheart, I need you to lean forward so I can get the electrodes off," she told him gently. "It's going to hurt, but I can't do anything about that."

With her help, he rolled far enough to one side that she could reach the round pads on either side of his spine. He sucked in a breath through his teeth as she removed the first one. Underneath was a sickeningly dark red burn in a perfect circle. My stomach twisted as I saw nearly a dozen pads trailing down his back. Olivia didn't flinch or pause, her nimble fingers finding and removing each one. Silent tears ran down my father's face when she was done, but he never cried out.

"Okay, Mystra," Olivia said, turning to the captain who had just finished clearing away the last of the wires from Gabriel's legs. He was wearing a comfortable-looking set of pants in the *Inspiration* blue uniform color. There was no shirt and no boots to his psi-pilot uniform. Apparently he needed a lot of bare skin to connect with the merge. "Get under his other side."

Mystra nodded and took his other arm. They got my father standing in one almost-smooth pull. Dad wrapped an arm around Olivia's shoulder for support but otherwise managed his own weight. He nodded tiredly to Mystra.

"Thanks, Captain," he said quietly, his voice raw. I wondered how painful the overload must have been. "Did we make it?"

"Thanks to you and Adora we've bought some time, but we'll need you again soon enough. Can you get to the Med Bay all right?" Mystra asked, moving quickly away from the sparking wreckage. A small line of crew members waited for her orders by the platform.

"Our POD is closer," Olivia said. "I can call Gloria if anything's worse than it looks."

Mystra nodded, then turned back to her command.

"I'm not teleporting anywhere, no matter how close it is," Dad said quietly to Olivia as they made their slow way off the bridge.

"I didn't figure you would, sweetheart," Olivia replied. "We're just going to take a little walk. Go as fast or as slow as you like."

Gabriel chuckled and then hissed as the movement set off the burns on his back. "Even my least favorite walks are better with you, love," he said, flashing an attempt at a smile.

I watched the two of them make their painfully slow way down the *Inspiration*'s main corridor; her shoulder under his to steady him while he put the other hand on the wall to keep her from taking all of his weight. They walked together silently, but it didn't take words to see the affectionate way their heads stayed close together and the gentleness of their fingers lacing through each other on her shoulder.

Olivia helped him ease down on the tiny, angular couch in their little living room and began rubbing ointment on the raw wounds that ran down his back. The way he watched her, even though he was exhausted and in considerable pain, was as tender as anything I'd ever seen. It made my chest ache. I'd never seen my father so gentle as when he reached up to touch her cheek in thanks for her ministrations.

Olivia's answering smile made the serious folds and creases of her advancing age fall away. For a moment, she was the beautiful young woman I'd seen in their wedding portrait so many years ago. Then concern drew her lips together again as she pulled strands of his hair away from the sticky ointment, finally tying it in a loose knot to one side in an effort to prevent causing more pain.

Even so, my father was so pale he might actually be called green by the time she was done dealing with the ruin that was his back.

"Well, at least it will heal clean," she muttered. "Your mother should be able to take care of it when she gets up in a few hours. After yesterday, I'll be damned if I'm going to wake her when I don't have to, though. I really thought she was going to do permanent damage to herself."

"She knows her own limits... unlike Adora. I don't know why I think I can keep up with that child," Dad groaned. He got to his feet unsteadily and headed in the direction of the bathroom. Olivia watched him go with quiet, concerned eyes.

"How long has it been since you ate something?" she asked. "No, don't answer that. I'll bet you haven't taken a break since breakfast. You can't push yourself like this without any fuel, Gabriel. No wonder you're nauseous. Ariel and I had a late dinner two hours ago."

Dad took his time in the bathroom. I didn't hear him retch, but there were a few long pauses that I suspected were a little dicey.

Liv shook her head and went to the tiny cooler in their minuscule kitchen. She poured a decent-sized glass of what looked like fruit juice. Then she went and knocked on the bathroom door.

"Gabe, let me in," she said.

The door slid open and my father's pale figure filled the doorway. With a scowl, Olivia put the juice in Gabriel's hand and told him to drink it all in small sips. Then she half-carried him to the couch before going back to the small kitchen to put together a bowl of rice and a sandwich with thick spread. I suspected it was a variety of nut butter.

"Eat," she said, placing the food on the coffee table and flopping onto the couch next to him.

A tiny tongue of psi-flame crept slowly out along the edge of the rice dish. I'd never seen my father's psi-energy at such a low ebb. He looked heavy-lidded and drawn afterwards, too, as he took another sip of the juice and lifted the rice bowl to his lips. For a few minutes there was silence as Olivia sipped a cup of tea, and Gabriel slowly made his way through the small meal she'd prepared for him. Halfway through, his hands stopped shaking, and the pace of his bites picked up as if he no longer had to fight through nausea to bring himself to eat. Even his color improved a few shades.

"Feel better?" she asked when he was done.

"Yes, thank you," he replied, getting to his feet.

"You don't have to get up," she said. "I'll take care of the dishes tomorrow."

"It won't hurt me to set them in the sink on my way to bed," he replied. He hobbled more than walked across to the little sink, his head down and his shoulders tight as if every joint and muscle were fighting him.

Olivia stretched, got up, and followed him into the bedroom. "I hate to bring up bad blood when you're not feeling well, but it's the only time you ever listen to me about this stuff."

"Come to bed, Olivia," he said. "You can read me the riot act in the morning."

"I should really go back and help Ariel in the Med Bay," she sighed, trailing into their oval-shaped bedroom as Gabriel pulled back the covers and fell into bed. He groaned in relief, curling onto his side. Olivia stepped to the bed and pulled a blanket over his waist before laying a gentle kiss on his brow.

"You were up before me," he chided her, "and you're quite a bit older than I am now, love. Take a rest and let the youngsters handle things for a few hours. Ariel will be fine on her own."

Olivia looked torn as he pulled his hand into hers. "She had a real crowd when I left..."

"Am I no longer patient enough for you, Liv?" he asked, pulling back the corner of the light sheet she'd draped over his waist. "There was a time you'd never leave me alone in this condition."

"That was before we had three kids," she pointed out, though she did put a gentle hand in his hair, "and before the Cat-Mantis started ganging up with your sister to tear the ship apart on the regular. Hell, this feels like a pretty good day for us lately. I'm putting you to bed in our quarters instead of in the Med Bay. I swear Adora isn't going to rest until she puts you in the ground."

"That's slightly unfair," he replied sleepily. "They were right on our heels to the very end today. Adora didn't have a choice. She'll probably eat the Mess hall out of every scrap of protein before she crashes, too. I can hear her from here."

"Your mother would have managed it without burning holes in your back," Olivia replied reasonably. She yielded to the tug of his hands enough to sit down on the edge of the bed. "And Gloria would have insisted you eat something at some point. Honestly, I don't know how Adora does it. It's nearly killing you trying to keep up with her."

With a small moan, my father wrapped himself around his wife, his arms coming around to encircle her waist while his knees and head pressed to either side of her small yet shapely hips. She ran a hand along the length of his arm encircling her waist while the other played absently with the soft hair at the base of his neck. I could see his shoulders relax into her touch and he gave another little sigh as his eyes faded shut.

"Take off the ship suit and hold me, Liv," he murmured, a note of entreaty in his voice.

She looked down at him, and even in the dark their eyes met.

"Goddamn it, Gabe," she whispered. "I will never be able to resist you, and you know it."

"That's why I love you so much," he said, nuzzling into her hip again.

"I know," she said, unzipping her ship suit. She pulled away from him just long enough to step out of it. Her figure was still trim for being in her fifth decade. Stripped down to bra and panties, she climbed into bed and pressed herself into his waiting arms.

They lay quietly for a moment, and I wondered if I was going to fall into a deeper sleep with them in the dream. That would be an oddly reassuring end to one of these vivid dreams. Certainly better than the other recurring one with my father in it.

"You do age you know," Olivia said softly into the dark.

"Hmmm... do I now?" Dad sounded mostly asleep. How he could possibly get comfortable with those burns on his back was beyond me. I wondered if he was actually falling asleep or passing out from exhaustion. Was there a difference? I was pretty sure there was. I, on the other hand, still felt strangely alert.

"It's not in your face or hair like the rest of us," Olivia went on, "It's here." She laid a kiss over each of his eyes. "Which is a shame really. I've always thought you had the prettiest eyes."

"I'm fairly sure they're still blue," he replied, a note of amusement in his voice. "At least, they were in the bathroom mirror a minute ago."

"As they always will be," she agreed, "But that's where you carry your pain. I can see it, even if others don't."

"What will I do without you?" he murmured, pressing his forehead to hers. "I swear you know me better than I know myself."

"You'll be fine," she whispered, kissing him to take the sting out of her words. "You'll see. It will be an adjustment, but you'll have the kids long after I'm gone. Ariel will make sure you're not lonely."

His sigh was heavier this time. "Just let me come with you," he whispered after a long pause. His voice was so quiet I almost couldn't hear it. "By the time you go, I'll already have had double what most men are given. I don't want to know what life is like after you."

"Don't you dare," she hissed, and I could hear the anger in her voice. "Don't you even think it, Gabe. I may not know everything, but I do know this: Cybele will be a better place because Gabriel Usuriel is in it. I want no part of helping him leave."

"I wish I had half your certainty."

"You want certainty? I'll give you certainty. Your mother and daughter are our lead medics and some of our strongest empaths. That means that I want you to think long and hard about what kind of mess you would be leaving for them to find."

"Now that is a morbid thought."

"Suicide is not glamorous or pretty, Gabe. It's an unnecessary death and that is always hurtful and ugly."

"Well... when you put it that way..."

"And I swear by everything you find holy, if you ever pick up a syringe again I will haunt you within an inch of your life. You will never have a moment of peace. I promise, you will rue the day."

He chuckled at that one. "Now that, I do believe."

"Don't make light of it. I mean it."

"I know you do, sweetheart. I'm not being flippant. And that much I can promise you. I never want to get into that headspace again."

"That's all I wanted to hear," Olivia sounded mollified.

I heard more than saw him kiss her. "I know. We've had this discussion once or twice."

She pushed away from him a bit. "Say it because you mean it, not because you know it's what I want to hear."

Gabriel groaned and started to roll over onto his back. He froze about an inch into the movement, and I could hear the pained hiss as he sucked in a breath through his teeth. "Can I claim injury on this conversation, Liv? I can't think straight right now. I just want to go to sleep."

"Sorry," she murmured gently, putting a hand on his chest. They were quiet again for a moment before Liv's soft voice said, "I just spend so much time worrying about you and the kids trying to keep up with that sister of yours. I swear she's taking years off my life every time she pulls a trick like this one."

"Yours and mine, both," he grumbled. "My back is killing me. I wish Mom would wake up and take care of these burns."

"Has she at least come to the top of her sleep?"

"No. She's still dead to the cosmos."

"As she should be. Twelve hours in the heart ship followed by nearly twenty-four in the Med Bay cleaning up after the wreck the Cat-Mantis made of our mining ship. Honestly, I should be more grateful for Adora. Without her we might have had to toss you back in the heart ship. If you had that much trouble with the psi-pilot, I can only imagine the mess we would have had if you'd attempted the heart ship."

"Mess... that's a good word for it." Gabriel sounded exhausted by the very concept.

"I like it better than 'corpse,'" Olivia said.

"How about I just stay away from that bloody thing?" Gabriel suggested.

"That's been a primary goal of mine for years, love."

"Glad to hear it. Someone has to be on team 'Keep Gabe In One Piece.' I swear, half the time it feels like the rest of the ship just wants to get as much power out of me as possible, regardless of what condition I'm in when it's over. Even Mom and Dad have thrown me to the wolves a few times. I think you and the kids are the only ones who have never come straight out and asked me to die for the ship."

"You've stepped in front of a few bullets for me over the years. And the kids."

"True. But you never asked me to. It makes a difference."

Her arms tightened around his shoulders again, and they clung to each other in silence.

"Speak of the devil," Dad muttered. Olivia glanced over her shoulder just in time for her face to be illuminated by the golden light of Gloria's entrance. "You shouldn't waste energy teleporting when you could just as easily walk," he chided his mother.

"What the hell did your sister do this time?" Gloria snapped, gesturing for Olivia to get out of her way so that she could have a look at Gabriel.

"Glad you're feeling better, Mom," Dad said, rolling onto his stomach while Olivia retreated to the wall. She pulled a thin cloth robe around her shoulders before coming to stand next to her mother-in-law.

"How did I sleep through this?" Gloria seemed to be asking herself more than Gabriel as she ran gentle fingers over the circular burns. "Sweet Fate, child, why didn't you wake me? This has to be incredibly painful."

"Yeah, it is," Dad agreed. "So let's heal it and get it over with."

"I've never healed burns this bad without an analgesic," Gloria said slowly. "All we have is morphine, but..."

"No," Gabriel cut her off. "Absolutely not. Not one drop and you know it. I'll take the pain, please and thank you. Now heal the damn thing."

Gloria sighed. "I can put you out for the beginning, but even that won't help by the end."

"Then don't worry about my comfort, and just do what needs doing," he grumbled.

"I'll hold his hand," Olivia said, sitting on the bedside and suiting action to her words. "Let's just be done, shall we? Gabe and I have both been awake almost twenty hours. I think we'd both like to get some rest."

Gloria nodded, a thin-lipped frown on her face. "All right, fine." She knelt next to Olivia on the bed with that utter grace she always commanded. Then she placed both palms on my father's back, and a shimmering golden glow picked up around them.

True to Gloria's warnings, my father didn't seem to be enjoying the healing. I watched his shoulders tense, and his grip on Olivia's hand tighten enough to make her grimace. Even so, he didn't scream or writhe away from his mother's energy. As the minutes dragged on, his breathing got ragged, and I heard Gloria make some small apologies as she moved from one burn to the next. When he finally conceded to a small whimper, Olivia hushed him with a hand in his hair. Aside from that, the healing was a silent affair that ended as quietly as it had begun.

"There," Gloria said finally, leaning back with a little less fluidity than she'd sat down with. "Not even a scar. At least you heal clean, kid."

"Mmmmm," Dad sounded like he was already half asleep. "Thanks," he said, rolling over and scooping up a pillow which he promptly buried his head into. I think he was out before Olivia and Gloria even stood up from the bed.

"Well, that wasn't quite as bad as I'd feared," Olivia said with a yawn.

"You should join him, sweetie," Gloria said, putting a hand on Liv's shoulder. "Trying to keep up with the kids isn't such a good idea."

"Oh, don't worry. I will," Olivia said, the edges of her mouth drawing down as she watched Dad's silent form. "Stella, lower lights by fifty percent." The AI dutifully adjusted the room's illumination, but Olivia made no move to join her husband in bed.

"What's wrong?" Gloria asked.

"Is he asleep?" Olivia hesitated.

Gloria paused a moment before nodding. "Quite soundly already. Poor thing's almost as exhausted as I was yesterday."

Olivia nodded, her eyes distant.

"Come now, child, what's bothering you?" Gloria prompted when the silence stretched too long.

Olivia's green eyes were dark as she looked up at my grandmother. "You'll take care of him when I'm gone, won't you?"

Gloria bowed her head, eyes closing as her golden hair fell forward to hide her face. After a moment, she tucked it absently behind one ear. "I'm his mother, Olivia. I've always tried to protect him. Unfortunately, he's extremely gifted at shielding. It's always been one of his strengths. Even passed out on narcotics, there were times

I'd have a hard time reading him." She gave a helpless shrug. "I'll do what I can, but you know better than most that Gabriel has a mind of his own. If he decides to do something foolish once you've gone, I'm not sure anyone can stop him."

"I know," Olivia said quietly, hugging herself while she watched her husband sleep. "Thank you for being honest with me. It probably would have just been easier to tell me a reassuring lie."

Grandmother inclined her head, then joined Olivia's silent observation of my father's slumbering back. "You know," she said slowly, "there is another option."

Liv raised one eyebrow. "Besides what?"

"Besides allowing time to do its work and abandoning the man who loves you far more than he loves himself." Gloria's voice had dropped to a conspiratorial whisper, and she glanced at the comm screen. Its lights were dark.

Olivia narrowed her eyes at her mother-in-law. "I didn't know you'd figured out a way to cheat death."

"It is as old as time itself," Gloria said with a tilt of one shoulder. "I certainly didn't come up with it. Vampires have been around almost as long as humanity, as far as I know."

"Oh," Liv sounded surprised. I watched as she considered the idea thoughtfully. "I suppose... we do have one of those on board, don't we. I have a habit of forgetting what D'nay really is." She paused, a slight frown on her face. "I'd be stuck at whatever age I'm turned, wouldn't I?"

"You might look it, but you wouldn't have the aches and pains of middle age. You'd be stronger and faster than a mortal, too."

"I'd also be technically dead half the day." Olivia didn't look like she enjoyed that concept. "Not to mention sensitive to the artificial sunlight in 'Ponics. And then there's the little matter of food."

"I'm sure Gabriel would be more than happy to exchange a little blood for his wife's life," Gloria pointed out. "As long as you stay under the influence of immortal blood, there are very few of the negative side effects you just mentioned. It's worked for his father and I for over a century."

"True enough," Olivia seemed to be choosing her words carefully. I could understand that. This seemed like it might be a touchy subject with my grandmother. "However, we've proven over and over again that Gabriel is not your match in the psi department. Who is to say his blood would work the same way? Or even if it did, how much might I have to drink to get the correct effect?"

"It's impossible to say without trying it," Gloria said softly. "But I can tell you exactly what your death will do to my son. You're his heart, Olivia. Even if he survives it, he won't be whole."

"He's lived through one heart transplant. I do have some faith in his resilience if I die of natural causes." Olivia looked at my grandmother with honesty and sorrow in her expression. "But if I'm eternally suffering because of a choice I've made for him?" She shook her head and I found myself agreeing that the fallout from that probably wouldn't have been pretty. "What if the partnership doesn't work? He'll accept the blame and likely take it out on himself. Or, even worse, what if the level of blood donation I'd need to stay my normal self is too much for him to sustain? Look at him, Gloria, he's at his limit these days as it is. We all are."

Grandmother's expression drew age lines around her mouth and eyes, her face set in an emotion that was painful to look at, let alone experience. I felt for her. There really wasn't a good option here. Knowing how things eventually turned out, my heart ached for Gloria even more. "The Cat-Mantis have been making life difficult the last few years," she agreed. "But it has to calm down again eventually."

"I'm not getting any younger," Liv said, "and I don't think I'd relish being a seventy-year-old married to a twenty-five-year-old for the rest of eternity. Fate knows I love him, Gloria, but even my vanity has limits."

"Which is why I bring it up now." Grandma still looked grim. "D'nay would probably have my hide for even suggesting all this, but after what happened with Orville..." she trailed off, eyes haunted. "I can't watch Gabriel kill himself with that poison again, Liv. Not if I can prevent it."

Olivia's response was to pull the eldest Usuriel into a tight hug. "I know, believe me," she whispered as Gloria's arms came up to wrap around her back. "If it was just the strangeness of it, I'd do it in a heartbeat. But Gabe has too many people riding on his shoulders already. It's pushing him too hard as it is; I can't add to it. Not now. If I were the one thing that pushed him over that edge... no.

It wouldn't just break my heart; it would probably kill a lot of people. You and I both know he's a big reason we've survived the Cat-Mantis so far. What would happen to the ship if he's not around to psi-pilot?"

"It would fall to Ariel, Hal, and Drex." Gloria sighed, leaning back and giving Olivia's arms a squeeze. "Not the answer you want to hear as a mother, I'm sure."

"Not an answer I didn't already know." Olivia matched the sigh with one of her own.

"Well, think on it," Grandmother said, tucking a few strands of hair that had fallen out of Olivia's braid back into their proper place. "Though, not hard enough for our men to hear. No use fighting about it if you don't even want to go through with it. And I have a feeling it would be a fight, at least in my household."

Olivia nodded, her face suddenly very tired. "I will consider it, though I doubt my answer will change. Bring me a solution that doesn't involve draining my husband dry, and I will be more than willing. Until then, though, I agree. Let's keep this discussion between us."

The room was beginning to darken and feel farther away as Gloria stepped back and glanced down at my father's sleeping form.

"Well, I should get back to the Med Bay. I've probably been away too long already. You should really get some sleep while you have the chance."

"Thanks for staying to talk." Olivia's voice was distant and seemed to echo, but even so I could hear her yawn at the end. I could hardly see the two women or the POD they stood in anymore. Everything was a dim blur.

"I'll see you the next time our shifts overlap. With as many hours as we're working lately, I imagine it will be soon."

"Sleep well." Grandmother's voice was the last thing I heard before I faded into the dark embrace of a deeper sleep.

Chapter 4

Lillian

I woke the next day to the smell of eggs and rice in the kitchen. After breakfast, Dad teleported me to the University with his usual easy grace. Once he faded from the room, I shook my head at how effortless he made it seem. I really had been spoiled by his strength as a child. With a resigned shrug at the inevitable disappointment that would be my next ride with Liam, I tossed on my workout uniform and trotted outside before taking off for the OW compound.

Liam's dark-haired figure was already there when I arrived, doing his stretches next to our usual practice mat. I nodded to him when I came in, but otherwise didn't acknowledge his presence as I started my warm up.

"Feeling any better?" he asked me after the silence had stretched long enough to go from expectant to uncomfortable.

"I didn't know I was doing poorly to begin with," I said, a hint of irritation in my voice.

"Okay, so you're still spore bent for some reason. Honestly, Gracie, just tell me what I did so I can apologize already. I hate it when you're mad at me."

"Who said you did anything?" I asked, glancing up at him.

He spread his hands. "Your attitude, that's who! Seriously, I've never felt more unwelcome during a visit than I did yesterday at Angelus Quietum."

"That doesn't mean you did anything," I pointed out. "Guilty conscience much? Is there something you want to tell me about? Something I should be mad at you for?"

"No!" he snarled, anger finally starting to kindle in those familiar blue eyes. It had taken long enough, I thought with a touch of annoyance. Apparently he hadn't gotten much of the Usuriel temper if it took this long to goad him into a fight. "Fuck, what is wrong with you? Did you hit your head or something over the break?"

"I don't think she hit her head, but she did give my wife a good scare," Jillian said as she walked towards us. I noticed that her black braids were longer than the last time I'd seen them, which was only a few days ago. I frowned at her.

"I didn't know you were married," I said.

Jillian gave me a look like I was losing my mind. "What are you talking about?"

"Did you get married over break? I don't remember you having a girlfriend."

"Amourie and I have been married for years," Jillian said gently, a look of concern on her plump face. "You came over for dinner a few weeks ago. Don't you remember?"

Liam looked equally confused, though I thought I saw a touch of vindication in his gaze. I think he might have been hoping I actually had suffered some kind of physical injury that could explain my sudden change of attitude towards him. No such luck, I thought bitterly.

"You don't remember having grilled salmon over at Jillian and Amourie's last month?" Liam asked.

Then it hit me.

Of course.

The timeline shifted when my blood killed Grayson. Without the vampire around to divert Amourie's affections, she'd ended up making a permanent attachment to Jillian. A shiver went down my spine at the number of ripples my unintentional time damage had done. What else had changed now that Grayson was unmade? It was impossible to know.

"Sure, of course," I lied, shaking my head as if I were amazed at my own lapse. "How could I forget! Sorry, I had a rough day just before break. I think my brain got a little scrambled."

"That's what Amourie said." Jillian sounded a little cautious. "You seemed upset and she had to take you back to Angelus Quietum."

I nodded. "Yeah, I think I went a little wild that night. Sorry if I scared her. Dad took care of me, though, and the rest of the break was actually pretty good."

Jillian glanced between Liam and me as if she knew this wasn't the whole story. When I didn't volunteer any other information, however, she patted me on the shoulder and offered a smile. "Well, I'm glad to see you're okay. Let me know if there's anything you want to talk about. I'm always happy to hear you out."

I returned a smile I didn't feel. "Thanks."

She walked off in the direction of the punching bags several feet away and started putting on gloves.

Liam turned to me, his eyes narrow with suspicion. "You might be able to bluff Jill, but I know you too well. You really don't remember that cookout, do you?"

My mouth formed a thin, unhappy line. "Let it be, Liam."

"No! You're my OW partner and, even if you don't want to admit it lately, you're still my best friend. As far as I know, we've never kept secrets from each other before. So what the hell happened over break? If it's affected your memory, I really should know about it. And I get that some of what was said between you and James is private, but at least tell me why you're treating me like something that just crawled out of a swamp and got goo all over your shoe."

"Ugh," I groaned and ran a nervous hand through my hair. He wasn't going to leave me alone about this and the longer I stalled, the more I sounded like my father. I was already turning into Gabriel more than I really wanted to lately. I opened my mouth to apologize and promise him I would tell him everything once we could find a place in private to talk, but I never got a chance to say the words.

"Gracie?"

Liam and I both looked up at the unexpected interruption. I didn't recognize the commanding, feminine voice immediately. However, once I saw her pale figure striding in our direction, my heart jumped into my throat.

"Ummm... are you talking to me?" I asked, as my sister, Lillian, came to stand in front of us.

Despite the fact that she was on the council, I rarely saw Lilly at the Overwatch compound. She was in her dress uniform today and looked every inch the OW officer. Her white hair was pulled back, leaving her face as sharp and flawless as only an elder child could be. As I met her pale blue gaze, however, all I could think about was her signature on the bottom of our father's execution order.

"Yes," she said, tilting her head at me. There was something reluctant about her expression, and I had a feeling this interaction was not something she'd done by choice. "I think we are overdue for a conversation, little sister," she said slowly, eyes traveling over my face as though she were trying to get a read on me. I saw the mild frustration in her expression that I got from a lot of powerful telepaths. Many of them were slightly unnerved by my complete and utter blankness.

"A conversation about what?" I asked, narrowing my eyes at her. This was the most words she'd ever spoken to me in the three years since we met.

"What else?" She sighed. "We only have one thing in common. Come on, there's something I want to show you and I don't have all day."

I glanced at Liam who gave me a helpless shrug. "Okay, I guess," I said, a bit off balance.

Lillian grabbed my elbow and teleported us directly to a clearing on the highest mountain top I'd ever been on.

"Whoa," I gasped, head reeling despite the relative smoothness of my sister's teleport. My ears popped at the change in elevation and my hair whipped around my head as the mountain breeze picked up its coppery curls. I wrapped my arms around my chest and shivered. "We could have just gone to my dorm if you wanted someplace private to talk."

"The seclusion is only a fringe benefit to this location," Lillian said evenly, producing two cloaks with the wave of one hand. She handed me one with a zigzag pattern of orange and white before wrapping a solid blue one around her own long, thin shoulders. Then she turned elegantly, head erect and back straight, and headed down a small dirt path in the woods.

Glancing around with a sigh, I realized there was nothing to do but follow her. Reluctantly, I did.

The woods were as deep and lovely as any terraformed part of Cybele. It must have been almost two centuries old because through the underbrush I spotted trees with trunks so thick I couldn't have wrapped my arms all the way around them.

Slowly, we moved up and closer to another, even taller peak to our left. Then, suddenly, the trunks parted and a sheer cliff with a long, switchback staircase carved into its side loomed ahead of us.

"What is this place?" I asked, coming abreast of my sister. We hadn't spoken as we walked through the forest, and Lillian hadn't so much as glanced over her shoulder to see if I was keeping up.

"The Sanctuary of the One Stone," she replied. "The heart of the Divinitas Faith."

"Divinitas," I echoed. "They're the ones who think we're gods, right?"

She tilted her head slightly and I took that to be a half-way agreement. "Divine emissaries may be a better term," she said in an authoritarian tone, and I was reminded that she was a professor at University. "Few Brothers will speak of their religion aloud, but those that do usually call us angels."

We'd made it to the foot of the stairs now and began our ascent. Lillian led the way, her sharp shoulders held at an elegant angle even as she navigated the treacherously narrow stair. My father was strong and graceful, but Lilly reminded me even more strongly of a dancer. She just carried herself as if every muscle was under perfect control. Her equally controlled voice drifted back to me over her shoulder.

"I heard Vanessa approached you about the order," she said as calmly as if we were discussing the weather.

"If you mean the death warrant on our father's head, then yes," I agreed, knowing she'd hear the Usuriel temper in my tone and not caring. Ever since Grayson died, I was finding myself less worried about social graces; they just didn't seem as important anymore.

"I am guessing that means you have not reconsidered." She did glance at me then, blue eyes incredibly intense in her ageless face.

I scowled at her. "When was the last time you had a civil conversation with Dad? Honestly, he's not the uncontrollable monster everyone seems convinced he is. I should know; I just spent the two day break with him. He hardly touched alcohol and he's keeping Angelus Quietum in pristine condition. I'm not aware of many unstable drug addicts that can run an entire farm by themselves."

Lillian frowned and turned back to her footing on the stairs. We were silent as we finished climbing the cliff.

Slowly, the trees got thinner and more scraggly while the incline of the rock on either side of us got steeper. After a while, I put out a hand to steady myself on the rock wall to my left while I tried not to look over the drop on my right. I knew I could fly, but despite my flippant comment to Liam, it was a new ability, and I was still a little nervous this high off the ground.

Finally, feeling as if I'd made up for missing my workout that morning, I was able to see the flat plateau at the top of the stairs. Dominating the space was a gigantic monastery, its sloped roof reflecting the sunlight like a celestial jewel. Now that I saw it, I was fairly sure I'd seen stills of the huge, red and green temple built into the mountain. I frowned up at its soaring, cylindrical columns and round, jade doors as Lillian and I walked up the last few flights of stairs.

With a last burst of speed, Lillian finished the stairs and stood at the top. She leaned against her knees to catch her breath, her lovely head tilted upwards to let the strong mountain breeze blow back the strands of her ponytail.

I caught up to her and paused uncertainly, staring at the huge temple. It seemed to blend with the surroundings in a strangely organic way. Even so, I felt a deep discomfort with what it represented. I knew being an Usuriel made me different, but I'd never felt like some kind of god. Not that I was sure what a god felt like. However, I was pretty sure they didn't get covered in bruises from OW practice.

"What I don't think you're understanding about our father," Lillian began once we'd caught our breath. She didn't look at me while she was speaking, rather her eyes moved over the peaks and domes of the temple that loomed like an overlarge rocky outcropping before us. "Is that you have only known him for a tiny fraction of his lifespan. He has good spells and you've been privileged enough to only experience him at his best. What I want to show you today is what the more long-lived of us already know: that Gabriel's sanity is as fleeting and ephemeral as his sister's and the consequences when it slips keep getting more dangerous with each episode."

I frowned up at Lillian but tried to keep my tongue civil. I knew a decade and a half was a heartbeat to the length of time she'd known our father. Even so, Gabriel was the person I'd run to when I needed reassurance of my own mental stability, and he'd been as steady and gentle as I needed him to be. I didn't doubt he struggled with depression, but I was still unconvinced that such an issue was dangerous to anyone but him.

Little did I know.

"If he's been in a 'good spell' for the last decade or so, why push to fill the order now? Why not just let him be and see if he can find a workable equilibrium? It's not as if he's hurting anyone in Angelus Quietum," I pointed out.

Lillian shook her head, though she still didn't look at me. "Because it won't last. He's a myopic narcissist and he doesn't do well without an audience in attendance. Now that you've left, it's only a matter of time before things take a turn for the worse. Hell, they're already heading there if his little stunt at the Landing Day party is any indication. Trust me, the man is dangerous when left alone for any length of time." She darted a glance over at me and, seeing my unconvinced expression, took a deliberate breath. "Well, you'll see what I mean in a moment."

So it was that my father's only two living children walked towards the Sanctuary of the One Stone while arguing the merits of his execution.

As we came within sight of the temple, a brown-robed, middle-aged man emerged from one of the cavernous jade doors. Though his gait was perfectly smooth, especially for a mortal his age, he nevertheless moved quite rapidly to intercept us. The loose fabric of his robe folded about him in a brown puddle as he knelt directly in our path.

Lillian sighed, but her face was still that arrogant blank mask she wore more often than not. "Stand," she commanded, though not unkindly. "Please."

Not looking up nor saying a word, the balding devotee did as she asked and got to his feet. Still, he did not veer from our path. Bowing deeply, the monk turned and walked back into the temple. Since he was clearly following the only route in, we were forced to follow in his wake. I thought I read a note of irritation in Lillian's face, but she said nothing. Thus, we entered the great, round portal into the monastery in silence.

The first thing that assailed me when I stepped into the temple was the sheer size of the place. From the outside, the surrounding mountains and cliffs made it seem small, but inside the true scale was revealed. The ceilings couldn't have been lower than six meters and quite possibly stretched to seven. The walls were massively thick, and I could see the perfect, rounded top of a barrel vault curving high above us. The corridor was so long and broad I felt as if I was peering into the heart of the mountain itself. In the distance, the veil of darkness hid the end of the hall as if it simply went on forever.

The light was dim, yellow, and flickering. I thought there were paintings on the walls, but in the poor light I had a hard time making them out. I spotted braziers at regular intervals along the wall and realized there were no electric lights here. Without really thinking about it, my flames rippled along my skin, and I felt them reach for the licking tongues of the brazier lights. Then, all the fire in the room flared upwards, casting brighter shadows along the walls and emitting a roaring sigh of acknowledgment. Suddenly, the paintings were extremely clear and my breath caught.

If I thought the graffiti of Sorrow in Skykyle earned the title of art, I was wrong. The masterful skill poured into these walls was incredible. I'd never seen my family portrayed with such glowing, gentle brush strokes. Even the paintings in my grandparents' home paled in comparison to the hyper-realistic and stunningly idealized figures that filled these murals.

And it wasn't just my father this time. Yes, he was there of course. Front and center, in all his fierce perfection, Gabriel stood like the darkly beautiful mystery he was. They'd even captured a measure of the pain in his gaze.

But it didn't stop with Dad. No, we were all there — Gloria and D'nay shone down from the top of the composition like the sun and the moon, hands reaching out towards each other in obvious passion. Adora's fierce androgyny was flanked by Vanessa's indomitable monocular gaze, the two women almost challenging the viewer to look away from their burning beauty. On the other side of my father, Ariel, Hal, and Drex seemed to glow, their red and blond hair a fiery counterpoint to Adora's pale, blue-tinged shadows. Spiraling upwards from our siblings, Lillian and I framed the composition on the far left; bright red light and pale blue shade as if we each echoed an opposing side of our father's legacy.

I looked into my own painted face and felt extremely small. Did I truly look so ethereal and commanding in person? The mural's fairly burned with power and idealized flames licked from the edges of my hair. I somehow didn't think I ever had such presence—at least I hadn't in the bathroom mirror that morning.

My eyes slid back over Gloria and D'nay to the other side of the painting. Dax and Evensong completed Adora's side of the mural. I recognized Dax's blond elegance, of course, but I'd seen very few stills of Evensong. I'd forgotten she was a brunette. She seemed softer and gentler-edged than her siblings. If I'd been guessing parentage by looks, I would have switched Lillian and Evensong. Captured by the artist's talented brush, however, every member of the first three generations looked every inch the divine heralds these monks believed us to be.

That was just the first of the murals. My mouth hung open stupidly as I took in the rest of the hall. There were dozens of them; all huge, detailed, and masterfully rendered. Several altars at the base of the largest images overflowed with half-melted candles and gleaming trinkets. My eyes darted over them, my senses so overwhelmed by the scale and artistry that I couldn't analyze each one with the proper attention it deserved.

My father and Adora psi-piloting the *Inspiration* filled the wall on the other side of the doorway. A little farther down from that, I saw Grandmother in full mother-goddess glow, her hand pressed to my father's bare chest as he rested with eyes closed on the lap of a red-headed woman. I assumed that was Olivia, though the artist had only hinted at her face as she gazed with adoration at Gabriel's prone figure. Past that, I thought I caught a glimpse of Adora again, her figure adorned with grapes and tobacco leaves.

We'd begun walking again. The murals passed more slowly than I thought they should and it reinforced the mind-bending scale of this whole temple. After a long walk—and passing several paintings dedicated to third-gens, including Dax healing the sick and Lillian surrounded by a rampant herd of horses—we came to an intersection. Natural light streamed in from our left. An arched doorway at the end of the second corridor led out to an open-air ledge where the carefully laid tile of the temple interior gave way to rough, natural stone. It was scrubbed and clean, but the cracks and fissures of the plateau's icy nights were etched in its surface.

"I'd say you're next." Lillian's voice was extremely dry. Startled from my observation of the mountain range framed by the archway, I followed her gaze to a section of wall currently being attended to by the Brothers. There were scaffolds built against it to allow the artists to reach the top of the huge, arching wall; in fact, several of them were painting away as we walked up.

True to Lillian's observation, the figure taking shape under the artists' brushes was indeed female and red-headed. When I saw the same stylized flames as the first mural's ringing the edge of the composition, I knew my sister was right.

My stomach clenched even as the monks turned and noticed us. Several of their eyes widened and then, one by one, they fell into little prostrate puddles of brown robes, their paint brushes falling where they may.

I opened my mouth to protest their absurd reverence, but Lillian put a hand to my arm. Startled, I glanced at my sister, and she gave her head a mute shake. Then, she turned to the Brother who had been leading us this whole time.

"My sister and I would like to contemplate the view privately for a few moments," she said.

The Brother bowed deeply to her, then retreated to the curve of the wall near the scaffolds. I watched as he sat cross-legged on the floor and folded his hands in his lap.

"Come on, let's finish our talk." Lillian didn't wait for my reply before striding quickly through the final arch and out into the bright sunlight. I followed in her wake, still unsure how to feel about this whole experience.

"I thought they mainly worshiped Dad," I said slowly once we were out of easy earshot of the monks. The view from the plateau was spectacular. The sloping Galloway mountains curved their tree-furred fingers to the mountain streams that fed Lake Angelus. I could just barely make out its glimmering surface in the far distance to my left. "I didn't realize they had altars for every member of the Family."

"Well, all of the first three gens get special treatment," Lillian replied and gestured to a dark shape seated on the very end of the ledge. "But you're right, Dad is a particular favorite."

We drew closer, and I realized the seated figure was actually a life-size sculpture carved from the same dark rock as the mountain itself. Closer still and I recognized the angle of his shoulders like I did my own. I felt strangely numb as I walked up to a perfect replica of my father's seated form. From the strands of hair that straggled away from his ponytail to the veins of his bare hands and arms, it looked as if the monks had abducted my father and painted him to match the stone. Glancing at his wrists, I frowned slightly and realized that he had quite a few more scars these days than when the sculpture had been done. I suddenly felt heartsick.

"Now that we're really alone, I can say what I've truly brought you here for," Lillian said, meeting my gaze defiantly. I was pretty sure what was coming next. Sure enough: "I know you told Vanessa that you weren't willing to complete the execution order on our father. I respect that decision even if I don't agree with it. However, before you close the matter completely, I feel you need all the facts."

I eyed the unnervingly life-like sculpture. "While this whole thing is rather... creepy... I'm not sure it's any kind of damning evidence. I mean, it's these monks that are kind of crazy, not Dad."

Lillian nodded, her face falling into something close to determination. "Well, then, will you at least hear me out?"

With a longing glance at Lake Angelus, I shrugged. It was the first time my sister had ever been willing to talk with me. The least I could do was listen to what she had to say. "Okay, fine."

"Thank you," Lillian said, her head lifting with the same supreme dignity I'd seen in Adora. "One of the most often-cited arguments for our father's sanity is that he survived Olivia and Hal's deaths without falling back to the morphine." Lillian glanced at the sculpture with something like contempt. She obviously didn't care for what it symbolized—both the man and the deity these mortals had built him up to be. "And I suppose there is some truth to that. He didn't betray his promises to his first wife immediately. No, he took a page from her book and shut down completely. He sat right there." She pointed to the sculpture and met my eye. "Every waking moment that didn't include eating, bathing or dressing for over fifty years. He didn't speak, he didn't smile, he didn't acknowledge another living being for nearly that entire stretch. He let an entire religious cult spring up around him without a single word of encouragement...or discouragement. And he has refused to set foot here ever since Ariel convinced him to leave."

I glanced between the opening to the monastery and the silent stone effigy. This whole trip was definitely like something out of a bad holo, I'd give her that.

"Now, you tell me just how stable that seems to you," she said, eyes flashing. "Because if this isn't enough to convince you, I can tell you a few stories about growing up with him at Angelus Quietum that were not horseback rides and yoga." I gave her a sharper glance at that one, and she made a disgusted face. "Yes, I've heard about how much he's supposedly mellowed out there with you." Her lip curled. "Sometimes I wonder if you've ever even met the man who raised me." She glared back down at the sculpture as if it could send her displeasure back to its subject. "The one who would have screaming fights with my mother before taking off to get black-out drunk with his damn sister. The one who would disappear for days and make Mom worry herself sick thinking he was dead in a ditch before coming home claiming he'd been too busy at the Overwatch to even answer her tap. The one who showed up to Mom's funeral so fucking intoxicated his own mother wouldn't let him into the service and had to carry him home and put him to bed."

I watched her face and realized that Lilly wasn't actually cold or emotionless. Now that the wall of arrogance was down, underneath it Lillian was actually angry. Not the kind of anger that came and went with the occasional unkind word or frustrating situation. No, my sister was angry the way my father was sad—perpetually and deeply ingrained in the fiber of her being. I remembered what Gabriel had said about his second marriage not working out. Clearly Lillian still carried the scars of that flawed relationship and, looking into her livid expression, I had a feeling I wouldn't be able to explain to her why a failed marriage wasn't grounds for execution.

"That's all you have? That's why you brought me all the way out here?" I asked, my own temper flaring. I was really getting sick of people trying to use my father's struggles with substance abuse as a reason to condemn him to death. "To complain to me about how shitty a father he was to you? Okay. Fine. Sometimes Dad isn't the best person in the world. I've had a few experiences with his less roses and butterflies side, too, believe it or not. But that doesn't mean he's dangerous or unstable. It just means he doesn't know when to put the damn bottle down sometimes. Last I checked, that wasn't an executable offense."

A sour smile twisted across Lillian's sharp features, ruining the usual Family good looks. Or maybe I just didn't find my sister's personality attractive. That was a possibility, too.

"You didn't live through it, so you don't understand. He was an alcoholic, yes, but that wasn't the real issue. The real problem was that he could never think past his own wants and needs. At least not far enough to give a damn about what his actions were doing to Mom and me."

Lillian broke off, her pale face reddening, and I suspected she might be fighting tears. When she continued after a moment, however, her voice was soft but steady. "And maybe you're thinking that the man has grown up a bit since then. First, may I point out that he was past his second century by the time I was born. He wasn't young by any stretch of the imagination. And things did not improve after my mother's death. If anything, they got exponentially worse. I assume you're familiar with Sorrow by now."

I thought about the late nights spent with Liam and James researching the urban legend spawned by my father's sixty-year drug binge. "I might have heard of him once or twice."

Lillian took my dry humor with a sneer of disgust. "Like I said before, you've only seen the tiny, lucid window of the last thirteen years. Before that, he'd been slowly going downhill for well over a century. If you talk to scholars on the subject, and I have, most of them agree his stability peaked during Olivia's lifetime. He was just over a hundred and fifty when she died, Gracie. He's over four hundred now. What does that tell you about the last two hundred and fifty years?"

I glanced between the statue and my furious sister. I tried to empathize with her anger, but couldn't find the energy. "That it's about damn time the man caught a break," I said evenly. Then, I met Lillian's eye. "Maybe that's why the universe was kind enough to give me this decision instead of you. Maybe Fate knew Dad deserved at least one stroke of good luck after centuries of being torn apart."

Lillian looked pretty pissed. But before she could get an angry word out, I cut her off. "No. You got your say. I heard it. Now, you get to hear me." I met her blazing gaze and pulled on the flames until I knew my own was equally incandescent. "You and Vanessa may have an execution order out for him, but the way I see it, that document is way out of date. It was signed before he cleaned himself up and spent a decade raising me in peace and quiet. So, unless something major changes, consider Gabriel under my protection. Anyone who tries to complete that order without a really compelling and urgent reason will have to answer to me."

"Gracie..." Lillian started but I stopped her with a savage glare.

"Tell the rest of the Overwatch. Make sure they all know. Vanessa can toss me out of the OW if she wants, but it won't change anything. I don't care if it's you or 'Nessa or Liam." That was a little bit of a lie, but I'm pretty sure my Usuriel blank face held. "Anyone who goes after Gabriel better like fire, because they'll be getting a lot of it. Without a single thought of warning."

I'd thought my sister was pale before. She turned white as a ghost despite the chill mountain air. "You mean that, don't you," she whispered, staring into my face with very wide eyes.

I thought of my father's strong arms wrapping themselves around me despite the splatters of Grayson's blood. I thought of the vulnerable expression on his face when he'd realized what I'd seen in my dreams, and again when he asked if there were any other ghosts haunting Angelus Quietum. I wondered just how shattered he'd be if he knew that Lillian and Vanessa were actively campaigning for his execution. I felt my expression harden into something resolute. "Absolutely."

Chapter 5

Vanessa and Politics

After that pronouncement, Lillian swiftly and efficiently delivered me back to my dormitory. She did linger in the doorway just long enough to discuss the dire political situation, however.

"It's only a matter of time now," she said, her eyes flinty shards of blue ice, "before Riland declares war on the Terrans. When that happens, they'll try to use it as a screen to mask their purge of the vampires. Mark me, it will be bloody and it's not going to stay on that side of the Provinces."

Finally, she was saying something I agreed with. It didn't make me feel much better, but at least we weren't at odds on this topic. "I know some people who are trying to stop it, but I think you're right," I replied, unwrapping her cloak from about my shoulders and handing it back to her. "War may be inevitable."

My sister took the manteau from me as if it were mildly contaminated. "If you really do care about Dad, you need to convince him to go to New Paradise," she said, not meeting my eye, "I've already put out a warning to the rest of the Family. If things go as badly as I think they will soon, we need to get the most vulnerable out of harm's way."

"Ummm... I'm not sure Dad counts as vulnerable," I pointed out, "any more than you or I do. And you really think he's going to leave Angelus Quietum any time soon?"

Lilly gave a fluid shrug. "Actually, I was more thinking that he'd be a nice layer of added protection for the new colony," she sighed, "If he's really doing as well as you think he is, it would be nice to have an elder child guarding our evacuation route."

My chest tightened at her phrasing. "So that's what New Paradise is? An evacuation route for the Family?"

My sister's face was grim. "We haven't said as much to the younger children yet, but between us... that's exactly what it is." She shook her head. "This whole mortals and immortals mingling thing is a failed experiment. It's damaging for everyone involved. Just look at what it's done to Dad... and the Divinitas Brothers... and Riland. No, it's not working, and we need our own place—a place where the mortals won't have to worry about us and our dangerous skills; a place where we won't have to worry about angry mortal mobs with pitchforks and torches. It's the only way we'll preserve the peace."

I frowned, considering her words. Her statements seemed short-sighted to me; mortals and immortals had been coexisting for centuries. Perhaps it caused problems here and there, but I felt as if Riland's violent intolerance was more to blame for our current conflict than the intrinsic nature of our diverse society. I opened my mouth to say so when Lilly turned abruptly away.

"It has been a long morning. I should let you get some lunch. I hope you will give some thought to our talk," Lillian said and, without another word, she disappeared in a shower of blue embers.

I sighed as the silence of the hallway rang in my ears.

"Yeah... I'll think about it."

***

The next week and a half I spent trying to focus on school. My studies had been sadly neglected for a while, and it wasn't even hard to make excuses to Liam about why our meals had to be short and functional.

For his part, Liam seemed to have decided I needed a little space. I was grateful for it, even if I found myself lonely in the evenings once all of my make-up work was finally done. After my tour of the Sanctuary, I'd found enough emotional stability to stop picking fights with my OW partner and our interactions were civil enough, if a little icy. I could tell I'd hurt him again and a tiny corner of my heart wondered just how many times I could damage our relationship before I broke it beyond repair.

Still, in all matters OW, we continued to be extremely well-matched partners. My stoic flames countered his razor wit and approachable humor with marked success. Even Vanessa, head of the Overwatch, commented on how well we were coming along.

I'd been afraid Vanessa would be upset about my disclosure of information to James, but when I broached the topic in her office, she shrugged it off.

"Anything that helps avert this conflict," she sighed. "I'd rather if you had told me first, but I don't think you've done any harm. In fact, truthfully, I think you may have prevented the whole thing from exploding. The Terrans seem to have headed off Riland's claims of attack pretty well. They have Landing and Skykyle mostly convinced that those avatars weren't their manufacture."

I felt like cheering for James at that news. "That's good, right?" I asked, glancing over at Liam. He stood several paces away, looking into the practice gallery. He liked to keep a healthy physical distance between us lately.

"The peace is holding for now," Vanessa agreed, rubbing her temple by her bad eye absently, "but tensions are still high. I'm afraid all it would take to set things off is an incident or two. So try to keep things low profile, if you can. The anti-Awareness sentiment is closer to home than you may think."

I thought of Malcolm and frowned. "Yeah, I've run into that once or twice."

"A lot of the younger children are heading to New Paradise, so at least most of them will be out of harm's way if things go poorly," Liam said, looking our way again. I knew his parents and siblings had made arrangements to take an extended vacation in the next few weeks. From what I could tell, most of the Family members under the tenth generation were trying to find ways to leave the continent. I knew Leesil had finally found that job opening on Hal and I was pretty sure her parents and siblings were planning to move with her. I didn't blame them. Even with the dense Usuriel population in Landing, I was beginning to draw unfriendly looks at University.

"I wish the first two generations would move in that direction," Vanessa sighed. "But Grandmother is determined to have Ileesia at the University Hospital complex, and Fate knows, her men won't be straying far from her side at this point. D'nay and Gabriel have closed ranks around her every time I try to set foot in Chronurea Valley lately."

"Between the three of them, I don't think anyone will be able to touch a hair on Ileesia's head," Liam pointed out. "And Riland would have to be barking mad to go after the first two generations all in one place. They're safe enough where they are, I imagine."

"I hope so," Vanessa agreed tiredly.

***

That night, I dreamed of Dad. The familiar filth of Adora's death scene wrapped its putrid stench around my throat. I only caught a flicker of one pale wrist this time; otherwise, I didn't even see my aunt. Instead, my father's gray face dominated the dream as I forced air between his still lips. It took until sunrise before his silent chest finally rose on its own and I sobbed in relief, rolling him over onto his side to bring up the poison I'd been locked in deadly competition with all night.

I woke with tears clinging to my sticky cheeks.

"Stella," I muttered, tapping my implant to summon the AI. "Time is it?"

"Oh four hundred thirty."

I groaned and peeled an eyelid open. The window was still black as pitch. I burrowed my head back under my pillow and tried to fall back to sleep.

A warm wind ruffled my curls. I moaned and poked my nose out from underneath my pillow. Sure as electricity in a socket, Ariel's glowing figure illuminated the center of my tiny dormitory.

"What do you want?" I demanded of the ghost. I gave up on sleep and threw the covers off my legs. My head still groggy, I groped for the little blue journal on my bedside stand. With one finger, I found the ribbon I used to mark our place and flipped open the fragile pages.

I frowned at the end of our last conversation. There was no additional looping handwriting to explain my sister's appearance. I glanced in confusion at the ghost. To my surprise, her hands were empty of her version of the blue book. In fact, her whole outfit was wrong. Instead of the neat, brown skirt suit she'd worn in every appearance since I was a child, she was dressed in a thin, loose, white shift and baggy, draw-string pants. Her arms wrapped around her thin chest, her knuckles white as if she were cold. She shivered, her green eyes wide as she stared around the room.

"Ariel?" I wrote her name in the book. She didn't react. "Ariel?" I said her name aloud this time.

Her gaze snapped to me and her mouth moved rapidly, but no sound came out. I shook my head in confusion and held up the book. She frowned, her brows knitting together. She reached for the book with one glowing hand. It passed through my skin in a warm wave.

Ariel jumped back as if she'd been burned, rubbing her hand and moving her mouth rapidly again. There was still no sound, but I suspected she was cursing.

"Ariel, are you okay?" I asked.

My usually composed sister shook her head at me, her red curls blowing in the ethereal wind that always accompanied her. At least something hadn't changed. Then, with a last terrified look, she turned away from me and ran through the far wall. The eerie glow faded with her and I was left alone in the dim blue of the comm's nightlight.

My stomach twisted. "Ariel?" I called again into the silent room. Her glow failed to reappear. I tapped my implant. "Stella?"

"Yes, Gracie?" The AI's silver face lit up the comm screen over my bed.

"Is everything okay at Angelus Quietum?"

The AI gave me a long, blank stare.

"I know he's probably asleep and you're not supposed to give me vital readings or anything but... do you know if Dad's okay?" I ran a hand through my red waves, pushing them away from my face. With Stella's artificial gaze meeting mine, the anxieties of dreams and ghosts seemed ephemeral and silly. "You know what, never mind. You don't have to wake him up. Forget I said anything."

Stella's gaze went distant, then she blinked and tilted her head at me. "Gabriel is asleep in his own bed. All vital signs are normal."

The air suddenly seemed cleaner and easier to pull into my lungs. "Thanks, Stella."

"You're welcome."

The comm screen went dark. I shivered, the ever-present dread in my gut bubbling as my anxiety settled. "Might as well start the day."

***

After washing my face in the sink, I tossed on my OW workout blues and took off for the compound. If I had to be up before the sun, at least I could get my workout in before I had to share the free weights with anyone.

Using my flames to fly through the early morning dark was invigorating, their orange tongues spiraling out and illuminating the dense terraformed foliage below me. I'd been traveling this way more often since my spat with Liam. While it took more energy, it was easier on my stomach than his seventeenth-generation teleportation.

The Overwatch compound loomed into view, its concrete and solar panels distinctly out of place in the middle of the woods. I alighted near the entrance and pulled out my badge. The "OW" on its circular surface glowed blue when my skin touched the metal, certifying me as the officer qualified to carry it. I held it up to Johnny at the door and he buzzed me through to the computer checkpoint. There, Stella scanned me before opening the inner doors with a whoosh of filtered air.

As a global organization, the Overwatch never

completely slept. The hallways were lit and I passed two fellow officers escorting an offender to a holding cell. The big gymnasium was empty of people, though. Its massive ceiling stretched into dark shadows, and the lights in Vanessa's office were black. Tossing my towel on the bench beside the free weights, I settled into my workout.

I'd just finished my first set of reps when raised voices drew my attention to the hallway.

"Well then, wake her up!" Vanessa shouted, slamming through the practice room door. The metal walls echoed with the violence of her entrance. I'd sparred with Vanessa before, and I knew my first cousin was incredibly strong despite her diminutive size.

"Fine. But she'll be pissed. Just letting you know." Camphor's dark figure faded away from Vanessa's side with a swirl of green motes.

The head of the Overwatch scowled at the place where her partner disappeared. Then, with a twist of her tiny shoulders, she marched towards the locker rooms on the back right wall. As she passed under a light, the dark stains across her hands and uniform glistened a deep red.

"Everything alright?" I called to her, drying off my neck with a towel.

Vanessa paused, her head snapping in my direction as if she hadn't noticed my presence. I knew my head blind status sometimes unnerved the high level telepaths, but Vanessa didn't usually let on that it bothered her. She stared at me with her one good eye, the other socket obscured by the black eye patch I'd never seen her without.

"No," she replied after a long silence. She rubbed at the scarred temple next to her bad eye. "I just had to execute a diplomat."

My stomach clenched. "Not..."

She waved one dainty hand to dismiss my fears. "No, no, it's not your friend. James, isn't it?"

I nodded.

"He's around your age, isn't he? Still in University?"

"He's a year older. But yes, still in school. Though they have him pulling double shifts at the embassy on top of the school work lately."

Vanessa ran a hand through her mane of black-and-white-streaked hair, then glanced at the dried blood on her palm and cringed. "Don't worry," she said, wiping her hand ineffectually on the hip of her tailored OW blue uniform, "this guy was older. And Family. Fates, I hate having to take out one of our own."

I swallowed hard and took a step closer to her. "What happened?"

Vanessa glanced around the empty practice room, then jerked her head in the direction of her office. "If you really want to know, why don't you come to my office when you're done down here? I'm going to get cleaned up, but it shouldn't take me long. I'll meet you there."

I glanced at the windows set high in the three-story wall behind me. The sky was turning a navy blue that spoke of gathering dawn.

"Okay," I agreed and moved over to the punching bags.

Liam came in just as I finished. "You're here early."

"I couldn't sleep," I muttered, giving the bag one last jab. It shuddered with the impact of my fist, which was much stronger than a mortal my size could have accomplished. Even without enhancing my punches with pyrokinesis, I could take down most men with a single blow. Despite his telekinesis, Liam's torso still bore the scars of our training bouts.

"Everything okay?"

"Actually, I was about to go meet up with Vanessa," I said, moving over to the bench and toweling off. "She just got back from executing a diplomat."

Liam's face went white. "A diplomat?"

"Not James," I reassured him.

"Gracie?" Vanessa emerged from the locker rooms in a fresh uniform, her damp hair no less wild around her petite shoulders.

"I'm coming," I called to her, tossing my towel over my neck.

"Bring Liam with you," she said, moving towards the back of the practice galley.

Liam lifted a helpless shoulder before falling into step with me. We walked through the slowly populating workout room, edging carefully around practice mats, balance beams, chained hoops, and weighted balls. Jillian and a few other OW officers watched us with mild curiosity as we disappeared into the back stairway.

After three sets of switchback stairs, I was regretting not suggesting Liam teleport us up to Vanessa's lofty perch. Camphor had already done just that, delivering a middle-aged mortal woman with thick spectacles and a halo of black, wiry hair. She glared at Vanessa with gleaming, intelligent eyes.

"Do you have any idea what time it is?" she demanded, adjusting her patterned dress over an ample figure. Her hands were covered in tiny wires and circuits and, unless I was mistaken, they looked implanted into her flesh. I had never seen such modifications before, and I had to avert my eyes to keep from staring.

"I apologize for the inconvenience, Doria, but you did sign a contract that includes an urgency clause," Vanessa said smoothly, settling herself in the wheeled leather chair behind the desk. "I'm afraid this couldn't wait until your normal hours."

"Hmmm." Disbelief was clear in the woman's tone. She planted her hands on her hips and gave the head of the OW a glare I would have wilted under.

Vanessa rubbed at her temple again, her mouth thin and flat. With a gesture, two boxes appeared above the desk with a shower of pale blue sparks. They floated over to Doria who plucked them from the air with raised brows. She pressed a finger to the opening mechanism and the lids lifted to reveal over a dozen holo disks. It was obsolete tech. Dad had a few old ones tucked away at Angelus Quietum, otherwise I wouldn't have known what I was looking at.

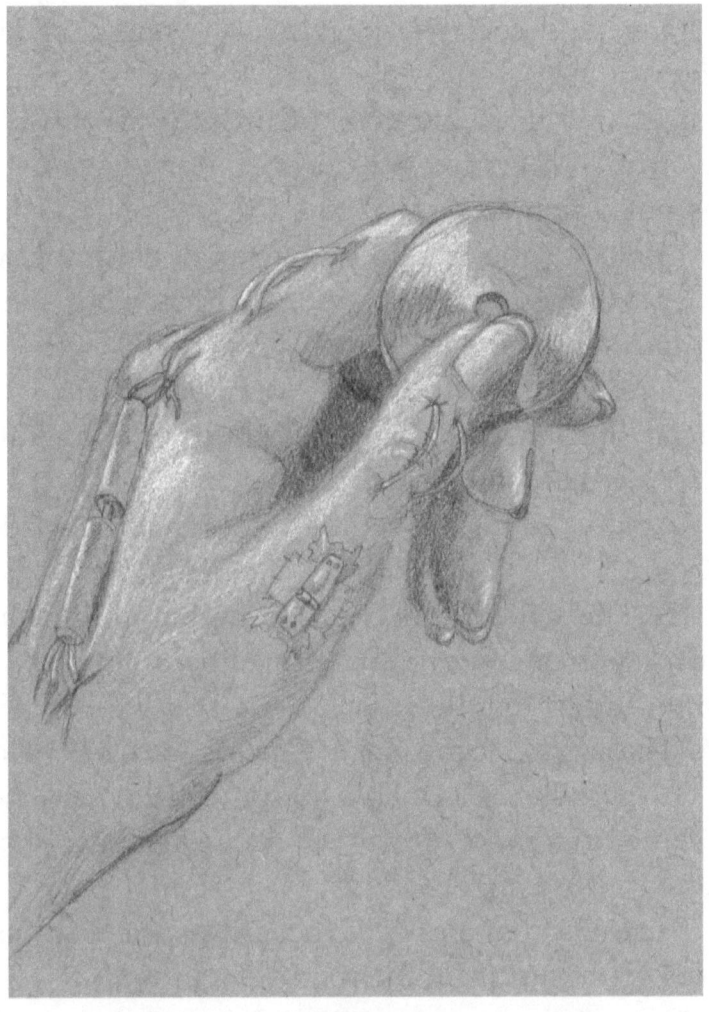

"Physical data storage?" One eyebrow quirked higher on the woman's mobile face. Her thick fingers pulled one of the gleaming cylinders from its case and held it to the gathering dawn light. "Newly printed, too." Her eyes narrowed, snapping to Vanessa. "Where did you find these?"

"Can you read what's on them?" Vanessa's voice was flat.

Doria waggled her head in an ambivalent way. "I can try. But I'll need access to a core. I don't have the right equipment at home."

"Stella," Vanessa said with a tap of her implant.

"Yes, Vanessa?" The silver AI appeared on the large comm screen hung over the desk.

"Grant temporary level 1A access to Doria Blackford. She'll need to work in your core for a while. Give her any help you can, okay?"

"Access granted. I look forward to working with you, Doria."

"I'll show her to the core," Camphor volunteered, gesturing with one midnight-skinned hand for the computer expert to follow him.

"Thank you, Camphor," Vanessa said, her voice tired. "Hopefully we'll be able to figure out where those disks came from more effectively once we know what's on them."

Doria nodded, her eyes focused on the disks as she followed Camphor from the room.

"Now," Vanessa sat straighter in her chair as she turned to me and Liam. "You're both friends with this Terran diplomat, James, right?"

"Yes," Liam agreed. "We've both known James for years. He stayed with Gabe and Gracie the year before the flood. I actually met him during the evacuation efforts."

"And you've been attending Landing University together?"

"We don't see much of him anymore," I said. "But for the first year or so we were... close." I thought of the days we walked across campus holding hands, James linking Liam and me with his gentle smile. My throat tightened.

"Has he ever mentioned someone named Damien Usuriel?"

Liam and I exchanged a meaningful glance. "Only once," I said slowly.

Vanessa leaned forward. "Go on."

"About... what... six months ago now?" Liam glanced at me for confirmation and I nodded. "James woke us up at the crack of dawn, all worked up about rumors of war between Riland and Terra Nova. Chattering on about anti-awareness tech and biological weapons. He mentioned Damien getting pissed enough to take a swing at one of the Riland ambassadors."

Vanessa took a deliberate breath, her one ice-blue eye moving between us thoughtfully. "Did he mention anything about Damien in your conversation last week, Gracie?"

"No. We mostly just talked about the rogue androids or avatars or whatever those mechanical monsters were in Riland."

"The ones you toasted?" Liam cocked an eyebrow at me.

"Yeah, those." I rubbed a hand against my workout pants nervously. The way James looked at me after seeing the pictures of those avatar-like creations smashed and burned to a crisp had bordered closer to fear than I felt comfortable with.

"Okay," Vanessa said, a fingertip tracing the scar that interrupted her left eyebrow. "I guess it's possible that this was a random mental break..."

I cleared my throat. "If you don't mind, 'Nessa, what exactly happened?"

Her eye closed and her head bowed. It was the first time I'd seen my cousin humbled. "We got a call about" — she tapped her implant— "three hours ago. Hostage situation. A coworker from the embassy was the one who called it in. She said Damien didn't show up for work. When someone went to check on him, they found his wife dead in the living room. Blood everywhere. Coworker said Damien had the kids upstairs and was threatening to kill them if anyone came up."

"Fates." Liam's long fingers wrapped around his throat.

Vanessa nodded her agreement with his horrified reaction. "I thought it best to handle this myself. I called in Camphor, and we were there within ten minutes."

"And? The kids?" I whispered.

Vanessa met my gaze with a dead expression. My stomach dropped. "From what we can tell, they were already dead." Her voice was hardly above a whisper, her jaw so tight her lips barely moved. "It was just bait to get the biggest guns we had on scene. He was a two-T— 'path and 'porter— and a damn strong one for being a twelfth gen. He had the whole house shielded. There was no way to know if he was a danger to those children or not."

I thought of the blood on Vanessa's uniform. "You neutralized him yourself."

She stared at her hands as if she could still see the blood on them. Then her head lifted and her chin tilted into that Usuriel arrogance I knew so well. "There are shitty parts of this job. Today was one of them."

"Oh, 'Nessa," Liam breathed. "I'm so—"

She cut him off with one raised hand, her eye closed and her expression tight. "Not now," she hissed. "There will be time for that later. Right now, we need to figure out what the fuck happened. Because at some point in the next sixty hours, I'm going to have to look at the grandparents of those two children and explain why their father teleported their hearts right out of their chests."

Bile rose in the back of my throat, but I managed to lock down my expression into utter neutrality. Most Usuriels didn't master the blank face until they passed a human lifespan. Mine was pretty reliable at only nineteen. One of the few perks of being raised by a four-hundred-year-old second-gen.

"Were there any signs of illegal activity? Drug use? What do his bank accounts look like?" I asked the questions rapid fire, using the familiar line of inquiry to ground myself.

Vanessa took a deeper breath. "Those were my first questions, too. Camphor looked up his financials. There were some large cash withdrawals. I'm thinking either extortion or drug use."

"Or both," Liam commented, his arms now folded across his chest.

"Or both," Vanessa agreed. "We found a suicide

note." She produced a slip of paper from the air to her left. It was wrinkled, and the edge looked torn from a spiral bound notebook. "It was taped to those boxes of disks."

"Interesting," Liam murmured, leaning over my shoulder as I took the offered paper.

"To the officers who find this," I read aloud. "I'm incredibly sorry. There was no other way. Damien."

I handed the note to Liam who took it gingerly in his large hands. "Fucking Fate," my partner muttered under his breath as he examined the paper.

"Well, you didn't kill an innocent man," I pointed out with a shrug. "His intentions were clear. He wanted you to kill him. This wasn't your fault, Vanessa."

"I know." She ran a hand through her striped mane. "But that's not how this is supposed to work. I should be able to diffuse the situation, get some answers for the family, hold a hearing. All of that comes before an execution."

"When things go right," Liam said, handing her back the suicide note. "You did what you felt you had to at the time, I'm sure."

Vanessa started to nod, then stiffened and held up a finger. She tapped the base of her neck, activating the rice-sized implant under her skin. "Yes? Doria? Okay. Okay, calm down. What is it?"

Liam and I raised an eyebrow at each other in the long silence.

"Alright, I'm coming. Okay! Yes! I'm coming. I'm coming. Alright. Calm down. We'll be right there."

Vanessa tapped off her implant.

"Doria found something?" Liam asked.

"We need to go," Vanessa replied sharply. "Take my hand."

Obediently, Liam and I took her child-sized hands in our own. With a wave of pale blue psi, the room dissolved around us.

Chapter 6

DNA

The core materialized in a wave of cool, filtered air, and darkness. Tiny blue lights flickered on countless black boxes of wires and circuits. Ropes of bundled wires as thick as my thigh rose like corded snakes to wrap coils around the edges of the room.

"I hope one of you knows something about genetics," Doria said, her voice coming from my right. She and Camphor sat silhouetted against the pale blue glow of a holo table.

"Only what I've picked up from Lilly over the years," Vanessa responded, crossing her arms over her chest and moving in their direction. Liam and I followed in her wake.

"You may want to call in an expert," Camphor said over his shoulder. His eyes burned a luminescent green in the dim lighting. "Because I think I know what I'm looking at. But this is the kind of thing we can't afford to be wrong on."

Vanessa planted herself between Camphor's standing figure and Doria's seated one, her good eye squinting up at the flickering double helixes rotating on the display.

"DNA?"

"Not just any DNA," Doria said, flicking a wired finger. New strands of proteins entered the display and scrolled next to the original chain. "This is Family DNA. It's labeled as 'Usuriel – elder child' in the database. And this is a viral strain. Look at the codes here and here." She pointed to two sequences that lit up, then zoomed in at her touch. "If I'm not mistaken, they code for the same exact proteins."

I frowned at Liam who shrugged. "What does that mean?"

"Like I said, I'm not an expert," Camphor said, turning those glowing green eyes in my direction. "But the file is listed as 'Solutions Project 3.' If I had to guess, we're looking at a biological weapon."

"One that's been tailor made for the Family," Doria murmured.

"Camphor, go get Lilly," Vanessa said, her eyes fixed on the blinking helixes.

Her broad-shouldered partner tapped his neck for the time. "I think she's in class at the moment."

"I don't care. Unless she's up to her elbows in neurosurgery, I want her here now."

Camphor nodded and disappeared in a rush of green sparks.

"And you two." Vanessa rounded on Liam and I. "I think it's time I had a conversation with this diplomat friend of yours."

"He's pretty busy lately," I warned, leaning closer to Liam.

"I think he can clear his schedule for this," Liam reassured me, putting a hand on my shoulder. "Especially if you and I are the ones to extend the invitation, Gracie. Where are we having our meeting?"

"In my office is fine, Liam. As quickly as you can get a hold of him."

I swallowed down the lump in my throat and nodded. Liam's power rushed up my spine and we vanished in a cloud of blue.

***

Liam knocked at James' door politely. I tapped my foot and tried to breathe through the restlessness in my stomach.

"So, what exactly did you two fight about after those damn avatars? The way you talked about it with Vanessa, it sounded like a pretty civil conversation." Liam arched a dark brow in my direction.

"Is he even in there?" I dodged the question, cringing inwardly at the waspishness of my tone. My boys used to bring out the best in me.

"Yeah, but I think he's asleep." Liam's eyes went distant. "Oh yeah, definitely asleep."

"I guess we'll just have to knock harder." I suited action to word, rapping my knuckles on the alloy door hard enough to sting. "James! Get up!"

A muffled curse issued from inside the dormitory, followed by a sliding crash.

"Last chance to tell me so I don't put my foot in a big pile of social shit," Liam muttered out of the corner of his mouth.

"As long as you do most of the talking, it'll be fine," I whispered. "You're always better with words than I am, anyway." I put a hand on his arm and gave him earnest blue eyes. "Seriously. Pretend I'm not here and we'll all get along famously."

"Okay..."

The door slid open, revealing a disheveled Terran ambassador-in-training and a dormitory so full of haphazard stacks of files and memory pads it was impossible to say which one had fallen over most recently.

"Gracie. Liam. What are you doing here?" James gasped, his eyes moving cautiously between us. "Did we have a breakfast date and I just forgot? Fates, I'm sorry. I've been all over the place."

Liam cleared his throat. "No, we didn't have anything planned. In fact, we're not really here on a social call."

James' blond brows furrowed and a few tangled locks of hair fell across his forehead. He pushed them back absently. "Is everything okay?"

"Actually, there was an incident earlier this morning. It involved a diplomat you might be familiar with. Vanessa was hoping you'd be willing to come down to the OW compound and tell us what you know about him." Liam struck just the right tone between gentle and professional.

"Ahhh... I don't know. I've got a class in—" he tapped his implant and cringed "—forty-five minutes. I should really get showered and dressed. Can it wait until this afternoon?"

"I think Vanessa was hoping for sooner rather than later."

James turned back to the room, scratching the back of his neck. "I've already missed so much class with this internship. I should really…" He trailed off, stooping to pick up some papers from the floor.

Diplomacy wasn't getting us anywhere. "Damien Usuriel is dead," I said flatly. "He murdered his whole family before committing suicide by Overwatch. I really think you need to make the time for this."

All the blood left James' face and his eyes got wide enough to show white around the edges. "Oh," he breathed, a hand coming up to cover his mouth. "Fates. His whole… but he has two kids…"

"Your professor will understand. Vanessa needs all the information you can give her," Liam said, his voice soft but urgent.

"Right. Yes. Of course." James cast about for a fresh shirt, finally pulling one from a basket of folded laundry on the floor. He sat down on the bed with it and stared blankly at the wall.

"Hey," I said gently, stepping closer to him. Guilt squirmed in my gut and I put a hand on his shoulder. "I'm sorry about your friend. I hate dropping this on you and then rushing you out the door. But Vanessa wants to have something to tell his family sooner rather than later."

James looked up at me, his familiar, mortal features reddening with the beginnings of grief. "Yeah, of course. And I want to help. I just… I don't… I don't know what I could possibly tell her."

"Anything you saw or overheard about him at the embassy might be useful," Liam said, tapping my elbow. "Come on, Grace. Let's give him a minute to get himself together. We'll wait for you right here in the hall."

James took a shaking breath. "Yeah. Okay."

Liam and I left the room, the door automatically hissing shut behind us.

"You could have let Vanessa drop that bomb," Liam grumbled, crossing his arms and leaning back against the wall.

"What's the point? No matter who told him, those two kids will still be just as dead."

"You have absolutely no tact, did you know that?"

"I told you to do the talking." I adjusted my workout shirt as an excuse not to meet his disappointed gaze.

"I was. Why didn't you let me handle it?"

I groaned and rubbed one eye. The grit of my shortened night's sleep ground against my eyeball. "It worked, didn't it? He's moving."

Liam's half-lidded expression communicated his opinion of our friend's current mental state.

The dread in my gut tried to twist itself into flames again, but all I could see in my mind's eye was James' heartbroken face. Fates, what was wrong with me? These were my boys—the only men I had ever loved besides my father—and the only expression I ever saw in their eyes anymore was disappointment and pain. With a massive act of will, I closed my fist on the flames in my chest.

"I'm sorry," I muttered. "You're right. I should have let you handle it."

My partner's eyebrow went up. "Was that an actual apology?"

I sucked air in through my nose and let it stream back out my mouth. "Yes. And not just for James." I jerked a thumb at the still-closed door. "I haven't been in a good emotional place lately. I don't know why I keep taking it out on you, but I can't seem to stop it."

Liam's mouth fell open. Before he had a chance to respond, James' door opened.

"Okay." Our diplomat looked a little red-eyed but otherwise steadier than he had earlier. "I'm ready to go."

"James—" I started, but he shook his head, a tiny upward tilt of his mouth forestalling my apologies.

"It's okay, Gracie. You're just being you." His faded-blue eyes crinkled affectionately at the corners. "I'm glad you and Liam were the officers to come, even if it's bad news. I've missed you."

I didn't have words for the grace James always gave me. Instead, I offered him my hand. He took it with an affectionate squeeze.

"We've missed you, too," Liam said. "Come on, we don't want to keep Vanessa waiting."

"Let's go."

My partner wrapped his long arms around our shoulders and the world shifted again. This time, Vanessa's office materialized in ribbons of blue psi.

Once the room stabilized, Liam dropped his arms from our shoulders and put a hand to his brow. Beads of sweat gleamed in the low track lighting.

"You okay?" I asked, putting a hand to his elbow. This many jumps, with this many passengers, this rapidly, usually took it out of my partner.

"Yeah, yeah, I'm fine." Liam reassured me. The flush of his cheeks belied his statement, but I let it be.

James stepped away from us, his head swiveling around the spacious, empty office. Vanessa's desk crouched under the comm screen next to the full-story window overlooking the practice arena. On the low window sill sat a small green vial and a figurine of a raven, a white feather tied about its neck with twine. James picked up the little figure, running a finger down the length of the feather, before setting it back on the sill.

The door plate chimed. Liam and I glanced up. My tall partner's lips pressed together.

"Evan," he muttered.

A loud knock was followed by Evan Kylar's clipped voice. "I hear you moving around in there, Vanessa! Open up."

"Should we open the door?" James asked quietly, moving closer to us.

"No," Liam whispered. "We should wait for Vanessa. She didn't say anything about him."

The next few blows to the door echoed like gunshots. All three of us flinched. "I'm supposed to be inspecting a unit right now, not waiting on you!"

The boys shifted nervously beside me. I scowled at the anxious way their shoulders hunched as the head of Riland Watch all but took the door off its hinges.

Evan's voice quieted, but I could still hear him clearly as he began a litany of profanity that would have made my father blush.

"Who is he?" James hissed, pulling us to the far wall near the window.

"Head of Riland's Watch," I whispered.

"Net search 'disagreeable mortal.' I'm pretty sure his picture is next to the definition," Liam put in.

"He's about as backwards as they come," I agreed.

"When they come for your head, Vanessa, don't come crying to me," Evan snarled, wrapping up his vitriol with an impact that actually set off the door alarm. Its piercing shriek filled the air with visible vibrations.

Liam and James clapped their hands over their ears. I charged over to the door plate and pressed my hand to it. The alarm shut off the instant the door slid open.

Evan stared at me from a few inches away, brown eyes wide at my unexpected appearance.

"Was that honestly necessary?" I growled, dropping my hand from the door plate to my side with a movement too fast and smooth to be mortal.

Evan bared even white teeth in something more menacing than a smile. "Where's Vanessa?"

I stepped back with one foot, angling my body to the mostly-empty room. "She's not here."

Top lip curling, Evan muscled through the doorway. I saw his aggressive movement coming in the shift of his weight and stepped back, otherwise he would have slammed his shoulder into mine with bruising force.

"Watch it," Liam protested, coming to stand at my

side.

"There's no need to be rude," James agreed, holding up his hands in the universal gesture of peace. "We're all waiting on Vanessa. I'm sure she wouldn't have called us here if it wasn't important."

Evan's eyes narrowed at James. "I don't think we've been introduced. You are…"

"James Galling." My young diplomat offered his hand. The Watch officer shook it, his lips pinched together in suspicion.

"Galling… that's a Terran name, isn't it?"

James nodded. "Yes. I'm an ambassador-in-training at the Terran embassy."

Evan's bushy black eyebrows arched in confusion. "What does Vanessa want with you?"

James spread his hands. "I am a telepath, which means I fall under the Overwatch's jurisdiction. When their officers tell me to be somewhere, I go."

"A mortal telepath." Evan leaned closer to James. "Interesting. You're the genetic manipulation variety, right? Not a Family mongrel?"

"Nope. Pure genetic tampering. Not an Usuriel Family member anywhere in my pedigree. Unless you count the Peace Child."

"Okay, then, telepath. What am I thinking?"

James' brow furrowed and he sent Liam and I a mortified glance. "You want me to read you? Here? In the OW headquarters?"

"Oh, come on. It's perfectly legal as long as I give consent. So I'm giving it. What do you need, a fucking form?"

"No—"

"So then just do it!" Evan cocked his head at Liam and I. "This guy a little slow or something?"

I needed to leave or Evan did because his sorry ass was about to get torched. "Leave him alone, Evan."

"It's alright, Gracie," James raised a calming hand in my direction. "I won't go past surface thoughts."

I rolled my eyes and ground my teeth, but held my tongue.

Evan smirked and leaned towards James. "Well?"

James met his eyes, then turned five shades of red. His blue gaze flashed to me for a heartbeat, then darted away.

Evan howled with laughter. "What do you know? The rumors of Terran telepaths aren't completely spore-shit! Who would have guessed?"

Fire was creeping around the ends of my hair, but it was Liam who cracked his knuckles and took a step closer to the Head of Riland watch.

Fortunately, I didn't have to decide if I was going to hold my partner back or help him beat Evan to a pulp because our standoff was interrupted by Vanessa arriving in a sigh of pale blue wind.

"Oh good," she said, loudly and abruptly. "Just the people I needed to talk to. Now maybe I will start getting some answers that make sense."

"You're not the only one who could use some answers. I do have other obligations besides dancing attendance on the Overwatch all day," Evan snarled.

Vanessa ignored his vicious tone, her head perfectly

erect as she walked around us and settled in her chair. "Three of my people are dead. If they were mortals under your jurisdiction, you'd have me waiting on you until the matter was resolved." She held up one finger to forestall his angry response. "I am simply asking for the same courtesy I show you. Now, there is a comfortable chair outside my office door. I suggest you make its acquaintance. I have some questions for Mr. Galling before I can speak with you."

Evan's mouth snapped shut, and if he'd been a pyro like me, I think smoke would have curled from his ears. Instead, he managed a very stiff bow to Vanessa before turning on his heel and marching double time out of the office.

"I'm afraid I won't be much help," James said apologetically, once the door had hissed shut behind the irate Riland watchman. "I haven't spoken to Damien in almost a week."

"That's more recently than any of us have spoken with him," Vanessa replied, drumming a thumb on the surface of her desk. "Why don't you pull up a chair, and tell me what you do know about him?"

Obediently, James pulled over one of the wooden chairs from the corner. While he was settling himself, Vanessa turned to Liam and I.

"Thank you for bringing him in so promptly. I will call you if I need someone to take him home in an hour or two," she said.

Liam and I exchanged a glance at the obvious dismissal.

"James?" I said his name quietly, stepping to his side.

"I'll be fine," he reassured me. "Thanks for the ride, Liam."

"Anytime." Liam's warm hand found my shoulder, and I didn't protest as he shifted the world under my feet again.

***

Fresh, clean sunlight warmed my face when we reappeared next to the cafeteria. Students and professors moved sedately around the stone walking paths, their unhurried movements and casual chatter a sharp contrast to the anger and tension of Vanessa's office.

"Well, that was a shitty way to start the day," Liam commented, adjusting his workout top. "I didn't get my workout in, but at least we can eat something before we head to class. Come on, I'll buy you a hot cup of tea at the cafeteria."

I gave him a half-lidded expression. "We're both students. Everything in the cafeteria is free."

"I didn't say I was going to break the bank," Liam teased, that good-natured smile curving his generous lips upwards.

I rolled my eyes and fell into step with him towards the eatery. "How do you do that?"

"Do what?"

"Make me chuckle even when I feel like crap?"

He offered me a bow as he put a hand to the

cafeteria's plex-glass door. "Glad to be of service, m'lady."

I shook my head at him, but walked through the door. "I'm not anyone's lady."

"I dunno, I've heard Professor Joan compare elder children to ancient Earth royalty."

"We joke about it," I allowed, taking a tray from the rack, "but it's not like we have actual political power. Usuriels can't even hold office, let alone rule anything."

Liam selected his own tray and got into line behind me. "Do you think the mortal watch would say a word about what goes on at Angelus Quietum or the Homestead?"

"The Overwatch would," I replied, taking a bowl of hot, spiced rice and a plate of eggs from the heated bar.

Liam shook his head as he chose his own breakfast. "Only because they have you now. You've heard Vanessa. The only way they can possibly hope to enforce anything on the top three generations is if you agree to carry it out. Before you joined, third-gens and up were a law unto themselves."

"They managed to take care of Adora," I muttered under my breath.

Liam placed a cup of steaming tea on my tray. "As promised, your drink of choice."

"Thank you."

My tall partner inclined his head to me, then led the way over to our usual table by the orange tree. We were quiet a while as we got settled and took the edge off of our hunger.

"So… do you finally want to talk about it?"

I froze at Liams' words, the spoon of rice halfway to my mouth. I cleared my throat. "About what?"

"You said you've been in a bad emotional place lately."

I shoved the rice in my mouth and chewed slowly to buy myself time. Liam sat silently, watching me with intent, Family-blue eyes.

"I said I was sorry for that."

"Yes, an actual apology from Gracie Usuriel. I should demand it in writing and hang it on my wall."

"Hey, I admit it when I'm wrong!"

Liam met my gaze thoughtfully. Finally, he nodded. "Yeah, once the fire dies down you'll usually own it."

"Thank you." I muttered into my rice.

"But you've been lit up for weeks. Ever since you had that fight with James."

Grayson's dying screams mingled with Amourie's heartbroken sobs in my head. I forced myself to swallow. The rice felt like a lump of alloy going down my throat.

"It was a bad night," I managed, taking refuge in my tea. Its heat soothed my frayed nerves.

"So like I said, you want to talk about it?"

Tears heated the back of my eyes, and I seriously considered allowing myself to curl into a sobbing heap on Liam's lap. He'd hold me and tell me everything would be okay and… and I knew where that led. Would we stop at holding? I knew what it felt like to kiss him; the thrill of his psi running down my back. I gazed up at his beautiful features—the best fusion of mortal and Family genetics—

and felt my meal twist into a knot of sick dread.

I tapped my implant for the time. "I should really get changed and head to the studio."

Liam's jaw tightened, his mouth pinching flat. He mirrored my time tap. "You don't have class for another hour."

"I know, but I promised Professor Blackmon I'd have something for critique today." I downed the last of my tea in two long gulps and picked up my tray. "I've barely had time to touch my clay all week."

Liam's expression told me what he thought of my excuse. "Will I see you for dinner?"

"Hopefully. Depends on how much homework Professor Tyler gives us. But let me know if you need help with James later."

Liam waved me away with one hand. "I can handle a simple transport myself. Enjoy your classes."

Grateful for his dismissal, I trotted over to the tray return. In the doorway to the cafeteria, I paused. Liam's long, lean figure was clearly visible across the large room. It might have been my imagination, but his head seemed lower and his shoulders more hunched all alone at our table. Guilt sent a painful pang through my already heavy guts.

I walked out of the cafeteria.

Chapter 7

Vampires and Ambria

I didn't hear anything else about the Damien incident for a while. Liam said James was very quiet afterwards and asked to be dropped off at the Terran embassy without giving any hints about what he and Vanessa had discussed. Other than a few lurid net articles and the usual whispered rumors among the OW and my mortal classmates, no one had any more information.

Even Jillian, who usually had her finger on the pulse of things in the Overwatch practice room, just shrugged when I asked her if Vanessa had said anything.

"Nothing that hasn't been all over the net," she said, pulling her black braids into a tight knot at the base of her neck.

"Oh well." I readjusted my gloves and took another few swings at my punching bag. "Just figured I'd ask."

"Never any harm in that," she agreed, stepping up to the bag beside me and starting her workout. We sweated and panted beside each other companionably.

"Where's Liam?" she asked, tossing back a drink from her water bottle.

"We got a bout in, but he left early. His classes start

at oh-nine-hundred today." Which was why I made sure to get here a little later so we could only spar once before he had to take off, I added mentally.

"I see."

The pace of my punches picked up. One, two, three, kidney punch, nose jab. I focused intensely on the movement of my arms and hands.

"It's too bad. You two used to be such a good team. I really thought you were going to be Vanessa's pick for number two, since Lillian's made it clear she wants to phase out of physical enforcement."

My strike faltered, breaking my rhythm. I bounced on my toes to regain my balance. "What are you talking about? We *are* a good team."

Jill's dark eyes held something close to pity. I shied away. "Not for much longer if you can't be civil. Liam's a sweetheart, and he'll put up with a lot, but even he has limits."

"We had a good conversation the other day," I protested, stripping off a glove. I wasn't getting back into my groove with this sick knot of dread and guilt in my gut. "I said I was sorry for how off I've been. Which, I suppose, I should say to you, too. I am sorry. I didn't mean to take my issues out on you."

"No harm done here," Jillian said, watching me with a hand on one hip. "But ya know, actions speak louder than words." She gestured to the empty bench where Liam and I used to put our towels side by side.

"Yeah, I know." I swallowed the lump in my throat and picked up my towel. "I've got class, too."

"Uh huh. Have fun," she said, turning back to her punching bag.

I left her behind, wishing I could leave the hollow feeling in my stomach just as easily.

***

Two days later, Liam turned twenty-two. Stella reminded me first thing in the morning that it was his birthday.

"You did set it in your calendar, did you not?" she asked when I scowled up at the comm screen. I was still toweling off after my shower and took the excuse of drying off to bury my face in the soft fabric.

"Yes," I muttered, pretty sure I was unintelligible through the towel. With a groan, I tossed the cloth away and rummaged through a drawer to find a clean set of practice clothes.

"Do you wish to send him a message?"

I flashed Stella a glare as I pulled on my blue uniform jacket over the practice outfit. Landing was in the midst of an unusual cold snap.

"Tell me you're not on team Liam, too," I hissed, settling the heavy material more comfortably over my shoulders before doing the buttons up the side. Jillian's words had been ringing in my head. Between her and my father, who tried to be tacit about his inquiries into my love life, but ended up being pushy anyway, I felt as if everyone was ganging up on me lately.

Stella tilted her head at me. "I was unaware Liam

had a team," she replied. "Are we discussing a sport?"

I rolled my eyes and waved a hand at her. "Nevermind," I said and walked to the closet. "No, I don't need to send him a message. I'll see him at the compound in a few minutes anyway. Thanks for the reminder, though."

"You are welcome," Stella replied and faded from the comm.

I sighed after she left and looked down into the little dormitory closet. It was less than half the size of my walk-in at Angelus Quietum. Even so, it was lockable, which meant I kept most of the valuable objects I had in there. My jewelry box, Ariel's journal and elixir, a few expensive pairs of shoes including the dreaded Morial heels, and the three Ambria dresses Dad and Grandmother had given me over the years all sat in the quiet dark. There were also two flat boxes at the back that I'd been trying to forget about lately. I pulled out the slightly larger one and set it on the bed.

I chewed on a hang nail, trying to make up my mind about this particular surprise. I'd ordered the Ambria dress tunics for James and Liam when my signing bonus for the Overwatch came through. It hadn't been long after James came back from his internship, when the three of us had still felt as if we might fall into a *ménage à trois* at any moment. I'd remembered how much they both admired my dresses, and I thought it would be nice for them to have something equally special for when we went out. It had taken almost the whole bonus, but even after our falling outs, I hadn't had the heart to send them back. They felt like a link to that moment when I still felt so optimistic and excited about where our friendships were heading.

I lifted the lid to the box and looked at the neatly tailored fabric. Liam's was Gabriellan blue to match his eyes, of course. Back in the closet, I knew James' was a light leaf-green that would compliment his honey-and-sunlight hair. I ran gentle fingers over the sumptuous fabric and knew it would be a dream to wear. It would also look amazing on him, I thought, envisioning Liam's strong shoulders in the gold-trimmed dress tunic. As they had since the Family party, my hormones knew exactly what they thought of my OW partner. I wished my heart was half as decisive.

Jill was right. I'd been pretty hard on Liam lately. If I didn't want to alienate him completely, this probably wouldn't be a bad idea. I hated to string him along, what with how fickle my emotions towards him had been lately, but by the same token, I couldn't deny that I did have real feelings for him. If anything, the anger I'd felt in his direction after Grayson's death was probably an indication of how much he actually meant to me. Like always, my damn father seemed to be right. I needed to make nice with Liam at some point, or I would really regret it.

"Okay," I murmured to myself, willing the nervous tremble in my stomach to steady. "It's not doing any good in the back of my closet. I have to give it to him sometime."

Before I could lose my nerve, I closed the box and picked it up. Hugging it tightly to my chest, I walked outside and took off for the OW compound.

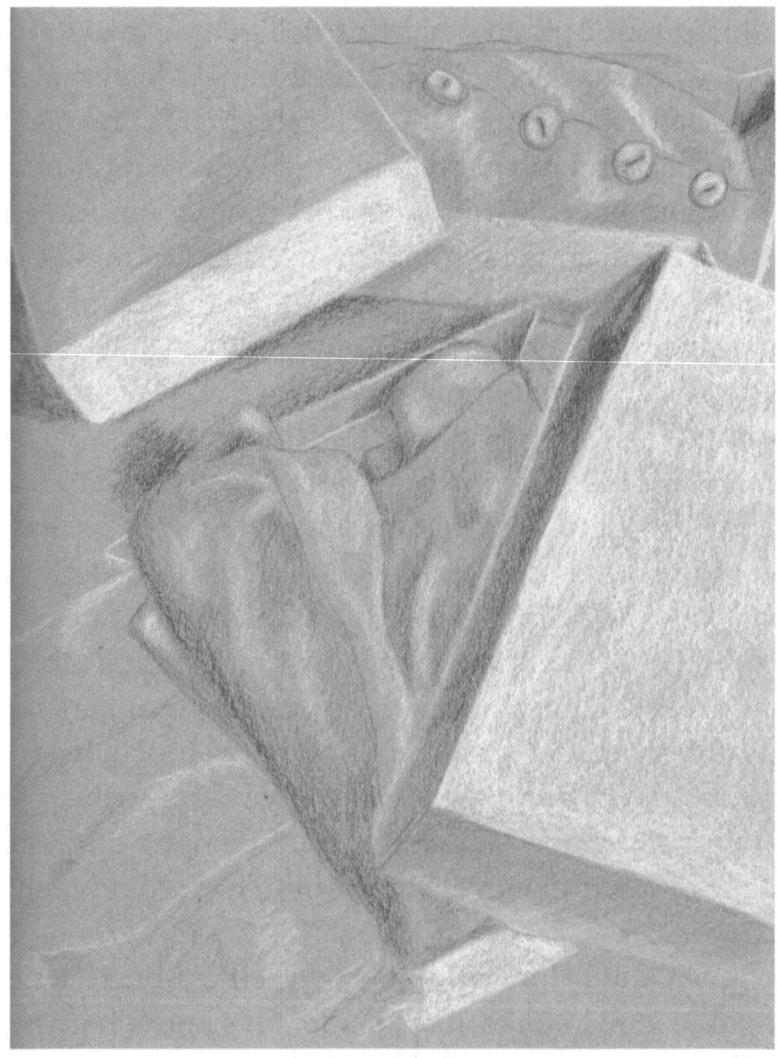

I'd been up early that morning so I beat Liam to the practice mat. Jillian and the other regular morning members of the OW workout were slowly straggling in. A few of them waved to me before heading to their usual equipment. Feeling more than a little nervous about my extravagant gift, I laid the box on the bench where Liam usually put his towel. Then, with nothing else to do, I began my own stretches.

It wasn't long before my OW partner showed up. He looked much more subdued lately, and I felt a twist of guilt at the shut down expression on his face as his long legs closed the distance to the practice mat. He didn't meet my eye as he walked up; instead he murmured a quiet, "Morning." Then, he turned to set down his towel and paused.

"Happy birthday," I said, watching his expression go from surprised to puzzled.

A genuine smile turned the corner of his lips up while his eyes glanced between me and the box. "You remembered?"

"We never made a big fuss about birthdays when I was growing up," I said, "but I've been waiting for an occasion to give you this for a while. I figured today would be a good day."

His dark brows arching with curiosity, he picked up the box and slid open the lid. I watched his face carefully as his bemused smile turned into wide-eyed shock.

"Gracie," he breathed. "Is this... what I think it is?"

"I got one for James, too, so don't feel too special," I told him, but I couldn't help a pleased smile from spreading across my face. "Do you like it?"

"I... I can't take this," he said, staring down at the tunic. "Honestly, it must have cost you over a month's pay..."

I waved away his objections with one hand. "Aren't you the one who used to complain that the elder children got everything? Looks, talent and money? Isn't that how you put it? Well, you've been pulling the weight of an elder child putting up with me lately. Perhaps it's time you got to enjoy a few of the perks of being friends with one instead of the downsides."

He swallowed hard, and for a second I thought he was going to cry. Then he shook his head ruefully and set the box down on the bench. With reverent hands, he pulled the tunic out of the box and held it up. Unless I was mistaken, it was going to be a perfect fit. It really did match the exact color of his eyes. When he glanced back at me there was a wide grin on his face.

"I think—no, I know—this is the nicest thing anyone has ever gotten me," he said, eyes bright. Then a hint of mischief sparked in them, and he was suddenly ten times as handsome. "This does mean you have to take me somewhere nice enough to wear it, you know."

That mortal dread tried to rise in my chest, but for once I shoved it away. Dad had said not to punish myself for Grayson. I had a feeling punishing Liam for it was equally unfair, and unhealthy. Without its oppressive weight, that iron hand of control I'd been using to clamp down on my attraction to my OW partner loosened just a touch. I found myself returning his grin with one of my own.

"I think that might be arranged," I said in spite of myself.

For the first time in weeks, his eyes truly lit up. I'd made the right decision giving him the tunic, I thought. I suddenly felt lighter than I had since Grayson died.

"Gracie and Liam." Vanessa's voice through our implants wasn't enough to completely wipe the smiles off of our faces for once. Even so, Liam and I exchanged a glance. This early in the day, her summons was probably not a good sign. In almost perfect unison, we tapped to accept her call.

"Yes, Vanessa?"

"We have a call for you," she said, and I heard the grim tone in her voice. "You'd better move. The mortal watch is already there, and they said there are mounting casualties."

I reached for my jacket and pulled it over my practice clothes. Liam rapidly folded his tunic before trading it for his own OW uniform jacket with a quick teleport.

"Just send me the reference image and we're there," he said, tapping to Vanessa. His eyes got that distant stare that said he was communicating telepathically. When they refocused, he held out a hand to me. I took it.

***

The old-fashioned manor where we solidified looked out over terraced rice fields. I didn't have to ask Liam where we were this time; I recognized southern Riland. This was the heart of vamp country—night labor was the backbone of the rice industry. The part that made

me nervous, however, was that the time difference was
enough for the sun to still be below the horizon here. If we
were dealing with vampires, they were going to be awake
for at least another hour or two.

Gunshots in rapid succession turned our heads
towards the back of the house. I glanced at Liam. The full
moon lit his face well enough for me to meet his eye
before we sprinted around the corner of the manor.

"Stay back!" I heard the man's voice before I saw
him. Another gunshot rang out, followed by the thick, wet
explosion as it found a target. Liam stepped in front of
me, a nearly transparent psi-shield sliding up in front of
him and wrapping around to encircle the two of us as we
neared the action; a wise precaution if we were dealing
with projectiles.

"I think we are going to need medical back up," I
said, tapping my implant to alert Vanessa.

We were too late for the gun to be a problem,
however. By the time we rounded the corner, the spray of
blood across the back wall made it clear that the vamp had
hit the carotid artery with his first strike. It was extremely
sloppy work.

Over the last few months of working with the OW,
I'd seen quite a few messes that vampires, mortals, and
Usuriels had left behind. Usually it was the mortals or the
Family that ended up drenched in blood from an injury,
either intentional or accidental. Almost every vampire
scene I'd ever been to was completely bloodless. After all,
it was too precious a commodity for them to waste it
across a floor rather than down their throats.

This time, however, the term 'bloodbath' seemed completely appropriate. This vampire had clearly lost every scrap of control, because he was covered in as much blood as he was managing to drink. It had completely soaked his shirt and plastered patches of his short hair to his head in dark spots. I had a serious sinking feeling that there was too much blood to account for just this one victim. My eyes found dark smears leading from around the other corner of the house. Liam closed the distance to the vamp with his long stride.

"Let the mortal go!" he barked at the vampire, flashing his ID. "We're Overwatch. Let him go, and step away."

The vampire rounded on him, blood still spurting from his victim's neck wound. The mortal's bullet had hit him in the shoulder, but the gaping wound didn't seem to faze him. He hissed, sharp teeth bared like a cornered animal. The moonlight caught his eyes and there wasn't a shred of sanity in them; just burning, desperate need and aggression. He launched himself at my OW partner. It wasn't the smoothest movement, but it held the supernatural strength of his kind.

If Liam hadn't been training with me on the regular, I probably would have been nervous. As it was, I knew he was perfectly capable of subduing a lone vamp; even one as gone in the blood lust as this one. With a few concise movements, Liam sidestepped the charge, grabbed the vampire by the back of his neck and used his own momentum to slam him head-first into a solid nearby tree trunk. Then, before his opponent could regain his stability, Liam seized the vamp's injured arm and twisted it firmly behind him.

Either the blow to the head or the pain of Liam's pressure on his injury finally managed to break the vampire's blood rage. With a gasp, his eyes went wide, and by the time Liam had forced him to his knees, I could see some humanity bleeding back into them. They darted around wildly, as if he wasn't sure where he was or how he'd gotten there.

"You have him handled?" I asked Liam, heading towards the mortal victim.

"No problem." Liam sounded grim as he looked down at the now trembling vampire. "Tell me your name and ID number." I heard him begin talking to the vamp in a quieter tone as I knelt to the mortal.

I'd known he was dead from the moment we came around the corner, but even so I had to check. In the moonlight, the mortal's face was a pale and waxy blue. His lips were so white I knew he'd bled out, but I pressed my fingers to his neck anyway. There was no pulse, though his flesh was still warm. With a groan, I leaned back from him and took in the cut of his Riland watch uniform with a rising sense of dread. An incident or two indeed; if this didn't set off Riland's mortal population, I didn't know what would.

"Did I... do that?" I turned to see the vampire looking at me with horror written across his blood-splattered face.

Fuck. He'd lost it so badly he didn't even remember what he'd done? This was an executable offense for sure.

In fact, I was pretty positive the vamp wouldn't survive the repercussions of this attack. But I had a feeling I'd have a harder time completing that order if the vampire hadn't been lucid at the time of the act. Then I glanced back down at the dead mortal and felt a lot less compassion.

"Yes, you did," I informed him coldly, sliding to my feet. Liam met my gaze and his frown deepened as I shook my head to let him know the mortal hadn't survived.

"You're in a world of trouble now," Liam informed his captive. "If you want to see another moon rise, I suggest you tell us exactly what happened."

"I... I don't know... it's all a blur," the vamp wasn't old. He looked our age, honestly, and from the way he was shaking in Liam's grip, I had a feeling he wasn't much older in reality either.

"Go back to the beginning," I told him, echoing my father's calm advice. I flashed on Grayson and shoved away a wave of empathy for the vamp. I hadn't been in any kind of altered state when I killed Grayson. It had been a complete and utterly unpredictable accident, I reminded myself. This, on the other hand, was uncontrolled blood lust. The vamps knew their instincts were dangerous, and they were responsible for keeping the mortals they fed from safe. This wasn't an unexpected accident. At the very best it was inexcusably negligent; at worst it was premeditated homicide. I tried to hold on to that knowledge as I met the vampire's terrified gaze. "Start with the first thing you remember clearly and work from there."

"I was supposed to be turned tonight. We'd gone through the whole ceremony," his voice was a little steadier when he said that, but it put another layer of dread in my gut. I suddenly had an awful feeling I knew what was going on and that perhaps this particular vamp wasn't as culpable as I'd thought. "My parents are spending the night at the Skylar's to make sure they're out of the way. There wasn't supposed to be a mortal within twenty kilometers. How did this happen?" He got a little panicky there at the end, and I was pretty sure he had to stop speaking just to keep from losing it.

Liam swore. He'd put it together, too. "Where were you being turned, Martin?" he asked. I noticed that he'd used the vamp's name. Clearly my partner was beginning to feel a little bad for the baby vampire as well.

"The bullpen around back," Martin said tremulously, looking over his shoulder towards a large barn slightly up the hill. The bloody smears led in that direction. That familiar dread sank claws into my ribs.

I took a steadying breath and walked over to inspect the vampire's injured shoulder. The edges of the mostly bloodless wound had only barely begun to knit together. That was consistent with a newly-turned vamp; I'd seen older ones heal that kind of damage in less than an hour, and at this rate Martin would be lucky if the wound was healed by tomorrow night. The tension in his body said that Liam's hold was still causing him quite a bit of pain.

"If Liam lets you up, can you take us to it?" I asked, exchanging a cautious glance with my partner. Slowly,

Liam nodded and took a little pressure off of the vamp's bad shoulder. Martin took a deeper breath and flashed me an uncertain look of gratitude. Seeing that the lack of pain wasn't going to send the young vampire back into an uncontrollable state, I stepped back, and Liam finished letting go of his wrist.

Unsteadily, Martin got back to his feet. He nodded too quickly, eyes deliberately avoiding the mess he'd made of the mortal by the wall. "Yes, of course," he said, head down and body language submissive. I think he knew it would only take a single false move to seal his swift execution. "I'll do whatever you say. Please," he flashed me eyes that were too wide. "I'm not dangerous... at least, not anymore. I don't think..." he swallowed hard and I think he was trying not to be sick, "I... I really didn't mean to hurt anyone."

"Do you remember being turned?" Liam asked, looking down at Martin with a cautious expression. My partner was probably ten centimeters taller than the vampire, which made Martin about the same height as my dad. The vampire looked young and unfinished to me, his round, soft features reinforcing the impression that he was under twenty. It was technically illegal to turn anyone under seventeen, so I knew he was most likely somewhere between eighteen and twenty-two, but he probably could have passed for sixteen.

Slowly, the vampire nodded. "I think so." He seemed a little unsure. "I remember taking Litta's blood and then... pain. The change hurt, a lot. They'd told me it would, though, so I wasn't scared. But then I passed out and..." his gaze was distant and he frowned, his head shaking slowly. "I know I woke up, but that's where it gets... confused."

"That's a word for it," Liam commented, glancing over at the slowly-cooling body of the Riland watch officer.

"Come on, take us to where you were going through the ceremony," I said, giving my partner a glare. "Maybe that will help spark your memory."

Martin nodded too fast again and wrapped his arms tightly around his doughy chest. When he made no move towards the barn, I gently touched his elbow. He jumped, dark eyes flashing too much white in my direction.

"Are you feeling off balance again?" I asked carefully, trying to phrase it so that he wouldn't think I was judging him. Fate knew I might have to take his heart and head by the end of the night, but that didn't mean I needed to treat him poorly in the meantime. I'd probably get more information out of him if he thought I was on his side, anyway.

"No... not exactly..." he said slowly, though his eyes strayed a little longer on my neck than I cared for. That's an even worse idea than you probably realize, little vamp, I thought. "I think... I just... you're really pretty." He said it in a rush and seemed a little horrified that he had. Then he pressed on as if he needed to justify sharing the sentiment. "I don't think I can be attracted to someone without... thinking about that right now. And I don't want to hurt you."

"Well, at least he's honest," Liam sighed, then rolled his eyes at me. "Why don't you show him that you can take care of yourself, Gracie?"

"You really can't hurt me," I reassured Martin, pulling up enough flame to encircle my shoulders and spill their orange light into the night. In their glare, Martin's hair was actually a dark blond. "Truly, I'm faster and stronger than I look. Number one, I can fly so you'd never catch me. And number two, even if you did, I can send you up in flames faster than you can tear my throat out. Even if you managed to get by Liam, which you wouldn't, there's no way you could harm me. Okay?"

Instead of looking threatened, Martin actually relaxed at this revelation. His nod was more solid this time, and he let me guide him by the elbow towards the blood-smeared corner of the barn.

I should have known it was going to be messy. Fates, nothing about this scene had been pleasant. However, the bull pen on the other side of that barn was something out of a horror holo. Even the strange androids up near the coast hadn't left such a grisly tableau.

The only thing I knew about turning a vampire was from my Awareness Theory class and OW training. From what I'd read and discussed in class, the traditional way to do it was in a secluded location with a large animal sacrifice. Back on Earth, a human sacrifice had been more common and resulted in what the vampires referred to as 'blooding.' That was a bond the individual vampires shared as part of a court, coven, or other collective community. Since blooding was banned here on Cybele, most vampires didn't belong to a group outside of their own immediate family, and there was no supernatural bond between a vamp and his or her maker. Blooded vampires tended to be stronger and have a larger array of powers as well, so keeping the first feeding to animal blood wasn't just humane, it also helped make the vampire population a little more manageable.

It seemed that Martin's makers weren't completely negligent. The bull they'd selected for the ceremony glanced up at us from the far corner of its pen as we walked around the barn. Next to the pen's closed gate were two crumpled figures.

Martin let out a gasp of grief, and he moved quickly to kneel between them, face stricken. I'd been afraid of this reaction, but at least it meant that our baby vamp hadn't been turned by someone random. It also meant that this was a true vampire family farm, and what happened tonight was closer to an accident than I liked to think about.

I glanced at Liam as the two of us slowly caught up to Martin's distraught figure. My partner looked as grim-faced as I did.

"No, no, this can't be happening." Martin was on the verge of real hysterics, his eyes darting between the two fallen women. "Litta... Mary... why? Why would anyone do this?" Covering his face, the young vampire began to weep audibly. My heart couldn't get heavier as I looked down at the red ruin that was the first woman's chest. Since Martin had said there weren't supposed to be any mortals around, I strongly suspected these two were his makers. As I've previously stated, taking out the heart was usually perfectly effective at preventing a vampire from rising again. It didn't really matter if these women were mortal or vamp; since it looked like someone had unloaded a high caliber weapon into both of their torsos, there was no question that both of them were irreversibly dead.

"They're gone, Martin," Liam said, almost gently. He covered his mouth and nose in a futile attempt to block out the smell of death before reaching over the first woman to take the vampire's uninjured arm. "Clearly, you didn't do this. Come on, there's nothing we can do for them now. The medics will come and take care of them in just a bit."

By this point, Liam had pulled Martin up to his feet, but the vamp was clinging to the front of my partner's uniform as if he really wasn't up to standing on his own. The look Liam gave me as he half-carried Martin over to a bench beside the barn was more than a little haunted. I swallowed hard and tried not to look at the two women again.

"I don't think that mortal watchman by the house had a gun capable of this," Liam commented to me, inclining his head to the blood trail that led into the barn. My stomach sank as I glanced at Martin again. I thought the vampire had been distraught earlier, but now he looked downright traumatized. He was clinging to Liam and shaking as if he wasn't currently cold-blooded.

"Take him to the other side of the house," I told Liam, impressed that my voice remained calm. Maybe I was getting used to these gory scenes, or maybe I was still just numb. The ringing white noise in my head suggested the latter. "You know, the side we teleported into," the one that doesn't have any bodies in sight, I implied. I was pretty sure Liam picked up my hint because he nodded.

"Are you sure you want to clear the barn by yourself?" Liam asked. "I'll only be a second."

"I'm pretty sure there's no threat in there, but if you want me to wait for you, I will."

He nodded. "I'd feel better if you did. Besides, I think our medical backup just arrived. I'll let them handle Martin for a few minutes. He could probably use a once-over anyway."

I looked at the silent, pink-tinged tears running down the young vampire's face and knew he wouldn't be trying to make a run for it. Liam would be able to keep a mental ear on his interactions with the mortal medics just around the corner anyway. "Okay," I agreed and in a flash, Liam and the baby vamp were gone.

I turned to face the slightly ajar barn door. I suppressed a sigh. The now-familiar reek of blood and death made my stomach roil badly enough without taking a nice, big dose. While I waited for Liam to return, I summoned a small fire ball to hover at my shoulder. The full moon had been bright enough to see relatively comfortably so far, but the shadows in that barn were deep enough that I knew we'd need better lighting. The bloody smears on the ground lit up with a sickeningly red color at my gentle night light's flickering.

"Well, this is a fun run," I groaned, trying to peer into the barn's darkness without actually walking into the building. I had a feeling I knew what was in there, and I wasn't looking forward to confirming my fears. I found myself tapping a foot nervously, trying to pass the time while I fought not to look behind myself at the two dead vampires.

"Okay," Liam said, reappearing to stand solidly at my side. I looked up at him at the same moment his eyes flickered down to me. Our gazes met and despite the grim situation, I realized I was extremely glad he was the one at my side. "Are you ready to do this?" he asked.

I suddenly had a strong urge to grab his hand, but I shoved away the impulse and nodded instead. "As ready as you are," I replied, my reluctance clear in my voice.

"Hmmm," Liam agreed, but we stepped forward together anyway.

We found almost exactly what I thought we would. I wasn't happy about it, but I also wasn't surprised.

The dead Riland watchman had a gun of a make and caliber I'd never seen before by his side. It looked big and fully capable of the damage to the two women's sundered chests. From the bite marks, it seemed Martin had torn this watchman's throat out as thoroughly as the other mortal's, though there was a little less blood splattered across these walls. It seemed the newly turned vamp had been hungrier the first time and hadn't wasted as much precious food.

"I was really hoping this one would still be alive," Liam groaned, rubbing one bloody hand on his practice pants. "Then maybe Martin would have stood a chance in front of the council."

"Yeah, me too," I sighed, and swallowed hard as

the stench tried to upend my stomach.

"Think they had any idea what they were doing?" Liam asked, raising an eyebrow. "Interrupting a turning, I mean?"

I shook my head slowly. "It's hard to say. Maybe. Seems like the kind of stupid thing Evan would send his watch into. He probably didn't even warn them that the most dangerous vamp in the place was the turnling."

"Oh, come now, that's just basic Awareness Theory," Liam protested.

"You really think the rank and file Riland watch went to University?" I asked, cutting a glance in his direction as we turned to leave.

"How stupid do you get? I mean, they live in Riland, for Fate's sake. If they're going to police vampires, they'd better know something about them."

"They don't technically police vampires," I pointed out as we exited the barn, and Liam put an arm around my shoulders to teleport us to the front. One little tunic and my partner was already taking liberties, I thought. I clung to the safe mundanity of that thought. It was a lot better than flashing on all of the bodies I'd just seen. "We're the ones who technically police the vamps. Which means there's technically no reason for the Riland watch to train their people on them."

"It also means there's technically no reason why they were here tonight," Liam growled as we solidified in the front of the manor. An emergency hover vehicle sat with its tailgate open and not a single mortal in sight. Martin perched on the edge of the EHV with a blanket draped around his shoulders while he stared off into space. "Let alone with anti-Awareness weapons. There's no reason to use a gun that big on a mortal. That thing was made with vampires in mind."

They were trying to make an incident, I thought, but I didn't say it aloud since we were nearing Martin's silent figure at the back of the ambulance.

"Where are the medics?" I asked, glancing into the empty hover vehicle.

Martin shrugged and winced as the movement hurt his shoulder. "They handed me a blanket and said that was the best they could do," he said hollowly. His eyes slowly traveled up to my face, and they reflected back the same buzzing numbness I felt in my extremities. "They're afraid of me. I could taste it on my tongue," he said quietly. Then he dropped my gaze again. "They should be. I'm dangerous."

"No, you're not," I said it before I could think about it. "Not more so than any other vamp, anyway." I instantly regretted my words. Even though it was true, I probably shouldn't be giving him any hope. Chances were, he'd be executed for this. I glanced at Liam. My partner looked as pained about the situation as I felt.

"This has been a hard night," Liam told Martin. "And it does look bad for you. But honestly, I think you may have a decent case for self-defense. That's what I'm going to put in my report, anyway."

The vampire looked up at Liam as if he couldn't believe the Overwatch would be so understanding. "You'd... do that for me?"

"Yes, we will," I said, putting a hand on Liam's arm and stepping closer to the two men. Around the corner, I heard the rustling of the medics bringing the first mortal watchman's body towards the emergency vehicle. I somehow didn't think Martin really needed to watch the casualties get loaded up. He seemed to be in a fragile enough headspace as it was. "But right now, why don't we go back to the OW compound? Liam and I will make an honest account to Vanessa and tell her how cooperative you've been since you came around. I'm sure the council will take that into consideration, along with the fact that you'd just been turned. There's a lot of extenuating circumstances here."

Martin looked between Liam and I, his dark eyes searching our faces for signs of a lie. Then, slowly, he nodded. "You're not what I expected the Overwatch to be like," he said quietly. "Thank you."

Liam inclined his head and put a hand to Martin's shoulder. "Ready?" he asked us both. When we nodded, the manor bled away.

Chapter 8

An Eager Beginning

We delivered Martin to the OW holding center where he was put in one of the vampire cells. Since the sun had risen on that part of the continent, he collapsed the instant we arrived, and Liam had to bodily carry him to the cell. At least he wasn't awake when those bars slammed home for the first time. I tried not to think about the fact that the cell was probably the last place Martin would ever see.

After that, Liam and I spent a ridiculous amount of time making our reports. First, we had to go back to the scene and record what we could of the carnage. Then we met with Vanessa, first alone and then again with Evan. We went over the story— with accompanying visual aids— what felt like a dozen times. By the time we were done, I was starving and shaking almost as badly as Martin had been at the end.

Vanessa seemed sympathetic to Martin's case, but Evan made it abundantly clear that anything short of a swift and public execution would be grounds for open conflict with the Overwatch.

"This is why we have a problem with you people and your corner on the Awareness population!" Evan all but shouted on his way out. "My people are dying, and you want to make excuses for the monster who killed them! Get your heads out of your asses and execute the parasite!"

Once he'd gone, Vanessa turned to Liam and me. "Go home," she said, looking at our exhausted faces. She sounded tired, too. "Eat something and get some rest. I'll make some comm calls and see what I can do, but it's not looking good for the kid."

"Let us know before you do anything, won't you?" I said, feeling a bit maternal towards the now defenseless vampire down in holding.

Vanessa nodded, her eye dull and almost as miserable as I felt. "Yes, that much I can do."

"Thanks," I said.

I exchanged a look with Liam who wrapped an arm around my waist, pulling me tightly against his body. I leaned my head against his chest and let his psi rise around me with that familiar lurching tilt. The close contact really did make it a bit smoother, but he was so tired I could feel his control waver a bit on the edges.

The University mess hall solidified in front of us, but we just stood there, looking at it. It had been weeks since we'd allowed ourselves this kind of physical contact. I think between the trauma of the morning and the relief that our relationship seemed to be thawing, we really couldn't bring ourselves to move away from each other.

Slowly, Liam's other arm found its way across my

shoulders, and he held me close against him, his cheek resting against the top of my head as if he wanted as much physical contact as he could manage. Rather than pull away, my hands slid over his, and my face turned towards his chest so that my ear could press to the safe strength of his heartbeat.

"Come on," I whispered after a few minutes. "We need to eat, or we'll both be on the floor here soon."

"I know," he murmured into my hair. "But I need this right now."

I swallowed hard and tried to tell the sick dread in my chest to shut up. Then, I remembered what Grandma Gloria had said to Amourie at the very end of Grayson's illness. Someday, I would wake up, and Liam wouldn't be there. It might not be tomorrow, and it might not be ten years from now, but that day would come. Even if our lives were simple and safe, my immortality meant I'd most likely outlive him by centuries. With this incident, I felt as if a war might spring up at any moment. Nothing felt simple or safe anymore. If we were going to be on the front lines, that day might come much sooner than I cared to think about. Nothing was promised except right now.

I turned in his arms and looked up into my partner's face. His eyes were that beautiful midnight-blue. I leaned against his solid chest and said exactly what I was thinking.

"I'm too hungry to keep standing here. But after the mess hall, I promise we can spend some more time just like this."

He tilted his head at me thoughtfully, eyes narrowing as if he suspected a trick. That was fair enough.

If I was a good, stable, and reliable OW partner, I'd been almost the opposite as a romantic partner. I held my breath. Had I damaged his trust in me beyond repair?

"I think I like that idea," he said cautiously. With a small, tired smile, I took his hand and led him into the dining hall.

I was a little afraid that our meal would be awkward, but it wasn't. If anything, we were more relaxed around each other than we had been in months. At first we both ate with single-minded intensity. But once we slowed down, Liam's hand found its way to the back of my chair. It was with less than a thought that I leaned the line of my body against his. My heartbeat picked up. After a decent meal, I actually had the energy to think about doing something with Liam other than take a nap. He must have had the same thought, because suddenly there wasn't much eating going on. The two of us turned to each other, and out of the corner of my eye I saw Liam set down his fork.

"Your room or mine?" he asked. I had the feeling he'd been hoping to ask that question for a really long time.

"Mine," I replied, thinking of the perpetual clutter that filled his dormitory. At least I knew my bed was clear.

Liam wasn't usually one to waste his energy on theatrics. In all honesty, he wasn't strong enough to have the energy to waste. This time, though, he banished the trays with a wave of one hand. Then he turned back to me with a very cautious look on his face.

"You're sure?"

I tilted my head at him and tried to see anything other than Liam Usuriel, my perfectly loyal and steady OW partner; the man I'd been trying and failing to keep myself from falling in love with for over a year. I didn't.

"Yes," I said, taking his face in my hands. "I'm sure."

I leaned up and into the space between us. There wasn't much of it left, so it hardly took a stretch to press my lips to his. I'd meant it to be a light, quick kiss; something to allay his insecurities and let him know that I was still attracted to him. Let's just say it didn't stay light or quick. Midway through, his power picked up around us, and when we finally came up for air, the two of us were sitting in the middle of my bed.

"Now what?" he asked, dropping the hand that had come up to the back of my neck as if he was unsure of how welcome his advances would be now that we were truly alone.

I nibbled my lower lip. "I've been overthinking this for way too long. It's about time we shut up and just take our clothes off."

He hesitated, and I could see a little reluctance in the set of his mouth, but he couldn't keep himself from quite literally lighting up with psi at the thought. Suddenly, his blue eyes were incandescent, and I took that to be all the answer I needed.

"Wait," he protested as I undid the top button to his OW jacket. I paused, glancing down into his face.

"I thought you said you needed to be held." I could hear the sensuality in my own voice. I traced my hand along the exposed skin at the opening of his collar until my fingers spread across the back of his neck. His eyes rolled shut, and his body relaxed helplessly into my touch. I felt a rush of satisfaction at how obviously irresistible he found me.

"Held is... one thing," he replied, his eyes opening and one hand forestalling my finger's distraction. I think he knew he'd give in rapidly to whatever I wanted if he didn't make me stop touching him. "Holding implies you care about someone and want to enjoy their company. What you're suggesting is a little more... mindless. I'm not sure I want to turn our relationship into that. I'm pretty sure I care about you too much. And knowing you, if the breeze changes tomorrow, I don't want you writing me off as something quick and easy."

I had a feeling he might be right, so I leaned back on my heels. "Okay, fine. What do you want to happen next, then?"

He considered that, his eyes traveling over my face as he came to a decision that put both fear and hope on his face. I had a feeling I wasn't going to like his answer. "How about I start by telling you that I'm stupid in love with you."

His words hit me a little harder than I'd thought they would, even if I was halfway expecting them. I took a bracing breath and caught myself running a hand through my hair. When I finally met his gaze, I gave a helpless shrug. "Fate knows why," I said finally. "I've been a complete bitch to you lately."

He sighed, clearly not thrilled with my answer but

not completely discouraged either. "I have asked myself the same question. Honestly? I think it's the contradictions."

"Contradictions?" I echoed.

"Yeah. It's like you somehow manage to be perfect opposites all at once." When I continued to give him a confused look, he went on. "You carry yourself like the royalty you were born to be, yet half the time you have no idea how privileged or powerful you really are. You're petite and beautiful, but you also hand me my ass on the practice mat. You're Gabriel's daughter, yet you had no idea who Sorrow was until I explained him." He lifted one shoulder, that familiar rueful smile coming across his face. "What other woman is ever going to be both sexy enough to pull off an Ambria dress at a Family party and strong enough to have my back at the Overwatch? There is no one else like you, Gracie. And I know that if I have even the tiniest chance on Cybele to be with you, I have to at least try."

"Well, there's always Vanessa and Lilly," I muttered, as much to hide my blush as to point out the flaw in his logic. "They're strong and they clean up at least as nicely as I do."

He waved a hand to dismiss the other third-gens as if they weren't some of the most beautiful and gifted women on the planet. "They're three-T's. What do they need me hanging about for? With you, I'm not just another pale, washed-out version of the first few gens. With you, I have useful skills that don't have to be as strong, because you more than make up for their lack. With you, suddenly I'm half of one of the best teams at OW, and I'm not a charity case—I'm valuable. I never thought I'd feel that way about my powers, but with you around, I do."

I considered him thoughtfully as he leaned on one elbow looking up at me, the top of his jacket undone to reveal the long, smooth curve of his neck. When he explained it like that, how could I blame him for falling in love with me? It made sense that he'd find me to be the perfect mix of someone who both needed him and could take care of him. Oddly enough, I found myself feeling very much the same way about him.

"Fuck," I said, staring at Liam and feeling like somehow I'd never quite seen him before.

"What does that mean?" I'd put the caution in his eyes with my own fickle behavior, but it still hurt to see him look at me as if he was waiting for the emotional blow. Just watching that echo of imagined pain cross his face sparked a sharp pang in my chest. He saw it in my expression because he frowned. "Gracie? Say something. Please. Am I wasting my time, or is there even a tiny chance that I might have more than just your attraction or your working partnership? I'm grateful to know I have those things, believe me, and yesterday I think I would have given up my implant just to get you in this bed. But now that I'm here, I'm not sure I can settle for either one of them. I want you; all of you. And if I can't have that, well, maybe you're right and we need to take a break from being friends."

I shook my head and took the smooth curve of his jaw in both hands. "You've had me for a lot longer than either of us probably realize," I murmured. His eyes met mine, and there was so much longing in them. I'd put this off far too long. His heart raced under my fingertips as I guided him up for another kiss. This one was much faster, I think because he wanted to make sure he hadn't misheard me.

While our lips were still pressed together, he came up to his knees. When he pulled away from me, he was once again a decent amount taller. His fingers traced the edge of my face, and it was my turn to lean into his touch. After denying my youthful flesh for so long, the physical contact felt incredible. My hands spread across his chest, and I considered trying for another button on his coat, but decided to respect his obvious desire to take things more slowly. Seeing as he'd been patient enough with my erratic emotions the last few months, it seemed only fair.

"Does that mean..." he left the sentence open for me to finish, obviously needing to hear me admit to some stronger emotions before he was willing to move forward physically. I didn't blame him, but it didn't make it any easier to find the words.

"That I love you?" I tilted my face up to his and tried to put the honesty of my words into my gaze. "I'm pretty sure I have for a long time, Liam. I've just been too... I don't know... afraid? Distracted? Stubborn? I'm not sure why, but it's taken me a stupidly long time to admit it to myself, let alone to you. I'm sorry if I've hurt you in the meantime. If it makes you feel any better, I've been pretty miserable over it a few times, too."

He shook his head, fingers finding the stray strands of hair around my face and brushing them gently away. "No, it doesn't make me happy to think of you hurting," he said. "But I can't tell you how amazing it is to hear you say that you love me. Can I hear it again?"

"I love you," I murmured, hardly more than a whisper really, but we were so close that it didn't have to be louder.

He put a finger under my chin, then gently tilted

my head and kissed the place where my jaw flowed into my neck. I felt that touch all the way down my shoulders and into the pit of my stomach where heat blossomed to wash up and down my spine. All that from one gentle kiss. I shivered with anticipation. I had a feeling sex with Liam was going to be a completely different experience than my first attempts at coupling.

I was right.

First of all, there is a magic to being with someone you're really in love with. For all that I'd fought it for a long time, there was no denying that I had real and deep emotions for Liam. Now that he'd finally forced the door open, my desire was a living thing that rolled up and out of the center of my chest at the simple sight of him. And it wasn't just hormone-fueled lust. No, I'd experienced that enough times now to know the difference.

And for all that I'd enjoyed James, I think even at the time of our date some part of me had known that relationship couldn't last. It had felt almost like a farewell or a tribute to the beautiful thing we could have been if we simply weren't exactly what we are. I'd known James, and loved him, but where that pairing had been a regretful ending, this one was an eager beginning.

The familiarity I had with Liam no longer had to do with the fact that he was Family. It had to do with all the times we'd sparred on a practice mat; the countless meals and conversations we'd shared at University; the thousands of times I'd seen him walking towards me with a smile on his face. It had to do with the fact that he'd teleported a loaded shotgun out of my face and taken on a blood-blind vampire in my defense. Hell, the blood stains were still on his uniform from that lovely incident. I didn't care. I watched the angle of his graceful fingers as he undid the clasps of my OW jacket and felt as if Liam himself embodied safety and home.

Then there's the fact that we were both Usuriels. I'd never been with a Family member before, and there really is a reason the Divinitas built shrines to us.

Once he'd gotten my jacket open and paid attention to my neck and collarbone, I shrugged out of the coat before reaching down for the edge of my practice shirt and pulling it off over my head in one smooth motion. My skin fairly glowed with my flames, as if they were rushing along the inside of my body just below the surface.

Liam watched me with eyes that flickered with blue light. When he followed my lead, pulling off his shirt, all that perfect, white Usuriel flesh was exposed in the afternoon light flooding in the window. Like my own slim yet strong figure, I could see where our OW training had sculpted the planes of Liam's torso into something lean and muscular. When I ran a hand across the magnificent breadth of his shoulders, his power rose along with my touch. My fingers sent blue sparks gliding along his skin as if he couldn't quite help his mind's response to me.

Then, I reached for his belt, and the look he gave me was drowning in blue psi.

Let's just say, I somehow managed not to burn the dormitory down.

This had been a long time coming between us, and perhaps that added to it, too. Liam was much more experienced than I, but I don't think he'd been with a lot of other women. Even so, our pairing was as open, honest, and complete as such an act can be. I remember watching the red and blue of our powers mingle and slide along our bare skin, casting wild shadows across the dormitory walls long after the sun had set in its own riot of color.

"I'm graduating from University at the end of this term," Liam said quietly as I rested against his chest, his fingers playing absently with a curl of my hair as we took a break from our amorous activities.

"Hmmm," I replied, awake but not interested in spending the energy on a reply.

"I'll have to find an apartment or something," he murmured, pressing his face into my hair and taking a deep breath.

"Are you planning to stay in the Landing area?" I asked. As a teleporter, he could live just about anywhere on the continent and still make it to OW practice every day.

"I haven't decided," he replied thoughtfully, shivering as I ran lazy fingers over his bare stomach. "I imagine it depends on what you want to do."

"Me?" I tilted my head so that I looked up the length of his shoulder at his face. He gave me a gentle smile.

"Yes you, my lovely firebird. Or am I still too forward to call us a pair now?"

I considered it, but didn't have the strength to even argue the point anymore. "No, I suppose there's no denying it now. You'll probably regret it, but I'm all yours."

"I sincerely doubt I will have any regrets about tonight," he said and kissed me. It was quick and gentle, but it felt as if it sealed something more solid between us. When he pulled away from me, however, his face was serious.

"What's wrong?" I asked, touching his cheek with one hand. It was an awkward position so I didn't hold it long, but it did pull his gaze back to mine. "I thought this was what you wanted."

"It is," he reassured me. "Believe me, I feel like I'm going to wake up from the best dream I've ever had at any moment." His mouth flattened into that grim expression again. "I just..."

"Just what?"

He shook his head again and pulled me tightly against his body, his cheek pressing to my forehead as his strong arms all but crushed me to his side. This wasn't sensual, it was more of what he'd asked for in the first place; holding me because he needed reassurance. Sensing his change in mood, I hugged him back, burrowing my head against his shoulder.

"Do you think that new gun we saw on the dead Riland watchman could pierce a psi shield?" he murmured, voice so low I felt it through his chest.

My own body tensed at his question, and I suddenly found myself clutching him to me with almost bruising force. With an act of will, I deliberately relaxed my shoulders so that I wouldn't give myself a stress headache and tried to think of something to say that was both reassuring and true. I didn't come up with much.

"I don't think vamps have psi shields," I pointed out, "and Martin managed to survive the attack on his makers despite the new weaponry."

"Probably because he was still passed out when they opened fire, and the watch didn't realize how dangerous he was until he was at their throats," Liam countered.

I tended to agree with that assessment, so I didn't say anything. We lapsed into silence, the room growing dim as the last puddles of sunlight faded to naught in the corner.

"Do you really think we're going to war this time?" I asked softly into the dark.

Liam didn't reply immediately. Instead, his fingers found my hair again, and he tangled their tips in my silky curls. "I've wanted to believe that we could avoid it," he said slowly. "That James and my mom and 'Nessa were all blowing things out of proportion." I felt more than saw his head shake. "But after the avatars and now this... I don't think Evan is going to stop provoking things until there is open conflict. If he's willing to send his own watch into almost certain death just for political gain..."

My chest tightened, and I shivered against him, my bare body and my thoughts growing cold.

"We'll be on the front lines," I whispered.

"Dear heart, we already were today," Liam replied. "That was an unprovoked attack. Martin may be getting the blame but truthfully, he's just another casualty. If we'd arrived in time for those mortal watchmen to see us, how much would you bet me they'd have opened fire in our direction?"

I didn't want to think about it, but my lover was right. There was no other reason for the watch to be at Martin's family farm. Somehow they'd known about the turning and went in with the intention of killing vampires. My stomach turned, adding nausea to my chill. With a wave of one hand, I summoned a small ball of psi-fire to hang above the bed. Its gentle light and warmth felt familiar and reassuring as it hovered above us.

Liam blinked up at the fire light, then down into my face. "Well, at least now I don't have to go into battle concerned about who is going to be in my bed at the end of it." He gave me a hint of his usual jovial smile. "In reality, it's probably best that we sorted ourselves out. This whole limbo thing has been a distraction we might not have been able to afford much longer."

I nodded my agreement. "Honestly, I already feel steadier knowing we're not at odds anymore," I said and realized it was true.

"Me, too." With one hand he tilted my head and gave me a gentle, lingering kiss. Afterwards, we were both beginning to glow again.

"I'm happy we sorted this out for other reasons, too," I said with a half-lidded smile.

"Hmmm... wouldn't want to go over them again for me, would you?"

"Probably easier if I just show you," I replied, shifting my weight so that I knelt over him, my long red hair falling like a curtain around his upturned face. Sweet

Fate, he was beautiful. A small, blue spark caught in his eyes despite their lazy, sensual expression. That generous, mortal mouth of his tilted upwards in a smile that told me he knew exactly what pleasures I was going to treat him to, and he was looking forward to every single one. Fuck, why had I put this off so long?

"Educate me, my love." He said it as naturally as breathing, but I think it was the first time he'd used that phrase. My love, I echoed in my head as I placed a kiss on his forehead. Then I watched his eyes fade shut as I began kissing my way down the curve of his neck. I could get used to being called that.

Chapter 9

Honesty Part Two

I wish I could end this story here. Right here. Resting in my dormitory with Liam's beautiful naked body laid out against my pillow, my father safely in Angelus Quietum, my grandparents happily awaiting Ileesia at their homestead and James asleep in his own dormitory a few meters away. My biggest regret at that point was Grayson, and while he was an honest tragedy, I think I was starting to learn to live with that accident. If I could pause time right there, curled up against Liam while we slept with the contented satisfaction of new lovers, I would do it in a heartbeat.

Unfortunately, that's not how time works, even for a fate like me.

Liam and I didn't leave my room that evening. I had a few snacks hidden in a dresser drawer and we nibbled on a few of those before tossing on some night shirts. Sometime well after dark we fell asleep tangled in each other's arms. That may be the most beautiful place I'd ever been.

It must have only been a few hours later that Liam woke me. He didn't mean to; in fact, I'm fairly sure he wasn't awake at the time. However, even in his sleep the pain was bad enough that he gave voice to it. I think that's what woke me initially, but the tension in his body as he curled around me pulled my consciousness the rest of the way out of my dreams.

"Liam?" I said his name softly, putting a hand to his arm where it wrapped around my waist. I heard him breathing rapidly and thought that perhaps he was having a nightmare. He whimpered in that dreaming way and I decided I was probably right. "Hey, wake up." I shook his shoulder and rolled towards him as much as I could with his solid weight blocking me. My bed wasn't large and Liam was a tall man, so there wasn't a whole lot of wiggle room.

"Gracie?" His voice still sounded half-asleep. His eyes flickered open, then he took a sharp, pained breath. My brain flashed on Grayson so fast I thought my heart was truly about to climb out of my chest.

"No, no, that's not possible." I was talking to myself out loud already. Can you say traumatized much? Even so, the instant I sent a nightlight to illuminate the room it was clear that Liam was sick. His face was a little too flushed and, now that I'd moved away from him, there was no reason for him to be curled almost double on the bed. With a groan, he wrapped a hand more tightly around his gut. I swore incoherently, stumbling back from the bed. My half-naked body fetched up against my desk as my brain raced in pure and utter panic.

"It's okay, Gracie, take a deep breath," he said, recovering a touch. He was still a bit out of breath, but he rolled easily to a sitting position, and after a moment he seemed just fine. "I'd say Gloria just went into labor... or rather she did sometime while we were asleep, and I wasn't shielding." He tilted his head at me. "You really didn't feel it?"

"Oh..." My body relaxed, my cheeks warming to something quite flaming. "No, no I didn't feel it."

Liam frowned at me. Between the echo pain and my odd behavior, he was now mostly awake. "I might be envying your iron shields later today," he said with a gentle smile. "Which is a good reason to try to get some rest now. I'm fine, I promise, I'll just have to keep a shield up while I sleep. It's a trick, but James showed me a technique that works most of the time. Why don't you come back to bed?"

Slowly, I allowed him to take my hand and pull me back under the covers. Even so, I was shaking all over. My body was much less yielding against his even as I snuffed out the night light.

"Gracie," he murmured my name gently and pulled me back into his arms despite the fact that I made no move to curl around him again. "What's wrong? And don't tell me nothing, because you're trembling."

I tried to force myself to slow my breathing, but it wasn't working. I shut my eyes tightly and tried to think about anything but a dying vampire and the gasp of pain that Liam had woken me with. Of course, the harder I tried not to think about it, the more my brain supplied images of the man I'd finally admitted I was in love with writhing in mortal agony.

"I can't do this," I gasped, pulling away from Liam

and sitting up on the edge of the bed. I wrapped both of my arms around myself and sat there hugging my torso as if I'd fall apart without the support.

"Lights at fifty percent," Liam said. Obediently the desk lamp came on. He pushed himself up to sit next to me and wrapped a length of the blanket around my shaking shoulders. Then he watched me quietly for a few moments while I forced my muscles to stop tensing so badly that I thought a joint might dislocate.

"I'm sorry," I whispered, feeling like I wanted to disappear. "I thought I could... but I can't..." I shook my head and stared across the room as if my desk had an answer.

"This has to do with what happened after the Riland avatar incident, doesn't it." It was more of a statement than a question. I was grateful that he didn't try to touch me at that moment. I didn't think my nerves could take it. "You haven't been quite yourself since then."

"Yes," I admitted, my voice barely above a whisper. I glanced at his concerned face and buried my face in my hands. "Fates, I... I should have told you this earlier. I wasn't exactly planning on our little tryst tonight but... shit. You're going to break up with me the instant I explain this one," I could hear my voice shaking even as I tried for a note of humor in that last statement. It was too true to carry the joke, and I just ended up sounding scared. "Either you'll think I'm crazy or dangerous or both."

"I'm already pretty sure you're both," Liam replied steadily. "But I'm also pretty sure that's why I'm in love with you. So, take a deep breath, and tell me what happened."

Obediently I sucked in air and tried to steady my nerves enough to put the situation into words.

"So… you know that James and I had a fight. And then I went to Amourie's."

Liam inclined his head.

"Well, I met a vamp there. One of the waitstaff. He introduced himself as Grayson. We… had a conversation. He suggested we take it to the back."

Liam's expression darkened, those little sparks that had been so sensual earlier igniting in anger. "Is that what this is about?" His voice was deadly quiet. "Did he—"

"What? No! He didn't hurt me. Well, no more than I asked for. The bite was small and hardly even qualified as an injury." I ran fingers over the now-smooth curve of my neck.

Liam's brow crinkled in confusion. "I don't understand. You think I'd judge you for being with a vamp? Come on, sweetie. You think I haven't checked out all of my options?"

"I wish it was just a one-night stand," I moaned, rubbing my eyes as an excuse to hide behind my hands again. "That was my intention, at the time. But that's not how it worked out."

"Okay." Liam squinted at me. "But, you did mess around with this Grayson vamp, right? You said he bit you."

"Yeah," I agreed. "Fates, I warned him I was untasted. It was the first thing out of my mouth when he suggested seeing a sunrise together. But he'd been with Amourie before and didn't think it would be a big deal. I figured he had more experience and knew what he was talking about. Proves both of us wrong, I guess."

Liam's eyes were getting a little wide around the edges. "Wait. So he took your blood and then…"

I stared at Liam's reflection in my mirror, trying to focus on his safe, familiar features. It didn't work. All I could see were tiny rows of blue lights and dark stains splashed across a couch.

"At first we thought it was just the change. When my blood didn't knock him out immediately, we assumed the fever and nausea were a side effect of his body coming back to a mortal state."

"Logical. But?"

"But instead of stabilizing after his heart started back up, things got worse. A lot worse. I called Amourie. She was angry at first, but pretty quickly she saw how sick he was. We called Gloria. She came and tried to override my blood with hers." I was staring at the corner of my desk now, but I wasn't seeing it. I couldn't look at Liam.

"Did that help?"

I shook my head.

"So… he…"

"Yeah."

"Fuck."

We sat in silence. Finally, I found my voice again. "That's not even the most twisted part of it." Liam held his breath. "Afterwards, there was this big flash of psi and everything changed. The back room became storage, not a lounge. Amourie was back on stage singing. Grandma wasn't even in the club. No body. No blood, except for what got on my arms and pants."

"Hold on." Liam put up a hand to stop me. "You're telling me this Grayson vamp dies and suddenly the whole world transforms?"

"Not the whole world. But parts of it, yes. I didn't understand at the time, but it was just the things Grayson affected. Everything influenced by or connected to him changed or disappeared the moment he died. According to Dad and the Anori database, it's a property of my blood because I have an affinity for time."

"Time? No, you're a firebird."

"Just because you have one power doesn't mean you can't have another. Apparently, I'm also a fate. Ever since I was a little kid, I've had dreams. Visions. Times and places I've never been—I experience them like I was right there." His wide-eyed expression almost made me burst into tears. "I know, it sounds like I'm crazy. After Grayson, I really thought I was going the way of Adora, too. Honestly, if Amourie hadn't taken me to Dad…" I took a shuddering breath. "Anyway, he told me that there are documented cases of this kind of psi in the Anori database. It's just super rare."

"That's a lot," Liam muttered, one hand covering his mouth.

"What? To find out you're poisonous and officially a time traveler in the same conversation? Yeah. A lot. That's one way to put it." I wrapped the edge of the blanket around my shoulders a little more firmly. It didn't matter. I still shook. "I tried to jump back in time and prevent myself from going to Amouries in the first place. But it didn't work. Even with a clear mental picture, I couldn't go back. Dad says it's because I fundamentally changed the timeline. After Grayson was unmade, there was no way to get back to the events that surrounded him."

"Let me get this straight. You unmade him? As in, he was never even born to begin with?" Liam asked, his tone extremely careful as if I were some kind of untamed wild beast.

I nodded miserably. "I got Stella to help me search the net for him. There's no sign that anyone by the name Grayson was turned in the last century. There were a few mortal Graysons down in Skykyle, but none of the pictures matched. From what I can tell, it's exactly like Dad said. I erased him from existence entirely."

Liam took a long, deliberate breath. With one hand, he absently rubbed his other arm as if he were suddenly cold. I somehow doubted the issue was the temperature. His gaze was distant for a moment, then he licked his lips nervously and said, "So, your blood is poisonous to vampires. What about other people? I mean, should we be careful if you get cut?"

I hugged myself tightly. "I hope it's just vampires. I mean, I had sex with Malcolm and he was fine, but there wasn't any blood involved. There wasn't any tonight either, but I think you can see why you scared me pretty good." I gestured to Liam, who tilted his head as if acknowledging my point. He didn't look quite as spooked since I'd pointed out the Malcolm thing.

"Maybe you ought to discuss this with Grandmother Gloria at some point. After she's recovered from having Ileesia, of course. It seems like she might be a good source of information on this kind of thing. She's certainly the only one who has ever been outside of our reality."

"That's not a bad idea," I agreed.

We both stared off into space as if neither of us really knew what to do with this situation.

"Well, assuming I make it 'till morning without being unmade," Liam said finally, "I haven't changed my mind about being with you."

I glanced at him a bit cautiously. "I just risked your life because I'm a hormone-addled twit. Why the hell would you want to be with me?"

Liam shook his head at me. "Vampires and Usuriel blood mix to make some really intense and unusual supernatural effects. Good old-fashioned sex is not even close to something like that, and you know it as well as I do. You didn't risk anything, especially since you've done it before without killing your partner."

"Yeah, that was pretty much what I thought, too," I admitted. "But when I woke up to you..." I couldn't even finish the sentence. I cringed just thinking about the conclusion I'd immediately jumped to.

"I think it's understandable that you got scared," Liam said quietly. "And I suppose I should be happy that the idea of hurting me has you so spooked. But I'm fine, and honestly, Gabriel and Gloria were right. You can't punish yourself for this. It was an accident."

"So was what happened to Martin yesterday, and we'll probably end up executing him for it."

Liam's hand found my shoulder, and the touch wasn't about sex. He was just my OW partner again; safe, steady, and reasonable as ever. I don't think I realized how much I relied on his insightful, calm logic until that moment. "Martin tore people's throats out. Even if he wasn't in his right mind, it was still a violent act. You, on the other hand, did nothing violent or threatening. Hell, you warned Grayson up front that you were untasted and might be dangerous. He took the risk anyway and paid the price. The result was unlikely, but he did know it was one of the potential hazards of his actions."

I looked at my best friend, partner, and now lover. I felt my face reflect the vulnerability I tried so hard to hide most of the time, but I couldn't help it. "Just because it was unintentional doesn't mean I'm not dangerous. Do you understand the risks, Liam? I'm a firebird; possibly the strongest that's ever lived. And now apparently a fate, whatever that means. I've already killed someone without meaning to. I'm not sure it's safe for you to get so close to me. I really don't know what I'd do if I hurt you."

"I think we're a little past those warnings, lover," Liam tried for gentle, but I could see a little of his twisted sense of humor in his smile.

"I know," I moaned, but I let him pull me into his arms. "That's what I'm worried about."

He took a deep breath, and I felt his chest rise and fall under my ear. As if they had a mind of their own, my arms wrapped around his waist, and I prayed to anything that might hear me that I could somehow manage to keep Liam safe. Between angry mortals, out-of-control vampires, execution-happy Usuriels, and my own crazy powers, I felt as if the world was getting more dangerous by the day. I wouldn't say it aloud to him, but Liam just wasn't strong enough to protect himself from something like me.

"You've been trying to drive me away," Liam said softly. "Well, that makes a bit more sense. And I appreciate the fact that you want to keep me safe, Gracie, but I'm your OW partner. Even if we're not dating, I'm around almost every time you call on your fire. I don't think kicking me out of your bed is going to be effective at keeping me out of harm's way."

"Fates, I know it," I muttered into his chest. Intellectually, I think I knew that, with the war gathering, keeping Liam close was the best way to keep him whole. I did have good control over my flames, as our enthusiastic yet fire-free pairing had proven. Chances were, he was much more likely to die from a psi-proof bullet than my own powers. Unfortunately, my emotions had decided that sex and death were now tied together, and I was having a hard time not tossing him out the door.

"Look at me," he said, and tilted my face up to his. I think he saw the fear in my eyes, because he kissed them closed. "We've done just about everything two non-vampires can do with each other tonight, and I'm just fine. If you want to worry about something, worry about what those damn mortals down in Riland are planning to send after us next. That's a legitimate concern. But don't be afraid that this"—he kissed me firmly on the mouth—"is going to hurt me, because it's not. If anything, being distracted by our relationship issues when I should be focused on having your back is much more likely to get me burned."

"I really hope you're right."

"I've been known to be from time to time," he replied. When that put a little half-smile on my face, he tapped his implant and said, "Lights out." The room sank into darkness, and I allowed him to pull me back into the safe warmth of the bed. I thought it would take me a long time to fall asleep, but when Liam's breathing evened out in an easy, painless slumber, I found myself quickly following him into a deep, dreamless sleep.

Chapter 10

Ileesia

The next day was strange for a number of reasons. Being a pair with Liam was its own kind of odd, but waking up in his arms was certainly not the worst part of the day. It felt so natural to kiss him before the two of us went into our usual morning routines. After my shower he showed up in my dorm, dressed and ready to go, and offered to teleport both of us to the compound instead of making me fly myself. With a shrug, I agreed. Once I was dressed, I enjoyed the fact that his teleport was so much smoother when we were pressed closely together.

The mood of the OW compound when we got there was downright somber. Most of the members were grim-faced and looked like they hadn't slept very well. Jillian looked a little better than most, but then she wasn't a telepath. Even so, her dark eyes were set and her generous mouth drawn in a serious line when she greeted us at the practice mat.

"I don't think things are going smoothly," she said when I asked her what was wrong.

I frowned. "What do you mean?"

"Gloria and Ileesia," Liam supplied, a distant look

on his face. He winced, and I could almost see him slamming down his shields a little tighter. "Gloria's in pain, but that's normal for labor, isn't it?"

"She's a little over three weeks early," Jillian said, glancing around at the hollow-eyed telepaths in the room, "and, even in that shielded birthing room, almost everyone felt the echo pain last night. I think Gabriel went up there around midnight, and he's helping keep the shields from leaking too badly, but even he can only do so much."

I nodded slowly. It made sense that Dad would be nearby, what with Grandma Gloria in such distress. I wondered if I should go up to the hospital to see if they needed anything. It probably wouldn't be a bad idea to bring some food after class, I thought. Dad would probably forget to eat unless someone reminded him, and clearly my grandparents wouldn't be thinking about such things at the moment. Making a mental note to grab something for Gabriel and D'nay from the mess hall at lunch, I started my usual stretches.

The rest of the morning was normal, if a little subdued. Even the mortals seemed on edge, though I'm not sure they knew quite why. Class was quiet, and I thought I saw a few of my more sensitive classmates looking a little green.

At lunch, Liam reluctantly agreed to visit the hospital with me and helped me pack some sandwiches for Dad and Grandfather. I wasn't sure they'd be interested in eating, what with the echo pain that was probably blasting them a lot worse than it was the rest of the Family, but at least I could offer.

If I'd thought the University was somber, the hospital was downright grim. Liam had to take a firmer grip on my arm the moment we stepped onto the maternity ward, and I glanced up at him with concern.

"You don't have to stay," I told him. "Honestly, it's a short trip back to class from here. I can walk no problem."

He hesitated a moment, then I watched the little color he had drain out of his face and knew Gloria was projecting another contraction. Liam nodded abruptly and gave me a quick kiss. "I'll see you at dinner," he said, then faded away with the usual sigh of blue wind.

I turned back to the curving hospital hallway and saw Dad watching me with a tired smile on his face. He must have just caught that little intimate interaction with Liam as he rounded the corner. I felt myself flush a nice bright red.

"Hey, Dad," I said, trying to play off my embarrassment. "How is Grandma?"

He closed his eyes and nodded as if that were an answer. Then he gave me a quick hug and a kiss on the top of my head. "She's strong. She'll be fine." He sounded exhausted.

"How long have you been awake?" I asked with a frown. "You look awful. Maybe you should let one of the third-gens take a shift?"

Dad shook his head and gave me another tired smile. "I don't think the rest of the Family would appreciate it if I took a break. Shielding is actually one of my stronger suits; even Lilly or 'Nessa wouldn't be able to keep this from bleeding to the younger children. Not that I'd be able to block Mom out long enough to get any real sleep right now myself."

I'd suspected as much, but I gave him a sympathetic grimace anyway. "Sorry. I guess my alloy shield continues to be an unexpected advantage."

"Indeed," Dad agreed with a yawn.

"I did bring you and Grandpa some lunch," I said, holding up the package of sandwiches.

His smile was a lot more genuine this time, even if I could still see the strain in his eyes. "Ah, now that is something I will take you up on," he said and put an arm around my shoulders to lead me farther down the hall. After a few twists and turns, we came to a little sitting area with a couch and two armchairs clustered around a low table. The nurses' station next to it was deserted.

"Where is everyone?" I asked, glancing around the empty hall.

"Hiding. Like sensible people," Gabriel replied, settling onto one of the armchairs with less than his usual grace.

"She's getting through the room's shields and yours badly enough to affect mortals?" I raised an eyebrow, feeling a little impressed at my grandmother's psychic strength. My father hadn't been kidding when he said I was the only person on Cybele who wouldn't feel Gloria's labor.

"Hmmm... strongest psi on the planet," he said. "I don't know how Dad's still in the same room with her. Dax at least has his own shields plus a decent null amulet."

I'd known such a thing as a null amulet existed, but they were rare. It made sense that whoever was attending Gloria would need something to block her out, however, and I found myself nodding as I took out the sandwiches and handed one to my father. He accepted and unwrapped it with a grateful look on his face.

"Sweet Fate, you are a lifesaver," he sighed, taking a bite of the roast beef and cheese. "I don't think anyone else would be willing to even set foot in this hospital today."

"Yeah, Liam almost passed out just teleporting in."

"Hmmm..." I'd caught him with his mouth full, and I was kind of hoping he wouldn't have anything to say about my relationship status. Of course, he was my father, so once he finished chewing, he did. "Congratulations on that, by the way. Glad to see the two of you finally got together."

I shook my head at him. "It was barely a kiss. How do you extrapolate a whole relationship out of that?"

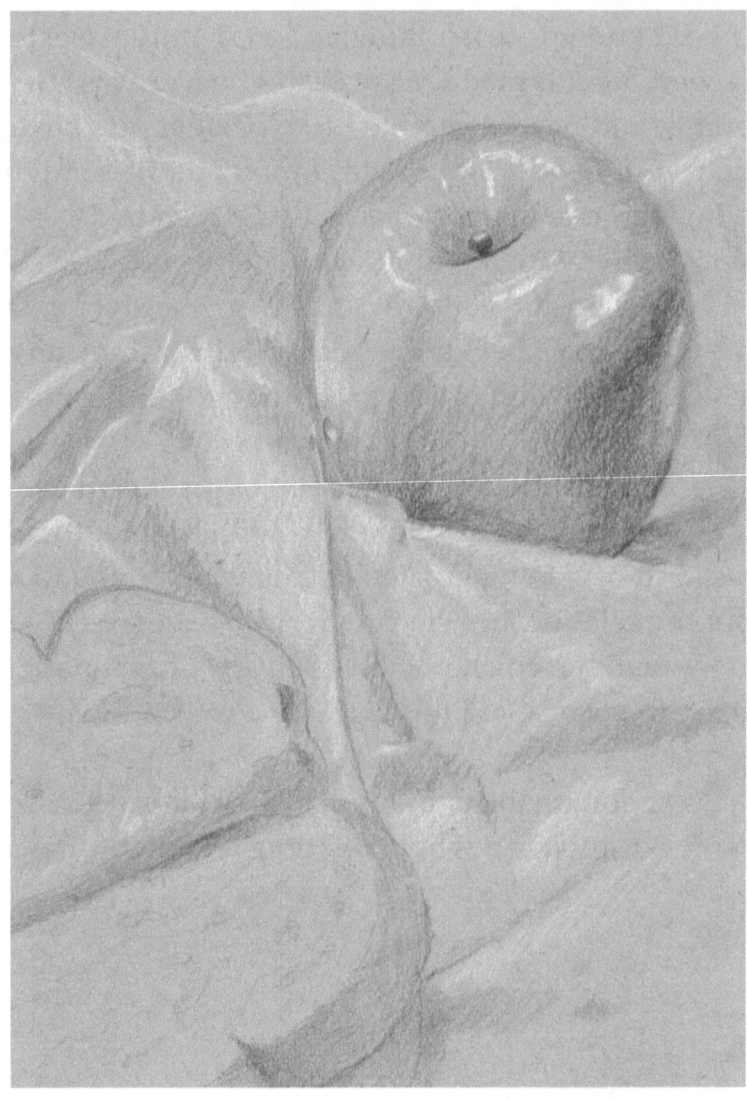

Dad gave me a look that told me he found my embarrassment rather amusing. "I've had one or two relationships, you know," he said evenly, "I know what they look like. Besides, you may be a null, but Liam isn't. I think every telepath he runs into today is going to know exactly what happened last night." I groaned and swore, ducking my head to avoid my father's gaze. He chuckled and patted my shoulder. "Don't worry, I didn't get any graphic details. He's mostly just happy. It's nice to see, actually."

A little relieved that Dad hadn't gotten quite so intimate a look at my sex life as I'd first feared, I managed a smile that may have teetered on the edge of a besotted grin. "It is quite a bit better than watching him mope around," I agreed.

"What about you?" Dad asked, tilting his head, "Are you happy about it?"

I made a show of considering his question, but really it didn't take too much thought. "Happier than I thought I would be, actually," I said finally.

"Good, that's the way it should be," Gabriel said with a nod and finished eating his sandwich. I watched him quietly, having already eaten at the mess hall earlier.

"Can I do anything else?" I asked when he'd finished and thrown away the parchment paper I'd wrapped the food in. "You know, to make things easier for you or Grandma and Grandpa?"

He shook his head, and his face turned bleak again. Judging by his expression, I had a sinking feeling Jillian had been right. Things were not going smoothly.

"Nothing to do now, but wait," he sighed and picked up the other sandwich I'd brought. "I'll give this to Dad if I can peel him away from Mom's side for two seconds. Thanks for checking on us, sweetheart. It means a lot."

"Of course," I said, recognizing the dismissal. He probably needed to focus on shielding, I thought, as he stood to give me a quick hug. "I'll bring dinner by in a few hours. Let me know if anything changes."

"I will," he agreed with another of those exhausted smiles and a wave. I returned the smile, then turned and walked off to class.

***

The rest of the day was more of the same. I didn't even ask Liam to teleport me to the hospital after dinner. He'd hardly touched anything on his plate and, by the time we left the mess hall, I could see that Gloria's pain was starting to leak through the edges of his shields despite his and Dad's best efforts. So, after walking my boyfriend back to the dormitory and convincing him to lay down for a while, I took the meals I'd prepared for Dad, Grandfather, and Dax up to the hospital alone.

By the time I got there, Gabriel looked like he had a splitting headache. He sat in one of the armchairs at the little sitting area where we'd eaten lunch with his shoulders hunched and his head in both hands. When I asked him if there was any change, he shook his head mutely. Then he quietly thanked me for the food, but made no move to touch it. Not wanting to distract him and make things harder, I laid a quick kiss on his bowed head, set his dinner on the little table, and went back to the dorm to check on Liam.

"Surviving?" I asked my partner as I stuck my head

in his doorway. He'd asked me to leave the door open so that I could just come back in when I got back from my hospital visit. When I didn't get an answer, I walked into the darkened room and shook his shoulder gently.

"Hmmm?" was his sleepy reply. I'd never had to put any effort into my shields, but from the way the rest of the Usuriels on campus were dragging about, I had to assume keeping them completely up for so long was exhausting for most telepaths. If he could sleep through the echo pain, I didn't want to disturb him.

I patted Liam's shoulder and said, "It's just me, love. Go ahead and sleep. I'll be in my room if you need me."

"Mmmmhmmm."

For a moment I thought about checking on James. He was a high level telepath, after all, and this couldn't be comfortable for him any more than it was for Liam. But when I tapped for him there was no response. I asked Stella about it, but all she could tell me was that he wasn't on campus. Well, I thought, hopefully wherever James was it was far enough away that Gloria's echo pain was at least dampened.

Satisfied that I'd done what I could, I went back to my room and started on some homework. The tension of the day must have been getting to me, too, because after reading a few chapters for my Advanced Awareness Theory class, I fell asleep in bed with my clothes still on.

I awoke in the middle of the night to the most eerie and bone-chilling sound I had ever heard. It was a rising, keening cry, as if everyone on the Usuriel wing of the dormitory was calling out in pain at once. Of course, that was exactly what it was, I realized as I came more fully awake. I'd fallen asleep with the door open, and it seemed a number of the other Usuriel students had as well. Even as I sat up and rubbed the sleep out of my eyes, that hair-raising wail swelled again. Male and female, deep and high, the chorus of agony filled the hall as the Matriarch projected her birth pangs into the talented minds of her descendants. Mixed in with the moans and whimpers, I heard several people cursing or begging for a reprieve. I swallowed hard and was never so glad of my head blind status as I was at that moment.

"Gracie!"

Liam's voice cut through the other cries, at least to my ears. I don't think it took me more than a minute to run down the hall, past the other doors where my extended family writhed with their ancestress' labor. I had a split-second to worry about why Dad wasn't able to shut out the worst of the echo anymore before I quite literally had my hands full with my distraught and pain-wracked boyfriend.

"What the hell are you doing?" I asked, catching Liam as he tried to stand in his doorway. "Honestly, why didn't you just tap if you wanted me?"

"Fates, Gracie, how do women do this more than once?" he gasped as I half-carried him back to the bed, his body shaking under my arm as I helped him lay back down.

"I'm not a mother, so I have no idea," I told him, straightening the twisted blanket and settling it over him. "I'm not sure I can do much to help, but if you can think of anything just tell me."

From down the hall I heard the moan rise again, and suddenly Liam's hand on my arm was crushing. He swore and pulled me down onto the edge of the bed. I don't think he meant to, that was just the direction his body twisted as Gloria's powerful mind projected its torment. Without really thinking about it, I suddenly had his head and shoulders in my lap as his hands clung to my upper arms in a vise-like grip. Thankfully, I'm a third-gen and stronger than most mortals despite my lack of telekinesis, because it took all of my strength to support him as he rode out that particular wave of agony.

"It... has to be... over soon... right?" he gasped once the contraction subsided enough for him to speak again.

"Sweet Fate, I hope so," I told him, even as the cries mounted down the hall, and my lover bowed his head as the wave of pain broke over them all again.

***

It took almost an hour and a half before the end came. That may not sound long, but it seemed like an eternity as Liam's moans and whimpers slowly dissolved into screams. If I flashed on Grayson about fifty times, I somehow managed to stay steady and calm for Liam. I knew that was what he needed from me right then, no matter what our relationship was. Friend, OW partner, or girlfriend, it really didn't matter which one I wanted to call myself. What *did* matter was providing a soothing voice and strong arms when he needed them. Just as he'd had my back so many times, this time I was the one who had to swallow the emotional pain and do what needed doing.

When it was finally over, relieved weeping replaced the cries of pain up and down the corridor. Liam took a few exhausted, cautious breaths before looking up at me.

"I don't know why, but Gloria's very upset," he said softly, voice raw and face utterly drenched in sweat. Nervousness of a new kind squirmed in my gut, and I considered tapping for my father. However, looking at the condition of my boyfriend, who had been a lot farther away from the main event than Gabriel, I thought better of it.

"Can you still hear her?" I asked.

He shook his head tiredly, then laid it on my chest as if he no longer had the energy to hold it upright. "No, not anymore," he murmured, already falling asleep.

"Come on, lay down before you pass out on me," I said, not unkindly. "Will you sleep better if I go back to my room?"

"No, please stay," his voice was soft but clear as he settled himself back on the pillow.

"Okay, I'll be right back." I trotted back to my room and made sure the door had shut behind me. It had. I went back to Liam's room, palmed closed the door behind me, stepped out of my stiff work-a-day pants and bra before climbing into bed next to him. He shifted his weight so that I could curl around him more comfortably, and then he promptly fell asleep. I, on the other hand, laid awake worrying about Dad, my grandparents, and Ileesia for a very long time.

Chapter 11

Family Ties

I woke to Dad's tap early the next morning. Liam was still asleep beside me, and after the rough night, I decided to step outside to take the call instead of waking my slumbering boyfriend.

"Hi Dad," I said, walking down the corridor to my own room. "How are Grandma and Ileesia?"

"Mom is recovering," Gabriel said, his voice low as if he were trying not to wake someone. "She lost a lot of blood, but Dax thinks she'll be able to go home in a week or so."

My heart sank at that assessment. The idea that my grandmother's Usuriel metabolism needed a week of hospital rest to recover was daunting. Dad had almost fully recovered from heart surgery in three days. I suspected things were a little more complicated than blood loss, but I didn't push him. "What about Ileesia?"

The pause was so ominous, my eyes slid shut as I stood in front of my dormitory door. "She's alive," Dad said slowly, "but she's not out of the woods just yet. We will see how the next few days go."

I swallowed hard. "I'm so sorry, Dad. Is there anything I can do?"

"Tell Vanessa and Lilly what I just told you," he said, his words slow and raw. "I don't have the strength to deal with repeating everything to them."

"Sure, I can do that," I said. "Have you even slept yet? Your voice is still tired."

"I'm heading to bed right now, I promise."

"Okay. Try to get some decent rest. I'll take care of 'Nessa and Lilly."

"Thanks," he said and tapped out.

Dutifully, the next thing I did was sit down at my desk and inform the rest of the third generation that our grandmother and Ileesia were critically ill. As experienced, high-level telepaths, I think Lillian and Vanessa may have gotten more information from the psychic maelstrom the night before than Liam and I did. Neither of them seemed surprised by the news in any case. They both peppered me with questions I couldn't answer, and by the end of those calls I knew why my father had delegated the task to me. I warned them that Dad said he was heading to bed so bothering him for details was probably a bad idea. Whether they heeded my warning and left well enough alone or not, I can't say.

The next two days passed in a delicate, waiting hush. Liam and the other telepathic Usuriels seemed exhausted but unharmed by Gloria's psychic storm. In between classes and OW practice, I spent a decent amount of time at the hospital. Once or twice, I had to flash my badge, and tell Reporter Joe to find something other than the maternity wing wall paper color for his headlines. Grandma Gloria was sleeping most of the time when I came to visit, her face pale and far more fragile than I remembered it. D'nay looked beside himself, alternately hovering at his wife's bedside and next to the tiny bassinet in the infants' critical ward. My father, on the other hand, just seemed utterly drained by his attempts to contain Gloria's suffering. When I came to check on them, he sat quietly watching his mother sleep with that familiar, shadow-ridden gaze.

On the third day, Gabriel showed up outside my dormitory. I knew things were either very good or very bad the moment his carefully controlled blue psi filled the corridor. My fear must have shown on my face, because he tried to give me a reassuring smile. I say "tried" because by this point he looked so utterly worn it was probably a minor miracle he was on his feet at all. I'm pretty sure it was the first time he'd left the hospital except to sleep since Grandma went into labor. I somehow doubted even those absences had been long.

"Dax says Ileesia's doing better. There's good odds she'll pull through," Dad said as I stepped closer to him.

"Oh, thank Fate," I breathed, putting a steadying hand to his shoulder. Whether it was to steady me or him, I'm not quite sure. I felt as if we were both at the end of our emotional ropes.

"You can say that again." Gabriel's relief was palpable. "You've been wonderful the last few days. Really, I'm not sure how we would have gotten through it without your help."

"Who, me? I just brought some food and warned a few gawkers away," I protested, dismissing his praise with a wave. "You're the one who managed to keep everyone sane. I was with Liam at the end. If the younger children had to deal with that for all twenty-six hours she was in labor, we'd be locking a few of them away at the OW compound to assess for mental stability."

"Ugh, it did get pretty rough for a while," Dad admitted. Then he gave me a strange little look, as if he were curious about something. "You really didn't feel a thing that whole time?"

I gave him a helpless shrug. "Not a twinge."

"You are a wonder," he said, touching my cheek. I thought I saw... something... pass over his face. Fear, perhaps, or dread. I'm not sure quite what to call it, but clearly he was still emotionally off-balance from the last few days, because with a small, distraught sound, he pulled me tightly into his arms.

"It's okay, Dad," I murmured, wrapping my arms around his solid chest and giving him a reassuring squeeze. "Go home. Get some rest. Dax and his people will take good care of Grandma, Grandpa, and Ileesia until they can go home."

"Gracie?" He said my name low and urgent, as if he were trying to deal with some kind of strong emotion. I tried to gently pull away from him, but he held on to my shoulders, pressing me against him as if he were afraid I might not be there when he let go. "I worry about you out there on the front lines with the OW," he whispered. "You know that, don't you? I'd be an utter wreck if anything happened to you."

I'm sure he was just feeling insecure. After the last three days of watching his parents and sister struggle, it would be enough to get to anyone. But his words sent ice to form in my stomach and Vanessa's words to echo in my head. "Another level of hell to explore," she'd said. I tried not to dwell on what an 'utter wreck' might look like in my father's universe.

"Don't worry, Dad," I said as steadily as I could manage. "I'm careful. And Liam has my back. He's not an elder child, but he's strong for a younger gen. You don't have to worry about me."

"Worrying is a parent's job," he replied, but he did let me pull back from him. When I met his gaze, he gave me a sad smile. Despite his unlined face, I could believe he'd been around over four hundred years. His eyes carried every one of them that morning.

"Go home, Gabriel." I used his name to address him for the first time in a long while. There is something powerful about using someone's name. James had once commented on the fact that I referred to my father as Gabriel more than most children might, and he'd seemed to think it was disrespectful. I didn't find it that way at all. It was the way my father had introduced himself to a lost little girl when she needed to be found. To me, his name was an invocation of that same presence; the ethereal man who had saved me all those years ago. "Go get twelve hours in your own bed. You'll feel a lot better for it."

With a little shake of his head, he gave me a slightly more genuine smile. "Okay, okay, I'm going. You just be careful in Riland, alright? I've heard some nasty rumors about what's going on down there."

"I will be, Dad. I promise."

***

After the trauma of Ileesia's birth, Liam practically moved into my dormitory, which was an arrangement I was quite content with. Falling asleep and waking in his arms filled me with a warm satisfaction that I carried with me around campus.

As promised, I took him out to a very nice restaurant in Skykyle. We both wore Ambria and looked good enough that the conversation in the establishment faded to naught when we walked in. Well, I choose to believe it was our good looks, and not the fact that we'd begun to get a reputation as one of the strongest teams at OW, anyway. I don't think Liam cared which it was. He looked just as amazing as I'd thought he would in his dress tunic and seemed as radiant as the full moon that night. Not that I was biased, or anything. Afterwards, we enjoyed taking the nice clothes off of each other just as much as we had showing them off in public.

Not long afterwards, I had a mishap in the art studio. I was in the middle of a wheel throwing unit in my advanced clay class. About an hour into our three hour class, I leaned the wrong way and spilled slip all over my pants. Professor Blackmon gave me an understanding smile and a wave. I gratefully trotted off towards the dormitory to find myself a change of clothes.

I normally didn't mind the three flights of switchback stairs that led up to the Usuriel floor, but in wet,

slimy pants—heavy with the granular remains of liquefied clay—I was heartily jealous of Liam's ability to teleport by the time I stepped onto our hallway.

"I can't, Liam. I know what it means to you."

I paused at my boyfriend's name. I recognized the
feminine voice, but for a moment couldn't place it. Then I
caught sight of Lorie Usuriel's blonde figure in the doorway to Liam's room. The afternoon light slanted in the
window at the end of the hall, silhouetting them in shades
of gold.

"It's just a thing, Mom." Liam's voice was low but
urgent. He pushed a very familiar box back into her arms.
"It can be replaced. Family can't."

Lorie shook her head, but her arms tightened
around the box.

"How much do you need?" I asked, stepping closer.

They both startled, turning to face me with wide,
Family-blue eyes. Liam paled while his mother's cheeks
formed little patches of red.

"What?" Lorie stammered, her grip on the Ambria
box white-knuckled.

"How much do you need?" I asked again, meeting
her mascara-clad gaze steadily.

Liam shook his head. "You don't understand,
Gracie. Dad lost his job over whatever that spore-wit
down in Riland's been spewing. We're not just talking
about a vacation. They have to break their lease and start
all over in New Paradise. You can't cover this."

I didn't glance in his direction. "Tell me how much
you need, Lorie."

Her voice cracked on the number. It was a sum that would have made Grandma Gloria's eyebrows raise. I tapped my implant.

"Stella?"

"Yes, Gracie?" The AI's smooth, artificial voice asked through my auditory nerve.

"I need to make a transfer of funds to the account of Lorie Usuriel."

Lorie's cheeks glistened with tiny, golden reflections while I finalized the transaction. I didn't have the heart to tell her that it hadn't even wiped out my savings. After next month's paycheck, I'd still have enough for two months' rent on the little flat Liam and I had been eyeing over in Skykyle.

When I was done, Liam's mother swallowed hard and offered me the box in her arms. I looked down at its smooth, white surface, then shook my head.

"It's Liam's. He can do what he wants with it."

She turned towards her son, lifting the box in his direction, but he backed farther into his doorway. "Keep it," he said softly. "Just in case you need it."

She bit her lower lip, her nose and cheeks now gone from rosy to red. She hugged the package tightly to her chest. "Okay. I'll keep it pressed for you."

Liam nodded.

With a whimper, she wrapped an arm around his waist and buried her face in his chest. Before he had a chance to respond, she flung herself in my direction and crushed her damp cheek to mine.

"Thank you," she whispered in my ear. I opened my mouth to reassure her that it was the best use I could think of for the money, but she leaned back and pinned me with a stare that held much more of that Usuriel steel than I'd ever seen in a younger child. Her fingers dug into my arm with bruising force. "I have no right to ask more of you." Her voice was so low I had to strain my ears despite our close proximity. "But please. Keep my son safe."

I met her gaze with iron of my own. "You have my word."

She left without looking back.

"You didn't have to do that." Liam's voice echoed in the empty hallway after the clatter of his mother's feet on the stairs had faded.

"We're partners," I replied, forcing myself to swallow past the fist in my throat. "We take care of each other." I reached for his hand. He didn't pull away, but he didn't return my squeeze. I frowned at him. "What's wrong?"

"I guess I'll be squatting in your room next semester. I promised Mom I'd send my salary until they both have jobs again. Which means I'll have nothing to live on after I graduate in a few weeks."

I leaned in his doorway, watching him pace the tiny, cluttered space. "I'll still have enough for rent."

He drew up short, his eyes wide. "Seriously?"

"It's a disbursement year for the Family trust, and Dad sent me my share. He says I'm working a career job so I'm an adult in his eyes, even if I haven't graduated yet." I put a hand on his arm. "You really think I'd leave you with no place to go? Come on, Liam."

He opened his mouth, then closed it again, shaking his head. "You have no idea what it's like to worry about money, do you?"

I narrowed my eyes at him. "What is that supposed to mean?"

"Nothing. Nothing. I'm sorry." He blew a breath through pursed lips and rubbed at his neck. "I... thank you. Thank you so much. Honestly, I have no idea how I can ever pay you back."

"It's not a loan. It's a gift." I ran gentle hands over his chest, reaching above my head to massage the tension from his shoulders. "Relax, okay? You don't have to worry about money anymore. Hear me? I will take care of you and your family. Leave that part to me."

"Grace," he murmured, allowing one hand to rest on the swell of my hip. "We just got together. I appreciate it, but don't make promises you won't keep. Especially not this one. I might hold you to it."

I met his fearful gaze, and for once the scars he reflected at me weren't from an emotional injury I'd inflicted. This one was old and worn, the kind of pain built over a lifetime.

"No matter what else we are or aren't, I'm still your partner," I said firmly. "I'll always have your back."

His big hands came up to cradle my face. I leaned into them. "Thank you."

"I love you, too."

He kissed me, warm lips covering mine. His arm wrapped around my waist, pressing me closer, and I remembered the whole reason I'd come to the dormitory in the first place.

"Oh, my clothes are filthy," I protested. "And I should really get back to class..."

Liam reached behind me and shut the door with a tap of the pad. Then he tilted my head to gain access to my neck, nibbling down it with swift, dainty kisses.

"Well, if you've got to take them off anyway..."

I laughed and reached for the top button of his shirt.

Chapter 12

Playground Games

A little over an hour later, it was time for Liam to head to class. Between the OW and this being his last semester, he couldn't afford to miss seat time. I reluctantly let him extract himself from my arms and watched as he disappeared in a shower of blue sparks.

After a quick shower and a trek back to my own room for fresh clothes, I should have gone back to class. Yet, despite the afterglow, I just couldn't shake a nagging feeling of resentment. With a huff, I sat down on my bed and crossed my arms.

A warm wave of wind tossed my hair about my shoulders. Ariel's faintly glowing figure materialized next to me, dressed in her usual brown skirt suit and holding her blue journal. At least something was back to normal. I picked up my copy of the faded little book from my bedside table and flipped it to our latest page.

"What's wrong, little sister?" Her looping handwriting scrawled across the page, appearing as if from nothing just the way it had since I was a small child. I thought about the first time I'd seen her as a terrified six-year-old fresh from a year in a government group home.

"I don't know," I wrote back honestly. "Liam said something earlier, and I can't get it out of my head."

Ariel's green eyes traveled over the cups, memory pads, art projects, and general clutter of my desk. In the big mirror above it, she looked like a coppery, incandescent shimmer.

"What did he say?"

"That I don't know what it's like to worry about money. But I do know. There was a time when I didn't have anything." I shivered, the cold damp of the group home chilling the pit of my stomach.

We sat in silence while leaves cast shadows through the window to dapple my growing collection of ceramic vases.

"I only ever saw the group home once," Ariel wrote. "When I came with Gabriel to collect you."

"That was the first time I saw you."

"Other than that, I don't know anything about your early years. Do you remember your mother much?"

I paused, a little surprised at the question. A child's nightmare rose in my mind. Pale skin, dyed-blonde hair, a white dress.

"Not as well as I used to," I replied. I ran my hand through my hair, pushing it back from my face. A thought came to me, and I turned to Ariel. "But I'm a fate. So I should be able to go back and see her again, right?"

Ariel's eyes narrowed. "I thought we agreed to keep spoilers to a minimum."

I held up a hand. "No, no, I don't mean talking to her or anything. She wouldn't even know me. We could just get close enough so I..." I trailed off, unable to admit that I no longer remembered my mother's face.

"I can't give you a reference image for this."

My hand found the thin gold chain around my neck. I wore this necklace almost every day. My fingers traced the little golden "G" and "U" Leesil had given me just before I went off to University. I hadn't always carried the Usuriel name. For the first six years of my life, I hadn't even known what I was.

"I have one," I murmured. "Just help me pull on the fire. I should be able to take us there."

Ariel studied my face. Then, slowly, she leaned forward and poured herself into me as she had so many times. The heat of my flames gathered, and I closed my eyes, fixing my inner vision on the broken swings and chipped paint of my childhood playground. A hot wind shivered over my skin, blowing my copper waves around my shoulders.

A high, childish giggle and the squeak of unoiled chains grounded me. I opened my eyes. Ariel and I stood next to a dented slide, its metal glaring harshly in the midday sun. I put a hand out to it and almost burned myself.

Ariel moved around the play equipment, in the direction of quiet voices. I followed in her glowing wake.

A busty blonde woman stood by the swings, and though the temperature was warm, she had a large, loose sweater on. It fell off of one pale, freckled shoulder and she pushed it up thoughtlessly.

"Higher!"

The little girl couldn't have been more than three. Her hair gleamed like fire in the sunlight, shades of orange and red too saturated to be mortal. Chubby, freckled cheeks split in a euphoric grin as her mother gave the swing another, stronger push.

The babble of voices announced the arrival of another mother with two children in tow. They carefully closed the sagging chain link fence behind them. Though they weren't dressed any differently than my mother and me, the newcomers gave the pair by the swings a measuring look. Then the mother shooed her children to play on the see-saw at the opposite end of the park.

Amaya. My mother's name was Amaya. I watched her face fall under the weight of that scrutiny, her shoulders hunching as she wrapped an arm around her waist.

"One more push and we have to go home, Gracie." Her voice cracked like dead leaves.

"No! I don't wanna!" My three-year-old self gripped the swing chains tightly, her round face screwing up into a tight ball of protest.

"I'll let you pick out some juice at the store." Mother dangled the treat as she gave another good push.

Amaya's eyes came up and for just a moment she met my adult gaze. Her eyes were sunken, a muddy hazel so dark it was hard to tell if they were blue or green. Yet the angles of her face, the worried set of her mortal mouth, the little lines around her eyes, everything about her was right in a way I couldn't describe.

"Can I help you?" she asked.

I tried to speak, but my pulse had become too large to fit words around. I dumbly shook my head.

"Come on, Gracie." Amaya pulled the little girl from the swing, her wary eyes moving between me and the other mother who had settled with a book on the park bench. "It's time to go."

"I want grape juice!" the three-year-old declared, tugging her mother forward with big, hopping footsteps.

"Yeah, yeah, grape juice," she agreed, opening the park gate which protested with a grinding squeal. The two of them walked down the cracked sidewalk before disappearing behind a graffiti-covered alloy wall.

I took a shaking breath and clenched my fists, willing away the distant tingle in my fingers. My gaze fell to the mother on the bench. She was now glaring at me over the edge of her book cover.

"Usuriels," she muttered, loudly enough that I knew it wasn't meant to be discreet. Then her eyes dropped to her book and didn't resurface.

I hardly noticed the heat of Ariel's touch before she'd fully enveloped me. Without a word, I pulled on my flames. In the blink of an eye, we were back in my dormitory.

"Goodnight, Gracie," Ariel murmured in my mind before her glow flickered out, leaving me cold and alone in the growing dark.

***

I didn't go to the studio that night. Instead, I wandered to the cafeteria early and watched the students come and go. Sitting by the orange tree, nursing a cup of tea, I observed the mass of humanity wandering by.

They talked and laughed, held hands and exchanged significant glances. Some of them, the ones alone like me, stayed immersed in their memory pads the whole time. I saw the full range of our diverse society, from younger children to pure mortals to a few individuals I strongly suspected were vampires lucky enough to partner Usuriels. Was it just me, or did the mortals' expressions falter when another Family member walked into the room? Did that Aware young woman duck her head away too quickly? Had this social discomfort always been there and I just hadn't noticed it?

Pulling out my own memory pad, I tapped my implant to sync with it. "Stella, what can you tell me about Evan Kylar?"

An image flashed up—a flattering still of a young man with his arm around a blonde woman, their tow-headed child in between them as they beamed up at me. If it hadn't been for a birthmark on the side of his neck, I wouldn't have recognized Evan.

"Evan Kylar is the head of Riland watch. He completed his training at Riland Academy and has been an active watchman for sixteen years. His wife, Cora, teaches the lower set. Their son, Justin, is twelve."

Cora looked like she taught six-year-olds. Her wide smile and sparkling blue eyes screamed innocence. I wondered if she had any idea how her husband behaved at work.

"You're here early, love. This seat taken?"

I tried to smile at Liam, but I knew it didn't reach my eyes. "It's the seat next to mine, so it must be yours."

He set his tray on the table and settled beside me. "What are you looking at?" he asked, picking up his fork.

"Evan," I muttered. "I'm trying to figure him out."

"That's enough to put anyone in a bad mood. But what's there to figure out?" Liam cut himself an aggressive bite of chicken. "He's a belligerent asshole, which

means he hates everyone he can't control. Since most people with Awareness fall into that category, he hates us the
most."

"You really think it's that simple?" I flipped
through the article Stella had pulled up on my memory
pad. It included a link to his net account and a few more
pictures of him in his Riland watch uniform.

"Sure. He's afraid of us. Some people react to fear
by trying to hide. Some people react by trying to kill what
they're afraid of." Liam shrugged and pointed at a picture
of Evan at a shooting range. "Guess which one he is?"

"Hmmmm." I tapped a crosslink and was rewarded
with an image of Senator Stafford's bulbous features.
"What about him?"

"He's even worse," Liam opined, starting in on his
salad. "At least Evan hates us because he really thinks
we're dangerous. That piece of spore-shit feeds people's
fear so he can control them with it."

I set down the memory pad. "I've always hated politics. Why does it feel like I'm always in the middle of
them, anyway?"

"Because they're not a game." Liam's eyes followed
the crowd as mine had earlier. "The assholes in power
treat it like one, but it's the rest of us who have to live
with the consequences."

I shivered. Liam put an arm around my shoulders,
and I leaned into his warm solidity. He smelled like rose-
mary, thyme, and home.

Chapter 13

The Calm

The next few weeks were strangely normal. Looking back, I feel like it was the calm before a storm — a little blissful oasis before everything went up in flames.

"Mom got home safely," Dad said through my implant. "I just finished getting her settled on the couch, and she's taking a nap while I cook us some lunch. I figured you'd like to know we made it okay."

I was nursing a cup of tea in the mess hall after Liam left for class. My own lesson started in about twenty minutes, but my mug was warm, and I didn't feel like moving yet.

"Yeah, thanks for letting me know. What about Ileesia?" I asked.

"Dax wants her to stay a few more days. Something about blood tests coming back and weaning her off of the oxygen."

I nodded even though he couldn't see me. "I guess Grandpa is staying at the hospital with her then?"

"Yes. It was hard on him, having to let me leave with your grandmother while he stays, though. You know how they are."

I inhaled the gentle scent of herbs and heat before

taking another sip of tea. "Wrapped around each other's little fingers, you mean? Yeah, I've noticed."

Dad chuckled. "Well, I know you have class in a few. I don't want to keep you."

James' tousle-haired figure walked through the mess hall door, and I caught myself just before I choked on my tea. Deliberately finishing my swallow, I cleared my throat and answered my father. "You're right, I should probably go. Tell Grandma I love her, and I'll comm you guys tomorrow when I get a chance, okay?"

"Sounds good, sweetie. Be safe. I love you."

"Bye Dad. I love you, too."

With a tap, I ended the conversation and turned my full attention to James. He wandered down the rows of heat lamps and warming trays, picking up a few items and stowing them in his bag.

Swallowing down the squirming weight in my throat, I got up to put away my mug just as he was filling his travel cup at the drink dispenser nearby.

"Hey, how have you been?" I asked gently, pausing at his shoulder, the mug clutched like a talisman in my hands.

"Gracie?" He jumped, splashing water all over his hand.

"Sorry," I apologized, finding a towel beside the drink machine and handing it to him. "I didn't mean to startle you."

"It's okay, it's fine, really," he babbled, mopping up the mess. The rings under his eyes were so dark I almost asked who hit him in the face. "It's my fault. My head's been under the Mystra Dam lately."

The tense knot in my stomach eased at his friendly, if tired, demeanor. "I know that feeling," I said, putting my mug where it belonged in the return window. "Don't they give you days off at the Embassy anymore?"

James rubbed the side of his face as if fighting a headache. "It doesn't seem like it. I'm sorry, I know we haven't seen each other in a long time, but I have a meeting in twenty minutes, and I can't be late."

"Is it with someone important?" I asked, eyeing his tangled hair.

He followed my gaze and hastily ran his fingers through the blond strands. It did little to help. "Any better?"

"May I?"

Something in his shoulders relaxed at my question, and his expression was that sweet, vulnerable kid I'd fallen in love with at Angelus Quietum. "Please."

With quick, steady movements, I worked through the worst of the knots and finger combed the lengthening strands away from his face and to one side so that it wouldn't fall in his eyes. "There. Much better," I said, giving his appearance an approving nod.

"Thanks, Gracie. I…" he trailed off as if afraid of what he'd been about to say. Awkwardly, we dropped each other's gaze, and he grabbed his travel cup, holding it tight to his chest to prevent another spill. "I miss you," he finally managed.

"I miss you, too."

Six months ago, he would have hugged me and laid a kiss on my cheek at this point. Now, the space between us felt heavy and wrong.

"You should probably go," I said, breaking our painful silence.

He nodded and turned to leave, but then paused. "I… um… I have a free evening next week. I'd love to have dinner with you. Just as friends, of course, if you're not too busy."

You're with Liam now, a back corner of my mind snapped. Maybe I should say something about my new relationship? I opened my mouth to say my partner's name, but I couldn't force it past the fluttering pulse in my throat. I coughed to clear it. "That would be great," I choked out.

"Really?" James' relief was worth the omission. "Great! Yeah. I, um, I'll send the day and time to your memory pad, okay?"

I nodded.

"Great," he said again, hefting the bag of food he'd been collecting and drifting towards the entrance. "I'll see you then! And thanks." He pointed at his hair with one finger and gave me the wonderful smile that always melted the inside of my ribcage.

"Anytime," I said, watching his familiar figure until he was through the outer door and lost to my sight.

***

A few days later, I received a lovely thank you note from Liam's mother for my gift. His siblings sent us a postcard featuring freshly terraformed tropical beaches. I showed these items to my boyfriend after our usual morning sparring round.

"That's cute," he said, picking up the postcard and

examining it closely. His expression softened at their signatures on the back, before picking up his mother's note.

"I thought so," I agreed, toweling off the back of my neck.

"Did you read this? Mom says they've found a small house for rent right on the beach." The smile that lit up his features was worth every credit I'd gifted his family.

"Yeah, I read that! Next time we get a long break, we should take a vacation down there," I suggested. "I could use some time in a beach chair!"

He chuckled and handed me the letters, which I put back in my pocket. "Just don't forget the sunscreen, or you'll spend the next month complaining to me about how many new freckles you have."

The whoosh and hiss of the main door announced Vanessa's arrival in the practice hall. She strode in our direction, the creases around her mouth sharp and defined in that way I'd come to recognize as bad news. I swallowed down a wave of dread.

"Everything okay, Vanessa?" Liam asked, arching a brow at her. I suspected he was picking up her mood telepathically as well as visually.

She came to a stop in front of us, her stride clipped and even more militaristic than usual. "No, not really," she admitted. Blowing a wild black curl out of her face, she met my gaze. "I'm afraid the Council has decided against Martin. His execution is to be swift and public, per Senator Stafford's personal request."

Dread twisted my guts, and I put a hand to my suddenly queasy stomach.

"Fates," Liam muttered, fingering his long throat.

"I'm sorry," Vanessa went on. Her eye was now fixed on the floor. At least she sounded as miserable as I felt. "I know the two of you got a little fond after bringing him in, and I can't blame you. But he broke the law and, unfortunately, my hands are tied."

My mouth was suddenly full of sand—dry and cumbersome—while my hands tingled and burned as if teleported to one of Hal's tropical beaches.

"Thanks for letting us know," Liam said. As usual, I was grateful for his ability to say the right things in hard moments. "We don't blame you."

Vanessa gave his sweaty arm a pat with her doll-sized hand.

"Would… would it be okay if I went to see him?" I choked out.

Liam shifted his weight beside me. "Are you sure?"

I didn't glance in his direction, keeping my gaze fixed on Vanessa. She licked her lips.

"I don't see why not." With a gesture, she pulled a slip of paper from the thin air to her left. "Here, let me write his cell number down." With a few swift motions, she scribbled down the number and handed it to me. "I'm sure he could use a visitor or two. I don't think he's had any since you picked him up."

The pain between my shoulder blades had nothing to do with our morning bout. I tucked the paper next to the letters from Liam's family.

"Are you sure you want to visit Martin?" Liam

repeated his question, his eyes following Vanessa's progress towards the stairs to her office.

"You heard 'Nessa," I said, hugging myself in an effort to ease the hollow ache in my ribs. It wasn't helping. "He hasn't even had a single visitor since he got here. We owe him that much at least."

Liam's sigh wasn't happy, but he put a hand on my shoulder anyway. "I know what the flatliner block looks like. I can get us most of the way there, at least. We'll have to wait for this evening, though, otherwise he won't know we stopped by."

I nodded because I couldn't get the words "thank you" past the tension in my jaw.

**

That night, after dinner, Liam shifted us to the vampire cellblock. As far as his shifts went, it wasn't a terrible one, but the solid silver bars that materialized around us still didn't help my equilibrium.

There were only five cells, but they took up the whole hallway. The floor was poured concrete and the walls a flat, white cinderblock. Behind us, the scrape of chair legs preceded Jillian's head poking around the corner.

"Everything alright?" she asked.

No, they weren't, but I nodded anyway.

"Just visiting a prisoner. We won't be long," Liam reassured her.

"Okay." Jill disappeared back around the corner, and we went back to looking at cell walls.

There were no windows. Despite knowing that this feature was as much for the prisoners' safety as for security, it didn't lessen my sense of claustrophobia.

Martin was the only prisoner on the block tonight. He was in the last cell—a five by five meter box with a bed, a sink, and a toilet. A plastic bag with the last, clinging remains of platelets and plasma sat in the sink, but otherwise the only difference between his cell and the other four was the silent, yellow-clad figure sitting on the bed. He had his arms wrapped around his knees, and his chin tucked to his chest.

"Hi Martin," I managed, clearing my throat.

He didn't move.

Liam and I exchanged a glance and he gave another try. "We just wanted to see how you're doing. Are they treating you okay down here? Is there anything we can get you?"

A low sniffle was the only answer. I stepped closer to his cell, resting my hands against the cool silver of the bars. "Vanessa told us... about the trial. I'm so sorry."

He rubbed his brow. From this distance, I could tell how red and raw his face was. "It's okay." His voice echoed in the empty space. "With Mary and Lita gone?" He gave a weak shrug, his eyes still firmly on the floor. "It's probably better this way."

I didn't know what to say to that. I turned to Liam for help, but the sorrow in his expression said he wasn't sure how to answer, either.

"I want you to know that we told Vanessa

everything, and if it were up to her, things would be different," I tried again.

Martin didn't lift his head at my voice.

"Is there anyone we could call? Any messages you'd like us to send?" Liam suggested gently.

The young vampire licked his lips nervously and finally met my partner's eye. "Is there any way I could… get a piece of paper? And a pen? You know, to send a letter?"

Liam made a small gesture with his left hand and pulled the desired items from thin air. He didn't usually spend energy on such theatrics, but if it cost him an uncomfortable amount of psi, he didn't show it as he handed the folded paper, pen, and envelope to Martin.

"Thank you. Sorry to make you wait around while I write it, but I'm not sure how else I'd get it delivered…" his voice trailed off, and he stared at the wall just to Liam's left with an empty, broken gaze.

"I'll talk to Jillian. If you leave it with her, I'm sure we'll find a way to get it delivered," Liam reassured him. "That way you can take a while to work on it without us hovering around."

"Thanks." Martin hugged the paper to his chest and sank back onto the bed. Those sorrowful eyes were fixed on the floor now.

"I guess we'll leave you to it, then?" I suggested, rubbing my neck.

There was no answer.

"Let Jill know if you need anything else before…" Liam bit his lip. "I mean, she'll know how to find us."

Martin gave a silent nod.

Liam laid a hand on my shoulder, and I leaned into his solid strength. In a swirl of blue motes, Martin and his cell block vanished into thin air.

Chapter 14

The Spark

Then came the day my world fell apart.

It began calmly enough. I woke up in Liam's arms, gave him a quick kiss, and jumped into the shower. Once we were dressed and ready for the day, my lover teleported the two of us to the OW compound where we took bouts with another set of partners. Training for the tourney had a more serious edge lately. I think every officer was keenly aware that we might be heading into a mass-casualty situation at any moment, and the rumors and whispers of psi-proof weapons were ever-present each time we came to practice. That morning wasn't any worse than usual, but I still remember being on edge as we went to the locker rooms to rinse off and change after our bouts.

My Advanced Awareness Theory class was normal, though I got a few dirty looks from mortals who passed me in the hall on the way there. I ignored the icy glances as always and, by the time I'd settled into my seat in class, I had already forgotten them.

On my way to the mess hall for lunch, I saw a very familiar and very unwelcome face.

What was it about Joe the reporter that heralded doom?

His balding, mortal head bobbed towards me on the walkway, and I seriously considered ducking into an empty classroom to avoid him.

"Ah! Just the Usuriel I was looking for! Gracie, can I get a word?"

Fates damn it, he'd seen me. Slamming down my Usuriel blank face to avoid giving him a look of pure disgust, I tried to walk past him without stopping. With unusual nimbleness for a mortal his age, Joe changed directions to trot in my wake.

"Come now, we've known each other a long time. You have to give me a comment on this story. It's the biggest news the celebrity section has had in ages," he puffed, clearly out of breath from trying to keep up with me. I deliberately lengthened my stride, hoping he'd wear out and give up. "Besides Ileesia, of course."

"When have I ever had a comment for you, Joe?" I snapped. "Go crawl back into whatever net-hole you climbed out of."

"Really? That's all you've got for your old friend, Joe?" He was panting now, but his next words were still horribly clear. "I can't believe you're still protecting the old man after this. She was your own mother, for Fate's sake."

I stopped dead in the middle of the walkway. I'm an Usuriel. I have fast reflexes. Poor Joe nearly plowed right into me. At the last moment, he managed to just barely skitter past my shoulder before turning around to face me, gasping and flushed.

"What did you just say?" I growled, eyes narrowing at him as he caught his breath.

"Amaya Blackmon. She was your mother, wasn't she?"

"What about it?"

Joe frowned up at me, clearly a little thrown by my ignorance. "You really don't read the celebrity net, do you?"

I scowled back at him. "Dad always says it causes more problems than it solves. From what I can tell, he's right. Now, what kind of slander have you dug up about my mother to parade about? As if going after my father and grandparents isn't bad enough. For Fate's sake, the woman has been dead for over a decade. Why can't you leave well enough alone?"

Joe's face became uncharacteristically cautious. In fact, there was something in his eyes I might even have called... gentle? Whatever that expression was, it was the kind of look you gave someone when you really didn't want to give them bad news. I knew. I'd been on the receiving end of enough emotional trauma over the years. Suddenly, I had a really bad feeling about this conversation.

"I hate to be the one to tell you this, Gracie," Joe said slowly, "but the Skykyle watch found your mother's body yesterday."

"Wait... what?" My head spun and I felt more than a little confused. "Why would they care about her body? I mean, she's been dead and buried for thirteen years."

"Who told you that?" Joe asked, and I didn't like the calculating gleam in his eye.

I didn't say anything, but I think the look on my face was answer enough.

"What... what are you trying to say?" I stammered, ineffectually trying to draw him out. It wasn't even a good attempt. In my defense, however, I was already pretty off balance from this whole conversation.

"Hey, Gracie!"

I turned back the way I'd come and saw James with an unfamiliar woman in the violet of the Skykyle watch heading in our direction. Feeling as if I were in a very strange holo, I waved to him. Joe raised a finger, but I ignored him.

"James!" I returned his quick hug of greeting. "I didn't think we were meeting until dinner."

"I was walking to class and this officer seemed lost. She asked me if I knew a Gracie Blackmon. At first I said no, but then as she was walking away I remembered that Blackmon was your mom's family name, wasn't it? I think she might be looking for you," he explained, gesturing to the young, blonde mortal woman beside him.

"Officer Jessica Coffing," she said, holding out a hand to me. "Nice to meet you, Gracie..."

"Usuriel," I supplied, shaking her hand. I wondered what isolated rice farm the Skykyle watch had pulled Officer Coffing out of if she didn't recognize the Family looks.

"Ah... yes... of course." She shifted her weight uncomfortably. With clumsy fingers, she pulled out her memory pad and tapped it to activate the screen. A still came up and she tiled the screen to me. "Do you recognize this woman?"

I looked at the image of the curvy woman with dyed blonde hair and felt a rising sense of dread. "Yes," I replied simply, "that's my mother, Amaya Blackmon. What is this about?"

James cleared his throat and tilted his head at Joe who was watching the whole exchange as if Landing Day had come early. "Perhaps we could get a little privacy?" he suggested to the reporter.

"Freedom of the press!" Joe snapped. "I have just as much right to stand on this walkway as you do!"

James sighed and looked tired. "Come on, Gracie, why don't we go to my room? It's quiet and just around the corner."

The number of difficult conversations I'd had in James' room was mounting, but I couldn't think of a better alternative. With a nod, I gestured for Officer Coffing to fall in behind James ahead of me. Joe trailed after us, but once James, the Officer, and I were in his room, my friend palmed the door shut in the reporter's face.

"Okay," James said, a grim expression on his usually gentle features. "Now, what did you want to talk to Gracie about?"

The Officer's eyes slid between James and me, a questioning look on her face. "Are you her boyfriend?" she asked.

"No, just a good friend," he said quietly, glancing at me. I saw the pain in that look. The satisfaction I'd found in my new relationship with Liam dulled the sharpness of that particular emotional wound for me. Even so, I quickly focused on Officer Coffing.

"Whatever you have to say to me, you can say in front of James," I told her. "I trust him. Now, why do you have a picture of my mother?"

Officer Coffing looked between us cautiously, then a grim expression came across her face. "I regret to inform you that your mother's body has recently been recovered in Skykyle City."

I shook my head, the world tilting underneath me. "Recently? She's been dead for thirteen years. Hasn't she?"

"That seems about accurate with the decay rate," Officer Coffing allowed. "However, she was never declared dead until yesterday."

"Well then, she's been... what, missing all this time?" James sounded amazed by that concept.

"No one actually filed a missing person report on her." The Officer had very pretty green eyes for a mortal. At that moment they looked apologetic. "Before she disappeared, Amaya was picked up twice for public intoxication and once for prostitution without a license. She checked in and out of three separate detox facilities in the last year of her life. It doesn't seem she had any contact with her family or any close friends who would have noticed when she disappeared."

Well, I'd strongly suspected my mother had the same issues as my father, but that didn't make hearing it stated so bluntly any easier. I gave a sad shrug and sat down on the edge of James' bed. "Even as a child I knew she had problems. She was declared an unfit mother when I was six."

"Yes, we found those records, too. They had been sealed until you turned eighteen, but now they are public record," Officer Coffing explained. "At the time of her disappearance, there was a new strain of lung rot going through the drug users of Skykyle. There wasn't a cure for it at that point and a lot of spore-addicts were dying. If anyone remarked on the fact that she'd gone missing, I imagine they assumed she'd overdosed or caught the lung rot and died in one of the spore-holes the watch was forced to burn. There were quite a number of condemned buildings that became graveyards in a matter of months."

I swallowed hard and silently thanked Fate for the random chance that my father had survived that particular hell. "So, is that what happened? She overdosed or died of lung rot and someone just now found the body?"

"No," Officer Coffing shook her head and her chin-length blonde hair fell in her face. She brushed it behind one ear, then looked at me critically. "You said you go by Gracie Usuriel now. I'm guessing that's your father's name?"

"I thought you said you had my paperwork unsealed," I replied. "Shouldn't it list my father as the one who picked me up from the group home?"

"Actually, that part of the paperwork was never properly filed." The Officer's mouth settled into a disapproving line.

My stomach sank again. Trust Gabriel not to submit the right forms if they happened to be inconvenient. I thought back to how quickly he'd pulled me out of that group home. No, I didn't think he cared much at all if the bureaucrats were satisfied with the legality of my parentage. One look at me and anyone could see that I was his. No one in the Family had ever questioned him when he claimed me as his own, so what did the government matter? We were Usuriels; practically a law unto our own. Out in Angelus Quietum, he'd had no need to prove paternity or to worry about someone brave enough to try taking me away from him.

"You really don't know who my father is?" I still couldn't wrap my brain around that one. Reporter Joe had put it together, I thought, so why hadn't the Skykyle watch?

"Is he an older Usuriel?" she asked. "Someone with connections to the first few generations?"

I exchanged a look with James. He gave me a helpless gesture.

"You could say that," I said. "My father is Gabriel Usuriel. He's... well I guess he's not the only living second-gen anymore. Now there's Ileesia, too. But up until a few weeks ago, he *was* the second generation."

The wide-eyed stare Officer Coffing gave me would

have been comical if this whole topic hadn't been so dreadfully morbid. "Gabriel... Gabriel Usuriel is your father," she echoed, sounding like I'd just kicked her in the teeth.

"You say that like it's a bad thing," James grumbled. I sent him an appreciative glance for the support. With a scowl on his face, he came to perch next to where I'd sat down on his bed. Officer Coffing looked between the two of us, then set a few memory pads on the floor to clear a place for herself on the hard little chair by the desk.

"I... I think this may be hard for you to hear, then," she said slowly, her mortal green eyes a little distant as if she were trying to figure out how to phrase things. Since I'd joined Overwatch, I'd had to navigate a few tough conversations myself. My stomach found another set of knots to twist itself into while I watched her gather her thoughts. When she glanced back at me, the nervousness in her face made my heart rate double. "The reason we found your mother is that someone was doing research into the Sorrow urban legend. They ran across a witness who named your mother as someone he'd been involved with. This witness even claimed that she was going to visit him the last time she was seen alive. You... are familiar with Sorrow?"

Sweet fucking Fate.

"Yes," I said quietly. "I'm fully aware of Sorrow."

"When this individual started digging into your mother's records, it seems they discovered her disappearance. This was brought to the attention of one of our cold case units and they obtained a search warrant for Gabriel... that is... your father's... properties in Skykyle."

I didn't want to hear the rest of this. I really, honestly didn't. I wanted to get up from that bed, walk out the door and start running as far and as fast as I could. I wanted to call on my flames and scorch Officer Coffing where she sat in James' chair before she could open her mouth again. I wanted to find Liam and hide with him in my bed until all of the scary truths went away.

They weren't going away.

I remember watching Officer Coffing's mouth move, the slightly lopsided mortal tilt of her lips etching into my memory as she undid every solid thing my life was built on.

"Behind one of his apartment buildings, we found Amaya's grave; along with at least fifty other individuals who died within five to ten years of her. We think she was the most recent victim, but we won't be positive until we're sure there aren't any more graves."

"At least fifty..." James echoed faintly.

"Victims?" My voice didn't sound like me. It sounded like something that came from a long distance away.

"Yes, I'm sorry, but we will have to inform the Overwatch of this. It's being investigated as a homicide... well... a series of homicides, really."

I couldn't breathe. I couldn't think. "That's... that's not possible..."

"I am terribly sorry, but I am afraid it is the truth. We are trying to identify the rest of the victims now, but Amaya's remains were the freshest we've found. We were able to match DNA without having to sample bone marrow. We had confirmation against the database this morning."

"No, there has to be a mistake..." The room spun and I staggered to my feet. I still don't know where I thought I was going, but if James hadn't caught me I would have hit the floor.

"Gracie!" I blinked up at James' concerned face as I clung to his arm and the wall to keep me upright. "Easy now, let's think this through. There has to be a rational explanation." He turned to Officer Coffing. "What makes you think these deaths were homicide? I mean, have you determined the cause of death?"

She shook her head slowly, eyes watching me with silent intensity. "No, most of the remains are too badly decayed to identify the cause of death so far. We have our forensic teams working on it." She gave us a sad shrug. "But fifty bodies in shallow graves on a vacant lot? It's pretty damning."

Yes, yes it was.

For a long moment, no one said anything. James' face alternated between concerned and distant, clearly torn between making sure I wasn't about to pass out and wrapping his brain around the situation. Officer Coffing shifted silently in her seat, her eyes darting between James and me as if trying to figure out how to mitigate the emotional shrapnel she'd let loose in the room.

For my part, it was all I could do to keep myself standing. Then, slowly, the world stopped spinning. In fact, my head felt quite full of that strange, buzzing emptiness that told me I was going into shock. I was extremely grateful for the calm that it washed over me and I embraced it, letting the ice flow into my spine and limbs, making them simultaneously more solid and yet somehow farther away. Then, when the screaming horror in my head finally succumbed to the numbness, all that Overwatch training kicked in, and I wasn't Gabriel's daughter anymore. Instead, I was the OW officer assigned to his execution order. I shook off James' hand and stood more steadily on my own.

"You don't have to worry about telling the Overwatch," I whispered. My voice didn't shake, though there was a vacant hollowness to its tone.

"I'm afraid it's protocol..."

I pulled my badge from my pocket and flashed it in her direction without meeting her eye. "Consider us informed." This time my voice was a touch more solid.

Her eyes widened, and her mouth turned into an almost perfectly round "O" of surprise. "I... I see..."

"No, you don't," I muttered, then I met her nervous gaze. What was in my eyes I can only guess, but if Officer Coffing's face was any judge, it was terrifying. Then I cleared my throat, gathered my strength, and managed to address her in something that approached my usual professional tone. "Your team can keep doing its forensic investigation. I'd like to read their report when they're done with it. Please forward all of your documentation to my personal net account. It's easy enough to find at the Overwatch database."

"Are... are you..."

"Thank you for your time and concern, Officer Coffing." I cut her off before she could stammer at me. I clung to the frozen tundra in my chest as I met her gaze. "Can you find your way out, or should James walk you to your vehicle?"

She'd had no idea what she was walking into. The grim furrows of her brow said she wasn't sure she liked it now that she understood. Officer Coffing hesitated, chewing her lip. When James gave her an equally useless shrug, and the dangerous gleam failed to leave my eye, she seemed to think that perhaps retreat was the better part of valor and got to her feet.

"I will be in touch, Officer Gracie," she said, apparently knowing enough about the OW to use my first name. "I can see myself out." I didn't move or say a word except to incline my head slightly to her. With one last spooked glance between James and me, she said, "I am sorry about your mother." And left the room.

Once the door shut behind her, James began speaking rapid fire as if his brain had been working through the whole conversation at a feverish speed. "Gracie, let's take a moment and get our heads around this. You don't have to tell Vanessa right away..."

"Oh yes, because she'll fail to notice my mother's name plastered all over the celebrity net! I might not read that trash, but just about everyone else at OW does." The numbness was slipping now that Officer Coffing had left the room. Fear and rage waited for me just beyond its calming presence. My hand had found the edge of the wall again, and I tried not to cling to it while I watched James pace.

"It looks bad, but you heard her. They don't even have a cause of death for those bodies yet."

Fury broke through the shock first. "He killed them! Why else toss them in a shallow grave without even a death certificate to give their families closure?" I tried to say my father's name, but dizziness bled through the numbness again and I had to pause to force it back. "He killed my mother, James. He killed Amaya and let her body rot in a back lot while he was off raising her fucking daughter!"

"That doesn't sound like Gabe," James protested. "Come on now, you're not a telepath, but you know your father better than that, and so do I. He's depressive, yes; I'd even say suicidal at his worst moments. But he's not violent, at least not towards other people."

"Tell that to Orville and Adora," I growled, another hot wave of anger rolling over me like the most beautiful, cleansing tide of fire I'd ever experienced. It made me feel steadier than I had since my mother's name fell out of Joe's greasy mouth.

"Think this through to the end, Gracie. If you run to the OW council with this now, they'll have an execution order on your father's head so fast the real facts won't have a chance to come to light. How will you feel if someone goes down to Angelus Quietum, does the deed and it turns out to be a misunderstanding?"

"He's had an execution order on his head for years!" I all but shouted at him. "He survived the Sorrow incident only because no one was strong enough or brave enough to try to complete it!"

James stared at me with shock. I'd almost forgotten how little I saw of him these days. It seemed impossible that he didn't know about the order, after its heavy weight had been dragging behind me for so long.

"The only reason that man is alive right now is because I wouldn't complete the order for Vanessa, and there's no one else with the right combination of skills to do it. Hell, Lilly and 'Nessa have been trying to convince me to go through with it for months. And I've been the one defending him!" The betrayal was bone deep. I felt as if the flesh over my rib cage had been carved away, leaving me bleeding and exposed. "I've been the one saying that he wouldn't hurt anyone; that even with as dark as things have gotten for him, he'd never actually ended up killing anyone." The laugh that bubbled out of my lips was painful. "I guess the joke is on me."

The room was too small and too hot. Feeling as if I might faint if I didn't get out, I staggered for the door. The whole of Cybele tilted, but I kept my gaze fixed on the door plate.

"You don't know that he killed those people, Gracie. Think about Sorrow's legend. He's a protector, almost a vigilante on behalf of the dregs of society. Murder doesn't exactly fit that narrative. If he'd been preying on those people, don't you think they'd warn each other away instead of into his arms?" James actually sounded incredibly reasonable at that point.

"If there's such a logical explanation for it, why didn't he ever tell me where my mother was buried?" I demanded.

James gave me a reproving expression. "Because he's a tight-lipped bastard about anything emotionally taxing?"

I shook my head. "No, he told me where Adora's grave is. Why not my own mother's?"

"He told you where Adora's buried?" There was shock in that statement.

The grimmest smile spread across my face. "Oh yes, he led me straight to it. Right after he admitted to euthanizing her for the OW. God, what a sick bastard, showing off her body to me like some kind of trophy. I should have seen it then, but I was too taken in by his performance of guilt and remorse!"

"Are you sure it was a performance?"

James' voice seemed to echo in the background as visions of Adora's horrific end rose in my mind's eye. I'd been living in the putrid filth of my father's truth for years now, but I'd loved him too much to see it for what it was. Even with my sister and cousin begging me to see Gabriel's evil, I'd still kept my eyes closed. Well, they were open now.

I was only a few feet from the door when James grabbed my shoulders and forced me to look him in the face. "Where do you think you're going?"

I met the mortal blue eyes of a man I'd loved since I was sixteen. Poor, naive, ethical James, said that tiny part of my brain still capable of rational thought. He was still under the delusion that the world was a pretty place. I thought of the gutted farmer in Riland; Grayson dying in Amourie's arms; Darius teleporting his children's hearts out of their chests; the Riland watchmen with their throats torn out; Martin in his holding cell waiting for an execution. No, the world was not a nice, neat, or pretty place. For too long I'd been like James – trying to believe that the safe, wholesome, peaceful part of the universe could win. Well, it just wasn't true. This was the final blow to my faith in humanity. I sucked in a breath and felt as if it were ripping my chest open.

"I'm going to get a knife." My voice was surprisingly steady.

James squeezed my shoulders, and even though I was easily strong enough to pull away from him, I hung limply from his grasp. "Think for a minute! You're letting your emotions overwhelm your sense! Tell me, honestly, what would the motivation be? Gabriel may be an addict, but he's never been irrational. There were pretty solid reasons behind why he went after Orville and Adora. What possible reason could he have for killing the mother of his young child?"

Finally the tears arrived. Just the image of myself as that scared, vulnerable six-year-old looking up into my father's face with unconditional adoration suddenly seemed like the most horrifying thing in the world. I'd thought he was an angel; my angel—the one sent by my mother to love and protect me. Instead, he was a devil; the monster who had destroyed any chance my mother ever had of getting better. He hadn't saved me. He'd stolen me, and he'd done it with hands soaked in my mother's blood.

"Don't you get it? That's why he killed her! People get into custody disputes all the time. The fact that she'd had a child by him and never said a word? That's plenty of motive for murder!" With a gasping sob, I twisted away from James. My friend let me go with a concerned look, his weight shifting to put himself between me and the door. I hugged myself tightly and dodged his gaze but didn't make a move to get around him.

"I still think it's stretching things," James replied, his voice still infuriatingly calm, "but okay, let's say some kind of argument over your placement somehow resulted in Amaya's death. What about the other bodies? You can't tell me Gabriel had disputes with all of them. He has a bad temper, but it's usually all talk. You're going to tell me he was losing it so badly and so regularly that he had to bury fifty people? That's insane."

"Gabriel's sanity is as ephemeral and fleeting as his sister's, and the consequences when it slips keep getting more dire." I tried to quote Lillian from memory, my gaze distant. I might have been off by a word or two, but the meaning was clear enough. Tears were rolling silently down my cheeks now, but at least I managed not to give in to a full-on breakdown.

"So... what... you're going to complete an execution order on him over this? Where's the proof? I mean, how do we even know that what Officer Coffing told us is true?"

I frowned at that one and felt a tiny sliver of the blinding emotional storm slip. It was as if I hadn't been able to see my usual reality for a moment until his words let me catch just the slightest glimmer of its safe shape through my buzzing haze. I brushed the tears away, swallowing hard. "Could you sense a lie from her?"

"No," he said cautiously, "but that just means she believes what she told us. If someone she trusts told her the lies, she wouldn't know the difference."

I sucked in a deeper breath, mind racing as I tried to think of a reason why the Skykyle Officer would lie. "Reporter Joe seemed to have the same information," I said slowly. "And he usually has good sources..."

"Like the Skykyle watch?" Jame supplied. "Honestly, who better to feed you a lie than the celebrity net? Even if you didn't read the article, everyone around you would."

I nodded slowly. "Evan," I murmured. "Or Senator Stafford. They could have lied to the Skykyle watch."

"Easily," James agreed.

"I need to go to Skykyle," I said. I might explode if I didn't teleport immediately to see the evidence of my father's homicidal past for myself. Without even thinking about it, I tapped for Liam. "Liam! I'm in James' room! Get down here, I need a ride!"

"James' room?" My boyfriend may have sounded the tiniest bit jealous. Since I hadn't expected it, I didn't think it was my imagination. However, I really didn't have time for relationship issues. "Is he... upset about it?"

"What? No, I haven't even told him," I snapped. James gave me a questioning look, and I dodged his gaze. Why did my boys always pick the worst moments for these conversations? I didn't have the headspace to be anything but pissed about it so I growled the next sentence at Liam. "Are you going to make me walk upstairs and find you, or are you going to teleport down here?"

"Relax, I was napping. Let me put on some pants, and I'll be down." His voice was cautious, as if he was trying not to set off my temper. Way too late, I thought.

"Good," I hissed and tapped out.

James' eyes were narrowed when I looked at him. "Tell me what?"

I groaned and rubbed my face. The shock and anger hovered in the back of my head like a strange white noise, but my semi-normal conversation with Liam had made me feel a little more myself. Even so, I didn't want to spend time emotionally hand-holding James through the revelation that the woman he was in love with and his ex-lover were now a pair. I needed to get to that apartment building in Skykyle before my sense of reality finished sliding off a cliff. Still, I doubted Liam would keep his hands to himself once he arrived. That meant I could either tell James now or let him find out when my boyfriend decided to greet me with a kiss.

"Liam and I..." I started, peering over my fingers at James. "We've been a pair for a few weeks now."

He tried to put up that pleasant, blank mask I'd seen before, but it couldn't hide the hurt in his eyes. "That didn't take you long," he murmured icily. I wanted to disappear into the floor.

Liam chose that wonderful moment to appear in the room with a sigh of blue-tinged air. He took one look at James' expression and put a hand on his hip. "And... you just told him, didn't you?"

"You mentioned it, and he asked," I said, spreading my hands.

"I'm standing right here, you know." James was usually so polite and positive. It was strange to hear bitterness in his voice.

"James, it isn't as if we don't care about you," Liam started, extending a hand towards our friend.

James shook his head and glanced at me with something between compassion and heartache. "It's okay. She offered to pair with me first, and I said no. I don't have anyone to blame but myself. I guess I just didn't expect her to go running to you quite that quickly."

"Wait." Liam glanced between us, his brow lowering to darken his face. "That's what your fight was about after the avatar incident? You asked him to pair, and he said no?"

"Is that a problem?" I asked, all those eager flames suddenly a heartbeat away. I felt them gather and knew I was probably glowing. "No, no, you know what, don't answer that. We don't have time for this. I have to get to Skykyle, and this is just slowing us down."

Liam gave me a look that had a touch of his own temper flashing. "What is so damn important down in Skykyle all of a sudden? Honestly, you woke me out of a dead sleep to come to our ex's room, and now you don't even want to sort out the mess you set up for me to walk into? What the hell is wrong with you, Gracie?"

I shied away from him and gestured to James. "You explain it," I said. "I can't. I'd light the whole building up."

I heard James sigh, but I was studiously looking at the far corner of the room. "The Skykyle watch came looking for Gracie this morning. Apparently, they found her mother's body in a shallow grave... behind Gabriel's apartment building."

"Fucking Fate." The shock in Liam's tone was gratifying. I dared him a small glance. He looked very pale. "Wait... I thought Amaya was long dead. I did some research on her back when we were all into the Sorrow thing. I couldn't find much about her in all of the databases I searched through. Just a few old arrest warrants and birth certificates for her and Gracie."

"But no death certificate?" James asked.

"No," Liam allowed. "I did think that was kind of odd. She just sort of fell out of the records without a trace."

My chest tightened, and the numbness tried to wash my vision gray. With a concerted act of will, I pushed down the crippling anxiety and reached for Liam's arm.

"I have to know," I whispered. I hated how badly my voice shook, but I couldn't help it. That same sick dread I'd had since Grayson solidified in my guts. "Please. I have to know if it's true or not."

"And if it is?" Liam asked slowly.

I took a deeper breath, but it didn't help. My heart still raced in my ears. "If it is, then I have to go see Vanessa."

"Oh, Gracie," Liam murmured, eyes sliding shut before he glanced back at me and went on. "He's your dad. And you're way closer with him than I've ever been with my parents. I remember how upset you were when he passed out at the Family party. You tried to say you were pissed about how he'd interrupted our date, but the real reason you were lighting up liquor bottles is because you couldn't stand the thought of him hurting himself. Even if Gabriel did this, I can't let you go after him. Not if I want the Gracie I know to come back afterwards."

The truth fell from my lips. "If he did this, she's already dead."

***

It didn't take much more convincing to get Liam to teleport us to Skykyle. James dug into his old Sorrow timeline and found decent reference images of Gabriel's properties in Skykyle City. The only one that had a vacant lot on the premises was also the first modest apartment complex he'd bought in the city. We all agreed that had to be the location Officer Coffing had been discussing.

"You don't have to come with us," I told James once Liam was satisfied he could visualize the location well enough to teleport.

He glanced between Liam and me, faded blue eyes unreadable. "I feel like I barely know the two of you anymore," he said quietly. "You are the two people I've probably been the closest to outside of my own family. But I've put my work over you both, and now..." he trailed off looking up at Liam with something that approached longing. Then he shook his head and turned to me. There was definitely some regret in his eyes when he met my gaze. "We started this whole research thing into your father's past together. Didn't you used to call us your boys?"

On a normal day, I think I would have blushed. This time, hot tears rushed up, and I nodded before quickly looking away.

I nearly jumped when James slid his hand into mine. I glanced quickly at him, then at Liam when he did the same on my other side. Each of them gave me serious, earnest expressions.

"What kind of a friend would I be if I let you face this alone?" James asked, his face tilting to Liam's. "Not that you would be, but this is pretty deep stuff. I think maybe you need both of your boys today."

Liam nodded, taking James' other hand. "We started this together," he agreed. "The three of us looking for Sorrow's darkest secret. Well, I'd say we've found it. Now we have to go check our primary sources."

I actually cracked a fragile smile at that one. Echoes of Professor Joan's old mantra—which I had repeated endlessly to both of my research partners—rose like a safe, warm bubble in the overwhelming sea of uncertainty. Maybe, just maybe, there might be a little glimmer of light left in my world after all. Knowing that I would dissolve into real sobs if I opened my mouth, I squeezed their hands and nodded.

"Let's go," James said.

Liam's power rose around us and the room bled away in ribbons of blue-tinged psi.

Chapter 15

The Flame

We arrived in Skykyle to a blast of cold wind. The city was north of Landing and we'd been in a cool stretch lately even near the University. Arriving on the roof of a large tenement didn't help; up above the buildings' sheltering walls, the chill wind was cutting. I embraced the cold—it anchored me to my body despite what spread out below that lofty perch.

I knew the instant we materialized. I had my answer. Officer Coffing hadn't been lying.

Even now, I have a hard time thinking about that scene. Not only is it one of the most painful places I have ever been mentally, it is also one of the grimmest things I've ever witnessed.

The valley between the building we were standing on, and the one next to it, was pitted with little pill-shaped holes. Their rows were slightly ragged, but for the most part evenly placed. They started at the very back of the lot and dotted forward, spreading like a virulent cancer towards the street. Even from this height, I could make out the lumpy forms under the respectful sheets the watch had placed over the remains in each one.

I'd told Liam the truth. The Gracie that woke up that morning in his arms was dead. I wasn't sure who had come in to take her place, but I was pretty sure I wouldn't recognize her in the mirror tomorrow.

I'd dropped Liam and James' hands and stepped to the edge of the roof without even thinking about it. Feeling as if I might be sick if I stared down at that morbid spectacle a second longer, my eyes strayed upwards to the building across from the one we were standing on. If I hadn't already been wrapped in ringing, icy numbness, I think my chest would have tightened at the sight of the huge, pale blue wings wreathed in stylized psi-fire that completely covered the three-story wall. For a long moment, I found myself unable to do anything except stare at the mural, its fading paint showing the bricks through in ragged patches.

"Gracie?" Liam's voice was cautious as he moved behind me. I imagine he wanted to reach out and comfort me, but I couldn't deal with that right then. Almost by instinct, I called on my flames and leaped into the air.

The watch had parked a couple of hovercraft at the entrance to the lot—half to deter onlookers and half to make sure they could control who came and went at the crime scene. A small knot of watchmen were clustered near one of the vehicles while another group used shovels and a holo-recorder to excavate and document the graves. It was near the first group that I spiraled down for a landing.

I'd seen a lot of suspicion on mortal faces lately, but the look I got from the two men and one woman that stood in their light, gray Skykyle watch uniforms was downright loathing. Seeing as we were all pretty sure this was my father's handiwork they were unearthing, I couldn't blame them. Grabbing what little composure I had left firmly with both mental hands, I pulled my OW badge out of my pocket and flashed it in their direction.

"Amaya Blackmon?" It had been a whole sentence in my head, I swear. But all that came out was a muttered slur of my mother's name. Seeing the officers' suspicious looks, I cleared my throat and tried again. "Which one is Amaya Blackmon?"

The three of them exchanged a wary look. I made a point of keeping the OW badge in sight, and all three studied it as I took a few steps towards them. Then, before I could get within easy striking distance, the woman gestured almost directly behind me. "She's the one closest to the street."

I stopped and turned, my heart beating so fast it might actually injure itself on my ribs. With a bracing breath, I stepped towards the grave the female officer had indicated. Gooseflesh rose across my limbs, and my palms were slick with sweat as my legs closed the distance to the ominous hole. Then I was staring down at the white sheet at the bottom of the pit.

With a breath of psi-wind, I felt more than saw Liam and James appear next to me. My vision had narrowed to the series of lumps and bumps, under the shroud and my whole body was shaking.

"Come on, Gracie," Liam murmured, one of his large hands gently coming to rest on my shoulder. "This is answer enough. You don't really want to see what's under there."

"No," I whispered. I'm sure it was hard to hear me over the wind as it howled in the man-made chasm of the buildings' walls. "I don't want to. But I need to."

"Gracie—" James started, but I rounded on them, eyes flashing enough fire that it caught in my hair.

"I thought you two were here to help," I hissed. "Well, Liam, are you going to pull back that sheet, or do I have to climb down in the damn pit and do it myself?"

Liam looked at me as if he knew the woman he loved wasn't in my head at the moment, and he was sincerely concerned that she wouldn't be back. I shared the sentiment. But if I was going to do this—if I was going to walk into my childhood home, look into my father's eyes and then put a blade into his mechanical heart—I couldn't have any doubt left. I had to know that the skeleton in this foul, stinking pit was in fact my mother. I needed the horror of that knowledge to be seared utterly and irreversibly into my brain, or there was no way I would be able to go through with Gabriel's execution.

"Please," I whispered, looking up into the face that had once been too much like my father's for comfort. Now, I realized with an odd sense of relief, I couldn't find a scrap of Gabriel in my boyfriend's gaze, despite the pain that was in his eyes. "I have to know."

Slowly, he nodded. With a somber glance down at the figure in the pit, he waved a hand, and the sheet slid away from the near-skeletal remains.

I won't traumatize you with the details. Certainly they are etched in my mind's eye. Sometimes I wonder if my father's real problem wasn't his longevity but his horridly accurate memory. There have been times I wished he hadn't passed it on to me. This is one of them.

Suffice to say, the woman had blonde hair. I could see that it had been dyed, and that her natural color at the roots was something darker; brown or perhaps red. She rested on her back, hands placed folded across her chest. What made my skin begin to crawl with tiny licks of flame, however, was the stained and tattered white dress that clung to her exposed ribs. I'd never seen that dress in person before, but I recognized it instantly.

A little girl's nightmare rose in my mind.

"Good bye, Gracie," she'd whispered.

And then, a flash of that white dress before savage pain pulled me from my sleep.

I didn't blink. I didn't cry. I didn't think.

The fire came down as if by its own will and lifted me into the sky. I'd already left the Skykyle skyline behind by the time I really knew where I was heading. Once I did, I realized I'd been subconsciously waiting for this day ever since the dream of Adora and that deadly bottle of wine. After how good Dad had been the last few months, I'd foolishly felt as if I'd managed to avoid it. How completely and utterly stupid of me.

The trees blurred as I passed over them, though I'm not sure if it was from speed or my tears. Even so, my mind was blissfully blank as the fire poured through it, roaring out with the precise control of flight so effortlessly I didn't even have to think about it. All I could feel was my flames consuming the churning anger in my chest and using it as fuel to send me closer to the Overwatch compound—closer to where Vanessa waited with an execution order and a knife.

Chapter 16

Vanessa

I arrived at the Overwatch compound in a blast of orange flames. I'm sure it was a more dramatic entrance than I'd ever made, but it felt so good to channel the fire that I was almost loath to shut them down despite the toll of the long flight. Adrenaline is an amazing thing, and I don't know that I'd ever been so high on the stuff. Despite missing lunch, and traveling from one Province to another on pure willpower, I still couldn't help the little scrawling lines of embers that slid around my shoulders and hair.

The guard at the gate took one look at me and buzzed me in. I didn't even have to break stride as I slammed through each set of double doors. I'm not sure what he and the other OW members who were gathered in the training gallery saw when I walked in, but their reactions said it was something truly fearsome. Their eyes widened, and the few people working out this late in the day stopped their activities to stare openly. The knots of worried whisperers, who had sprung up in recent months in the corners and corridors of the Overwatch compound, all fell silent as I approached, their faces turning pale when they met my burning gaze. Then I was past the common areas and into the corridors of the OW offices. I took the stairs two at a time, hardly touching them as I glided up to Vanessa's office.

"There she is!" James' voice startled me as I rounded the corner. To my surprise, Liam and James were leaning against the wall just outside Vanessa's office. I think it says something about my state of mind that I hadn't even considered that they would reason out where I was going and jump ahead of me.

I slowed my aggressive charge towards the office door just the slightest, flashing back to how my boys had waited for me outside my art classroom the day I'd first found out about my father's morphine habit. If only tonight would end with such an easy return to equilibrium as that day had. A hot, painful prickle threatened in the back of my throat. I looked anywhere but at Liam and James as I strode purposefully towards Vanessa's door.

"Wait, Gracie, please." James sounded as if he'd been screwing up the nerve to say this for a while. "I know it looks bad now, but you don't have all the facts yet. Come on, Professor Joan taught us better than this. We need to explore all of the possibilities before we do something irreversible."

If I'm honest, there was a tiny little voice of reason in the back of my head that agreed with him. However, like my sense of hope and optimism, it couldn't seem to make itself heard through the blazing fire in my brain.

"You don't have to do anything except stay out of my way," I growled over my shoulder. I palmed open Vanessa's door.

Vanessa, an unfamiliar mortal woman in Riland's brown watch uniform, and Evan looked up from where they were sitting at Vanessa's desk. It appeared they were poring over some kind of documents, since they were all holding memory pads and styluses. My cousin scowled up at me as I burst into the room with a shower of orange sparks. Her face grew concerned as she took in my expression, and then something close to puzzled as she caught sight of Liam and James following in my wake.

"Gracie? I'm a bit busy at the moment," she said, eyes flicking from me to James to Liam and back again. "Can you wait outside until we're done here?"

"I need to speak to you alone." My voice was a flat, gravelly rumble.

"Now see here," Evan started, getting to his feet, "you can't just barge into a private meeting—"

"I'll do it."

My simple statement was said over his bluster, but I know my cousin heard me perfectly. She held up a hand, and Evan fell silent. He stared at her in wide-eyed shock, and I knew she'd just said something unkind in his head. Any other day I would have been giddy to see Vanessa put the head of Riland watch in his place. Today, I was just glad the burning urgency rushing through me wouldn't have to wait through some Fate-be-damned meeting.

"Christa, Evan, will the two of you sign the rest of the paperwork, and wait for me down at Martin's cell? I'll join you there once I'm done with Gracie," Vanessa said.

"Will this delay the execution?" Christa asked, lumbering to her feet. Her middle-aged figure was solid but slow, her movements deliberate. My OW training spotted what might be old injuries to her back and right knee; I could see it when she shifted her weight. I found myself fixating on those small details so that I didn't have to listen to the doubts James' last appeal to reason had put into my head. Irritation flared and I pulled up the image of my mother's decayed corpse. The horror and blind rage instantly drowned out any shred of uncertainty.

"No, no, we should be able to do it tonight," Vanessa reassured her, waving a hand for them to leave the room. "I'll be down shortly. This shouldn't take long."

Reluctantly, Evan and Christa gathered their things and left the room. As they passed me, however, I got a better look at their expressions. The woman's reflected the caution bordering on fear that many mortals seemed to feel towards individuals of Awareness, especially these days. Evan's, however, held anger and something else. I wasn't quite sure what to call it, but it was a strong emotion. Disgust? Jealousy? Loathing? I couldn't be sure, but it twisted his rugged features into something grotesque. If my head hadn't been bursting with its own powerful emotions, I think I would have recoiled from the glare he gave me. As it was, I stared him down with fire-drenched blue eyes.

Once the door slid shut behind them, Vanessa turned to the three of us.

"The last I heard from Lillian, you were threatening to light up anyone who so much as considered going after Gabriel," Vanessa said evenly, her ice-blue eye sliding from one face to another as if she were measuring each of us. "Now you come charging into a meeting with the head of Riland watch with your entire entourage in tow, essentially demanding I drop everything and hand you the knife. What the hell happened?"

Suddenly, I was incredibly glad Liam and James were there, because all I had to do was gesture to them.

"You tell it," I hissed.

"It might be easier if I just show you, 'Nessa," Liam said slowly, stepping forward so that he was closest to the desk. Vanessa met his gaze, and they were silent for several heartbeats. I watched her face lose what little color her pale skin had to begin with. Then, her eye darted back to me.

"Fates," she whispered. "I was afraid of something like this. It was only a matter of time. I thought we'd gotten lucky down in Skykyle and escaped a real tragedy once you came along but... oh, Gracie, I'm so sorry."

I held on savagely to the angry flames in my chest and shoved down the tears that leaped up at her gentle sympathy. "I guess this means we have something in common," I told her, my voice sounding clipped and painful. "The same bastard killed both of our mothers."

Vanessa looked at me as if I'd just punched her in the teeth. Then, slowly her eye narrowed and she nodded. "You actually mean to do this."

"Yes." My voice was suddenly steady. "Yes, I do."

"Vanessa," James breathed, "don't allow this. Look at her. She's not thinking straight right now. Please, use some common sense. You won't just be executing Gabriel, you'll be destroying Gracie, too. We have a war coming, you know it as well as I do. Can the Family afford to lose two of its strongest members right now?"

The head of OW met my diplomat's eye, and I saw the same silent communication pass between them as I had with her and Liam a moment ago. I don't know what they said, but James went white.

"Yes," Vanessa murmured. "I figured the net would catch wind of this pretty quickly. Do you have any idea what kind of chorus is going to go up for Gabriel's head in the next few days? We'll be lucky if the mortals don't burn half of Skykyle down themselves." She shook her head and her face was grim. "I can't even protect that young vampire down the hall, and he's a hell of a lot more innocent than Gabriel. Now that this is public, even if Gracie wasn't willing to go through with it, Lilly and I would have to handle it in the next sixty hours. If we didn't, I think we'd have that damn Riland death squad down in Landing picking off Usuriels inside a week."

If I'd had room for fear, I think Vanessa's words would have terrified me. However, at the moment, I didn't have space inside my head for anything but murderous rage. With an impatient growl, I leaned forward and met my superior's eye. "Can you give me the knife already so that we can all get this over with?"

Vanessa frowned at me and I suspected she might agree with James about my current mental state. Then she seemed to think better of it and slid open her desk drawer. With one hand she pulled out the same long, alloy blade she'd shown me before and a small cloth. She polished its surface carefully before sliding it into a leather arm sheath.

"Did Jillian show you how to use one of these?" she asked.

To answer her, I shrugged out of my casual jacket and handed it to Liam. I rolled up my sleeve and strapped on the sheath. The blade fit snugly against the inside of my forearm, tracing the length of my pulse. With a graceful flick of my wrist, I unfastened the clasping mechanism and the knife flowed easily into my hand. It was an assassin's trick as old as Earth itself. Mortals probably had to practice for years to get the movement right on one of these things, but I was Family; an elder child. I'd mastered it in a week when Jillian had brought out the bladed weapons for Liam and I to train on.

"Good," Vanessa said. There was something approaching regret when she searched my face, but she didn't say anything except, "Remember—one strike. Two ribs up and to the right. Make sure you tilt the blade upwards slightly so you don't just graze the thing. You want him dead in moments, not just bleeding out. He's too dangerous to injure. It has to be a killing blow."

I knew the anatomy. We studied it at University and in OW training. Since we were expected to execute vampires, every member of the Overwatch knew how to deal a fatal heart-blow. I hadn't done it on someone living yet, but I'd never missed on the dummy practice.

"He won't even know what happened," I said, my voice so soft even I could barely hear it. "Don't worry, I'll give him a better death than he deserves."

Slowly, Vanessa nodded. Then she tapped her memory pad a few times before extending it to me. "Put your hand on the pad," she said. The formal execution contract glowed at me. Feeling as if it wasn't mine, I put my hand on the pad. It lit up, the computer accepting my biosignature. Vanessa pulled the pad back into her own lap and looked over the document to make sure it was completed. With a resigned breath, she looked back up at me. "It's done. Be sure that you report back once... it's over. We'll make sure someone comes and delivers the body back to his parents. They deserve that much."

Her words opened a tiny door at the back of my head that screamed in horror at what I was about to do. I quickly slammed it shut again, but not before I'd envisioned the look on my grandmother's face when her firstborn's body was delivered to her door. Those doubts James had been stoking staged the best rally they'd yet managed, my chest clenching with an emotional pain so deep it felt physical. You're committed now, I thought to myself, and tried to hold on to the savage rage that had sustained me thus far. It mostly worked.

"I'll go with her, Vanessa," Liam said, glancing between me and the head of the Overwatch. "I can wait at the edge of Gabe's range. Somewhere just outside Carol's farm should be safe enough. Gracie can tap for me when it's done, and I'll bring the body back with us here. It's probably best if we don't just leave it out at Angelus Quietum, anyway."

"That will work nicely," Vanessa agreed. She glanced between the two of us. "Good luck."

Without another word, I grabbed my jacket from Liam. I was still pulling it on as I turned on my heel and strode out of the room.

***

"Whoa, slow down!" Liam caught up to me in the hallway, his hand finding my shoulder. I shrugged him off, but his long stride easily kept up with me anyway. "You don't need to waste your strength flying when I can teleport you. Honestly, I don't know why you didn't just wait for me out in Skykyle. I've told you before, if you want to go somewhere all you have to do is ask."

"I needed to clear my head," I said. And I knew you and James were going to try to talk me out of it, I added internally.

Speaking of our blond diplomat, I heard his footsteps rapidly following us as well. With a groan, I stopped at the top of the stairwell and turned to face my boys. It seemed I wasn't going to be able to outrun them, so I might as well just deal with them. I think it said something about my state of mind that I'd tried leaving without them in the first place, but I wasn't clear headed enough to be that self-aware. Instead, I turned around and gave them both the full brunt of my unleashed temper.

"Gracie—" James started, his face distraught as he trotted to a halt, panting.

"Liam, take him back to the University. This has gotten way too dangerous for him," I commanded. In Vanessa's office I'd managed to put my flames back in their box for a while. Now, I could feel them creeping up along my spine again. I didn't fight it. The angrier I was, the more likely I'd be able to put a blade in my father's chest before I lost my nerve.

Liam glanced between me and James, then shook his head. "No, I don't think that's such a good idea. I know you're not listening to reason right now, but James has always had the coolest head of the three of us. Besides, he's seen the inside of Gabriel's head. If anyone knows how he thinks, it's James. I think he might be a good person to have along for this."

I gave them both a furious glare, but their faces told me arguing was a moot point. My boys were along for the ride, whether I wanted them to be or not.

"Fine, but make sure the two of you stay well back. Gabriel will read you like a memory pad the instant you're in range," I grumbled and put a hand on Liam's arm.

"We won't get in the way," James reassured me as he grabbed Liam's other hand. "But I have a feeling you might need us afterwards. You know... as moral support."

One to carry Gabriel and the other to carry me. The thought went through my head as I glanced between them and realized they were bracing themselves for the worst. I hadn't allowed myself to consider any other possibility than a completely swift and deadly execution. The grim look on James and Liam's faces told me they'd had a few other ideas about how this might end. Perhaps it wasn't a bad idea to have a little extra back up, even if it wasn't OW trained. James was a very strong telepath—he'd be able to hear trouble coming even before Liam. If something happened to me, I wanted my boys to be able to get out of the way before an enraged second gen went the way of his sister.

"Okay," I said softly. It was barely more than a whisper, "Let's go."

Liam did as he was told.

Chapter 17

The Unraveling

We materialized on the edge of the forest just on the far side of Carol's farm. A few cows and their calves dotted the ridge above us, but her two-story house was several rolling hills away. That was good, since we didn't want her picking up on us, either. Whatever their relationship really was, I had a feeling she'd warn Gabriel in a heartbeat if she overheard what was in Liam and James' heads.

"We'll wait for you right here," Liam said, his face serious as he met my gaze. "Tap for either of us when it's done."

"Or if you get into trouble," James added.

I nodded, dropping Liam's arm and stepping away. Suddenly, I found myself unable to look at either one of them. My loyal, steady boys—the ones who had always taken care of me when things fell apart. I wanted to feel affection for them, but such a tender emotion would utterly destroy the fragile equilibrium I had at that moment, so I shoved it away. My heart was racing so badly I knew I'd be shaking soon if I wasn't already. I had to either act, or fall apart. If I was going to do this, it had to be now.

"You can still change your mind, you know," Liam said gently. "Even 'Nessa would understand if you decided not to go through with it. Underneath it all, he's still your dad."

I deliberately pulled up the image of that lot with all the open graves scattered like droplets of blood from a killing wound. That is what Gabriel really is, I told myself, underneath the civilized mask. He's a deadly weapon with no safety. If I walked away this time, how could I live with myself when he inevitably began to tear apart the people around him again? I thought of Adora reaching for him even as her body shut down from the poison he'd handed her. I thought of my mother's eyes in my dream when I was six—so sad and full of love for me. I thought of the rotted sockets they'd been, staring up from the ground at me earlier that morning. White-hot rage gathered in my core again, and the flames came boiling up over my skin like a living thing. I felt more than saw my boys take a few steps back as a sheet of fire came down around me.

"I'll tap when it's done," I managed just before the flames lifted me in their wake. Then I gave myself over to their fury and soared off towards the place I once called home.

I landed in the front yard of Angelus Quietum with a little more fire than I'd intended, searing a circle into the carefully-manicured grass. I paused and forced myself to put all those flames away, down into their usual, safe core. If I wanted any kind of element of surprise, I couldn't march in glowing like a Landing Day firework. It took several deep breaths, and a lot of mental control, but I hadn't been training most of my life for nothing. After a few minutes, my body still felt like a plucked string, but there weren't any licks of flame dancing about my shoulders.

Clearing my throat, I squared my shoulders and walked as calmly as I could to the front door. My body felt numb and distant as I placed my palm to the door plate. It slid open easily to reveal a dim living room. The afternoon sun slanted through the windows, but there weren't any lights on.

"Dad?" I called into the silent space. My voice echoed as I took in the couch and armchairs. I caught a glimpse of my OW portrait on the wall and felt a sharp stab of anxiety in the pit of my stomach, but I reined it in and stepped into the room. The door shut with a quiet snap behind me as I moved deeper into the house.

The kitchen and dining area were just as silent and empty as the living room. There really wasn't a reason for Gabriel to be in the bedrooms at this time of day, so it was more likely he was outside working. Just to be sure, however, I tapped for Stella.

"Hello, Gracie," she said, bleeding up from the twilight like a silver ghost.

"Hey, Stella." I tried to make my voice as normal as possible. If Carol would warn Dad, Stella was practically an extension of my father's psi. If she suspected anything, my mission would get complicated fast. "Any idea where Dad is?"

"Are you alright?" the AI asked, frowning at me. "Your vitals are elevated."

"I haven't been feeling well," I said, putting a hand to my head as if bothered by a headache. It wasn't even completely a lie. I was fairly sure I was going to be violently ill after everything was said and done today. My stomach gave a sickening lurch, and I quickly hauled my thoughts back onto the task at hand. I just had to get through this, and then I could completely lose it.

"Should I call for Gloria?"

"No, no, it's nothing that serious. Stress mostly, I think," I protested. "OW and school. It can get a little overwhelming."

"Is that why you are here?"

"No," I lied quickly. "There's just something I need to talk to Dad about. It shouldn't take long. Do you know where he is?"

"He left the house a little over an hour ago. I believe he was heading to the barn to take care of the horses for the evening," the silver AI said evenly.

My heart sped up another notch, and Stella's eyes narrowed at me. "Thanks," I said, trying to cover my response. I turned on one heel and walked rapidly to the back door.

I palmed it open and came nose-to-nose with Ariel.

I should have expected her. My ghostly sister had never been as affected by my alloy shields as the rest of the Family. Her blue eyes blazed into mine from inches away as she completely blocked the doorway. My already-shot nerves tried to roll the flames out and over the entire house, but I managed to hang on to my control by the barest edges of my fingernails.

She didn't move, and for a long moment we just stared at each other.

I broke first, my head going down though my spine stayed straight. "Stay out of my way," I snarled. Then I plowed through her with a determined twist of my shoulders.

Regret.

It flooded me so hard I almost stopped dead right there in the doorway. That edge of white-hot rage still simmered in my breast, however, and I held onto it as I forced my way through my sister's ephemeral body.

"*Don't do this,*" she whispered in my mind.

Then I was past the ghost and charging across the back porch towards the barnyard.

"Gracie?"

I heard Gabriel's voice as I trotted down the back steps two at a time. Of course Stella had warned him of my arrival, I thought. Mentally I cursed myself for calling her up. But then, he'd have seen me eventually. This wasn't a disaster, I told myself even as Dad's familiar figure stepped out of the barn and slid the door shut. The hinges groaned in protest, and I knew he still hadn't oiled the damn thing.

He turned towards me. The roaring numbness filled my entire body, making me feel as if I were floating and disconnected to it. What little feeling I had was very aware of my pulse high up in my chest. It threatened to choke me while my face burned, as if every capillary under my skin had burst.

Gabriel — at that moment I didn't want to call him my father — looked better than the last time I'd seen him, right after Ileesia's birth. He was exactly as I remembered him growing up — those perfect Family proportions making him elegant and powerful at once. He was wearing his usual work clothes, a simple shirt and denim pants with a jacket worn unfastened over top to keep out the chill. All that long, dark hair was tied back, though a few waving strands fell forward to frame his face in that way so many women had found alluring over the centuries. I wondered if that was what attracted my mother to him. The flames roared in my chest, and I closed the distance between us.

"Is something wrong, sweetheart?" He frowned at me as I slowed to approach him. Strange to think that a monster would wear such a beautiful face. "Shouldn't you be in class right now?"

I caught a glimpse of another glowing figure behind his shoulder, but my vision had narrowed to his face and chest. Nothing else seemed to matter except coordinating the movement of my hand and his rib cage so that they came together in just the right angle. The Usuriel blank face I'd practiced for so long slid over my features so naturally it was almost reflex.

Without breaking stride my left hand reached for his shoulder, almost as if I were about to embrace him. He must have read that as my intention, because his right hand began to come up to my back as well.

I flicked my right wrist, and the dagger fell easily into my palm. I hefted its solid weight and finished calculating the movement I needed to put it squarely between his ribs. I met his midnight-blue eyes with my own.

Without a word, I struck with all the savage strength his divine blood had given me.

As my arm curved in that deadly arc, several pairs of small yet strong hands grabbed hold of my wrist and elbow. They pulled against my momentum as if they meant to prevent the fatal blow. I'd lined everything up perfectly in my head, and with as many months of OW practice as I'd put in, there was no way I was going to miss this close to an unsuspecting target. Yet I'd had no warning that this interference was coming, and suddenly the dagger's trajectory was pulled down and to the right.

I may not be a telekinetic, but I am an elder child and I was about as adrenaline-high as anyone can probably get. Despite those mysterious hands, I managed to complete the movement and plunge the blade into Gabriel's torso. I felt it land solidly in his flesh, all six inches sinking in with surprising smoothness. The blade was extremely sharp. However, instead of landing in his chest as I'd intended, the dagger pierced the slim, muscular wall of his midriff.

Gabriel gasped at the unexpected pain, his hands coming up to my shoulders for stability more than to ward me off, I think. He held my gaze, blue eyes wide, shock written clearly across the sculpted planes of his too-perfect features. "Gracie..."

"You killed my mother, you bastard," I growled and wrenched the knife from his side with one quick, unmerciful movement.

He cried out as the blade left his flesh; fingers digging deeply into my shoulders. His breath came in ragged gasps, and I could feel the rush of his power tangling my hair up and around my head. For a moment I felt sure the near-miss would be a fatal mistake on my part. He was a second-gen, after all, and even if I was his favorite daughter, I somehow didn't think that would matter to the man who had buried my mother in a back lot. If I was going to survive this execution, I had to finish it quickly.

My arm went back, ready for another try at his chest, when I caught sight of his expression. There was no anger or aggression as he watched me with those ancient eyes. There was only love and incredible remorse.

"Sweet Fate, Gracie... I'm so sorry," he whispered.

Suddenly, where there had only been a few hands on my arm, now dozens tore at my shoulders, my waist, my legs. With a blinding flash of... was it my flames? Was it Gabriel's psi? Was it something else altogether? I couldn't be sure. But abruptly a bright light exploded in my face, and I was torn out of my father's grasp by reaching, groping, insistent hands that dragged me down and threw me across the barnyard. I gave a terrified shriek before I landed in a dazed heap several meters away from where I'd stabbed Gabriel.

My head spun, and my body felt bruised but otherwise unharmed. The knife had been ripped from my grasp and lay, glittering with dark blood, about a meter from where I crouched. When my vision cleared enough to look up, I glanced back towards Gabriel. But instead of seeing my injured father, I was greeted by an utterly surreal sight.

The Skykyle watch was probably right when they said there were fifty bodies in that lot. I'm fairly sure that's how many ghosts surrounded me, their faintly glowing auras sending their hair dancing about their transparent features. Unlike Ariel, these phantoms were blue-tinged and even more insubstantial. However, their sheer numbers made it impossible to see Gabriel's fallen figure through their densely clustered bodies.

"Gracie?" I heard Gabriel's voice from the other side of the apparitions, and I wondered fleetingly if he could see them. His call was followed by a sharp intake of breath, and the next words were choked. "Are you alright?"

The intense irony of the fact that I'd just stabbed

him in the side and Gabriel still seemed more concerned with my well-being than his own did not escape me. However, pissed was still a mild adjective for how I was feeling towards him, not to mention that I was a little preoccupied with the large throng of ghosts that had decided to show up at this most inopportune moment. Then all concern for Gabriel went out of my head as the ghosts' ranks parted and four individuals stepped out of the crowd.

Ariel and Olivia weren't a surprise. They glowed more golden than the others around them, as if there was something a bit more alive about them somehow. However, the two women in between them made my heart actually skip a beat as it slammed against my ribs.

Adora's proud androgyny looked down its perfect nose at me, her eyes holding mine in an icy stare. With one hand, she guided the shorter woman who walked next to her as if lending her moral support.

I almost didn't recognize Amaya. My mother's face wasn't sunken or sick anymore; instead it had the rounded, full curves of someone who was healthy and happy. Her hair was no longer the stringy, dyed blonde I remembered. Now it fell about her shoulders in long, red ringlets. She looked down at me with blue-green eyes so sad it made me swallow hard just looking at them. Even so, I couldn't tear my gaze away from her soft, loving face.

"Mom," I gasped, shifting my weight so that I was on my knees looking up at her.

The Family women stopped several paces away, but my mother kept walking until she dropped to one knee in front of me. It was a simple, mortal movement, utterly lacking in the fluid Usuriel grace. Even so, she was the most beautiful woman I had ever seen. Tears were silently flowing down my cheeks now. I was transfixed by her otherworldly gaze, those beautiful, peaceful eyes seeming to see straight into my very core.

"Why did you stop me?" I whispered. "He deserves to die for what he did to you."

Amaya gently took my face in her hands. Her fingers felt like cool mist on my skin. She shook her head sadly at me before placing a kiss on my forehead. Then, with a movement that I recognized from Ariel's trips in time, she lunged into my body.

Instead of Ariel's burning warmth, Amaya was freezing ice. And rather than communicate with words or emotions, she dragged my consciousness down, deep, past the normal sorts of dreams I had each night and into the depths where my mind could see times and places I'd never been.

Chapter 18

Sorrow

The world was a white, soft haze. I floated serenely through it until a figure materialized from its gentle light.

Amaya.

She sat on a medical bed, her feet dangling off the ground as she wrapped thin arms around her tiny waist. She looked far worse than the last time I'd seen her physically, however this was the woman I remembered from my other dream: deathly pale with dyed-blonde hair. Her eyes were sunken deep into bruises of flesh, and the hollows of her cheeks made her face almost skeletal.

Though I couldn't see a door, I heard the soft whoosh of air off to our left that indicated someone had walked into the room. Amaya glanced up, dull eyes watching the green-clad medic as he pulled up a chair from the mist and seated himself.

The medic didn't speak right away. His aged, mortal face avoided my mother as it wandered about the room, a somber expression on its wrinkled features. Finally, he cleared his throat and looked at the memory pad in his hand.

"Hello Amy."

"Doc," she replied when it seemed clear he wasn't going to continue without a response.

Another clearing of his aged throat. "I'm afraid I have some rather bad news. This round of anti-fungals hasn't been effective," he said slowly, glancing at Amaya. "Just like the last one."

She blinked at him slowly, her eyes dark and hollow. "I know," her voice was barely above a whisper.

"You're still using, aren't you." It was a statement, not a question.

"Can't work if I've got the shakes," she replied, eyes still distant. "Girl has to eat."

"A girl has to breathe, too," he pointed out.

She rubbed one arm. "Too late to worry about that now, I guess." She covered a body-wracking cough with one stick-thin wrist. When she put it down, there were blood smears on her sleeve and lips. "How much longer, then? Since your meds are useless."

The elderly medic sighed and gave her a pained look. "If you were clean... a few months. As it is? Weeks, at best. It's impossible to say exactly, but... not long."

There was a touch of shock on her face at that pronouncement. She hid it well after a moment, but I saw it cross her once-lovely features. I, on the other hand, had a really horrible feeling that the shape of this situation had just completely changed again.

"I'm very sorry," the doctor sounded as if he actually meant those words. "Weren't you telling me about your little girl last time you were here? Is she with relatives? Maybe you could make arrangements to see her."

Mom shook her head sharply and coughed again, shoulders tight. "Na, my baby don't need to see her momma dying," she whispered. Even so, her eyes were too bright.

"There are facilities that can help... ease the end. You don't have to die out on the street, Amy."

She shook her head and levered herself off of the bed. From a chair I hadn't seen before to her left, she picked up a stained jacket and wrapped her arms around it as if for comfort.

"I'd have to be clean for those places," she grumbled, staring at the floor. Then, for the first time, she looked at the medic with just the tiniest amount of pride in the tilt of her head as she made her next statement. "Besides, I'm a South Skykyle girl; tit to grave. There's only one place we go for that."

"Isn't morphine a little expensive?"

"I have a bit put up..." Her face was suddenly very sad. With as steadily as she seemed to take a terminal diagnosis, I wondered what had the power to put such a tragic look in her eye.

"Here." The medic produced a small purse from his coat pocket and pulled out enough money that Amaya's eyes widened. For a moment I thought she would refuse it, her faded, blue-green eyes darting between the doctor and the bills he'd put in her hand. Then, she closed her fist around them and shoved the money in her pocket.

"Thanks," she muttered and took a step towards the door.

"That would pay for a pretty nice hotel room, if you just wanted a warm place to overdose. You don't have to go to him, you know."

"I have some business with him anyway." Amaya glanced over her shoulder, a small frown on her face. "But even if I didn't, anyone who goes to Sorrow knows how to overdose by themselves," she said, her voice quiet but more in control than it had been for most of this conversation. "The point is that you don't have to go alone." She met the doctor's eye with some of the intensity that I recognized as her real personality. "Wouldn't you rather die in someone's arms?"

"I suppose... that does make some sense," he admitted. "Though, are you sure you can trust that the rumors are true? His sister made a real mess down in Riland a few years back. He might be dangerous."

"No," she said softly, turning away again, "he's not. Not to me, anyway."

***

The mist shifted, tongues of white clouds rolling across my vision until a hallway bled out of the formless dark. A gray door crouched at the end of the corridor, and Amaya's figure, now wearing the familiar white dress, walked towards it unsteadily.

I didn't want to see the end of this.

If I'd been corporeal, I would have closed my eyes or tried to run away. Since I was in Amaya's dream, I could do neither of those things. Instead, I watched as my mother raised a hand to knock on the door.

Before her knuckles could reach the painted wood, the doorknob rattled. With the barest of whispers, the gray door cracked open. It was pitch dark inside the apartment.

"Can I help you?"

I was prepared for it, but the pure anguish I felt at my father's voice was indescribable.

"Hello, Sorrow," Amaya murmured into the shadows.

There was a long silence. Mom put a hand out to push the door open a touch farther.

"I thought I told you not to come back." His voice wasn't angry, but it wasn't happy, either. Amaya froze.

"Please…" There was a note of pleading that I'd never heard in my mother's voice before. "I know the price. I have the needles."

He appeared in the inky maw so suddenly that Amaya stumbled back a step. Somewhere on the cold ground back in Angelus Quietum, my chest ached as I watched my father's figure bleed from the darkness.

Sorrow stood in the doorway, his muscular shoulders covered by a plain, black, sleeveless shirt. His face was so pale it seemed to glow in the dark room while the waves of his dusky hair faded into the shadows. The twisting mass of scars along the inside of his wrists and elbows were bare and clearly visible against his white skin.

"This is a one way trip," he rumbled.

"I'm counting on it," she said and pulled a pair of syringes from her pocket. She waggled them under his nose. "It's the strong stuff. Will it work?"

"We'll find out, won't we?" he said and stepped back from the door. The blackness instantly swallowed him up.

Amaya paused, eyeing the dark apartment with a touch of apprehension. She licked her lips and fingered the needles in her hand. "They said you could make it... clean. That it would be..." she trailed off, voice uncertain.

Sorrow didn't reply. A light came on, illuminating a tidy living room with hardwood floors and a brass floor lamp. The tension went out of her shoulders, and Amaya stepped into the room. Unfortunately for me, the dream followed after her.

The living room had an overstuffed couch and, to Amaya's left, there was a table and four chairs. Everything was clean and uncluttered which made me wonder just how much time he spent there.

A small gasp pulled my attention back to my mother. Her eyes had closed, and I saw that Sorrow had come up behind her, gently pulling her hair back and laying light kisses up the side of her neck. The expression on her face was so sad and enthralled at once—it was that, more than the unexpected sensual overtones between my parents that made me uncomfortable.

"I will make it as gentle as I can," Sorrow murmured.

Slowly, she turned to him and gazed into his face. From her expression, she found him as beautiful as every other woman who'd ever laid eyes on him. With one hand, she reached up and ran fingertips along the chiseled line of his cheekbone. He closed his eyes, tilting his head into her caress.

"Thank you," she whispered. She dropped her hand, and if his strong arms hadn't come up to catch her, I think she would have fallen.

"I'll take care of everything. Just relax," he said with a surprising amount of tenderness. He carried her as if she weighed nothing down the short corridor and into the bedroom.

Gently, he undressed her, lingering over her limbs with light touches. He kissed her palms and her forehead, stroking back the hair from her brow. She watched him with half-lidded eyes, her fingertips coming up to return the affection when his face or shoulder was close enough.

Finally, he lowered the lights and tucked her into bed. He slid out of his shirt before joining her, pulling her into his arms and letting her rest her head against the strong, broad plane of his chest. His skin was flawless save for that thin, white scar that ran up the center of his sternum. Her fingertips found and traced that raised line of flesh almost absently. For a moment they lay together quietly, and I could almost believe they were just a normal couple enjoying each other's company. Then, from the thin air to his left, Sorrow pulled out the needles.

"Last chance," he murmured, kissing the top of her head.

She raised her face to his and kissed his lips. "You'll touch my mind, won't you," she murmured. "We'll have no secrets."

He kissed her again, more deeply this time. I watched her melt into him, body relaxed and yielding to his touch. She sighed as he pulled away.

"No secrets," he agreed. "You're sure then?"

Mom nodded, stifling a cough as she burrowed against his shoulder.

I felt a wave of sick dread as he lifted the first syringe to his lips. With his teeth, he pulled the cap off the needle and held up his own wrist. She watched impassively as he injected the drug into the large vein there.

I'd never actually watched my father use before. There was a kind of morbid fascination that washed over me as he took a deep breath and his muscles seemed to shed any tension they'd held. He took a long blink and I watched the ever-present melancholy in his gaze fade away. Gently, he turned to Amaya and touched her face.

Suddenly, another layer of this twisted situation became clear. The moment his skin brushed hers, Amaya's face softened and her shoulders relaxed. Her sigh echoed his and she watched through hooded eyes as he uncapped the next syringe. The soft light from the bedside lamps twisted and bounced on the long needle as he slid it home in his wrist.

The two of them took a simultaneous little gasp of pleasure. It was so intimate. I felt almost as if I was watching them have sex. Yet instead of being a clean, wholesome expression of love or passion, this was a twisted, morbid joining that reeked of death, not new life. It would have been tragically awful to watch even if they hadn't been my parents. As it was, I felt as if the heartache would choke me as two of the people I loved most on Cybele deliberately tried to leave our world behind.

"She's yours," Amaya whispered, her dilated eyes still open just a touch.

Sorrow's brow creased slightly, his gaze distant with both the telepathic link and the drug. The smallest frown came over his face, as if he were trying to comprehend what Amaya's mind was telling him through the fog of the high.

I saw it when he finally understood.

The expression on his face was quiet anguish. His eyes flickered rapidly, seeing things I could only guess at. With what looked like a massive effort, he turned his head towards my mother, dawning horror on his face.

"What have you done?" he gasped, voice thick with the drug but still managing to convey his distress at her actions. Which part he found most awful—the fact that they had a child together that he knew nothing about, or that she hadn't told him about me until after he'd shot up a fatal dose of morphine—I'm still not sure.

"Be him for her…" Mom was fading and I could hardly make out her words. I had a feeling Dad understood her perfectly through that lethal telepathic link, however. "Be Gabriel… for our little girl."

My father's response was a shuddering breath that could have been a sob.

"Shhhh," Amaya hushed him, her eyes sliding shut.

Dad fought the drug a little longer, breathing coming faster despite the morphine's pull. In the end, though, it was too much for him. I watched him realize it; silent tears sliding down one perfect cheek even as he gave in to the grip of the drug.

"Gracie..."

Chapter 19

Reality

"Dad!" I came out of the vision with a terrified shout. I must have collapsed to the ground when my mother rendered me unconscious, because I sat straight up from a prone position. I took a great, heaving gasp and buried my face in my hands as I tried to wrap my head around everything I'd just seen.

It hadn't been murder. It had been mutual suicide. Only my father, damaged angel that he was, had a pacemaker.

"Ten years on either side and this would have been my lucky day." His words to my grandmother all those years ago suddenly made so much fucking sense. Of course. He'd been waiting for the day that damn mechanical heart finally threw a glitch at just the right moment. True to his luck, instead of quitting any of the fifty-odd times he'd put a fatal dose of morphine in his arm, it waited until he'd cleaned up and was trying to raise his twelve-year-old daughter.

It was about then that my brain caught up to itself and realized I'd just tried to complete an execution order on the man who had pulled himself out of a suicidal depression to come and get me out of that group home. The strange monster I'd somehow substituted for my kind, sensitive father evaporated into nothingness as I realized I'd known the real Gabriel all along. I'd just let Vanessa, Lillian, and the Skykyle watch talk me out of my own instincts and into attempted murder.

Horror isn't the word.

"Dad?" I looked around wildly, rising to my feet before I really had a chance to figure out what was going on.

The barnyard was mostly empty in the slanting rays of the setting sun. The large gathering of ghosts had disappeared along with Adora and my mother. However, there was still one apparition in attendance, and she was standing directly in front of my father.

Gabriel had fallen to his knees, one hand pressed to the gash I'd opened in his side. A dark stain was spreading across the lower half of his shirt, but he hardly seemed to notice. Instead, he was looking up with a rapturous expression at the glowing woman gazing down at him.

It was the first time anyone else had seen my ghosts. There was something vindicating about that in itself, I suppose. But at the time, all I could feel was terror that perhaps this meant my father would soon be joining them as a phantom himself. Even as I watched, Olivia reached out and ran fingers through his hair before letting her hand come to rest against the curve of his jaw. Gabriel took a sobbing breath that hissed through his teeth, his eyes rolling shut at her touch. I'd thought he'd been tender with Amaya at the end, but that interaction didn't hold a candle to the emotion on his face now.

Slowly, I approached the pair. Fate knew, I didn't want to interrupt them, but I could see the red creeping across the fabric of Dad's shirt and knew he was losing blood.

Just as I was within a meter or two and was considering saying one of their names, Olivia moved. Taking Gabriel's face in both of her hands, she bent and kissed him. He made a small noise, deep in his throat, that I didn't think was about physical pain. Then, as Ariel and Amaya had done to me, she poured herself into him. I'd never seen it happen in the third person before. It was rather incredible to watch. Like a glowing wave, she dissolved into a swirl of gold and red light that washed over his skin before fading into thin air.

"Gabriel?" I said cautiously as he wavered, eyes still closed and breathing shallow. Then, without a sound, he collapsed limply to the ground. "Dad!" I shouted, diving for him just in time to catch his head and shoulders before he could connect with the hard packed dirt.

"Dad? Dad, can you hear me?" I said quickly as I pulled his unconscious form more securely into my arms. When he didn't stir at my voice or hands, I braced his shoulders against my right arm so that I could put my left to his injured side. My hand came back absolutely covered in blood.

Finally, my common sense kicked in and I tapped my implant, ignoring the wet texture of blood against my neck as I did so. "Liam! James! I need help now! Get Gloria!"

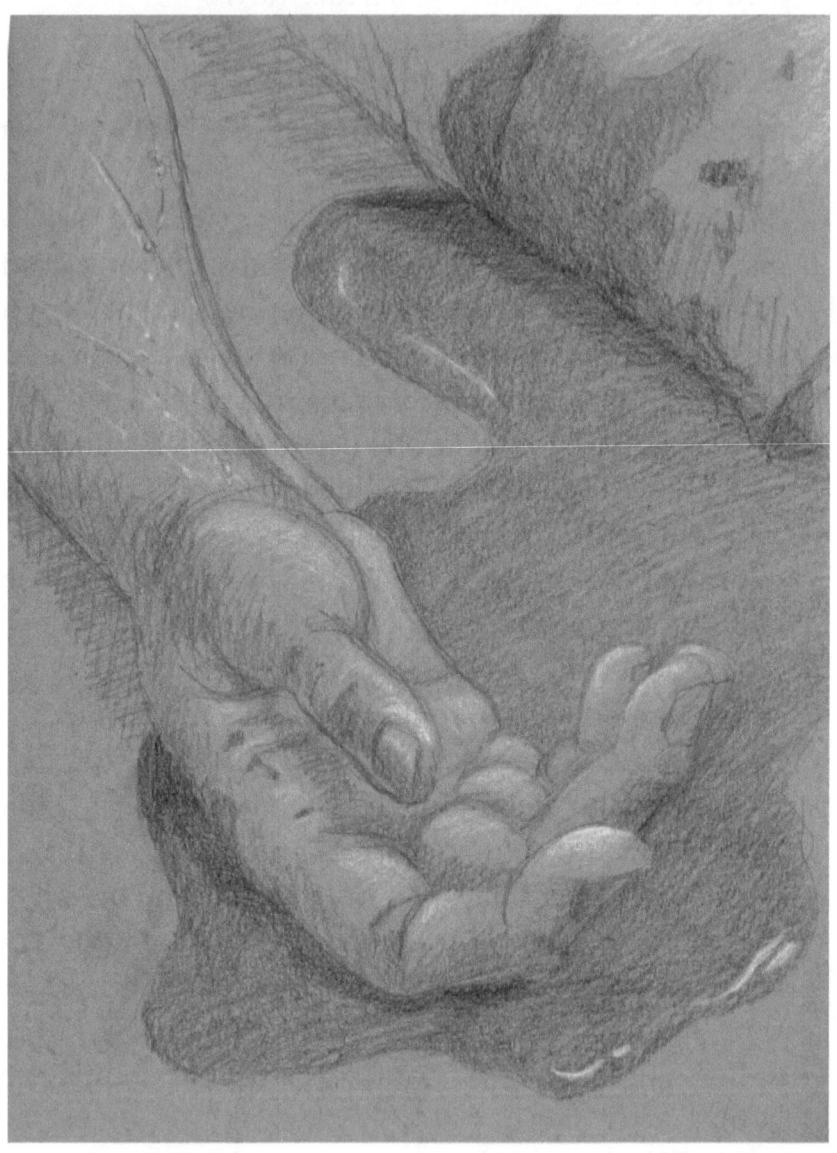

I'm not sure my boys heard the last of that because Liam teleported in so fast I hardly had time to press my hand back against the small but deep wound in my father's side. My partner's psychic wind tossed my hair about my shoulders, tangling it in a few of Gabriel's dark strands. As James and Liam appeared by the porch steps, I tried again to rouse my injured father. His eyes flickered slightly but didn't open.

"What happened?" Liam asked as he and James trotted to my side.

To my great relief, James didn't wait to figure out why I was holding Gabriel rather than trying to finish him off. He took one look at the scene and pulled off his light jacket. Tearing off a decent-sized part of the sleeve, he knelt beside me and pressed the absorbent fabric against the wound in Dad's side. "Gloria's on her way," he said to me quietly, face gentle and serious. "What made you come to your senses?"

"We were all wrong about Sorrow." I took a ragged breath and realized there were tears running down my face. I didn't have the hands to brush them away, so I blinked quickly and tried to use one shoulder to clear my eyes enough to see the boys' concerned expressions. "He wasn't a protector or a patron saint. He was a way out—a suicide pact. Those addicts were sick, probably most of them dying of lung rot. He let them ride along on an overdose so they wouldn't have to die alone."

"Fucking Fate, Gracie," Liam sounded about as horrified as I had been. I dodged his gaze and looked down at Gabriel in my arms. He was far too pale for my comfort, but whatever Olivia had done seemed to be preventing him from feeling any pain. His expression was peaceful despite the rough handling James and I had given his wounded side. I pulled his head more tightly against my shoulder, hugging him to me as if I could somehow undo the damage I'd done.

How could I not have seen it? All the pieces had been right in front of me. My mind spun as I tried to make sense of the sudden change in direction everything had taken. Anger rose in my chest, and I wasn't sure if I was more furious at myself for being so easily misled or at my father for being such a close-mouthed bastard about his own dark history.

Because it was painful and dark and horrifying, this secret that had been hovering on the edges of my vision my whole life. That much I couldn't dispute. But it wasn't malicious nor was it vindictive. In fact, from what I'd seen with Amaya, my father had given those addicts as much control and comfort at the end as he could afford them, as well as every opportunity to change their mind. The act itself might have been heartbreaking, but it wasn't dangerous to anyone who wasn't already terminally ill, or at the very least actively suicidal. Certainly it wasn't the kind of situation that warranted the use of deadly force to prevent it.

"Well, I'm not sure how you figured it out, but that does sound a hell of a lot more like Gabe," James said sensibly, pulling me out of the guilt-soaked reverie I'd fallen into. His hands were already covered in blood as he focused on applying pressure to the gash. "I don't care what Vanessa says. I've seen the inside of his head. Like I said before, suicide I can believe; not so much on the murder."

"That's a good question. How did you figure it out?" Liam asked as he knelt on the other side of Dad's still form, one large hand coming up to help me steady his shoulders.

"I'm a fate," I whispered, then glanced up at my partner through a screen of tangled red curls. I'm not sure what he saw in my face but his eyes got very wide. "Like I told you before, sometimes I just see things. The vision could have been better timed, but I trust the source. Amaya's death was a mercy killing."

Liam nodded slowly, his Family-blue eyes glancing between me and Gabriel cautiously. "Okay. Let's say that it's true. Sorrow has always been associated with overdoses, so I could believe that much. But if he let them ride along, how come he survived when his passengers didn't?"

"Olivia and Leeda's heart," James said evenly. I glanced gratefully in his direction. Liam hadn't been kidding when he said the diplomat had the coolest head of the three of us. His hands were steady on Dad's side even as he looked up at us. "That's the part of the story I know the best. I'm a Terran, after all. Without Gabriel's mechanical heart, my ancestors would never have come to Cybele."

My partner frowned. "What, so his heart just doesn't know when to quit? That doesn't make sense. Morphine is a depressant for more than just the heart. His breathing would shut down, too. Even if he survived being without oxygen that long... I don't care if he is a second-gen. The man should be brain dead."

Before either James or I could answer, Gloria erupted onto the scene with a blast of golden wind. When

I say erupted, I mean it. She was still carrying a little more weight from her pregnancy with Ileesia, but otherwise she seemed quite recovered from that ordeal. She was in a simple shirt and loose pants, but that didn't lessen the surreal sight of her as the golden light of her power streamed over us. Blazing, blue eyes took in the situation with one fierce glance and I ducked my head, unable to meet her gaze.

"For Fate's sake, what happened?" she demanded, dropping to one knee by James.

"A bit of a misunderstanding," James replied smoothly, shifting to one side so that she could reach Gabriel's injury more easily.

"Liv?"

Everyone's attention was instantly on my father's pale face as his eyes flickered open. I felt a rush of relief as I realized his comatose state was in fact ghost-related rather than strictly from blood loss.

"Gabriel, do you know where you are?" Gloria asked, one hand already pressed to his side, a gentle golden glow surrounding the wound.

Dad made a sound that suggested his mother's ministrations were not comfortable. "Liv... she was right here..."

"He's not delusional. She was just here," I said quickly. The expression on everyone's faces as they looked at me would have been still-worthy had the situation been a little less grim. I sighed and looked down at my father. "What did she show you, Dad?"

Gabriel gave me confused, blue eyes. "Something about Vanessa," he said slowly, "And a green vial—" He cut himself off with a gasp of pain and his right hand found my left arm.

"How bad is it?" I couldn't help myself from asking as I wrapped my hand around his forearm to give a little extra support. He clung to me with enough strength to make my shoulders ache, but I wasn't about to complain. With him conscious and Grandmother's healing hand on his side, I was hopeful that the consequences of my err in judgment would be erased rapidly. Thank Fate Ariel and the others had come in time, I thought.

"Bad enough," Grandma Gloria muttered, her face intense as she focused more glowing energy on Dad's side. "This was some hell of a misunderstanding. A few inches up and..." she shook her head, letting her voice trail off even as her eyes flashed up at me. "What were you thinking?"

I looked away again, anger and shame warring for dominance as I tried not to meet anyone's eye. "I..." Tears rushed up and I couldn't answer her.

Fortunately, James' calm voice did the talking for me. I found myself once again incredibly grateful I'd let him come along for this dreadful run. "The Skykyle watch came to the University today. They told us they were investigating Gracie's mother's death as a homicide. With Gabriel as the presumed guilty party."

"It wasn't just the watch. Vanessa has been trying to convince Gracie that her father is dangerous for months. It's been eating at her since the Riland avatar incident." Liam sounded disgusted. "Seeing Amaya's body was just the final tipping point."

"Amaya?" Grandmother sounded pissed, but when I dared a glance up at her, those blazing blue eyes were boring into my father rather than me. "You never explained Sorrow to her? Fucking Fate, Gabriel, I told you leaving her in the dark was going to bite you! Letting the mortal watch come and be the ones to tell her that her mother's unmarked grave is on your private land? No wonder she's after you with a Fate-forsaken knife! It would have served you right if she had put it between your ribs!"

Dad's breath hissed between his teeth and he gave the assembled a pitiable expression of frustration. "I tried to explain," he protested, "but honestly, you try having that conversation with a six-year-old!"

"I didn't stay six forever, Dad!" I shouted at him. "Fates, I could have killed you! Why wouldn't you just tell me? She was my mother! And I thought..." I couldn't put it into words. It was too horrifying—both the concept and what I'd done because of it.

"I did try to explain." Gabriel's voice was sounding fainter and his grip on my arm wasn't quite as firm as it had been. Suddenly, fear trumped anger again and I looked down at him in time to see his head start sinking back down to my shoulder.

"Gabe?" Grandmother's voice was now more concerned than upset. "Stay with us, kid." Leaving one glowing hand on his waist, she quickly put the other one up higher, closer to his chest. The glow brightened and Dad got some color back.

"So it's true?" Liam asked slowly, glancing between me, Gabriel, and Gloria. "Sorrow was assisted suicide?"

"Among other things," Grandmother grumbled. She suddenly looked very tired, but she put both hands firmly to Dad's side, and the glow around them grew to something so bright I had to look away from it. "Why don't you explain it, Gabriel? I think you owe your daughter that much."

"What else is there to explain?" Dad's tone was borderline pissed, and I saw from his expression that whatever Gloria was doing to his side had increased in discomfort as well as illumination. He did glance at me, however, and a softer expression came over his features despite the strain still in his eyes. When no one else spoke and James, Liam, and I simply watched him with silent, expectant eyes, he groaned.

"Sorrow... fuck... I never liked that name, anyway," he muttered. "But Gabriel was dead and people had to call me something. I guess someone said it and, when I didn't complain, it just stuck." He sighed, purple shadows gathering in the corners of his mouth. "So what exactly do you want to know? I'm an addict. I have been since the *Inspiration*. Sometimes I can get the better of it. But when things go really badly... like they did with Adora... let's just say I lost the fight that time." He glanced at me with wounded eyes. "I thought you knew this. We've certainly fought about it once or twice."

"She knew about the drugs, just not the fifty bodies on your lot," Liam clarified.

I shot him an annoyed look. As if Dad needed an excuse to shut down again. It had taken a dagger in the side to get this much out of him on the topic. I was really hoping for a little more detail before he decided his past was no longer open for discussion.

"Fates, will you heal that already," Dad grumbled, craning his neck at Gloria. His hands had been tightening on my arm as she worked, and I was sure I'd have bruises where his fingers dug through my jacket. It felt like a small penance for my stupidity, however, so I said nothing. With a pained gasp my father tensed, fighting not to writhe away from his mother's hands. "Whatever you're doing, it hurts like hell. What's taking so long?"

"Answer the boy, Gabriel," his mother hissed. I hoped it was my imagination, but the set of her eyes and mouth was looking a little strained to me. Fear began to squirm in the pit of my stomach again.

"How did Sorrow end up being a way out for those addicts?" James prompted gently, and unlike Liam, there was no judgment in his expression, only interest and compassion. He'd seen the inside of my father's head, I thought, he understood just how difficult this conversation was for Dad. I think he also suspected, as I had begun to, that Gloria was taking advantage of my father's guilt to keep him talking and alert. Well, it was nice to hear some honesty out of my father for once, and if it had the added benefit of keeping him alive, all the better.

Dad swallowed hard, and I watched him push the physical pain away with a conscious effort. When his eyes cleared, his expression was less temper and more of the anguish he used the anger to hide. When he spoke again, his voice was quiet with emotional as well as physical pain. Despite James and Liam's presence, it seemed my father actually felt I did deserve a little bit of difficult truth today.

"The truth about the overdoses?" He took a hissing breath. "Honestly, the first time was an accident. Girl I was dating figured out how to ride along on a high. One day, I woke up and... she didn't."

"Fates, Dad," I couldn't help the words from slipping out of my mouth, even if I knew he would probably resent my pity.

"Well, you can imagine how pretty things were after that." His mouth twisted in a pained smile.

Liam and James' faces were somber. Neither of them looked surprised by the grim truth behind Sorrow, but they weren't taking joy in hearing it either. If I was honest, that was about the way I felt about it, too.

I looked back at Dad who winced, as much to dodge our gazes as because of anything his mother was doing, I think. "For a while after that, my overdoses were just for me. Obviously, they didn't work very well, but there it is."

"Why didn't you just eat a fucking gun?" Liam grumbled. "If the morphine wasn't doing it..."

Dad raised an eyebrow in my partner's direction, his usual sarcastic gleam flashing wickedly in his blue gaze. "You're an OW-trained three-T. Think you could keep yourself from stopping a bullet if you knew it was coming?" he asked Liam. "Be honest."

My boyfriend looked a little uncomfortable with that question. When my father didn't drop his gaze, he gave a quick shrug. "If I was determined enough... maybe."

Dad's laugh sounded painful, and he crushed my arm a bit, but his eyes were still clear when he looked back at Liam. "Keep lying to yourself, kid." He shook his head. "No, you've been trained too well. And that's after catching bullets for less than a decade. I've had centuries of putting up a psi-shield the instant I pull a trigger. It's reflex. Trust me, I got desperate enough to try it once or twice."

"Well, that's something I didn't know," Gloria said, flashing a small scowl at her son.

He groaned and shifted uncomfortably in my arms, but didn't snap at her. In fact, his face was looking rather drawn again. "Yes, well, I'm not proud of it. And if I'm honest, I wasn't extremely serious about those attempts. I knew you'd most likely be the one to find me and... forever is a long time to carry around the image of your son's brains splashed against a wall." He gave Liam a significant look, as if daring him to dispute this rather compelling reason for leaving a less mutilated corpse.

"Okay, so you wanted to end things, but you weren't willing to go farther than an overdose," James chimed back in. "How did the other addicts get involved?"

"That new strain of lung rot," Gabriel replied with a groan, lifting his head a bit again. I think he was trying to lean forward so he could see James and his mother more clearly from around my shoulder. But the movement must have tensed the muscles along his side because with a gasp of agony he went rigid in my arms.

"Easy," I said, taking the opportunity to shift my grip on his shoulders. My arm was beginning to ache from supporting his weight, despite Liam's help. I glanced at Gloria, about to echo my father's question about what was taking so long, but the intensity of her gaze as she bent to her task made me hold my tongue.

"I'd never seen... anything like that lung rot." Dad's voice was weaker, but it still pulled my attention back to his face. "It was as if everyone around me was sick. I felt their pain constantly, like a background noise I couldn't drown out... not without a needle anyway." He took a ragged breath and was silent for a moment before going on. "The first one I deliberately took with me couldn't have been more than fifteen. Fates, he was so young. I'm not sure if he would have frozen to death or coughed his lungs out first, but either way, I couldn't leave him on the street. So I took him home, gave him the first decent meal he'd had in Fate knows how long and let him sleep in my bed while I took the couch. The kid was so grateful in the morning, but also so fucking sick. I'm not a healer, but I've seen enough death to know what it looks like. He begged me to make the pain stop. So I did. Just like I did for all the others. Just like I did for Amaya."

His eyes flickered up at me, and I could see he was losing strength again. Even so, his expression was so remorseful I could hardly meet his gaze. "If I'd known... Gracie... Fates, I wish she'd come to me about you sooner. It might have saved all of us so much pain."

We were all silent except for Dad's ragged breathing and the gentle hum of Grandma Gloria's healing energy as it surrounded his waist.

"If you did it enough times, I guess word would start to get around," Liam mused quietly.

"I may also have let it be known in a few spore holes that a pair of needles would be sufficient payment for a clean death," he admitted. "So... there you have it. Sorrow in all his fucking glory. Truth enough for you, Gracie?" Dad was looking awfully pale again, and he'd rested his head against my shoulder as if he didn't really have the strength to hold it up anymore. I wasn't sure which was tying worse knots into my guts—knowing what kind of hell my father had actually gone through, or worrying about why this healing was taking so damn long.

"Truth enough for me," I agreed. I wasn't crying anymore, but my voice was still painful as the next words came out in a rush. "I'm so sorry, Dad. I can't believe I... I don't know what was wrong with me. I should have gone to you about Mom, not Vanessa. Please don't blame James and Liam. They tried to talk me out of it. I... I just wasn't thinking straight..."

"Been there," he muttered, a small smile creeping across his face. I didn't like how his gaze drifted past my own, however. He was getting worse, not better, even though I knew Grandma Gloria had to be dumping a massive amount of healing psi into his side. I had a bad feeling that was increasing by the moment.

"Do you want me to call Dax?" Liam asked Gloria quietly. I felt as if we'd been kneeling on this hard ground forever, and my back had joined my arms in their complaints about supporting my father's solid weight.

"I know you still have an infant at home," James put in. A very polite way to point out she might still be weak from giving birth, I thought.

Gloria shook her head, face grave. "I'm not at my best, but this should be a simple healing. I don't think the issue is me. There's something very wrong with this wound," she said slowly, giving Dad and me a cautious glance. "Gracie, where's the weapon you used on this? Where did you get it?"

"It's over there." I met James' eye and indicated with my chin where the knife had fallen. Obediently, the diplomat got up and trotted over to retrieve the grisly weapon. "Vanessa gave it to me when I signed the execution order."

Dad's expression sharpened enough to shoot me a surprised and rather wounded look. Well that answered another question. He hadn't known about the order. I guess my hints the night of Grayson's death hadn't been explicit enough for him to piece it together. Well, there had been a lot going on that night.

"Don't worry," I reassured him, "I don't care if Vanessa kicks me out of the OW. I won't be completing that order, and neither will anyone else; not if I can help it."

James came back and handed the knife to Gloria who frowned at it. Maintaining her healing energy with one hand, she took the knife in the other and held it to the fading light.

"You may have already completed it."
Grandmother's voice was soft—dangerously so. When I
met her gaze, there was a bone-deep fury in her ethereal
features. "This blade is poisoned. I'm not sure with what,
but it has to be strong. That wound is eating energy like
nothing I've ever seen before."

Dad swore.

Ice poured into my veins, and my stomach clenched
hard on the thin air that currently occupied it. I hadn't
eaten in hours, but I suddenly felt as if I was going to be
sick. "Wait... what?"

"Vanessa," Liam hissed. He exchanged a glance
with James, who nodded.

"She was shielding hard in her office. Even when I
opened up to her, I knew she was hiding something,"
James said slowly. I'd nearly forgotten his solid presence
at my shoulder, but I was incredibly grateful for his
steadying hand as it found my back. "She must have
decided she needed a little extra insurance on this
execution. You know, on the off chance you had a change
of heart part way through."

Gloria swore herself and threw the knife so hard it
stuck straight up in the dirt by her knee.

"Give him to me," she said, alloy control holding
her voice in check. I caught a glimpse of her true
emotions, however, as she met my gaze with licking blue
flames in her eyes. "I can keep this at bay for a while. But
you need to go back to Vanessa and get the antidote to
whatever it is she used on that thing. Failing that, we at
least need to know what poison she used. Anything this
strong, the counteragent will be as deadly as the poison if

given by itself. I can't risk experimenting on him."

Feeling as if Cybele was falling from under me for at least the second time that day, I obediently allowed my grandmother to gather her son into her arms. Dad's face was paper-white again, but his hand clung to mine as Gloria lifted him off of my lap.

"Gracie..." My chest clenched at how weak Gabriel sounded.

"Vanessa isn't going to just hand over the antidote," Liam pointed out as I slid to my feet, my hand still in Gabriel's.

My eyes darted between my father and grandmother, heart pounding as I tried to wrap my head around the idea that Dad was still dying even with his mother's best efforts. Gloria's expression was pure fury despite her silence, while Dad looked like he was fighting just to stay conscious. In only these few moments that Grandma Gloria didn't have her healing hand on his injury, my father's skin tone had gone an unhealthy gray, and his eyes were obviously having a hard time focusing on my face.

"Well, let's just reason it out, then," James said, getting to his feet beside me. "She knew who Gracie was going after with that knife. She picked out this poison specifically for Gabriel. It has to be something that he wouldn't have a tolerance to, so probably not a narcotic or opiate. And it has to be deadly enough to overpower a second-gen metabolism with only a minute dose."

"Which narrows it down to about three or four compounds that I can think of," Gloria snapped. "Two of them actually have antidotes, so we'll hope it's one of them. Even so, I can't just try one when it could just as easily be the other. If I'm wrong, I'll kill him just as surely as letting this run its course."

"Can't you just keep him alive while the poison does run its course?" Liam suggested. "I mean, isn't that what we've just been talking about with the whole Sorrow thing? The man's practically been poisoning himself for a living, or at least for that stretch he was. Won't his mechanical heart just let him wait it out?"

"If only." Gloria's mouth made a hard line across her face. "This isn't something as tame as morphine. It's not just a depressant. It's acting more like... an acid? That's the only thing I can compare it to. Now that it's in his bloodstream, I have to stay a step ahead of it or it will begin dissolving his organs one by one. So unless his mechanical heart can survive being liquefied, I suggest you find the antidote."

I tried to keep the horror off of my face for Dad's sake, but when I looked down at him again, his eyes had slid shut. I didn't like the angle of his head as it curled against his mother's shoulder; it didn't look quite natural.

"Okay, so we get the antidote," James said, his steady calm exactly what we needed at that moment.

"I guess we could just go through 'Nessa's office," Liam sighed. "Though I imagine we'd be in a world of trouble if she walked in on us."

With a savage glare, Gloria met Liam's gaze with her own. "You want to discuss a world of trouble? No, you tell Vanessa I sent you. If she tries to put you off, tell her this." My grandmother turned and looked me straight in the eye. In that moment she wasn't the nurturing, healing mother-goddess I'd grown up with. No, she was a raging flood that swept away deep-rooted trees; she was a lightning strike that split ancient stone in two; she was a wildfire that devoured cities whole; she was all that and more—a force of nature distilled and contained in that deceptively tiny, beautiful body. When I say I trembled before her, I am not using a figure of speech. "Tell her that if my son dies, I will put an end to this Overwatch nonsense once and for all. And I will start by cutting off its ugly, one-eyed head. I don't care if she is my own granddaughter. She knew Sorrow's nature long ago. She also knew that anyone who went after my son would have to deal with me." The expression on my face must have revealed my surprise, because she gave a very bitter laugh. "What, you actually thought she was afraid of a passed-out junkie down in Skykyle? Please. The only reason that execution order hadn't been filled all these years is because I promised her I'd have the head of anyone who tried to complete it. I think she was hoping your youth and the 'misunderstanding' of your mother's death would be enough to protect you from me. She may have been right. However, it will not be enough to protect her if my son dies because of her poison—either emotional or physical."

I swallowed hard and looked at my father one more time. His eyes were still closed and his breathing was coming in small, pained gasps. Mortal dread had become a close companion of mine. I felt its familiar grip on my rib cage as I squeezed Gabriel's hand. An eyelid lifted just enough to let me see his pain-dark eyes slide in my direction. I flashed on Grayson so hard it took every ounce of control I had not to lose it right there. But Liam and the OW had given me a little practice on that front lately, so instead of collapsing into helpless tears, I laid my father's hand across his chest with as much tenderness as I could put into the motion. Any other day, I would have laid a kiss on his brow, but I somehow felt as if I'd lost that right. So instead, I stepped back and gave my grandmother a firm nod.

"I'll figure out what she used," I said, feeling an echo of that deadly rage I'd so lost myself to earlier lick back up inside my breast. This time, I was fairly certain its target was more deserving. "Don't worry."

Grandmother looked down at her son with one more concerned glance. I saw the fear in her eyes, then, and it put more terror in my chest than her anger, terrible though it was, ever could. "Be quick," she said. "We'll be waiting at the homestead."

"We'll convince 'Nessa," Liam said, coming to my side. James was already behind my other shoulder. Between the two of them, I suddenly felt a lot steadier. "Take care of Gabe. We'll get the antidote to you."

A last savage glare was Gloria's only reply before she and my father faded into a swirl of golden sparks.

Chapter 20

Truth

Gabriel and Gloria had hardly faded from the barnyard when Liam's psychic wind picked up around James and me. The world tilted and bled wildly before solidifying into Vanessa's dimly lit office.

Beside me, Liam took a sharp breath and staggered, only James on his other side keeping him on his feet.

"I'm okay, I'm okay," my partner said quickly as James and I turned to him in concern. He steadied himself against the large wooden desk. "See if you can find whatever she used on the blade. I'll be fine in a minute. I'm just tired."

Too many jumps, I thought, mentally counting the times Liam had teleported today. The more passengers, the faster he wore out, and we'd easily passed his usual three-to-four-a-day comfort zone a while back. Cursing myself for not paying attention to him and this horrible day for being... well... horrible, I gave my boyfriend's arm a squeeze before turning to raid Vanessa's desk drawers.

"You've been amazing today," I told Liam, even as I started rifling through the contents of Vanessa's desk. "Sit down before you fall down. We don't need any more injuries tonight, and we'll need you to get the antidote to Dad in a minute. After that, I promise you won't have to teleport for the rest of the night. Grandma and Grandpa won't care if we sleep at their place. Or, Fates, Dad or Gloria can send us home. Seriously, save your strength for just one more jump." I was rambling, but it kept me from completely losing it, so I let my mouth talk while I dumped papers, styluses, memory pads, storage chips, official seals, and several other weapons including a stun gun and two other knives onto the floor. Beside me, James was doing the same to the other side of the desk. The clutter next to him looked equally useless, and my stomach twisted again as the last of Vanessa's drawers were searched with nothing even remotely resembling poison or an antidote in evidence.

"It has to be here," James hissed, surveying the mess with both hands on his hips before he began dumping the clutter back into the drawers. "That poison was fresh. She has to have the container here somewhere."

"Unless she teleported it in and then put it back wherever it is she keeps it," Liam suggested, still looking as if he were fighting a headache as he sat in one of the plush armchairs. "She's a three-T, remember?"

"Her office is probably more secure than almost any other place on Cybele," James pointed out, head swiveling around the room as if he were looking for anywhere a vial of poison could be hiding. "The only people who can get in here are OW members or other teleporters. And then they'd have to have a reference image to 'port in. If that poison is as deadly as Gloria thinks it is, this would be the safest place to keep it."

Suddenly, I had a thought I really didn't like. As if I were in a nightmare, I turned to the window sill overlooking the practice gallery. Like Vanessa's office, the gallery looked dim and deserted. That was a little more unusual at this time of day, but I didn't think about it much at the time. Instead, all my attention was focused on the little green vial sitting next to the sculpture of a white raven. Sick dread making my hands shake, I took the half-dozen steps between the desk and the window before snatching up the vial.

"Oh no." My voice was low and the fear in my gut felt like I'd been the one stabbed. "No, no, no... this can't be happening..." The words were horrifyingly clear as I read them, however. TT123-G. I read the numbers and letters on the vial's side written in Ariel's looping hand with a feeling of utter dread. Unlike the elixir in my closet, however, the words "Warning—Poison—Immortal Death" were scrawled clearly underneath the coded designation.

"Gracie, what did you find?" Liam asked, looking a little more alert as he turned towards me.

"Is that it? Did you find it?" James sounded as anxious as I had been to find the poison. It was nice to know I wasn't the only one who felt some urgency about helping Dad. However, if this was what I thought it was, we were in a lot more trouble than any of us had initially realized.

I glanced up at James, my pounding heart making my cheeks burn. "Oh, I hope not," I breathed.

"Hey, 'Nessa's coming!" Liam called.

James swore and started shoving objects back into the disheveled desk. I charged towards the door. Before I got half-way across the room, it slid open to reveal Vanessa and Evan.

'Nessa looked exhausted and grim-faced, her hands covered in blood up past her wrists. Evan, on the other hand, looked like a cat with cream. Both of them glanced around the room when they caught sight of me, and I had a sinking feeling they were looking for my father's body.

"Where's Gabriel?" Vanessa asked as she strode into the room, confirming my suspicion.

"At the homestead," Liam replied. It wasn't even a lie, but it also didn't reveal the fact that I hadn't gone through with the execution. I would have appreciated my boyfriend's cleverness more if I weren't currently on the edge of panic.

"Is this what you used on that blade?" I demanded of Vanessa, shoving the vial in her face.

She frowned at me, ice blue eye taking in the terror in my expression with more than a little confusion. "What does it matter now?" she asked, obviously jumping to the conclusion Liam had hoped she would.

"Because this isn't just poison!" I all but shouted at her. "Do you even fucking know what this is, Vanessa?"

"Ariel's poison," Evan said evenly, brown eyes flashing dangerously. "I would assume it's strong enough to deal with an Usuriel, even an elder child. Your sister dealt with the immortality genome, so whatever she labeled as poisonous was obviously designed with the strongly Aware in mind. It's even labeled 'Immortal Death.'"

Well, his logic wasn't bad. I glanced wildly between him and Vanessa, trying to wrap my brain around why the head of Riland watch even knew the first thing about Ariel's experiments. After a moment of failed calculation, however, I decided it didn't matter and turned back to Vanessa.

"Answer me." My voice was a low, dangerous growl. "Is this what you used on that Fate-forsaken blade you gave me?"

"I needed something strong enough to take out a second generation morphine addict." She met my gaze with something that approached defiance. "He's tried and failed to poison himself enough times. I needed something a little less mundane. Ariel's poison certainly fits that description." She narrowed her good eye at me. "Is Gabriel dead, or isn't he?"

I'm a null. Her powerful mind could try to read me all day and not get anywhere. Not so much for my boys. I watched her gaze flicker in their direction. Her lips curled.

"You fucking idiot," I swore at her.

Her expression of disgust deepened. "Excuse me?"

I didn't have time for Vanessa's stupidity. I turned away from her, feeling as if my fire was about to explode through the entire compound.

"If Dad dies—when—fuck—if Dad dies from this stuff—" I could barely force the words out, but if I didn't I was going to send the whole place up in flames. I scrubbed at my face and started again. "You Fate-be-damned moron! You sent me after one of the oldest individuals on the planet with Temporal Mortis! If he dies, four *hundred* years of history goes up with him!" I pivoted on one toe and faced the room again. James, Vanessa, and Evan were looking at me like I'd lost my mind. Liam, on the other hand, had horrified understanding beginning to spread across his face. I met his eye, feeling as if I needed someone else to appreciate just how fucking doomed we all were. "You, me, James, every Terran on the planet... hell, maybe even the whole fucking colony!" I snapped my fingers in Vanessa's face. "He dies and we all vanish! Poof! Disappeared as if we never even existed to begin with!"

"Grayson," Liam whispered, his eyes round as dinner plates when I turned my attention back to him.

"Exactly," I hissed. "I haven't just killed Dad. I've unmade the entire colony!"

"Wait... what is that poison called? Temporal Mortis? Time poison?" James' nimble mind seemed to be wrapping itself around the concept faster than Vanessa and Evan. He shot the head of the Overwatch a terrified glare. "Why would you use something when you don't even know its properties?"

"It's clearly labeled 'poison,'" Vanessa shot back at the diplomat. "That was property enough for my purposes."

"Gracie, how do you know that vial is Temporal Mortis?" Liam asked, getting to his feet. He towered over almost everyone in the room.

"The Anori database called Temporal Mortis one of the three Immortal Deaths. Plus, it has the same codes Ariel used for experiments using my blood," I groaned, showing my boyfriend the bottle. "If she managed to make her immortality elixir from my blood, it stands to reason she'd also have come up with its opposite."

The words were hardly out of my mouth before I realized what was staring me right in the face. I felt my body and face freeze in an expression of shock.

"What is it, Gracie?" Liam took the vial from my suddenly numb fingers. I swallowed hard as a wild smile spread across my face.

"I'm the fucking idiot!" I crowed, grabbing his shoulders with both hands and giving him a shake. "I've had the antidote all along! Ariel's Usuriel in a bottle! The immortality elixir—it has to be the antidote! It's in my closet at University! Come on, we don't have much time!"

The sound of a safety releasing from a gun cut through my urgency. Liam's body tensed under my hands, and the two of us turned in almost perfect unison to face Evan's cold, dark gaze. His weapon had the same sleek, strange lines that I'd seen on the most recent mortal tech, and it was aimed directly at my head.

"Evan?" Vanessa's voice held the even calm one used when dealing with someone unpredictable and dangerous. My already speeding pulse jumped up a notch, making me dizzy and sick. "Think about this. The riots are bad enough. Do you want to give my people another reason to go after your troops? Gabriel is one thing; most Usuriels have already written him off as dangerously unstable. But if you shoot Gracie there will be a world of vengeance coming down from the Family."

"Shut up, 'Nessa." Evan's voice was low and had far more control than I was comfortable with. "You're utterly useless. Sending little Gracie to do a job you should have handled yourself years ago? I should have known you'd take the coward's way out." His upper lip curled in disgust, but his glittering eyes didn't leave my face. "No, I'm done playing politics with you." His face shifted again, this time a feral smile coming across his rugged features. "Now, little firebird, what kind of elixir did you say you have in your closet?"

"Liam," I breathed, trying to keep my voice as quiet as I could. "Get us out of here."

"I can't," he hissed back. "'Nessa's blocking me. Same goes for teleporting the gun."

I swore.

"Evan." James. Oh, sweet, innocent James. I'd almost forgotten he was in the room for a moment. He stepped out from behind Vanessa's desk with his hands raised. "Let's be reasonable here. No one thinks or acts their best with a gun aimed at their head. Put the weapon down, and let's discuss things calmly and rationally."

"Oh, hello, Terran." Evan's tone dripped with contempt, but his gaze did divert from me and my partner. "I wonder why you're in the room. I was under the impression that this was the Overwatch. I thought they were an Usuriel-run institution. Yet here you are, turning up uninvited just like always."

"Put down the gun, Evan." Vanessa sounded dangerous enough that, if I'd been a mortal, I think I would have run. The head of the Riland watch, however, simply turned and aimed the pistol at her head instead. She was a lot closer to him, so the muzzle of the weapon nearly touched the smooth skin of her forehead.

"Why? I've just evened up the odds. The simple act of standing in the same room with you is having a gun aimed at my head. Now that I finally have a weapon that you can't teleport away or shield out, you actually pay attention to me. Strange. Not so much fun when the tables are turned, is it?"

"You've made your point," Vanessa hissed, her eye flashing ice. "You and I both know you don't need that gun to get your way, so stop waving it in my face, and tell me what it will take to get you out of my office without bloodshed."

Evan sneered at her, but he did aim his weapon at the ceiling. "Well, since it seems I can't even trust you people to do your own damn jobs, I'd say that Cybele could use an Aware police force that has a little objectivity." His eyes were coal-black pits as they stared into mine. "Trained people, not an incestuous cult. You want me out of your office, Vanessa? Give me the ability to build my own army of psychics. Give me Ariel's immortality elixir."

My brain scrambled, spinning in horrified circles as I tried to think through a fog of hunger, terror, and bone-deep exhaustion. To be quite honest, I'm not sure how I was on my feet at that point, let alone coherent, so I suppose the fact that I started screaming at him might be slightly excusable.

"Are you deaf or just plain stupid? I told you, we're all completely fucked if Dad dies before I can get him that elixir! Every descendant Gabriel has will be erased as if we never even existed! Me—" I jabbed my own chest "—

him —" I gestured to Liam "—hell, even James! The peace child would never have been born without Dad's bad heart to trade for!"

"Who knows if Adora or Vanessa would have turned out the way they did, or if they would even have been born at all, if Gabriel wasn't around," James pointed out sensibly. "In fact, there's a very good chance the *Inspiration* would never have been built and launched without him. D'nay and Gloria were a driving force behind the generation ship. Without a child to protect, would they have been so eager to flee the other immortals into space?"

"And even if it was launched, how many times did Gabe save the ship? Without him as psi-pilot, the *Inspiration* probably wouldn't have made it to Cybele." Liam was catching on to this little thought experiment. Sweet Fate, I hoped that was all it stayed because the memory of Grayson's bloody death and the unalterable new timeline that had sprung up afterwards made the prospect of our unmaking all too real in my mind.

Evan narrowed his eyes at us. "Ariel was a geneticist, not a psiologist. I can believe she solved the immortality conundrum. But a poison that alters time itself? How is that even possible?"

"How do I make fire? How does he move objects with his mind?" I asked, gesturing between Liam and I. "How does Gloria's blood bring her husband back from the dead? Usuriel powers don't always make sense. Sometimes you just have to accept that they do, in fact, work. And I'm telling you, this is how my blood works. Trust me when I say, I've found out the hard way, that this particular power is very real, and very irreversible."

"This was made with your blood?" I didn't like the calculation in Evan's voice, but I didn't have time to dance around things. "Now I know you're mad. Ariel died before you were even born."

"Gracie," Vanessa tried to warn me, but panic and the knowledge that every moment wasted was a moment closer to the unmaking of my entire reality made the words come tumbling out of my mouth.

"Time isn't quite... linear with me around," I said. "It's too complicated to explain, but I'm not crazy! The Anori database talks about people like me; people who have an affinity for time. We're called fates."

"When did you find out about this?" Vanessa asked, narrowing her eye at me.

"Dad explained it after my first accident with this stuff," I gestured to the bottle of doom in Liam's hand. "I knew I had some kind of affinity for time since I was six, but it wasn't until a lot later that I really understood what was going on. But as for my blood, it was around the time James came to stay with Dad and me that Ariel asked me for some blood samples, and I agreed. Both the poison and the elixir are derived from those samples."

It was the most I'd ever explained my time travel to anyone except Dad and Liam. I watched the faces in the room as I laid my darkest secrets bare. Liam was unsurprised, of course, since I'd explained most of this to him before. James seemed thoughtful, as if his diplomat's mind was already spinning the angles to figure out how we could use this to our advantage. Vanessa was still watching me cautiously, and I could see some skepticism, but her expression also held a decent amount of calculation. Evan, on the other hand, was looking at me like I'd utterly lost my mind. I quickly addressed Vanessa for the last part of the diatribe. I had a feeling I'd win her over before the head of Riland watch.

"Don't you see? That's why I think the elixir might work as an antidote to the poison. They're from the same source. I don't even know for sure if it will work, but we have to try. Otherwise..." I glanced between Liam and James and felt my heart clench again. My mistake was going to sentence us all to death. No, worse than death. I shoved that thought away and was immediately treated to my mind's vision of what was most likely going on at the Usuriel homestead at that moment. My father's imagined screams echoed in my ears and my body suddenly felt extremely cold.

"Go get it," Evan said evenly, dark eyes burning into my own. "Bring the elixir right back here—" there was a sickening click as he cocked the pistol in his hand before aiming it squarely at James' head "—or I'll make sure we have an incident with the Terrans before I come after you."

Liam must have been straining against Vanessa's mental block for a while, because no sooner were the words out of his mouth than the familiar blue psi picked up around us and the world dissolved into streams of color.

Chapter 21

Hard Choices

I've complained about my boyfriend's teleports before. Let me just say, that was one of the most wrenching, sickening, terrifying jumps of my life. Afterward, Liam and I were both sick.

As an elder child, and not one that has ever been much for overindulgence, I don't think I'd ever actually puked before. Nausea had been an emotional response for me, not usually a physical one. When we materialized in my dorm room, however, both of us sank to our knees heaving. Nothing came up for either of us, I think, but it was one of the most painful and blindingly helpless moments of my life thus far.

I recovered first, gasping and clawing my way up the edge of the bed before staggering to my feet. I tried to get my breathing back under control as I reached unsteadily towards the closet. Thankfully, the room wasn't large, and it only took a few steps before I could lean on the wall for support while I fumbled a hand to the closet's door plate.

Behind me, I heard Liam stop retching and begin pulling himself to his feet. "I'm sorry," he gasped, voice raw and painful. "That was probably the worst 'port I've ever done."

"It's okay. We haven't eaten since breakfast, and you've been jumping every five minutes, not to mention taking twice the passengers you're used to," I told him as I slammed open the closet doors and practically dove for the back. I snatched up the little vial of Ariel's elixir, its smooth glass safe and cool in my palm, and suddenly I felt as if I could breathe again.

Then I caught sight of the remaining oblong box in the back corner of my closet. I immediately envisioned the leaf-green Ambria dress tunic inside it and felt sick panic rise again.

"Did you find it?" Liam asked, interrupting my dark thoughts. I clutched the vial to my breast and glanced over to see my boyfriend leaning heavily against my dresser. He looked awful; sweat drenched and hollow-eyed as if he'd just run the length of the training gallery fifty times. I was going to have to ask him to jump again, I realized. Guilt squirmed in my chest.

This was all my fault. Dad dying a slow and horrible death in Chronurea Valley, James held prisoner by a mortal so vicious he made most vampires seem tame by comparison, and now Liam looking as if he might do permanent damage to himself if I kept pushing him past his limits. The three people I loved best in the world, all suffering because of my stupidity.

"What do we do now?" I whispered, even though I knew the answer. I looked up at Liam as he came to his full height, his broad-shouldered figure rising easily two heads above me. I'd felt small beside him before. but at that moment it was comforting to lean into him and find my face pressed to the center of his chest. His arms came up around me, and I could feel how out of breath he still was as I hid my face in his shirt.

"How sure are you about the Temporal Mortis? I mean, could it be any other kind of poison?"

I shook my head miserably. "No. It makes too much sense. That vial looks just like this one. Even Ariel's handwriting and the codes match. And what else but a poison made for immortals could make Dad that sick that fast, even with Gloria pouring healing psi into him?" I looked into the face of the man I loved and tried to put all the honesty I could into my gaze. "I know it sounds absolutely crazy, but if you've ever trusted me, Liam, please, believe me now. Everyone we know and care about is going to be worse than dead if you don't."

"Well… then I'd say we have to get this to your dad," he said quietly, and I could hear the heartbreak in his voice. *James*, my own heart whimpered, but I knew he was right. If Dad died while we were trying to negotiate with Evan, we would all be unmade, James included. He was dead either way. Tears rushed up, but I couldn't afford the time to indulge in them. So instead, I swallowed hard and laid my palm flat against his chest, trying to focus on the steady beat of his heart to keep me grounded in the here and now. We're not dead yet, I thought.

"I'm so sorry, love," I murmured, "but we have to jump. It would take too long for me to fly."

"I know," he replied softly and rested his lips against my forehead. They were too cold, and I worried that the next jump might actually injure him. Even so, what were my choices? Liam would be as erased as I was if we didn't get to Gabriel in time. I felt his hand shaking as he tangled it in my hair, and I was fairly sure he was gathering the strength for the next teleport.

"Wait," I said quickly and slid out of his arms far enough to grab two apples and a container of nuts from a dresser drawer. I dodged to the tiny sink by the door and washed my hands thoroughly with soap before rinsing both apples. I tried not to think about my shower after Grayson's death as I watched the pink water run down the drain. Before I could dwell on the time I was wasting with this little break, I stepped back to Liam, pressing one of the fruits into my partner's hand as I quickly took a bite of the other. "We aren't any good to anyone if we're on the floor."

He gave me a look as if just the sight of food made him want to retch again.

I made a face and forced myself to swallow my bite of apple. "Seriously, half the reason you're feeling sick is because you haven't eaten in hours. We don't have the time to rest, but if I want to make it to our next destination in one piece, we need something to run off of besides adrenaline."

With a little shake of his head, Liam obediently took a bite. He chewed quickly, swallowed and raised an eyebrow before demolishing the rest of the fruit at record speed. "This has to be one of the shittiest days of my life," he said, "but damn this apple tastes amazing."

"Hunger makes everything better," I pointed out, dumping half of the nuts into his hand. The two of us were silent as we made short work of the small meal.

"Okay," he said with a nod. "I think I can make it to the homestead without passing out now."

I felt more steady myself as I stepped back into his arms. "I'm sorry I've dragged you into all this," I said, trying to keep my composure. I just had to keep it together a little longer, I told myself. Even so, the guilt was crushing.

He caught my chin with one hand and tilted my face up to his as his other one came around my waist, pulling me tightly against him. "If this has been a hard day for me, it has to be something out of a nightmare for you. Honestly, Gracie, I don't know how you aren't over in the corner sobbing. I would be. But that's you. Tough as alloy until everything's over with." The corner of his mouth quirked higher, coming as close to a smile as I'd seen all day. "Come on, let's go take care of your Dad, and then we'll come up with a plan to get James back. Once we're all safe again, we can both have a full-on meltdown. I promise."

I swallowed hard and nodded. This time, his teleport felt much more solid.

***

"You just missed them!"

Those were the first words out of Grandfather's mouth as he strode rapidly across his living room, a sleeping Ileesia held carefully against his chest. Liam and I had materialized in my grandparents' dining room, the wooden table and chairs at our back as we faced the living area. Outside, the sun had fully set, and the house was lit with the gentle glow of two floor lamps on either side of my grandparents' sitting room.

"What do you mean?" I asked D'nay with a frown, stepping out of Liam's arms to face the distraught-looking vampire.

"Gabe took a turn for the worse." My grandfather's face was grim. "Gloria was losing him, so she teleported them down to Stella's core. She seems to think merging with the AI's generators will give her the strength to buy him some time."

My whole insides froze at his words. I knew what death by Temporal Mortis looked like. If Gloria felt the need to merge with Stella, my father had to be in extreme distress. Horror and guilt chased each other through my guts, but I shoved them down. Like Liam had said, we couldn't afford to lose it right now.

"Why didn't she take him to the hospital?" Liam asked, "Dax and the other healers are there, and Stella has generators in that basement too, doesn't she?"

D'nay gave us a worried frown. "Haven't you been on the net? There are riots all over Cybele. The hospital was one of the first targets. Last I knew, it was still on fire."

"Fates save us." Liam sounded as terrified as I felt. I put a steadying hand on his arm and turned back to D'nay. We would have time to worry about the political situation once we weren't all about to be erased from history.

"Where's the merge interface?" I asked quickly. "We've only been to the core once, and I didn't see one when we were in the control room with Vanessa."

"There's an outside entrance. It's just through that door. I'll give Liam a reference."

"Thank you."

"Please tell me you have the antidote," D'nay said, nodding, stepping closer to Liam, and meeting his eye. My partner got that focused look that meant he was reading the image Grandfather was providing. "I've never seen Gabe this sick. And I remember his heart transplant quite clearly, so that's saying something."

Mortal dread was beginning to feel uncomfortably familiar. I pulled the vial out of my pocket for him to see. "If this isn't it, we're all in real trouble," I said honestly, "but I'm pretty sure it should work."

"Go, then," D'nay said, those Family-blue eyes a little too wide as he met my gaze. I'd never seen my grandfather really afraid before. A whole new level of panic tried to rise, but instead of giving in to it, I backed up until I was pressed tightly against Liam's side. He wrapped strong arms around me as Grandpa watched us with silent urgency. "Quickly."

Liam teleported without another word.

Chapter 22

Consequences

Now comes the hard part.

Up until this point, things were bad, but reversible. If I'd been able to give Dad the antidote right then, I'm fairly certain he and Gloria would have sorted things out with the uncompromising efficiency and fair-minded justice that had been the hallmark of Cybele society since the launching of the *Inspiration*. How much we as a people had relied upon their strength and consciences, I don't think anyone quite realized up until that point.

Perhaps if Liam had been a touch stronger and able to teleport rapid-fire through our destinations rather than forcing us to pause for a break, we would have caught them at the homestead and things would have turned out differently. Perhaps if we'd gone back to Evan to negotiate before heading to the core, everything might not have spiraled so badly out of control. Perhaps if I hadn't been an easily manipulated, fiery-tempered little idiot, I wouldn't have stabbed my father in the first place and caused all these problems to begin with.

Oh, hindsight. You shining, clear thing of beauty.

Suffice to say, that is not how it happened.

Liam's teleport was getting rockier again, but we managed to arrive in the clearing next to the computer core complex in one piece. My head hadn't even stopped swimming when I realized we were in trouble, however.

First of all, my boyfriend staggered as we landed and had he not already been tightly pressed against my steadying weight I think he would have sunk to his knees again. Even in the dim moonlight I could see that his face was too pale.

"Liam?" I said his name with low urgency as I turned in his arms and put my hands out to catch him in case he fell.

"It's not me," he said, recovering his footing with a shake of his head. "We need to get that antidote in there now. Gabe's in real trouble."

Another wave of fear washed over me as I realized he was reacting to my father's echo pain, not the disorientation of too many teleports. Taking a gasping breath in an attempt to steady myself, I grabbed Liam's hand and started charging towards the small alloy door in the hillside that led into the computer core.

We had only taken a few strides when Liam said, "Gracie, I don't think we're alone." A wave of headlights and the wind of several incoming hover vessels verified my boyfriend's statement. The noise of their landing was drowned out by a rumbling peal of thunder. I didn't turn around.

"You must think I'm incredibly stupid."

Evan's voice caught me up short only a few meters away from the door. I didn't have time to worry about the damn mortal watch, however, so the pause was only momentary. With renewed determination, I all but dragged Liam with me towards the core.

The sound of half a dozen safeties being released, followed quickly by the same number of rounds being chambered into decent-sized rifles finally made me freeze in my tracks. The elixir won't do Dad any good if it's splattered across the door to the core, I told myself. Why, oh, why did today have to be the day we finally ran into the rumored psi-proof guns?

"Typical arrogant Usuriel bitch," Evan said. I heard him cock his own pistol as Liam and I turned to face him. The sight that greeted us made my flames leap up in my chest like a wild beast.

James was slightly taller than the head of the Riland watch, but he still looked incredibly young and afraid as Evan pointed his gun at the back of his head. Vanessa stood behind Evan's left shoulder, glowering at the proceedings as if she disapproved of the whole situation. On either side of them, six mortal watchmen in Riland brown aimed at Liam and me with those same over-powered rifles we'd seen used on Martin's makers. I tried very hard not to envision the red ruin the vampiress' chests had been after their encounter with those guns. The headlights of the hover vehicles they'd just stepped out of cast dramatic shadows across the clearing and turned my night vision into streaming spots.

"Running around doing whatever you please regardless of the consequences to the mortals around you." Evan tilted his head at James. "If this is how you treat your friends, I'm glad I'm not one of them."

"Evan, honestly, you have to let us go," Liam said. There was anguish in his eyes as he looked at the barely contained terror on James' face. They'd really loved each other once, that tiny, calm corner of my mind thought. A flash of lightning lit up the entire clearing, followed by an ominous roll of thunder.

"Please," I added my voice to Liam's, pitching it to carry over the still-grumbling sky. "We're running out of time! I know you don't want to believe me, but it's true! If Dad dies, we're all going to vanish without a trace!"

"I don't think you understand," Evan snapped. "I'm not here to negotiate with you. I'm here to let you know that I don't make idle threats. I promised you a Terran incident if you didn't come back with that vial. So here it is."

"No!"

Liam and I shouted it at the same time, but it was Vanessa who was close enough to grab his arm and force it away from James' head as Evan pulled the trigger. Unfortunately, she was quite a bit shorter than the head of Riland watch and despite her significant advantage in strength, the angle of his arm was bad for her reach. She managed to angle the pistol away from James' head, but there was still an explosion of red as the gun went off. The force actually spun James around, a guttural cry torn from his lips as he collapsed to the ground, his right shoulder torn apart in a shower of blood and fragments of bone.

I'm an elder child. I'm fast. With my fire unleashed, I'm even faster.

This time Liam beat me.

I was on his heels as my partner swooped down on our fallen friend in a blaze of blue psi. With one hand he pulled James to his breast while he angled himself to shield the diplomat from Evan with his own body. His psi barrier rose up, reflexively more than purposefully, I think, since clearly Vanessa would have used her psi to stop the bullet if it hadn't been resistant to their telekinesis.

I made it to James' side a heartbeat later, falling to my knees next to them. One hand steadied myself on Liam's shoulder while the other went to James' writhing form, helping my partner pull him into the shelter of his arms. There was blood everywhere, soaking into the knees of my pants and coating my hands for the second time that day.

For a breath that lasted a lifetime, the image of James' helpless, bloody figure seared itself into my flesh, scarring itself into the very marrow of my bones.

Evan's voice shattered my frozen thoughts. "Bitch, what is wrong with you? Are you trying to get your people killed?"

"This has gone far enough, Evan. Convincing Gracie to give up the elixir is one thing, but if you think I'm going to let you waltz around slaughtering innocent people..."

"Let me? Fuck, Vanessa, you just did it *for* me earlier tonight. I've seen a lot of dangerous vamps, and I somehow don't think little Martin qualified. Don't act like your hands are clean in this."

By this point, I'd followed James' own example from earlier and pulled off my jacket to put pressure on his shoulder wound. His breath was hissing through his teeth and he'd buried his head in Liam's chest, his good hand tangled in his ex-lover's shirt. The harsh lighting painted the blood covering his chest and shoulder a patchwork of red and black. Thunder rolled in the electrically charged air.

Grayson, Dad, James—the list of people I'd watched bleed out was getting disturbingly long and, somehow or other, they all seemed to be my fault. My emotions, already stretched to their breaking point, gave up and left my head an empty, buzzing white as I tried not to look at the agony on James' face. It didn't stop his pained whimpers from tearing holes in my chest and gut.

"Hang on, James, it's not that bad," Liam lied, leaning his forehead against the diplomat's as he kept up a low, steady stream of quiet encouragement. "Gracie and I have you. Everything's going to be okay if you just focus on my voice."

As if from a long distance, I heard Evan and 'Nessa bickering as if a man wasn't dying at their feet. "Martin killed people. In a strict interpretation of the law, he was guilty," Vanessa said, sounding like she was trying to convince herself more than Evan, "but James has never hurt anyone. Hell, he's a diplomat. He's the definition of a civilian. No, I've put up with a lot from you the last few months, but this crosses a line. I won't be an accessory to crimes against the charter."

Evan's voice dripped with contempt. "Oh, stop with the attempt to grow a conscience. You're going to shut up and put up with whatever I say and we both know it. Now, get that vial from Gracie before I have to put a bullet in her other boyfriend. Or should I say cousin? Either way, I'm sure they're fucking. You people are completely disgusting."

While 'Nessa and the head of Riland watch argued, Liam glanced up at me with eyes that were more deadly serious than I'd ever seen from him. "Run, Gracie," he whispered, his free hand coming up to take over for me at James' shoulder. "Get to your dad."

I took a ragged breath, my heart hammering so hard I felt as if everyone present must hear it. I looked at Evan and Vanessa, but they were pretty well engaged in their argument. All those mortal watchmen were still aiming at me with those huge rifles, however, so rather than leap into the air and possibly draw their fire towards Liam and James, I stood slowly and began to back away from my boys.

To say that leaving James bleeding on the ground was difficult is not even close to the emotional reality of the action. In a day full of traumatic and shattering moments, that one ranks as one of the most wrenching. The fact that Liam was still next to him, staunching the wound but also offering his vulnerable back as an easy target for half a dozen psi-proof gunmen, only made it exponentially worse. The only thing that kept me moving was a combination of my father's suffering only a few meters away and the knowledge that when I did pull on my fire it would draw the gunmen away from my exposed boys at their feet.

A gust of wet wind dampened my face and made my curls stick to my neck.

My fingers found the vial in my pocket and slid it into my hand. Without even thinking, I pressed it against my chest, holding it like a talisman to ward off the impending cataclysm that I knew could strike at any moment. I clung to it as I forced myself to make every movement smooth and slow until I was far enough away from my boys to be sure any stray fire wouldn't hit them.

"Oh, no you don't." Evan looked away from Vanessa just before I leaped into the air. A heartbeat away from my mad dash, 'Nessa's attention turned to me as well, and I felt the warm rush of her psi as the elixir faded from my fingers and materialized in her hand.

"'Nessa! No!" I cried, lunging forward with my hand extended, fully intending to snatch the vial away from her.

The boom of one of the rifles startled me, and it was without thinking that I moved between the sound and Liam's exposed back, my fire coming up like a curtain around us. It wasn't a psi shield and it wasn't impervious to bullets, but at least the watchmen couldn't see Liam and James to take aim with my flames in the way.

Fortunately for me, the watchman who fired wasn't a very good shot. His bullet did nothing more than raise a cloud of dirt near where I'd been standing. My flames, on the other hand, were close enough to the mortals that even Vanessa and Evan took a step back.

"Hold your fire," Evan snapped at his troops. Then his dark eyes flashed to me. "Same goes for you. Unless you want me to simply let them execute the three of you."

Obediently, the mortal watchmen aimed their guns upwards. Glancing between them and Evan's expectant expression, I slowly eased down my flames as well.

"Vanessa," Liam's voice behind me was quiet but urgent, "why are you doing this? I get him—"my boyfriend flashed an angry glare over his shoulder at Evan"—but you're one of us. You know Gabriel didn't really murder anyone. Not in cold blood, anyway. He may not be completely innocent, but he doesn't deserve to die like this. I know you can hear him as well as I can. Even if you don't believe Gracie about the poison, why are you letting him suffer?"

Vanessa looked at the vial in her hand. Another flash of lightning lit her face clearly and her expression was extremely sad. "Because if I don't do as Evan says, he'll kill your family, Liam," she said quietly, but I heard her clearly before the roll of thunder drowned out James' choked sobs. Then her eye met my gaze, and even though the icy blue was hidden by the harsh light, I felt its chill all the way down to my core. "I'm sorry, Gracie. I didn't know what that poison was when I used it. Honestly, we still don't know for sure what it is. You're making a lot of assumptions and the truth is, without Ariel to tell us, there's no way to know for certain what will happen when Gabriel dies." She took a deep, sorrowful breath. "But I do know exactly what will happen if I don't give Evan what he wants. His people have a dirty bomb planted in New Paradise. They'll trigger it if the Overwatch doesn't go along with the Riland watch. Over a hundred Family men, women, and children will die."

"A dirty bomb?" I echoed, confused. "Like… radiation dirty?"

"More like a biological weapon," Evan explained. "A more permanent solution to the Usuriel problem. I'm a watchman, not a scientist, but the way they explained it, there are a few key DNA sequences that the virus targets. It shouldn't affect mortals even if your people do bring it over to the mainland. Which I personally find comforting, since I've been told it's a very painful death."

"If you take that, you won't be mortal anymore," Liam pointed out, nodding to the vial. "It's made with Usuriel DNA as the main ingredient, so the virus would go after you just as easily as it does us."

"Perhaps." Evan shrugged and held out a hand for the elixir. "But either way, I have access to the vaccine. Senator Stafford isn't an idiot. He knew we needed a bargaining chip, and if we manage to come to a peaceful solution to this problem, I'm sure you can negotiate access as well. However, either way it falls for the Family, I won't have to worry about it."

"Vanessa," I gasped, "why haven't you sent someone to disarm the thing?"

"Because I can't." She sounded utterly resigned, and I wondered just how long she had been dealing with Evan and Garret Stafford's threats.

"It's a double blind plant." Evan was obviously proud of this idea. I could hear it in the smugness of his tone. "No one knows where the bomb is, not even me. The person who placed it doesn't even know what it is. All I know is that my order unseals the firing mechanism. Once that order is given, there is no turning back. The person actually detonating the device doesn't know what his actions are doing, either. Good luck figuring out something no one actually knows, my dear telepaths."

Vanessa gave me a helpless look and handed Evan the vial.

My chest froze.

He accepted the elixir and uncorked it, peering into the vial with one eyebrow raised.

"If you believe me about the immortality elixir, why don't you believe me about the poison?" I hissed at him, holding my flames in check by the barest of threads. My body was trembling, and the white numbness was screaming in my ears, but somehow I was still standing, my body a wedge between Evan and my boys. My red curls tossed about in the growing wind, even as fat drops of rain ran icy fingers down my neck. "I'm not lying. You're going to get all of us killed... worse than killed."

The head of Riland's watch squinted at me with thinly veiled contempt. "Because clearly stabbing your father has completely unhinged your mind. Time poison? Really? You're as crazy as Adora was. All of you get to that point. For some it takes longer than others, but in the end, it's the Usuriel way—arrogant, unstable, and strong enough to burn buildings down with a thought. Somewhere, a perverse god has to be laughing." He shook his head in utter disgust. "Well, I for one am not going to cower in fear anymore."

And with that, he drank the vial in one swallow.

I didn't have the strength to lunge for him or shout a warning. I felt hollow, pithed, as if everything that mattered in the world was slipping through my fingers like smoke in the wind. I watched through a fuzzy, white haze as Evan doubled, dropping the vial to the ground. Golden light rushed up around him.

A sudden blast of light and wind, as if a huge amount of psi had just gone off, lifted my hair and made my eyes sting and water. I put up a hand to shield my face.

In that moment of confusion, when golden light was streaming over the entire clearing, the line of Liam's back leaned against my legs and suddenly the world bled away into blue motes.

Chapter 23

Daughter of Sorrow

I was falling from a great height in the darkness. All around me, it pressed inwards, crushing my chest until I couldn't breathe, couldn't see, couldn't think. Was this the end, my brain wondered. Was this what it felt like to be unmade?

And then, suddenly, air.

My starved lungs sucked it in desperately as I fell to all fours, the solid wooden floor of Angelus Quetum's living room cool and safe under my palms. I gasped and wiped at my face, tears streaming down my cheeks, though I managed not to retch this time.

"Gracie?" Liam sounded utterly winded, his voice raw and low behind me.

My brain felt as if it were moving through a thick, viscous fluid. I turned slowly to look at Liam over my shoulder and saw that he was staggering to his feet with James still in his arms. The diplomat looked incoherent with pain, high keening gasps escaping his lips as he twisted in my partner's arms. His right arm hung uselessly against his side. I didn't move as Liam shoved one of the small tables out of the way and ungracefully laid our injured friend down on the couch.

"A little help over here would be nice," he hissed at me, exhausted eyes flashing some Usuriel temper in my direction.

Slowly, I shook my head. "What's the point?" I whispered. "We're all dead anyway."

"Excuse me?" Liam and James had been my steady, encouraging companions all day. Through this nightmare excuse for a run, I hadn't heard a single complaint from either one of them. Now, though, Liam looked pissed. If I'd had any energy left to empathize, I would have. If I were him, I'd be pretty damn mad at me, too. As it was, I stared at him with a blank, hollow-eyed expression as the ringing numbness made every breath echo as if from a long distance away.

"Get up," my partner growled, eyes boring into my own. James gave another gasping cry, and Liam glanced down at the diplomat before returning his glare to me. "Get over here right now, Gracie Usuriel!"

If he hadn't taken such a commanding tone, I doubt I would have had the strength to do as he said. As it was, my limbs moved of their own accord as I stumbled to my feet and stood next to the couch.

"Look at him," Liam snapped, venom dripping from his tone. "This isn't a faceless stranger! This is James—our James! The one you were so in love with that you put me off for six months! Or don't you remember that part?"

I cringed at his anger, that icy numbness cracking like a fragile frost. Underneath I glimpsed an echoing depth of grief and despair so deep I couldn't see the bottom of it. If I slid into that abyss I would surely drown. After today, perhaps that wouldn't be such a bad thing.

"He's still breathing, Gracie." Liam didn't sound like he had the energy to yell anymore, but his tone was urgent. "He's still alive. Do you want to keep him that way or not? Because if you don't start moving, it's not an 'if' question about what's going to happen."

It's not an "if" question about what's going to happen either way, I thought. But the intensity of Liam's anger did manage to penetrate my inertia enough to let my brain latch onto the immediate situation. I blinked hard, trying to shut out the dark wave of doom long enough for my OW first aid training to kick in.

"Okay," I breathed, gripping the back of the couch to keep my balance before heading towards the linen closet.

"Where are you going?" Liam called. I could hear James' cries increasing in volume, and the old sofa creaking as his body twisted away from the painful, but life-saving, pressure Liam was putting on his shattered shoulder.

"To get some antiseptic," I muttered, using the words to keep myself grounded even though I knew Liam probably couldn't hear my answer, "and some blankets and towels. We have to keep him warm or he'll go into shock."

Going through the house looking for what I needed was surreal. I kept expecting to look up and see Dad around every corner as I went into the bathroom to grab the soap. As I passed my OW portrait, I had to clamp down hard on the urge to rip it from the wall. My hands were too full, and James' condition too serious for me to indulge in such childishness. But believe me when I say, I wanted to.

Liam's hand fell from his implant as I walked into the room. "Jillian and Leesil aren't answering my taps," he said. "I even tried Landing's emergency line, but no one's picking up."

"Fates. Well, that might be a good thing. Emergency services would just give our location to Vanessa," I snapped. "Sit him up," My hands moved rapidly, pouring the soap into a basin and soaking a washrag in the water as Liam levered James into a seated position on the couch. I was grateful to my partner for goading me into action, because my brain felt blissfully empty as long as I was doing something. I wasn't even shaking as I pulled James'

torn and bloodstained shirt away from the wound and pressed the soapy rag into the jagged hole.

"I thought you were supposed to elevate a person's feet if they had blood loss," Liam commented, one hand on the back of James' neck, the other offering the diplomat's good arm some support. For his part, James bit down on a scream as the soap burned into his exposed flesh.

"I don't want to send the couch up when I cauterize this," I replied evenly, keeping my vision and attention focused completely on the task at hand.

"Cauterize it? His collar bone is shattered. He could lose the use of that arm."

"Better than losing his life," I retorted, "and unless you have the strength to jump us to a healer, it's the best I can do."

"I'm not sure I could jump across the room right now," Liam sighed, "and with the hospital on fire, I have a feeling Dax isn't going to answer my tap."

"It's okay." Both of us glanced at James. His voice was breathless and raw, and he leaned so heavily against Liam I was fairly sure he wouldn't be able to sit up on his own. I think Liam and I had assumed he wasn't lucid enough to follow our conversation. But his eyes were open now, and his expression, though pained, was alert. "I'm a Terran. We don't have the same technological taboos as the Provinces. Once I go home, they can repair any damage Gracie does to my shoulder. Just get the bleeding stopped."

"Okay," I agreed quickly, trying not to think about how much this was about to hurt him, "Hold him still, Liam." I flashed an apologetic look at James. "Sorry in advance."

"Just do it," he whispered, pressing his forehead against Liam's torso and taking a firmer grip on his arm.

I'd never called my flames on living flesh before. I'd used the fire to enhance a punch or blast someone back, but I'd never aimed directly at muscle, bone, and skin to set it alight. I can honestly say, it isn't an experience I would care to repeat.

Afterwards, James was violently ill before all but passing out in Liam's arms. I tore up enough sheets and towels to bind his shoulder tightly, but at least the burned flesh kept the wound from continuing to leak his life away.

Almost a year ago at the Family party, I'd seen Liam pick up and carry my passed out father with very little effort. I think it said something about how tired my boyfriend was that he staggered as he carried the semi-conscious diplomat to my father's bed. It was the largest one in the house, and I think Liam shared my instinct to give a little extra room to our injured friend.

While he settled James under several spare blankets and the heavy comforter on the bed, I raided my father's bathroom cabinets for painkillers. For a drug addict, there wasn't a whole lot. It was both a relief and a frustration that the strongest thing my father had in his cabinet was acetaminophen.

"This is all we have," I sighed, bringing the bottle out for Liam's inspection.

"He's probably better off with whatever liquor you can find," was my partner's resigned reply.

I looked down at James. He was shivering, but his eyes weren't open, and little bright spots of color in the center of his cheeks were the only indication that he had any blood left in his body at all.

"I don't think he could keep anything down right now anyway," I said and sat down heavily on the other side of the bed. I looked at Liam and didn't like the shade of his complexion a hell of a lot more than I did James'. "Why don't you come sit down before you pass out on me, too."

My partner slowly shook his head, a lost look in his eyes as he hugged himself and stared down at James.

"Fates, Gracie," he murmured. "How did we end up here?"

"Liam—" The guilt I'd managed to hold at bay while we took care of James came slamming down on me again, and I buried my face in my hands, leaving bloody smears against my cheeks. The rest of what I meant to say came out in a gasping sob. "I'm not Gabriel's daughter. That was Ariel. No, I'm Sorrow's." I held out my blood-stained hands to him. "Do you understand the difference? Everything I touch turns to ashes. Everything I love dies."

"Gracie—" Liam moved towards me, but I recoiled, my body convulsing with the weight of what I'd done and its consequences.

"Don't touch me!" I cried, twisting my shoulders away from him. I heard more than saw him hesitate a hand's breadth from where I sat. I let the tears come, then, because I couldn't stop them. They blended with James' blood on my face and made it a hot, sticky mess.

Liam waited a moment, making sure I wasn't going to lash out at him again. Then his hand slowly found my shoulder. When I didn't pull away, he gently sat beside me and pulled me into his arms. I leaned into him, unable to find the strength to reject his comfort. Then James made a small sound of pain from the other side of the bed, and I forced myself to shy away from Liam's safe arms.

"No, no, this is what I warned you about to begin with," I sobbed. "I'm dangerous! Fates, if I haven't already unmade us, I'm going to find a way to get you killed anyway. Don't you see? You need to take James and get away from me."

He didn't listen. Instead, my lover took my face in both of his hands and kissed my forehead, his large, warm thumbs brushing away the tears and blood from my cheeks.

"You made a mistake. Admitted, it's a pretty damn big one. But you aren't the only one who is guilty here. Gabriel should have told you about your mother. Vanessa should have, too. You certainly didn't poison that knife. And you sure as hell didn't shoot James. So what are you really guilty of? Believing the people around you who are supposed to be your superiors and friends? Trying to do your job? At worst, you can cite an Usuriel temper, but that's a Family flaw none of us can completely avoid." He kissed my forehead again and pulled me back against his chest. His shirt was still damp with James' blood, but I didn't care. All my protests worn out, I clung to him as if he were the last solid thing in my world. I'm pretty sure he was.

"What are we going to do?" I whispered, body tense despite the fact that my head was now tucked into the space between his chin and shoulder. "Dad's still dying. We can't just wait around to be unmade."

Liam sighed and glanced at the door to Dad's bathroom. "I don't know that we can do much for Gabriel right now. Hopefully Gloria is right, and her merge with Stella will buy him some time while we come up with a plan. But before I can think straight, I need a shower and some food."

I looked at him like he was crazy to be thinking about such mundane things at a time like this. But the more I tried to think of something else that might help Dad, the more my empty stomach clenched, and my head let me know that it wasn't happy with being denied food for so long. Its dull ache, plus the disgusting feeling of drying blood on my pant legs, finally convinced me to go along with Liam's plan.

So, Liam and I took turns watching James and showering before I went into the kitchen to find something to eat. I brought back the usual cold meat and cheese sandwiches that were a staple in my father's house. I don't think the two of us said a word as we sat on the bed and devoured every scrap of beef and bread I'd managed to scrounge up.

I tried to wake James enough to eat something, but he lost even more color just looking at the offerings. I did manage to get some fruit juice, a double dose of the mild painkillers, and a few bites of bread into him before he turned an even more sickly shade of green and refused any more. I decided not to push things and resettled the pillows around him before letting him fade back into the half-sleeping daze he seemed to be hovering in.

By that point, I'd taken a few of the mild painkillers myself, and between them and the food, my headache was starting to fade. In fact, I felt more clear-headed than I had since I ran into James and Officer Coffing that morning. Sick dread still sat like a lump of molten alloy in my chest, and I think some part of me was still waiting to be unmade at any moment. But clean, well fed, and in familiar surroundings, I found my brain suddenly able to process the situation a lot more clearly.

"Liam," I said slowly as I sat beside James on the bed. Liam had stretched out his long frame along my other side, and his eyes were closed, though I was fairly sure he wasn't asleep. Being sandwiched between the two boys on the big bed took me back to nights of research in James' room at University. If I pretended I was back there, my heart rate actually dropped a little, and I felt once again like I could think more clearly.

"Hmmm?" My partner sounded exhausted. I tangled a hand in his hair and realized it was the longest I'd ever seen him wear it. It still wasn't past his ears, but the dark strands did fall across his forehead in an appealing way.

"I think I need to go back. Time jump, I mean. If I go back to earlier today, I should be able to convince myself not to go through with the execution order," I said.

Liam's eyes opened, and he gave me a thoughtful frown. "Didn't you try that with Grayson? You said it didn't work."

"I tried it after he died," I pointed out. "Not when the poison was still going through his system. I think if I'd time jumped then, it might have worked. But I was still figuring out the time travel thing at that point and didn't even think about it as a possibility until he was already dead. Which meant the timeline was already altered, and I couldn't get back to the original."

"This stuff is enough to make my head hurt," Liam complained, rubbing an eye. Fed and clean, it seemed my partner was having a hard time staying awake. He'd teleported enough times today, I thought, plus some heavy lifting. Between that and the emotional roller coaster, I couldn't blame him for being tired. "But... okay. So you're saying that because your dad's still alive, the timeline hasn't been altered yet. Which means you can still go back and fix things?"

"I think so. I mean, if I can... I have to at least try," I said. "I think it might be a little dangerous, though. I've never tried it completely on my own. Without Ariel as a guide... I don't know how much control I will have. I've almost put myself into shock with it before. I was a lot younger, but even so, I felt like I should warn you before I attempted anything."

Liam's somber gaze moved over my face. "So, I guess I should stay up and keep an eye on you while you try this thing?"

"Most likely a good idea. Though if it works, hopefully I'll be waking up in your arms in the dormitory instead of here." I ran my fingers through my hair and caught myself doing it. I suddenly had a vision of Dad writhing in agony down in the core that was so real I could almost see the black lines of Temporal Mortis climbing up his torso. Quickly, I tried to refocus on the image of Liam and I safely in my bed back at University. There, I told myself, if you do this right, you can be back there tonight.

"Okay," Liam said. "Do you think it would be safe enough for me to go get some tea? If I'm going to be up for any length of time, I'm going to need some caffeine."

"I don't think that would be a problem," I said, "But I'm not waiting on water to boil. Every second we spend talking about this is one more that my dad spends suffering."

"Good luck, then," Liam said.

I nodded and laid back on the empty side of the bed. Liam stepped away, eyes cautious as if he weren't sure how safe it was to be close to me when I made the jump. I didn't think it would be hazardous, but I wasn't completely sure so I didn't say anything. Instead, I glanced over at James. His face was pale except for those little spots of flush in his cheeks, his eyes closed and his breathing ragged.

Dad and James, I thought. The first two men I ever loved. Both of them were riding on my shoulders now.

I closed my eyes and envisioned Angelus Quietum as it had been earlier in the day. I could see it clearly, the afternoon light streaming in the windows as I walked through the living room with that thrice-be-damned knife.

I reached towards that moment and pulled on the flames.

The world fell away under me, bending and twisting in a riot of color.

Chapter 24

Paradox

Cool air slid over my skin, and I opened my eyes.

Afternoon light poured in the windows of my father's house, painting the furniture around me in soft gold tones. I was on the ground laying next to the couch, I realized, turning my head the other direction so that I could see the fireplace. There was no blood or bile from this evening's misadventures splattered across the floor, so I knew I'd managed some kind of a time jump.

Then, the light outside flickered, and I caught what sounded like a snippet of conversation echoing from a long way away. Frowning, I pushed myself to a sitting position.

The sight that greeted me was unlike anything I'd ever seen.

There were a dozen people in the room, but they weren't solid. I could see through them just like ghosts, their transparent bodies flickering and glowing as they moved through Angelus Quietum. However, unlike the ghosts I was familiar with, these didn't seem to stay much longer than a few seconds; they appeared just long enough to make out familiar features and perhaps an activity before they flickered into nothingness again.

There were dozens of Gabriels. Sitting by the fire, reading on the couch, hanging pictures on the wall, pulling on a jacket or shirt.

A little redheaded girl came running around the corner, and I realized I was looking at a seven-year-old me. She laughed and ran up to one of the versions of Dad, giving him a quick hug around the waist before dashing off to disappear into the kitchen. He smiled after her, face amused and indulgent, before he too faded out with a flicker of light.

I took a step around the couch and nearly jumped back as I heard a sob. Directly beside me on the sofa, Dad and I sat, clinging to each other. I was grown this time, looking almost the same age as Gabriel. My hands and arms were splattered with blood, and my face was red from crying. Dad looked concerned but steady, and I heard his voice for just a moment before the two of us dissolved into sparkling embers.

"How many pictures are in this room?"

A terrible crash from the kitchen drew my attention, and I took a step farther into the house. A little girl of perhaps nine with white hair and Usuriel features flickered to life, her slim body pressed against the wall with her hands clapped over her ears. I suddenly heard raised voices from the kitchen, my father's and a woman's.

"How much sooner would you have been home if you hadn't gone out with your fucking sister?"

"Leave it be, Lauria," Gabriel snapped. He didn't slur, but I could hear the drink in his voice. "Fates, you wonder why I don't want to come home! It's like being ambushed!"

"If you didn't always come home drunk, I wouldn't yell!"

I heard Lillian stifle a sob before she and her parents' fight faded away.

I stepped into the kitchen to the sound of another piece of ceramic shattering. This time, my father was alone by the counter. He'd dropped a tea mug but didn't seem to be paying it much attention, his shoulders tense as he paused, trying to take a deeper breath. It seemed rather unsuccessful, since the next thing he did was unbutton the top of his shirt and try again, hand pressing against the center of his chest as if it were the source of his distress.

"Dad?" I heard my own voice outside on the step and sure enough, twelve-year-old me burst through the door. "Dad? Are you okay?"

Before my father could answer, both figures flickered and disappeared into nothing.

The sound of a cup being set down on the table behind me made me turn. However, instead of my father, Lauria, or myself, I saw another redheaded woman who looked strangely familiar.

"Olivia?" I murmured, watching the ghostly figure set the table as if it were the most normal and natural thing in the world. She didn't look old, as I knew she would have been after landing on Cybele. In fact, she didn't look past her early thirties, her hair untouched by gray and her freckled complexion unlined. She set four places, I noticed. Then she looked over her shoulder and smiled.

"Hello, love," she said as my father came up behind her and wrapped his arms around her waist.

"Dinner should be ready soon," he commented, laying a kiss on the top of her head. "Should I call the kids in?" I caught a glimpse of his eyes, and the soft contentment in them made me feel as if I'd never met this Gabriel before.

She turned in his arms and gazed at him with a gentleness that was almost too intimate to look at. "How soon is soon?" she asked, flashing him a mischievous grin before taking his face in her hands and kissing him. "The kids seem pretty happy out there at the moment."

His smile deepened into something sensual, and he glanced over at the oven. "I could put it on low for a while..."

The two of them flickered out, fading into thin air just like the rest.

Through all of this, I felt ephemeral, faint, almost as if I were one of the flickering ghosts who slid through my childhood home. The one I hadn't seen, but knew must be here, was Ariel. With a frown, I put a hand to the door plate for the back door. It unlocked with a click and pushed open for me easily. I walked onto the porch.

Figures. Hundreds of them. Dad, Lauria, Lillian, myself, Adora, Gloria, D'nay—even James and Liam— they all flickered and slid in and out of solidity around the grounds of Angelus Quietum: James and Dad by the lake having a lesson while I did my martial arts beside them; Lauria pushing a small Lillian on a swing; Dad hauling firewood; Me, riding on Charcoal; Adora appearing in a cloud of blue sparks. There were too many to count.

With a frown, I noticed several individuals I didn't recognize. Olivia appeared again, holding the hand of a small girl with red curls. A boy a few years older with dark hair and green eyes appeared directly on their heels before the three of them flickered out. Then I caught sight of those two children again, slightly older this time, chasing each other across the grass as they laughed and shot colorful sparks at each other.

I startled when suddenly Liam appeared and trotted up the stairs directly through my body. I backed away from him, fetching up against the door, before he disappeared as abruptly as all the others. I stood in the doorway, hand braced against its cool solidity, trying to wrap my brain around what was going on.

Were these ghosts? Echoes of other times? Certainly the episodes of my own past seemed to suggest that. If that was the case, where was I? In between moments? Somehow outside of linear time? How did I find the moment I was looking for, and when I did, how did I interact with it? None of these figures seemed even remotely aware of me, even when they ran straight through my body.

At just that moment, the door behind me slid open, and a very solid-looking version of me stood there with burning blue eyes. I turned at the movement and stood there, staring at myself from inches away with an incredible feeling of sick dread rising in my guts.

It hadn't been Ariel in the doorway.

It was me.

I met my own gaze, so full of deadly rage I'd had no right to level in my father's direction. How did I make my past self understand? Before I could speak, however, she lowered her head and charged through me.

"Stay out of my way."

I felt her burning fury as she passed, white-hot and blinding. I wanted to grab her and shake her; to punch her in the face and tell her to sit down before she got everyone killed; to throw myself between her and Gabriel before she could make the biggest mistake of our lives.

"Don't do this."

And then she was past, sliding down the steps two at a time, all that Family grace making her move like liquid muscle.

"Gracie?"

I heard my father's voice as he stepped out of the barn. My heart clenched, and I belatedly dashed after her—me, fear lending my feet speed as I caught up to where she was approaching Gabriel's unsuspecting figure. I watched my prior self carefully measuring the strides, angling her shoulder down and back to give her thrust enough power to take out his heart in one blow. That little flick of a wrist was so elegant, so smooth, almost like breathing in its casualness, and suddenly the blade was in her hand.

"Is there something wrong, sweetheart? Shouldn't you be in class right now?"

"Dad, run! Get away!" I shouted as I lunged for my past self, trying desperately to gain a hold on her arm before she could finish the fatal movement. What would happen if she pierced his heart with a Temporal Mortis tainted blade? Would the death by massive trauma prevent the poison's effects from taking hold? Or would everyone just be unmade in one, split-second blink of an eye?

It didn't matter, I decided, as I grabbed a hold of her wrist, focusing all my strength and will on being corporeal enough to prevent the catastrophic stroke. I knew one person who wouldn't survive that heart strike and, after everything, I just couldn't offer Gabriel up to that cruel knife. My flames rose up, seeming to lend my hand a measure of solidity.

Suddenly, another set of hands slid next to mine, landing in my past self's elbow. A third set grabbed her forearm, and together the three of us pulled back, fighting against the deadly momentum of her blow.

She was strong. I could feel the fire of her anger giving her strength, making her impossible to stop completely. Even so, we skewed the angle of the blade so that it no longer drove straight at his heart but instead landed in the muscular flesh of his side.

"Gracie…"

I heard his pained gasp and closed my eyes, my hand sliding away from my former self's wrist. I'd failed to change the timeline. But that meant…

"You killed my mother, you bastard."

I didn't have to open my eyes to know what happened next. There was a sick, wet sound as the past me wrenched the knife from Gabriel's side. I heard my father's strangled voice as he bit down on a cry.

Suddenly, all around me there was wind and movement. I opened my eyes to see that the two figures who had helped me in thwarting the first thrust had been joined by a plethora of others. It was impossible to say who it was that had come to Gabriel's aid first, though the two closest to me now were unsurprisingly familiar. I caught a glimpse of a very young and vital Olivia next to the slim yet powerful ice of Adora. Others crowded in now, as well, dozens of flickering figures that shifted and darted around the act of violence at the center of this strange place out of time. Ariel, her fierce features their usual unsettling mirror of my own, found a place at my past self's other shoulder along with the blond perfection of her brothers. Two other Usuriels joined them, a woman with green eyes who mirrored Ariel and I with an uncanny likeness and a man who looked enough like Dad that it took me a second glance to realize he wasn't another version of Gabriel.

Others, mortals by the look of their features, also slid up and around us but they seemed less substantial. I thought I caught a glimpse of Amaya in their flickering crowd, but there were too many for me to easily pick out individual faces.

"Are you going to just stand there?" Adora hissed at me.

Startled, I quickly joined the rest of my family as they wrapped their hands around my past self, clutching at any spare inch of skin as we tried to use our combined strength to prevent the tragedy that was about to occur. Even so, we weren't solid and very clearly my past self had the advantage of corporeal form. She didn't even seem to feel us.

"Sweet Fate, Gracie… I'm so sorry," Dad whispered.

"No!" I shouted as the bloody knife went back again. This was when something had happened, I thought, something that stopped that final blow.

Me, I thought.

It was me.

With a lunge, I pulled on my flames, throwing myself between Gabriel and the other Gracie. There was a blinding flash as time itself stretched, wavered, tore. I felt it, leaking like a sieve and suddenly allowing all those ghosts to bleed through, grabbing my former self and throwing her as if she weighed nothing across the barnyard.

"Gracie?"

My father's voice seemed to come from a long distance as the world swam and bled around me in streams of color.

"Are you alright?"

That was the last thing I heard before everything went black.

Chapter 25

Gloria

"Gracie? Can you hear me? Come on, love, open your eyes. Please, Gracie. I need you to wake up."

Liam sounded terrified.

That was my first thought as I struggled up from the black depths that tried to pull me back under. My head pounded to the rhythm of my heartbeat, and my eyelids weighed several metric tons. With a massive effort, I managed to open them enough to see my distraught lover.

"'M okay," I managed to mutter, feeling as if my mouth was full of cotton. With a frown, I wet my cracked lips and tried again. "Calm down. I'm not dead."

Liam took a weak breath of relief and kissed my forehead. "Thank Fate. You gave me a good scare, there. It's been almost an hour and your lips were starting to turn blue."

"S...sorry," I stuttered, my teeth chattering as my whole body began to shiver violently. "I d...didn't have a w...whole lot of control on the return trip."

"You're freezing," Liam said, a concerned expression on his face. With a quick movement, he pulled off his jacket and shirt before pulling back the covers and sliding into the bed next to me. With a nudge, he slid me over so that he could pull the edges of the blankets mounded on James to cover me as well. "Come here," he said and wrapped himself around me, the warmth of his body burning through my thin shirt. Almost involuntarily, I leaned into him, pressing as much of my cold skin against him as I could manage.

"I take it you weren't able to change the timeline," my partner murmured, giving a little shiver himself as my freezing flesh sapped away his heat.

"No," I groaned, "but I did save my dad from being unmade on the spot, I think. So… there's that."

"What do you mean?"

I tried to explain as best I could about the flickering figures and the strange interaction I'd had with my former self. When I described how Adora, Olivia, and the others had come to my aid, he shook his head but didn't interrupt me.

"So… is that what happened the first time?" he asked when I was done.

Slowly, I nodded. My body was still shaking, but my voice was steadier now. "I think so. Yes, almost exactly."

"Is this how your other trips in time have been?" I appreciated how calmly Liam accepted my wild abilities. If I hadn't seen it for myself, I would have thought I was going crazy. I understood why Evan doubted my sanity.

"No. I've never seen anything like this," I replied, thinking of the flickering parade of figures. It had been so real, and yet so dream-like.

We lapsed into silence until James whimpered quietly in his sleep beside us, and we glanced at his side of the bed.

"What time is it?" I muttered, trying to bring another burst of shivering under control.

"Almost midnight," Liam replied, tapping his implant before going back to smoothing my hair. It was an absent gesture, as if he simply needed to reassure himself that I was still alive and in his arms.

I took a shaky breath. "How much longer do you think Dad has?"

"No way to tell," my partner said. "Any idea why this time jump was different than your other ones?"

I'd been thinking about that, and despite the raw exhaustion in my brain, I had a few guesses. "I've never jumped without Ariel before," I said slowly, "so I think that may have been part of it. I'm a fate, but she's not. Maybe my powers work a little differently when I'm on my own."

"Teleporting isn't any different no matter who gives me the reference image," Liam said. "As long as I have a clear memory of where I'm trying to go, I'll get there. It doesn't matter if it's my memory or someone else's."

That was a fair comparison, so I nodded, my head burrowing a little more comfortably against his bare shoulder. My shivering had finally subsided, but I felt utterly drained. I had to focus carefully on each word to make sure it didn't slur from fatigue.

"Well, we're dealing with Temporal Mortis. I think something about it may be... damaging? Bending? I'm not sure what it's doing to the timeline, but I don't think it's completely stable around that event. Also, I'm pretty sure the last blast of fire that I pulled down to save Gabriel did something strange. There are a lot of variables going on right there. I don't think I can risk going back again. Dad warned me about paradox, and I'm already getting uncomfortably close in this case."

"No, I don't think any more time jumps are a good idea," Liam agreed, pressing me tightly to his chest.

I let him hold me before speaking gently. I knew he would seriously dislike the conclusion I'd come to. "Well... perhaps not to undo things," I murmured, "but I do think I have to make another jump."

"What? Why?" Liam looked down at me, fear already riding his eyes again. The unmaking wasn't real to him, I realized. He was going along with me because he loved me, and he knew I was genuinely afraid of the Temporal Mortis. I think he even half-way believed me, but it was still very abstract to him. The look in Liam's eyes told me that finding me still and cold on the bed had left him far more terrified of watching me time jump again than anything that might happen when Dad died.

If we don't fix this, I'm dead already, I thought, but I didn't say it as I touched his face. My hand felt as if it were moving through molasses, and I had to blink hard to keep my eyes from sliding shut. Even so, I knew I didn't have the time to rest. Dad could succumb to the Temporal Mortis at any moment, dragging everyone I cared about into oblivion with him.

"If I can't prevent Dad's poisoning from happening, then I still need the antidote," I explained. "And the only place to get it is Ariel's lab."

"She only made the one vial, though, didn't she?"

"I don't know that for sure," I admitted, "but even if she did only make the one, I'm the main ingredient. I know I can physically time jump to Ariel's lab in the past. I've done it before. On that side of history, there won't be as much urgency. She should be able to make more immortality elixir for me to bring back with me."

I glanced over at James. His eyes were ever so slightly open, his chest rising and falling rapidly as if he were having trouble getting enough air. Under the blankets, I slid my hand over to his and squeezed it tightly. His eyes opened just a touch more and flickered in my direction.

"I'll get at least two doses," I said. "One for Dad and one for James. Maybe an extra just to be safe."

Liam was shaking his head and clinging to me tightly, as if he were afraid I might simply disappear if he let me go. "No, Gracie, please. At least sleep a few hours first. I know you're worried about Gabriel, but you won't help him if you put yourself into a fatal shock trying too many jumps in a row. You've been going all day and calling it stressful is a major understatement. I know my strength is tapped out. Even third-gens have to rest at some point or they will hurt themselves. Wasn't it a psi overload that injured your father's heart to begin with? How can you help anyone if you put yourself into cardiac arrest?"

"No, you don't understand. This stuff unmade Grayson in less than an hour. I know Gloria is holding it off, but Dad has to be entering the final stages by now. I can't sleep while he's..." I couldn't say it. The echo of Grayson's final screams made my heart rate surge again, and I clung to James and Liam, trying to breathe past my fear.

"Stella's wired in here, right?" Liam asked, sliding away from me and pulling on his shirt. I caught a glimpse of his torso in the lamplight before the stained cloth covered it again. "Why don't we check on Gabe? Will that make you feel better?"

I hadn't even thought about the fact that Stella would be able to connect us to Dad and Grandma. A rush of anxiety made me sit up and tap my implant.

"Stella? Are you there?"

The figure that bled from the room's dimly-lit shadows wasn't the usual AI. In all the years I'd worked with Stella, I'd never seen her hologram alter so much as a hair. This time, however, I hardly recognized her.

Silver and gold swirled around this woman like sparks of psi as her piercing silver-blue gaze flashed between Liam, James, and I. Her features were more Usuriel than I'd ever seen them; that arrow dart of a nose and high cheekbones distorting Stella's usually rounded face into something sharper and more dangerous. She was shorter than usual as well, her traditional hourglass figure suddenly more petite and fine-boned.

"What happened? Why are you here at Angelus Quietum? I thought you were out looking for the antidote," the AI snapped, and I blinked in surprise. Of course, it made sense that Stella would seem different with Gloria merged in her core. I wondered what she looked like when Dad or Adora merged with her.

"We had the antidote, but Evan stole it. We're trying to come up with a plan now to get more," Liam said. "How's Gabriel? Gracie's been beside herself with worry about him."

I had, quite literally, been beside myself over the situation today. I wondered briefly if whoever coined that phrase had been a fate.

Stella-Gloria's face looked as grim as I'd feared. "It's taking all of our strength to keep him stable. Even so, he's dying by inches. I'd say we're less than ten hours away from permanent damage."

I felt my chest ease a touch. Ten hours. We could actually get something done in ten hours. How bad were things when I was relieved to hear my grandmother describe Gabriel's condition as 'dying by inches?'

"Can I see him?" I asked, feeling as if I needed confirmation that he wasn't breaths away from the edge yet.

The merged AI shook her head. "You don't want to see him like this, Gracie." She met my eye somberly. "I want you to be honest with me, child. Can you get this antidote in the next half-day? Because if not, I can't keep him like this in good conscience. If it's just pointless suffering..."

"Yes! Yes, I can get it," I said quickly. "Honestly, Gloria, you have to keep him with us! If he dies, the entire Gabriellan line could be undone!"

She scowled at me and, unlike Evan or Vanessa, I didn't see doubt in her gaze. Instead, I saw the first flickerings of fear.

"If you had the antidote, you must have figured out which poison Vanessa used." Gloria's merge sounded suspicious, her strange, metallic eyes darting between Liam and I.

"Yes, we figured it out," I said miserably. "It's Temporal Mortis." I pulled the horrid vial out of my pocket, tilting it so the holo-cameras would be able to see it. "Ariel used my blood to make it a few years back. I had no idea she had until we found the vial in Vanessa's office, but the label and symptoms match."

Gloria and Stella had both been around a very long time. "Ancient" is a mild way to describe either one of them. If my math was correct, Gloria had to be pushing a full millennium by now. Stella was slightly younger than my father, but not by much. Between the two of them, there was easily fifteen hundred years of experience staring at me from that merge. The pure horror on her face as she looked at that vial couldn't be faked. Just like me, they knew exactly how real and devastating this was. And while it was nice to see someone take this situation as seriously as I did, seeing the knowledge of our doom written across the face of the most powerful creature on the planet was enough to twist my stomach into a new level of knots.

"You're a fate?" I watched as her eyes darted, seeing something in the merge that wasn't here and now. "Stella... knew that somehow. Or at least suspected." The merged AI's brow knit together, then refocused her gaze on me. I suddenly had a distinct feeling Gloria was the dominant personality in this merge. "I assume you've already tried and failed to go back and alter the timeline."

How she knew that, I didn't ask. I just nodded mutely, unable to keep the anguish out of my features.

"Such events are difficult to alter. They warp the fabric of reality around themselves, making knots even experienced fates have a hard time unraveling." There was a huge amount of sorrow and loss in her gaze as she looked at me. She thought we were already dead, I realized.

"I can get more of the antidote, though," I rushed to say. "All I have to do is jump back to Ariel's time. She should be able to make more with my blood. I know it still alters the timeline slightly, but it shouldn't even get close to the temporal damage I did. I don't think it should make any more knots than there already are. Please, you have to keep Dad alive long enough for me to at least try."

She shook her lovely head slowly, eyes so old and so full of heartache. "There is no antidote to Temporal Mortis, child."

Her words made my blood run cold. Then, I remembered what Ariel had said when she showed me the elixir. "They said it couldn't be done," I whispered. I swallowed hard against the rapid flutter of my heartbeat as I met her strange, combined gaze. "I think Ariel may have done it. I don't know if she ever told anyone besides me, but she did manage to create an immortality elixir. She said the Anori database claimed it was mythical, but she managed it because of the unique properties of my blood. She tried to convince me to deliver it back in time to Olivia, but I didn't want to risk being unmade. It seemed like a little too much paradox for me. So she let me keep it. That was the vial Evan stole."

"An immortality elixir for Olivia? Hmmm... yes that would have been a rather ingenious solution to that problem. I knew Ariel was looking into the immortality genome, but I always thought it was for Bryce, not Olivia," the Gloria-Stella merge mused, her ancient eyes seeing things that had happened long before I was ever dreamed of. "Oh my, that would have solved a host of problems." She shook herself sharply and seemed to refocus on the present. "But in the here and now... yes. If she did in fact manage to create Temporal Vivas, it should, in theory, counter the poison nicely. You really think you can get a hold of more?"

"If she made it once, she has to be able to do it again!" I sounded a little desperate, even to myself, but it was our only chance, so I clung to it. My brain was an exhausted fog, and my body was sore in a dozen places, but I pushed through it with savage determination. "She really seemed convinced that the elixir was the only way to help Dad. If I tell her he's going to die without it, I'm sure she'll be willing to try again."

"So it's real." Liam sounded as if he were the one going into emotional shock this time. "If you don't get that antidote, we're all... gone."

"History will change. It will be as if Gabriel was never even born," the merge said, though not unkindly. "I imagine it will unmake the colony. Without Gabriel, I doubt Gloria's marriage to D'nay would have survived its first fifty years. She was always terrified that other immortals would show up and exact vengeance on D'nay for his attachment to her. Without a child who needed both of his parents, she may have simply tried to minimize the damage of the relationship by breaking it off. She'd done it before. Even if she had stayed, she and D'nay wouldn't have been as determined to get off world so quickly." Her eyes were suddenly stricken with grief. "Stella... Adora... Ileesia... Olivia, Ariel, and the twins... the *Inspiration*... Cybele... everything we've built in the last four hundred years... gone as if it never was."

We were silent as Liam, Gloria, and Stella came to grips with the reality of Dad's undoing. I'd already processed this particular emotional blow, but despite the horribly grim situation, my mind and body were so exhausted that I simply sat there staring miserably into space with them.

James made a small sound, and I roused enough to check on him. He was trying to struggle into a sitting position, though the effort was clearly taxing. His waxy skin was covered in sweat as I moved closer to offer help.

"Easy," I said gently. "It's just Gloria and Stella. No need to push yourself."

"How's Gabe?" he asked breathlessly, clinging to my arm with his good hand; clearly he hadn't been coherent enough to follow the first half of our conversation. It took a decent amount of my remaining strength to pull him into an upright position, and even then most of his weight was leaning against my shoulder. I wrapped an arm firmly around his waist, trying not to jostle his injured arm while still getting a strong enough grip to prop him against me.

"Dad's very sick, but Grandma Gloria says he's not in immediate danger," I told him.

Liam looked in our direction with an anguished expression. "James got hurt pretty badly trying to deliver the antidote. You don't have contact with any healers you might be able to send our way, do you?"

"Have you looked on the net lately?" the merge asked, her face even more bleak as she glanced between the three of us. When Liam and I shook our heads, she waved a hand and summoned several little circular sub-displays. In their glowing confines, smaller holos showed us exactly what was going on around the continent.

Vanessa and Evan had described the state of the Provinces as "riots." Looking at this footage, that was a major understatement. Skykyle and Riland City were both ablaze. A dozen Overwatch members attempted to face down a violent mob on Skykyle's once-shining streets. I thought I saw Jillian's dark braids in their company before the mortals took over the holo-camera's view of events. In Riland, dozens of those avatar-like androids rounded up groups of people and loaded them into large hovercraft. Several members of the fearful crowd made a darting run away from the vehicles but, despite their obviously inhuman speed, the androids caught them with little effort. I saw one android pin down a young woman and tear her heart right out of her chest in one smooth, unnatural movement. Down in Landing, the hospital was a smoking ruin. I saw running figures nearby, the glow of psi and the flash of gunfire darting back and forth in the background.

"It's difficult enough for me to split my concentration between Gabriel and this conversation," Gloria-Stella admitted. "I can't take the time to go looking for a healer right now. But if I had to guess, I'd say they're all going to be pretty busy at the moment, anyway. You're probably safer staying there and doing what you can for James on your own. At least Angelus Quietum is in the middle of nowhere. You won't be in danger of getting caught in a crossfire any time soon." She looked at me sharply. "You *will* get that antidote to me. Once your father is on the mend, I can have a look at James. Then Gabriel and I will have to see what we can do about this conflict Riland has stirred up. As they say, when it rains..."

I took a breath to settle the renewed sense of dread in my stomach. I didn't have the energy for panic anymore, but the lead weight in my gut was starting to make me feel physically ill again. "Liam wants me to sleep a few hours before I try another jump. Do I have the time? Or do I have to try it now?"

The merge's gaze got distant, and I suspected she was focusing on my father's condition. When her eyes refocused on me, they looked worried but calm.

"An hour or two should be safe enough," she allowed. "Time travel is tricky as it is without being exhausted on top of it. Gabe and every one of his descendants is dead without that antidote, so I'd say it's better to err on the side of caution. Even so, don't oversleep. I'm pretty sure I can buy you another three or four hours, but past that we're in dangerous waters."

"Don't worry," Liam said somberly. "I'll set multiple alarms. Two hours is better than none."

The merged AI nodded, her face suddenly blank, and I knew she was paying attention to Dad rather than us. "I need to focus on keeping a step ahead of this poison," she said after a pause. "Let me know when you have the antidote. We'll figure out the fastest way to get it into Gabriel then."

"Go ahead. You look after Gabe, I'll look after Gracie and James," Liam said, eyes serious. "I'll let you know the instant we have the elixir."

With a last nod, Gloria and Stella's merge faded from the room.

Chapter 26

And

Liam set his implant's alarms while I settled James into a little nest of pillows I'd pulled out of the linen closet.

"I'm so... cold," he whispered as I tucked the blankets around him, his eyes so full of pain I could hardly look at them.

Thinking of what Liam had done for me earlier, I slid out of my shirt.

"What are you doing?" Liam asked as I began climbing into the bed next to our injured friend.

"Come on," I replied. "He's not a random stranger. He's our James, remember? He's hurt and afraid, so I'm going to hold him."

There was definitely some jealousy in Liam's Family eyes at that statement. I'd almost forgotten how unhappy he'd seemed when he found out that I'd offered to pair with James before him. He'd brought it up again right after we teleported here, I realized. It must be really eating at him if he felt the need to throw relationship issues in my face when we were in the middle of triage.

I paused, sitting in my bra next to James' shivering

form while I tried to decide how to handle my jealous boyfriend. Strange, I thought, even in life-or-death situations my boys somehow managed to make my life emotionally complicated. Or perhaps it was the stress of such dire situations that brought out our insecurities, I mused, as I watched the confusion and hurt on Liam's face.

"Don't look at me that way," I told Liam. "You're the one who slept with him. The farthest James and I have ever gone is kissing and that was years ago. Wasn't it the two of you who got so involved in each other that you completely ditched me at Amourie's the first time we tried to go out?" My boyfriend did flush a bit at that one, but he didn't uncross his arms or move towards me. "If anyone should be concerned and jealous here, it should be me."

"I almost forgot about that incident," Liam admitted. He met my eye with something approaching embarrassment. "I think I was afraid that, with you at school, James was going to forget about me. After all, how could I compete with an elder child?" He gave a small, self-deprecating laugh.

"Gracie?" James sounded so pathetic. "Liam? Please don't fight."

"Why did it have to be a competition?" I asked Liam before turning to James and climbing under the covers to assist our wounded diplomat as he settled himself against my shoulder. "If it were up to James and me, the three of us would have ended up in bed together that night."

James curled around my warmth with a sound of such profound relief that I found myself pressing my cheek to the top of his head. I tried to be gentle as I helped James find a position for his injured arm that didn't pull on the wound too badly before tucking the blankets and pillows more firmly around him. With one boy finally situated, I reached out my free hand to the other.

"Come on," I said again. "That was forever ago, but I think we can still fix our mistake. It shouldn't be an 'either or' situation with us. One way or another, we always seem to end up as an 'and.'" My boyfriend frowned at me, clearly unsure what I was getting at. "James *and* Liam. Or, if you prefer, James *and* Gracie."

His gaze slid over to James' face. I could feel the diplomat's uneven breathing and knew the expression on his face was probably rather pitiable. Liam's saturated blue eyes went to me one more time, and I saw the vulnerability in them.

"He's not a baby Gabriel," he said softly.

"Neither are you," I told him, holding that intense gaze. A wave of exhaustion came over me, but I fought through it enough to keep my train of thought. "I'm sorry I ever said that. It wasn't fair of me to compare you to Dad. And it wasn't the real reason I put you off, as you seem to have figured out. But the truth is, I love both you and James, and right now I'm too tired to pretend that I don't."

Slowly, he pulled his shirt off again. They were both so beautiful, I thought, how did I ever get so lucky to have two men like James and Liam so in love with me? Well, with as dreadful as my luck had been lately, I suppose something had to go my way.

"Is that okay with you, James?" His voice was so gentle. "Even after we got together behind your back?"

James nodded, because I don't think he had the strength to do much else.

Liam didn't need any more encouragement; he climbed under the blankets and curled around my other side. With a deep sigh, I pressed my face first into his hair and then into James'. Liam settled himself more comfortably against my breast before putting a hand to James' face, gentle fingertips wiping away the clinging drops of tears and sweat. The diplomat gave a shuddering sigh and relaxed more fully against my side.

"Liam *and* Gracie," James whispered into the bend of my neck.

"Exactly," I murmured, my head leaning back onto the pillow. My arms wrapped around the smooth, strong curves of their backs and my eyelids finally lost their battle with gravity. Pressed to either side of me, I felt their breathing slow even as my own followed suit. That's the last thing I remember before I passed out.

***

Two hours later, Liam's alarm woke me out of the
perfect darkness of a dreamless sleep. If it was possible, I

felt worse after the nap than I had before, my eyes stuck shut and my head swimmingly off balance. James' flesh felt chill beside me, and I realized I was covered in sweat, both his and mine.

"Come on, Gracie, you remember what Gloria and Stella said," Liam groaned. I felt the movement of his arm as he rubbed the sleep out of his eyes. He was comfortably warm on my other side, and through my post-sleep haze I felt a squirm of worry. James was definitely too cold, I thought. "We need to get up."

"I remember," I moaned, eyes rolling under my lids in protest. With a deliberate mental effort, I pulled up the image of Grayson at the end. A hot wave of adrenaline rushed over me, slamming into my head with a sickeningly painful suddenness. Well, I might have a headache, but I was awake.

I felt Liam's long-limbed frame disentangle itself from my side and I finally managed to pry open one eyeball. The light from the lamp on the bedside table felt like a dagger in my cornea.

"James?" I murmured, putting my now-empty right hand to the diplomat's face where it rested in the bend of my neck. His flesh was cool and clammy under my fingertips, and my chest tightened when he didn't respond to my voice or touch. With both eyes open and my head beginning to clear, I gently lifted James' injured arm from where it had fallen across my waist. "A little help over here?" I called to my partner.

With a gentleness that belied Liam's large size, we carefully eased James onto his back. Even with our best efforts, we must have jostled the wound quite a bit as we rolled him over. I found it disturbing that James didn't even flinch, his body limp and pale under our hands as we carefully covered him with a few more blankets than we had before. When we finally had him settled, Liam and I exchanged a worried glance.

I thought about Martin and how he'd been up and walking with the very same injury that dreadful night in Riland. I hugged myself tightly, feeling rather chilled without a shirt. I was too used to dealing with vampires and the Family. It was easy to forget just how fragile mortals really were. James might be a telepath, but his body was as human as any other mortal. If I didn't come back with that elixir quickly, I had a feeling the diplomat might just beat my father to the grave.

"I'm going to splash some cold water on my face," I said, turning to Liam. "I need to be truly awake for this. Can you make us some tea? I don't think staring at him is going to help James any, and I need something hot in my stomach."

"I can do that," Liam agreed.

"Thanks," I said and headed towards the hallway bathroom. That had always been my shower growing up, and I needed the grounding feel of my own spaces to get my head right before this jump. I can't afford to make a mistake, I thought, as I forced my exhausted body to go through its morning routine.

"Focused and awake," I told myself as I leaned over the sink, scrubbing at my face in an attempt to force myself into clearheadedness. "I'm going to Ariel's lab just after I left. She won't even have time to leave the room before I show up." I closed my eyes and envisioned the lab as it had been the night she'd given me the elixir. "Tell her about what happened with Dad and James. Convince her to make more of the immortality serum. Bring it back here, send Liam with one vial to the core for Dad while I give James the other." I recited it to myself several times, envisioning each step as clearly as I could while I soaped my face and went through the motions of wakefulness without my conscious thought.

Finally, I was as focused as I was going to get, so I shut off the water and leaned back, face burning. I stared into my childhood mirror. I'd been right the day before. I hardly recognized the person who gazed back at me with those haunted blue eyes. Whoever she was, she looked utterly drained. I turned away from the mirror, my face settling into a determined grimace.

With rapid fingers, I pulled my hair back into a functional braid before going into my old room to dig up a fresh shirt. I found a casual work-a-day farm top that felt as comfortable and familiar as a second skin, along with one of my lighter jackets. Then, as I passed the bathroom again, I quickly took a few more of those mild painkillers in a vain attempt to combat my pounding headache.

"Okay, Dad, I'm as ready as I can be," I breathed, walking back into the bedroom to check on James.

If it was possible, the diplomat looked even worse than before. I watched carefully to make sure his chest did in fact rise and fall. It did, though the breaths were more rapid and shallow than I thought normal. With a small frown, I straightened the twisted blankets before sitting down next to James on the empty side of the bed. He didn't react at all as I adjusted the angle of his injured arm, trying to make it as natural as possible.

"James?" I said his name gently and ran my fingers through his hair. Its blond strands were soaked with sweat, and I could feel the ominous chill of his skin. "Can you hear me?"

There was no response. He lay still as the dead, his lips now progressing past white and into a faint blue. Pushing down that ever-growing lump of sick dread in my guts, I laid shaking fingers against the large vein in his neck. His pulse fluttered against them, fast but weak.

"How is he?" Liam asked, walking in carrying the teapot in one hand and a full basin of water with the other. Several mugs and towels followed in the air behind him. Ah, the beauty of dating a telekinetic, I thought as one mug drifted to my hands, and Liam brought over the teapot to fill it.

"Not good," I said, taking a long sip of tea. It scalded my tongue, but felt good sliding down my throat. I'm running out of time for James, I thought, and quickly took a final sip before setting the mug on the bedside table. "I have to make the jump now. I'll try to be back before you even know I'm gone."

"Okay." Liam gave me a worried look as he set down the teapot and basin next to the bed on the floor by James' side. "Be quick, but also be careful. It won't help anyone if you don't come back in one piece."

"I know," I told him, taking a shaky breath as I laid back on the empty side of the bed again and closed my eyes.

"Gracie?" I glanced at my boyfriend one last time. Love, fear, hope and a myriad of other nameless emotions played across Liam's features as he looked at me from where he stood beside our injured friend. "I love you," he said, voice hardly above a whisper. "Please come back to me in one piece."

I glanced between him and James. My boys. No, we were in a war now. These weren't children's flirting games anymore and our relationships were far more than teenage flings. They were my men—the ones I'd run into a burning building for. In fact, I had a feeling that was exactly what I was about to do. "I love you, too," I murmured.

Then, I closed my eyes, envisioned Ariel's lab and called on the flames.

Chapter 27

Last Chances

For the second time in less than five hours, I fell through bleeding, spinning colors. I'd never been on so many teleports in one day, and certainly this was the most I'd ever jumped on my own power. Like Liam, when he'd pushed himself past his limits, this 'port was more than a little rocky. I spent several breathless moments in limbo before Ariel's lab finally solidified under me.

Quick, booted footsteps were the first thing I became aware of as the ground finally rose up to support me, and I took a gasping breath that burned in my lungs.

"Well, hello, Gracie." A gray-haired Ariel looked down at me as she leaned against one of the long shelves of test tubes, a pair of spectacles perched on the end of her sharp, Usuriel nose. I thought I caught a note of irritation in her voice. "I was wondering when you'd show up."

I tried to sit up, but the world spun violently around me, and I all but collapsed backwards, catching myself at the last moment on one elbow before I could hit the ground again. A wave of nausea rushed over me, and for a second it was all I could do not to be sick.

"Hmmm, you don't look very well, little sister," Ariel said, concern coming in to color her tone. "Look at me."

Obediently, I glanced at her. It was a mistake. The motion set off that spinning sensation again, and if she hadn't knelt to catch me, I think my head would have connected painfully with the floor.

"Over-extension," my sister diagnosed, meeting my eye and giving me a knowledgeable frown. "I don't think I've seen an elder child this worn out since the *Inspiration*. What have you been up to, my dear firebird?" With that usual Usuriel grace, my sister pulled me into her arms and stood as if I weighed nothing at all. "No, no, don't answer that. There will be time for explanations later. You need to rest."

All the events of the last day crowded close to my lips, but somehow I didn't have the strength to say a word. I felt the rush of Ariel's power come over us as she teleported somewhere. I tried to see my new surroundings, but my vision had narrowed into a small, dark tunnel, and I couldn't seem to form a coherent thought for more than a moment. Liam had been right, I thought dimly as my sister lowered me onto a soft, flat surface. Thank Fate he'd insisted I get those two hours of sleep or I just might have put myself into heart failure with this jump.

That was the last thought I had before darkness took me.

***

I woke to the smell of rice and eggs being cooked on a stove. It was such a safe, familiar scent. I drifted in a hazy half-sleep, listening for the cluck of Angelus Quietum's chickens or the gentle tinkle of china as Dad made breakfast in the kitchen.

I opened my eyes to a strange ceiling. Reality came crashing back down on my head.

"Dad! James!" I sat straight up in the little bed, my heart pounding fit to burst out of my chest. I looked around wildly, trying to figure out where I was.

The little bedroom was cluttered but tidy. Framed stills of red-haired little girls in pigtails and blond boys in *Inspiration* ship suits adorned the walls. Stacks of memory pads, old toys, and rolled up diagrams cluttered the tiny bedroom. The single bed I was sitting in, a rough-hewn wooden desk, and a chest of drawers were all that fit in its cramped, rectangular space. Above the desk was a nice-sized window which was open to let in a comfortable breeze.

Taking a steadying breath, I slid out of bed. My legs seemed relatively steady, though my head still ached dully. Feeling a bit disoriented, I looked out the window. The familiar stone facades of the University greeted me. There was something off about them, however, I thought with a frown. Glancing from building to building, I realized that the newest wing of the Fine Arts center was missing, as were two dormitories.

Before my brain could fully process the changes, I heard the rush of air as a door opened directly behind me. I turned, my fire rising up as I startled, wreathing my hair in a halo of embers.

"Oh! I'm sorry." Ariel gave me a gentle smile as she stood in the doorway, holding a tray of steaming breakfast food. "I didn't mean to scare you. Are you hungry? I imagine you must be. You've slept almost fourteen hours."

Fear sang through my body at her words, but I quickly reined it in. I'm in the past, I reminded myself. Dad and James aren't even hurt yet, let alone dying. On this side of history, we have all the time in the world. I forced myself to take another deep breath.

"Yes, thank you," I said, sitting back down on the bed. Ariel placed the tray beside me. Now that I let myself think about it, I was starving. I fell upon the food with a single-minded intensity while Ariel pulled up the small wooden desk chair. She sat leaning against the back of the chair, her chin propped on one fist as she watched me devour her offerings.

"So." Her voice was a bit cautious but not afraid. I glanced up from my meal at her. "Are you going to explain to me how our father has been poisoned? Or are you going to make me guess?"

I swallowed hard, the rice turning into a lump of stone in my throat. I set down my spoon and studied her face, my mouth still working to clear out the suddenly unwelcome food.

"How—" I started.

Ariel cut me off with a sharp shake of her head. "It's in the name, you foolish little thing. Temporal Mortis. Time Death. He's not just sick in your time, he's sick in every time. Of course, I'm assuming that's what you're here about but... no, I'm not wrong. I know the source isn't here, and it can't be in the past, because he'd already be dead. So it has to be echoing from the future." Her green eyes blazed into mine. "Your future. Now, are you going to answer me?"

I stared at her wide-eyed, feeling extremely stupid. Of course. That was the nature of Temporal Mortis. It killed the individual at every point in their timeline. The Anori database had said as much. Which meant it made sense that Dad was sick here as well as in the future. I closed my eyes, trying to wrap my brain around the intricacies of the situation, and failed.

"How bad is he?" I asked, feeling guilt and heartache weighing like stones in my chest. "How much time do we have left?"

"Bad enough," Ariel replied, "but I'm guessing your time is far enough away that the poison is moving more slowly here. Last I checked, Grandmother had him on an IV for fluids, but otherwise Dad is holding his own. For now."

I took a deeper breath, though the guilt still felt razor-sharp inside my rib cage. IV fluids probably meant he couldn't keep anything down. I tried not to think about how miserably ill he had to be and instead focused on the fact that Gloria hadn't been forced into the merge just to stabilize him yet. We still had some time here.

"It's my fault," I admitted. "I didn't mean to poison him, but... Fates... it's a long story."

"I suspected as much," Ariel said coolly. "Seeing as you're the only person I've ever discussed my time research with. I didn't mention the poison to you, that I know of, but it wouldn't take too much thought to reason it out."

I shook my head. Her logic wasn't bad, but she was still jumping to the wrong conclusion. "No, no, I didn't have any idea you'd even made Temporal Mortis until after Dad was poisoned."

"Well, then, how did it happen? And how could it be your fault?" she asked, confusion written across those familiar features.

"We don't have time for the whole story right now," I said. "Just... tell me this. How long does it take to make the antidote?"

"Antidote?" She raised an eyebrow. Then, suddenly, understanding washed over her face. "You mean the immortality elixir. Wait—yes, that just might work! Where's the vial I gave you? If you give it to Dad before the poison runs its course in the original time stream, it just might counteract the effects!"

"I can't," I said miserably. "That vial was... lost. Like I said, long story. But I remember you said the main ingredient for the elixir was my blood. So, here I am." I gestured to myself. "How long would it take to synthesize more?"

"From scratch?" Ariel looked a little horrified at the thought. "Fates, it took me twenty years to make the first vial."

"Twenty years," I echoed, feeling a fresh wave of panic. "Dad will never last that long..."

"No, no, that was a lot of trial and error." Ariel waved a hand to dismiss my outburst. "I never intended to make more than one dose. But if I have a fresh blood sample... three days? Maybe four if something comes up, but I imagine it shouldn't take much longer than that."

I suddenly felt like I could breathe again. "Okay, do you think he'll make it that long? On this side of history, anyway?"

Her gaze got distant again before she nodded slowly. "It's cutting things uncomfortably close, I think, but if it's our only chance... what choice do we have?"

I swallowed hard and met her eye. "Do you think you could make three doses? I know I need at least two, and the way things have been going lately, it feels like having a spare might be a good idea."

Ariel frowned and eyed me thoughtfully. "That's a decent amount of blood," she said slowly, "and you're exhausted as it is. I don't think it would take much more time to make a few more doses, but I'm not sure you should be donating quite that much. Not if you want to get the elixir to the future in one piece."

"How about just two doses, then," I begged, unable to keep my desperation out of my eyes. "Please. I don't care how much blood it takes. I need two at the absolute minimum."

Ariel's face was solemn as she considered me. Slowly, she nodded. "Okay. If you provide the blood, I'll do my best to make two doses of the elixir." She raised one slim finger at me. "On one condition."

"Anything," I breathed.

"I want to hear this whole story," she said, green eyes narrowed at me. "It seems to me there's more going on here than just an accidental poisoning."

"You might say that," I admitted.

***

We hardly finished that conversation before Ariel had us back at the lab, drawing my blood and sending vials of it through various machines. True to her predictions, I felt a bit lightheaded after the amount of plasma she emptied from my veins, and I watched her through half-lidded eyes as she bustled around the laboratory. She'd pulled up a large, leather armchair for me to sit in and draped a lovely, hand-sewn blanket across my lap before charging into her work with far more vigor than I'd expected from someone her age. She had to be over a hundred and fifty, I thought as she loaded yet another centrifuge with minute quantities of my blood and set it spinning.

"Okay, now I can listen," she said, pressing a few more buttons and tapping her implant. I assume she was setting some kind of timer. "I'll have to toss over the other group in fifteen minutes, but until then"—with the wave of one hand, she summoned a holo-recorder and tripod which she neatly set up in front of me— "all I want to do is hear exactly how this mess happened in the first place."

"Ummm... I don't know if I should tell you everything," I said, feeling a little uncomfortable with the camera. "This is kind of... spoilers or something, right? I mean, isn't it kind of dangerous to know too much about your own future?"

Ariel shook her head and those silver curls tumbled out of her bun, framing her face much the way Gabriel's dark waves so often did. For a moment, I saw so much of our father in her face that I had to look away. I hoped wherever Gloria was caring for him in this time, she'd managed to make him comfortable enough to rest. It physically hurt to think about how much he was suffering because of me.

"I'm in my last decade, Gracie," Ariel said softly. "I'm not like you and Gabriel. I won't continue on forever. And Usuriel aging isn't even the way mortals' is. It's more like fits and spurts. I watched it happen to Drex twenty years ago. We stay youthful for a very long time, but once age decides to catch up with us, it's a very rapid downhill slide."

"Wasn't Drexil younger than you?" I asked, slightly confused.

She nodded, green eyes extremely sad. With sorrow in her gaze, her resemblance to Gabriel was even more marked. "Yes. Only by two years, but—yes, I watched time catch up with my baby brother and knew it was going to be my turn very soon." She glanced down at her wizened hands and smiled that melancholy smile I'd seen on our father's face so many times. When she looked up at me again however, there was acceptance rather than grief in her gaze. "It's not so bad, really. Having an endpoint makes the current moment sweeter. I've always told myself so, anyway." She tucked a lock of gray curls behind one ear. "And I've lived a full life. I traveled the stars; built a new home; had my career and explored a passion project or two on the side; enjoyed my lovers; chose my husband; raised my children—I even got to look after a dozen or so grand-littles over the years." She tilted her head at me slightly and her voice became soft. "But here at the end, I find it isn't regrets that keep me up at night so much. I thought it would be, but it's not. No, I worry about the future. I worry about what will happen to the people I love once I'm not here to take care of them anymore."

"You worry about Dad." I matched her hushed tone, but the words were too true not to be said. My sister met my eye as she nodded.

"Among others. But yes, I do think I worry about him the most."

I ran my hand through my hair, and caught my sister looking at me with a somber expression. She wasn't the only one who mirrored Gabriel, I thought, and dropped my hand. "There is some cause for concern there," I admitted.

"Obviously." Her tone turned dry, and she raised an eyebrow. "At the moment he's dying, so I would say there is definite cause for concern."

I cleared my throat and looked anywhere but her and the holo-recorder.

"Listen, I understand it's strange to discuss. You're probably as used to hiding your time powers as I am used to keeping the more... dangerous... aspects of my research under closed covers. However, this is the first time Temporal Mortis has been used in millennia. It's also the first time a fate has been born here on Cybele. My own curiosity aside, I feel I owe it to the scientific community to document this situation. Even if no one else can view it for another few centuries without risking paradox, it would be a travesty not to take advantage of this unique window into the nature of reality itself."

I stared at her for a moment, then slowly nodded. She was a scientist down to the marrow of her bones and one that had been raised by a historian no less. Surely Olivia's careful journaling and record keeping had made an impression on her adoring daughter. Well, I'd already injured the timeline pretty thoroughly as it was. What was one more potential paradox between sisters?

"Okay," I said, glancing between her and the camera. "Where do you want me to start?"

"Well, perhaps begin with Dad's poisoning. How did that happen?"

I groaned and scrubbed at my face. "Not my most shining moment," I admitted, "and it's really complicated. How about we work up to that one?"

"Okay." Ariel gestured with one hand and one of the little wooden stools slid over from the wall for her to perch upon next to the holo-recorder. "You seem pretty determined to get more than one dose of the Temporal Vivas. Care to tell me who else besides Gabriel needs a dose of immortality?"

"James," I murmured, taking a calming breath as anxiety fluttered its dark wings in my gut. The image of his face, pale and cold on the pillow, made my shoulders tense with urgent dread. When I glanced back at Ariel, the question was on her face. "He's... well... a very good friend of mine. And the Terran ambassador to the Provinces. He

got hurt trying to help me get the elixir to Dad. I think—"
I cut myself off, unable to finish the sentence. I think he
might be dying. The words echoed in my head anyway
and even there I knew they were a lie. I didn't have to
guess. I'd seen death enough times now to recognize it.
Without help, I knew what the end would be for James.

"You're good friends with the Terran ambassador?"
Ariel asked, sounding as if she'd like a little more detail on
that topic.

"He stayed with Dad and I for a few months right
after he came to the Provinces," I explained, "and we've
been at University for a few years together, now, too. I
don't see him as much now that he's on active duty with
the embassy, and I'm always off with the Overwatch, but
he's still one of my... best friends."

"Wait, you're a member of the Overwatch?" She
raised an eyebrow at me. "No, no this will never work.
We're jumping all over the place and not getting any
closer to making sense. We need to back up and start from
the beginning."

"The beginning?"

She nodded, green eyes somber. Abruptly, she held
up a finger and tilted her head before tapping her implant.
"Hold that thought. I'm going to go switch around those
samples. You think about where to begin so that this
whole story makes sense. All of it—the Overwatch, the
poison, the time powers, Dad, your friend James. We have
a couple of days, so I want all of it. You think, and I'll be
right back."

With a small frown, I watched her get up and head back over to the complicated set up she had on the tables a few feet away. The beginning, I thought, as I watched her open the huge, circular machines and begin rearranging vials. Where should I start, I mused. With finding out about my mother? No, that didn't explain my knowledge of Temporal Mortis. With Grayson's unmaking? No, that didn't explain Liam, James, or the Overwatch. With going off to University? No, that didn't explain how I found out about my time powers, or my real relationship with Dad.

Dad, I mused. It somehow always did come back to Gabriel.

It only took a few minutes for Ariel to get the machines running again, but by the time she came back I was pretty sure I'd found my starting place.

"Okay," she said, settling her slim frame back onto the stool. "Have you figured out how to begin?"

"Yes," I said, meeting her green eyes. "It all started out with a question. Who is Gabriel Usuriel?"

***

The next two days passed in a strange blur. Ariel and I kept the machines running around the clock, sleeping in shifts so that we could keep moving around the samples every quarter hour. By halfway through that first day, I'd watched her do the first few steps enough times that it took very little instruction for me to pick up the process.

In between swapping out vials, eating, and sleeping, we passed the time by recording my story. Ariel was an excellent audience and a keen observer of detail. Her sharp, intelligent questions often coaxed me into adding more depth to the tale than I might have otherwise.

Finally, towards the evening of the second day, I caught up to that last, fateful day. I'd been so involved in the telling of the story I had almost forgotten the anguish of its ending. Feeling as if I were experiencing it all over again, it took me several tries before I was able to tell Ariel the whole of how I'd ended up there. As it was, there were a few points where I found myself speaking through my tears and, by the end, my hands were numb and shaking.

"That was the last thing he said to me," I murmured, voice gone past raw and into painfully soft long ago. "Gracie, I love you. Please come back to me in one piece."

"Oh, little sister!" Ariel was sitting in rapt attention on her little stool, tears hovering on the edge of her eyes as well. "What did you say back?"

"I love you, too," I said with a helpless shrug. "Then I jumped." I spread my hands. "And you know the rest from there."

She nodded, green eyes shining. "That is quite a story. A pity no one will be able to hear it again for at least a century. But there's too much potential damage that could be done with this knowledge. If Dad or, Fates, Adora got a hold of it" — she looked grim — "no, I think it might be best if you took this footage with you when you jump forward. With a little editing, smoothing out, a few details here and there, it would be a very nice addition to

Stella's archives. But on this end of history, it's just too dangerous to leave lying about." She gave me a genuine smile that made her look quite a bit younger. "Thank you for sharing it with me, though. I know it was painful at points, but at least now I know what we're up against. Not just Dad's illness, but a pan-Cybele war." Her expression sobered, and she got that distant look that telepaths got when they were using their mental senses.

"How's Dad?" I asked softly. I'd caught this expression on her face quite a few times during my telling, especially when the topic came around to Gabriel and his issues. Up until now, I'd managed to redirect my anxiety into the storytelling. But with everything out in the open and the holo-camera shut off, I found my thoughts circling back to the urgent situation at hand.

My sister's gaze refocused on my face. She looked bleak. "Not well."

I swallowed hard and glanced over at the machines that were busily refining my blood into my father's last chance.

"Are we going to make it in time?" I couldn't help the words from falling out of my mouth, though truthfully I was a little afraid of the answer.

"We have to," my sister said somberly, "or there won't be a colony left to worry about."

***

The last day was a little more tricky when it came to preparing the elixir. I'd fully recovered from my jump and the blood donation by now and, if I was running a bit of a sleep deficit from helping Ariel, it wasn't even close to the exhausted stupor I'd been in when I arrived. No, with my mind and body beginning to recover and Ariel too focused to interact with me anymore, all I could think about was Dad suffering over at the hospital next door and James waiting on me back in my time.

In a vain effort to distract myself, I fiddled around with the holo-camera, re-watching sections of my interview with Ariel and losing myself in the multitude of ways in which my life had gone wrong. Sometime in the late morning, I discovered that the camera could download a transcript of the holos onto a memory pad. Suddenly, I was able to go back and edit what I'd said; add more description here or take out a misstated word there.

Ariel's careful measuring, mixing, boiling, and stirring didn't seem to be slowing down anytime soon, so I turned back to the memory pad and began refining my account into something that approached coherence. I'd always been gifted in written communication and, as I sat there waiting for my sister to finish my last hope for making right all of my glaring mistakes, I found myself becoming incredibly involved in perfecting this account of how they had come to be in the first place.

By the time the sun began to sink below the horizon on the third day, Ariel finally turned to me with accomplishment filling her weathered features.

"Two doses of Temporal Vivas," she said, not a little pride coloring her voice as she flourished each vial. "Sealed, settled, and ready for consumption. And done in record time, if I do say so myself."

"Thank Fate," I breathed, standing and taking a vial in each hand. Then my relief crumbled, and I looked at Ariel with a frown. "How am I going to take these with me? I project my clothes and other small objects with me when I physically jump back in time, but I'm not sure I take anything physical with me when I make the return trip."

"Well, now, that is a problem," Ariel conceded, wrinkles gathering into a thoughtful expression. Then, her sharp eyes met mine, and she gave me a grin. "No, actually, I don't think it is. Come on, I think we need to take a quick trip to Angelus Quietum."

Chapter 28

The Fear of Time

The world bled and spun around me, but this return jump was much more controlled than my last one. I settled into my own flesh on the bed beside James with a strange wave of cool wind. With a gasp, I sat straight up on the bed, all the aches and pains from earlier in that dreadful day coming back with an angry vengeance. If it meant I was back in time to save James and Dad, I would embrace every bruise.

"Gracie?" Liam's voice came from my left, and I turned toward him, my vision obscured by several red curls. The room still felt slightly unstable, its familiar white walls distorting as my head swam. How long was I gone? Judging by how distraught my lover looked as he sat in a small wooden chair next to James' side of the bed, it had been long enough. "Tell me you have it."

The room finished settling around me as I nodded. "Yes," I said, a bit breathless. The relief on Liam's face was worth the rough time jumps. "Yes, I got it. It's just in the other room."

"The other room?" My boyfriend sounded confused, but I'd already shifted my attention to James. Our young diplomat was downright gray, and it took quite a bit longer than I thought it should before I saw his chest rise. The source of Liam's distress was suddenly very clear. Without taking the time to explain, I climbed off the bed. "How did you manage that?"

"Ariel and I hid it in her time," I said, already halfway across the room. My heart was pounding, and it was all I could do to keep myself from saying the words aloud. However, I couldn't prevent my mind from repeating the mantra that seemed to have moved into my brain in the last three days I'd spent with Ariel.

Please don't let me be too late. Please, please, please, let me have time to save both of them.

"Find a vein," I called back to Liam as I picked up speed, all but running by the time I hit the hallway. "He's too sick to take it by mouth, so Ariel sent me with a syringe. We'll save time if you already have a tourniquet tied by the time I get back. He's so dehydrated that's the only way we'll be able to find one."

Liam followed me to the bedroom door, looking slightly bewildered. Once I gave him instructions, however, he seemed to shake himself and get a sense of purpose.

"Okay." I heard his agreement echo down the hallway as I darted into my childhood bedroom and rushed to the closet. "I can do that."

My old mirror reflected back my image, and I caught sight of a terrified woman with wide, blue eyes before I flung the door open. The silent dark of my walk-in greeted me, and I tried to take a deeper breath as I shoved the clothes out of the way to reach the very back wall.

"Sweet Fate, please," I breathed, running my fingers along the edges of the little trick board Ariel and I had installed in the wood paneling. We'd made the fit tight, since we couldn't risk Dad stumbling across it, and a century's worth of grime made the wood stick to itself. Even so, I finally managed to get my fingernails around the barely visible edges. With one last pull, the board came off in my hand.

"Thank you," I gasped and snatched up the contents of our little time capsule. With fingers gone clumsy with haste, I tucked the ancient memory pad into a back pocket before grabbing the vials and syringes, one of which I uncapped with my teeth as I all but flew back down the hallway.

"He's ready," Liam said as I nearly ran into him on my way to James' side. I glanced down at his handiwork and nodded, shoving the vial into his hand.

"Open that," I hissed, fingers already exploring the pale blue veins a strip of torn cloth had made firmer and more apparent on James' uninjured forearm. His flesh was far too cool in my grasp as I picked up his hand and put it in my lap. My friend didn't stir in the least, his eyes closed and his breathing shallow as I waited for Liam to figure out the vial. "Come on, hurry up," I snapped at my partner.

"Tell me you're not going to waste that on a diplomat."

My insides froze at the sound of Evan's voice. My flames leaped into my chest, adrenaline making my head spin again as I stared, wide-eyed, from James' still form to meet the angry, incandescent gaze of Riland's head of watch.

Evan looked different than the last time I'd seen him. His features were smoother and just a little more even; as if the artist who sculpted his face had gone back and touched up the angles of his jaw, nose, and cheekbones to make them just a bit more... right. The muddy brown of his eyes was now a glowing amber that swirled with golden sparks, and his dark hair had deepened to something approaching my father's saturated midnight locks. Even so, his thick, mortal build remained unchanged, making Vanessa look ephemeral and slight as she stood at his shoulder.

"You got what you wanted, Evan, now go run your fucking war," Liam growled. "Let us deal with the mess you left behind in peace."

"Fucking Usuriel parasites," Evan grumbled, shaking his head at my partner as he stepped closer to the bed. "You're all arrogant assholes. Honestly, how do you survive being around each other without constantly blowing things up?" He waved his own question away with one hand. "Forget it. I've come for Gracie, not you or your pet Terran. I suggest you keep your mouth shut and stay out of the way before I decide you're too dangerous to ship off to New Paradise."

"Liam's Overwatch. He's part of the deal," Vanessa

hissed, blue eye flashing in Evan's direction.

"The deal isn't official until my troops have an unlimited supply of immortality elixir," he snapped, not even bothering to turn towards her as he spoke.

"That wasn't what we discussed!" Vanessa was pissed. "You said you'd disable the weapon and allow the rest of the Family, including surviving Overwatch, to leave peacefully for New Paradise if I delivered Gracie." With a gesture, my cousin indicated me. "Well, here she is. I knew she wouldn't be far from her shadows, and I was right. Now give me the disarming codes, and let me, Liam, and the Terran boy leave in peace."

"Fuck, 'Nessa, why didn't you just snap his scrawny neck when you had the chance?" Liam hissed, eyes flashing. Even so, I could see his fingers working to wiggle the cork out of the vial. It seemed sitting for a century had given it a tight fit.

"Don't think I haven't been tempted," Vanessa snarled, her teeth bared in frustration as she glanced at the head of Riland watch. "But unfortunately, he and Garret Stafford are both biologically keyed into the explosive in New Paradise. If either one of them dies, the other is the only person who can call it off and then it's a very short window. So unless you think you can convince Senator Stafford to be merciful right after we've murdered his right-hand man, I think we ought to restrain ourselves."

"See, little shadow? I'm not nearly as stupid as you think I am." Evan's voice dripped with condescension. "Now, give me that vial, and step away from the blood donor."

I hadn't heard anyone call James and Liam my shadows before, but I didn't object to the characterization. However, by now I'd recovered from my shock at their unexpected entrance, and I'd already decided that whatever the head of Riland watch wanted was less important than getting the elixir into Dad and James' veins as fast as humanly possible. Pulling the second syringe out of my pocket, I pressed it into Liam's hand.

"Get that vial to Dad," I hissed at him under my breath. "I have another for James. Go. Now."

"Oh no, you don't," Evan snapped and suddenly the weight of his psi slammed into me, making the air syrupy-thick and hard to breathe. "No one goes anywhere with my elixir!"

"*Your* elixir?" I snarled through clenched teeth, giving him a savage glare that slid a burst of flame around my shoulders. "Do you have any idea what I've gone through to get this stuff after you wasted the first dose?" Another burst of fire surged around me, but I was too angry to clamp down on it. I felt more than saw Liam take a cautious step back.

"Yes, mine," he growled, amber eyes drowning in golden psi even as the weight of his uncontrolled Awareness continued to grow, making my chest ache. "Just like you. Now, unless you want me to scour every damn scrap of Usuriel DNA besides your own off of the face of the fucking planet, I suggest you come quietly."

"I don't know what kind of lies my cousin has been feeding you, but I'm not going anywhere with you," I said, meeting his burning gaze without fear. I was Gabriel's daughter, after all. I'd been dealing with people who could snap my neck with a thought since I was six. Despite the obvious strength of Evan's newly-made psi, I doubted he had the control it would take to get past Liam, Vanessa, and I together. I wasn't intimidated by his theatrics. He might be able to stop Liam's teleport, but I was pretty confident that my flames would be unaffected by his mental block. Once James was stable, I'd get the other vial to Dad if I had to fly it to the core myself. "Now, let me get this elixir into Dad and James. After that, we can have a conversation about your request for my blood. Until then, however, I suggest you sit down and shut up. Liam?" I turned to look at my partner and held out a hand. "Would you please finish getting that vial open?"

The blow connected with the back of my head so suddenly I didn't have a chance to duck. I pitched forward, catching myself on James' legs as pain shot through my skull and bright lights exploded in front of my eyes. I gasped, completely blindsided, then Evan's hand grabbed me by the back of my hair and wrenched my neck up so that I was forced to look at him.

"I don't think you understand who you're talking to, you little cunt." His voice was so deadly calm. "You're mine. Bought and paid for. Now hand over that vial, or I will start my purge of Usuriels with your pretty boy here."

I should have been afraid. That piece of my brain that was normal, sane, and halfway mortal told me that this man was dangerous and most likely going to kill me if I made a false move. Yesterday, I probably would have listened to that calm, sensible voice of self-preservation inside my head. But today, I was too far past my limits and suddenly, my father's wonderful Usuriel temper didn't care what condition I was in at the end of the confrontation. For that split second, the only thing I cared about was that Evan was the one who had hurt James; the one who had prolonged my father's suffering; the one who seemed to keep getting in the way at just the moment I was about to get the spinning wreck my life had become back on track. In that moment, fury took over and — for the first time in my life — I truly lost control of the flames.

With a wordless cry they rose, blasting up and outward with a force that bowed my spine. They boiled up and over my skin — a scalding wave that enveloped my flesh but didn't consume it — before slamming into Evan so hard it actually took him off of his feet. If he hadn't reflexively put up a psi shield, I have no doubt I would have incinerated him on the spot. As it was, I didn't just slam him into the wall. No, I sent him fully through it with such an inferno of orange and red that the crater of drywall and insulation he came to rest in was still smoldering as I slid to my feet. My vision was wreathed in flame as I advanced on the Riland watchman, my head nothing but a screaming pit of rage and fire.

"Gracie, don't!" Vanessa's voice just barely penetrated my red haze. I ignored her.

The look on Evan's face as he stared up at me said that his death was written in my gaze. For all of his new found powers, I was a fully trained member of the Overwatch and one of the most powerful third-gens ever born. He was right to cower before me, because there was no mercy left in that churning maelstrom he'd unleashed.

Liam's scream, on the other hand, stopped me in my tracks.

I turned, my red curls blending with the flames as they tossed about my head. If I lived another thousand years, I would never forget that turn.

It was horrible for two reasons.

The first was that, as my gaze passed over the bed, I realized that this distraction had already cost me half of my heart.

James.

I was there when he took his first breath.

I was there when he took his last.

I didn't see it. It wasn't a gasping or dramatic scene. No, he'd slipped down into death so silently I hadn't even realized it happened until that glance told me I was too late.

There's something distinctive about death. Perhaps it's a particular pallor, or the way the eyelids relax just a touch and let still, sightless eyes gaze up at nothingness. I'm not an empath or telepath of any kind, but I knew James the way I knew few other people. All it took was that glance to know that he was gone.

For a moment, I wasn't sure if I was still breathing. The whole world seemed to pause, crystallize, squeeze in on my chest as if my own heart wanted to stop beating along with his.

Then Liam gave another wordless cry, and I finished the turn, my vision coming to where Vanessa had teleported to my lover's side. Her hand was on his shoulder, and I could see the blue blaze of her power wrapping around his body like contained lightning. He'd fallen to his knees, one hand still gripping the vial while the other clenched hard on his chest.

"Don't make me do this, Gracie." Vanessa's voice was low and full of regret. "Step away from Evan or I'll overload your partner. He's a Gabriellan male; it doesn't take as much to put them into heart failure as the rest of us. I don't want to, but if it is between one seventeenth-gen and the entire Family... I will kill him."

I shook my head, tears blurring my vision as I looked between Evan and Vanessa. The head of Riland watch wasn't trying to get up from where I'd tossed him. Rather, he pressed a hand to his side and watched me with wary, calculating eyes.

Vanessa, on the other hand, looked quite serious about her threat to overload Liam. Her good eye met mine steadily, genuine fear and anguish in her face.

"I can't give Evan the elixir," I murmured, my voice echoing and faint in the rushing roar of my flames. "I know you don't believe me, but Dad's death really is going to unmake the entire Gabriellan line. Liam's just as dead if I give up to Evan." I held her gaze and saw the utter grief in her ice-blue eye.

"Better the Gabriellan line than all of us." My cousin's voice wavered, as if even her iron discipline was struggling with this sacrifice.

I shook my head, my gaze straying back to James' body. The tiny sliver of his sweet, gentle blue eyes that had slid open in the relaxation of death reflected the flickering light of my flames as they stared emptily at the smooth, white ceiling.

"You don't understand," I said. "Gloria herself said Gabriel's disappearance would unmake the colony. Without him, there would be no *Inspiration*. No Adora or Adoran line. No Terrans. All of Cybele, gone in the blink of an eye."

Her hand slid from Liam's shoulder, and he took a gasping breath, falling to all fours. My heart was so numb and full of grief that it hardly reacted to the fact that he wasn't in immediate danger anymore. I watched my lover recover with an oddly detached sense of relief.

"If that's truly the case," Vanessa said slowly, drawing my attention back to her, "then we're all dead either way. The whole Family... gone."

A flicker of light just a touch brighter than the dancing flames already sparking along the edge of my vision caught my gaze. Feeling as if I were in a dream, I knew before I turned exactly what I was going to see.

Standing beside my father's dark wooden wardrobe was his first wife. Olivia stood, clothed in the traditional colonial ship suit, her auburn curls tossing about her slim shoulders in that same ethereal wind that all my ghosts brought with them. She looked young and vibrant, her freckles the only blemishes on her milk-white skin. On either side, her children flanked her; Ariel, Harold, and Drexil on her right, and the two other Usuriels I'd seen in the strange time warp here at Angelus Quietum on her left. The girl's green eyes couldn't have come from anywhere else but Liv, I thought, and the boy was such an echo of Dad there couldn't be any doubt about paternity.

"No, not the whole Family," I murmured, looking into Olivia's fierce, intelligent gaze. Fates, there was alloy in that woman's face. She'd never met my eye before, I realized, for all the times I'd seen her. This was the first time she'd ever acknowledged my presence. There could be no doubt that I had her undivided attention, however. I felt a rush of existential dread as a golden spark of psi caught in her eyes. "Just me and Lilly."

"Wait... what?" Liam sounded like he was figuring things out first. I spared him a glance and saw the utter anguish on his face as he processed what I'd just said. Vanessa's expression was mostly confusion, but that didn't matter. She didn't have to understand.

"What the hell is going on?" Evan had his feet back under himself, pain as well as temper in his voice. "Vanessa, burn him out! Teach her she can't just throw a temper tantrum and expect to get what she wants! Fucking toddlers, the lot of you!"

I ignored him and took a step towards Olivia. It brought me closer to the foot of the bed where Liam was also getting to his feet. One hand still pressed to the center of his chest as if there were still some lingering twinges, but his expression was more worried than pained.

"Gracie," he breathed, "what do you see?"

I took another step, and it brought me directly in front of my lover. Vanessa was only a hand's breadth behind him, but her slight frame was completely blocked from my view by his broad shoulders. For a moment, I looked up into his face, and it was as if we were alone.

"Don't worry, love," I said softly, touching his face

gently. "Afterwards, you won't even remember me."

"No." For a moment I regretted the fact that he understood my nature enough to grasp what was about to happen. This was the only grief my end would ever get, however, and I clung to the horror in Liam's eyes as proof that I'd somehow made a difference in this life. "No, Gracie, you can't. There has to be another way, a different time you could jump to, some way to undo all this without erasing you completely."

"Maybe there is," I agreed, "but I've run out of time to find it. Dad's not going to last much longer, and I can't risk being wrong again. Once we're erased, it's for good. Some things, once they're done, can't go back to the way they were before."

I took his face the rest of the way into my hands and, before fear of the unknown nothingness ahead of me and regret for the future we'd never have together could overwhelm me, I pulled him down for one last kiss. Liam leaned into me, as if he wanted to put two hundred years of love, passion, and companionship into that one press of lips. Tears burned my eyes as I pulled away, and I couldn't look into his face afterwards. But I did slide my hand into his and take the second vial back, tucking it beside the other one in my pocket.

"Bitch, you are useless. I guess I have to do everything myself."

I felt Evan's psi pick up again, blazing hot pressure against my skin.

"Don't worry about him, Gracie," Liam said softly and against my better judgment, I dared a glance at his face. There were tears streaking down his cheeks, but his eyes were calm and determined. "Nessa and I will take care of that stinking sack of shit."

"I..."

"I know. Me, too." The sorrow in his gaze put my father's to shame. "Go save the Family."

I did as he said.

Olivia was only a single step away now, her glowing hand outstretched gracefully. There was serenity in her expression as her green eyes met mine; as if she had all the time in the universe to wait for me. Perhaps on her side of reality, she did.

There was an explosion behind me, and the psi in the air suddenly increased to a crushing weight. I dared a last look over my shoulder and was greeted by a maelstrom of swirling blue and gold that quite literally tore the ceiling and walls apart into fragments of floating debris. Liam and Vanessa were blue torches, their power surging over their flesh like a second skin. Evan lashed out at their controlled auras with the raw, savage, unfiltered strength of an untrained elder child. Arcs of gold electric-like psi burst and snapped along the smooth edges of Liam and Vanessa's shields. Just as I turned back to Olivia, I caught a glimpse of a tongue of gold shattering Liam's shield and sending him to the ground.

I didn't wait to watch more. With one last, quick glance at where James lay still on the bed, I swallowed hard and slid my hand into Olivia's.

Her flesh felt like a warm wind under mine. I met her emerald gaze and nodded.

"I'm ready."

Like Ariel had so many times before, Olivia poured herself into me. She smelled like old books and hot tea as she rushed over my body in a warm wave.

She said nothing as her mind slid over mine, but I felt her love for Dad and her children clearly; deep as the oceans and bright as the sun. I tried to let that feeling comfort me as the image of a gently curved, alloy-walled hospital room flooded my mind.

Then, I pulled on my flames one last time.

Epilogue

Dear Dad

That is how I came to be a girl almost three hundred and fifty years out of time, sitting in the Med Bay of the *Inspiration* watching my father sleep. He doesn't seem to be in too much pain, and for that I'm grateful, even though I know it's just a side effect of how far I am from the main event. Even three and a half centuries away, the black lines of Temporal Mortis still streak his chest and arms, radiating up from the unclosable wound in his side. The blankets and bandages cover that part of his torso, but I can see the streaks of poison across his shoulders and reaching dark fingers up into his neck.

Olivia is here, of course. She's asleep, too, her head pillowed on one arm next to his shoulder on the bed while the other hand rests in his. That's right, even with him deathly ill, they fell asleep holding hands. Fates, they're adorable. How much would most people give to have a relationship like that? The kind where someone knows all of your flaws, all of your secrets, all of your scars, and still loves you to the end of time and back?

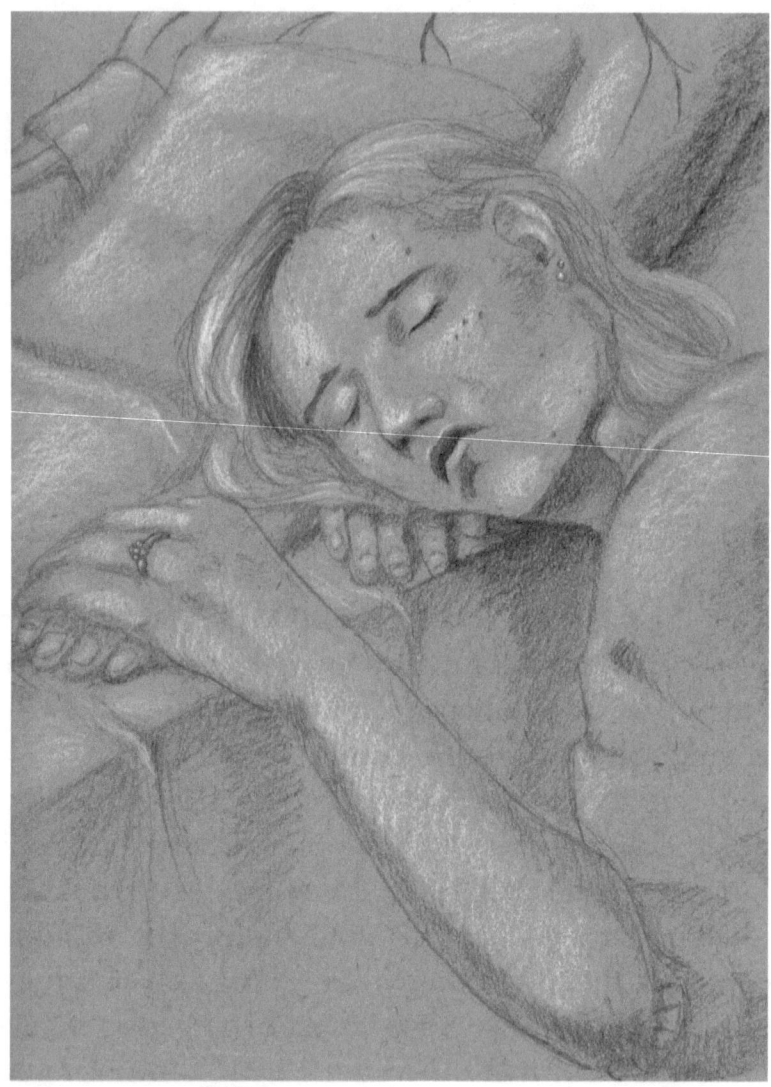

Now I'm just stalling.

So here I sit, finishing up this account of how I got here so that I can put off the inevitable. I came here for one thing. It's sitting in my pocket right now.

But I just can't bring myself to stop writing and wake Olivia up. I know that at some point I will. I'll give her the elixir and tell her what it does. I'll explain that if she loves my father and their future children, that she'll take it on the spot. I'll give her the other vial and tell her about Bryce; impress upon her the utmost importance of not allowing D'nay to make any more vampires. Without other vampires, there would have been no Riland Massacre; no White Woman. Fate knows what mischief Adora will get up to anyway, but at least her story won't end there with a poisoned bottle of wine and the near-death of my father's sanity.

And I'll give her this.

I'm kind of hoping this memory pad will be my bite mark, if you will, the splattered blood across my clothes after Grayson. I'm hoping it will be a little tiny ripple in time that lets people see a future that could have been and maybe encourage a few of them to make some different choices.

I started this account by asking a question, you see. Who is Gabriel Usuriel? I have a few answers.

A farmer. A drug addict. A pilot. A psychic divine emissary. A suicidal patron saint.

But those aren't the ones that matter. Here are the ones that do.

The man who put himself in danger by psi-piloting ships past light speed to keep his shipmates safe.

The man who put his life on hold to fix a failing dam and then rebuild an entire community after the flood.

The man who spent over twenty-four hours as close to his mother's agony as he could bring himself to shield the rest of the Family from her pain.

The man who, after fifty years of addiction, swallowed his pride and went to his mother for help getting clean when he found out he had a little girl who needed him. And then he stayed clean and mostly sober for over a decade so he could raise her in the peace and quiet she deserved.

D'nay and Gloria's son. Olivia's husband. Ariel's father. Adora's brother.

My Dad.

That's the man I choose to think you are, Dad. That's the man I choose to think will shine through once you read this and have Olivia at your side. I won't get to know that man, in all likelihood, but I have faith that he'll make Cybele a better place.

I'm not sure what will happen when Olivia takes this elixir. In fact, I'm pretty sure no one really knows. Ariel had her kind, gentle answers, but I've seen the reality of the world too many times to believe in happy endings anymore. My optimism died with a handsome, young diplomat whose only infraction was being my friend. I'm a fate, after all, and my instincts tell me that I will be following Grayson into non-existence. So be it. It was my doubt, my mistake, my blind temper that got us here. If my unmaking redeems me, I will embrace it.

Gabriel is starting to stir, and I think I need to stop writing and give Olivia the vials. I'm not sure how to end this, though, so I guess I'll end it the way my father always did his letters to me in school.

Good luck. Be safe. I love you.

Your Daughter,

Gracie

Glossary

Angel's Foot - a drug made from the spores of specific mushrooms native to Cybele. Use and exposure can lead to lung rot, a degenerative respiratory disease that is fatal without prompt treatment.

Angelus Quietum - Gabriel's farm on the banks of Lake Angelus, in the foothills of the Galloway Mountains situated halfway between Skykyle and Landing.

Awareness - A slang term for any individual outside of the mortal norm, usually with some kind of psychic powers.

Cambria - a species of giant, house-sized mushrooms that populated Cybele before the terraforming.

Cybele - The colony world settled by the Usuriels and their moral crewmates approximately two hundred and seventy years before Gracie's birth.

Death's Head - a species of fungus that populated Cybele before the terraforming. Their spores can cause a range of respiratory issues, from shortness of breath to asphyxiation and death.

Divinitas - A group of religious extremists who believe the Usuriel Family are actually divine emissaries that have come to lead mankind in the correct direction.

Firebird - a slang term for a pyrokinetic, someone who can conjure or control fire.

Hal - a large, tropical island south of the main continent on Cybele. It was named for Gabriel's son, Harold, who died along with his husband, Sam, in a shuttle accident shortly after landing.

Heart Ship - the original psychic drive of the generation ship, *Inspiration*. The heart ship was designed to allow Gloria to merge with the four main engines and achieve faster-than-light travel. Gabriel's one and only attempt resulted in a near-fatal injury that later required his heart's replacement, while Adora eventually took over the majority of Gloria's shifts in the heart ship.

Holo - a three-dimensional projection of light that can move and be set to synchronized sound.

Inspiration - The generation ship that brought the colonists from Earth to Cybele around the year 100 AT (after takeoff).

Landing - Also known as Inspiration Landing. This is the original settlement where the colonists landed from the *Inspiration* and began terraforming Cybele. This is also the location of Landing Hospital and University—the most advanced and only major such institutions on Cybele.

New Terra - a mostly-frozen northern continent of Cybele, inhabited by the Terran people.

Overwatch - the psychic police force run by the Family.

'Porter - an individual who can teleport.

Provinces (the) – a group of self-governing territories with a loose central government located on the main continent of Cybele. Skykyle, Landing, and Riland are all Provinces.

Psi - a shortening of 'psychic,' this refers to any power or ability wielded by an individual of awareness. It is often used to describe the energy generated by such powers as well. The amount of psi energy an individual has at their disposal is influenced by the individual's innate strength, their physical health, and their access to resources such as food, water, and sleep.

Psi-pilot - The term for a less-power-intensive psychic interface than the heart ship. The original psi-pilot replaced a damaged organic relay on the *Inspiration*'s main bridge. This allowed two telepathic and telekinetic individuals to merge with the engines at once, creating a solution that was actually better than the original. Later, smaller shuttles and the mining craft were also fitted with psi-piloting interfaces that allowed them to achieve faster-than-light speeds.

Pyrokinesis - the psychic ability to conjure or control fire. Shortenings include "pyro" and "firebird."

Riland - a province and city on the main continent of Cybele. It is home to the largest vampire population and was the location of the White Woman Massacre.

Skykyle - a province and city on the main continent of Cybele. It is the most densely populated city on Cybele and is the location of Gloria and D'nay's Landing Day party.

Spore-bent - slang for "angry" or "upset." Taken from Angel's Foot addicts who are looking for a fix.

Stella - The main AI of the generation ship, *Inspiration*. She was later fully integrated with several libraries and databases on Cybele, including the Landing University library, and Overwatch's mainframe.

Telekinesis - the psychic ability to move objects with one's mind.

Telepathy - the psychic ability to read thoughts. Almost all telepaths are also empathic, which is the ability to read emotions, with the notable exception of Adora Usuriel.

Teleportation - the psychic ability to transport objects and people from one place to another with one's mind. Also known as "'porting."

Terran - the Terrans were another space faring group from Earth. Originally a group of researchers, the radiation created by their vessels' faster-than-light drives proved to be disastrous to their health. This prompted advanced medical research, including the technology to replace organic organs with inorganic parts. Now settled in New Terra, Terrans use robotic "avatars" to interact with the world while keeping their flesh bodies safely cocooned in nutrient tanks. Avatar technology is outlawed in the Provinces on the mainland of Cybele, including Riland, Landing, and Skykyle, which forces Terran diplomats and visitors to abandon their avatars and interact "in the flesh."

Three-T - a psychic individual who has all three of the big "T" abilities - telepathy, telekinesis, and teleportation.

University - the largest institution of higher learning on Cybele. It is located at Inspiration Landing. Also known as Landing University.

Usuriel - the surname of most psychic individuals on Cybele, also known as the Family. The Usuriel Family consists of all individuals who are descended from the bloodline of D'nay and Gloria Usuriel. Once someone marries an Usuriel, they adopt that surname, regardless of gender. All blood descendants of D'nay and Gloria possess some amount of Awareness, though the type and strength of their psychic powers varies widely.

Vampire - an individual infected with a blood-borne curse, usually transmitted by drinking the blood of someone who is also infected. Blood to blood contact can also transmit the curse. Individuals with vampirism enter a dormant state during the day in which they are indistinguishable from a freshly-dead corpse. Exposure to sunlight will cause intense, painful burns and is often fatal if exposure is prolonged.

Vampires can only gain nourishment by feeding on the blood of the uninfected. However, many of these traits and attributes are altered when a vampire consumes the blood of an Usuriel.

ABOUT THE AUTHOR

Abigail Silver grew up in Pennsylvania and currently lives near Charlotte, NC with her husband, son, and fur children. When she's not reading, writing, or drawing (which is rare), she enjoys blasting music with the windows down on long road trips.

ACKNOWLEDGMENTS

Before I go any farther, I feel I owe you, dear reader, an apology.

I'm sorry.

This trilogy started out with such child-like wonder and gentle, family relationships. Then, as Gracie grew, her problems grew with her until, at the end of Visions of Fire, we glimpsed the brutality that lurked in her blood.

And now, here in this final volume, we have seen the devastation that is the end result of so many mistakes, not least of which were made by Gabriel and Gracie themselves.

I once made the mistake of setting this book on the shelf for over a year and then picking it back up, when my brain had forgotten a little bit of its trauma. After I finished, I felt a bit like I'd been hit by an emotional truck of my own making. So, if I've injured you or made you weep, I do apologize.

But if you've come out the other side with questions, replaying the death spiral of those last fateful days in your head and thinking 'if only they would have!' And perhaps, in a secret corner of your brain, a small voice whispers that this was a rather beautiful final storm, and my, wouldn't it be nice to write or paint or in general create one of your own that crushes the heart and brings forth the same exquisite agony?

If so, my friend, congratulations.

You've figure out the point of it.

If you do feel inspired to create in some way, I would love to see the results. My email is always open at abigailsilverwriting@gmail.com.

Or you can write and complain about the brutal ending. Either way, I appreciate fan mail.

So now, on to the people who made this project possible.

First and always to my family, especially my parents and brother for being my forever support. To my mother for her excitement when I told her I was going to illustrate this trilogy, and then for faithfully reading each installment, even though sci-fi and fantasy are not really her thing. To my father for our deep conversations about the history of things, the many angles that politics offers us, and a willingness to apply logic in any situation. My brother for late night chats, genuine enthusiasm for audio book recording (perhaps that will be next?) and fantastic reading recommendations. To all of you, thank you for being the rock that I grew from and that continues to be a source of comfort, peace, and stability in a chaotic world.

To my loving husband and our brilliant, mischievous little boy, I cannot thank you enough for making space for my creative process. You understand that it is part of who I am and love me that way. There can be no higher accolade than being your wife and mom.

I am incredibly lucky to also have a family of writing who has gathered around me and supported me over the years. I would certainly not be where I am without them. The first on this list must always be my editor, Harlow Kelly. She is such an integral part of the Usuriel Multiverse that I can't imagine what it would be without her. From endless discussions of logistics to micro-analysis of character motivation, she is truly the kind of sounding board that is utterly irreplaceable. I am humbly in her debt and so privileged to call her my friend.

The other beta readers and critique partners on this journey were no less critical. I could not have made this journey without them. They include J.A. Waters, Jordie Nichols, Jessica Ritchey, Jessica Blasko, Rachel Greene-Phillips, Theresa Gonzalez, Ann Darlington, George Beckman, Marisa S, Paula Braley, Rebecca Amiss, Ernie Fink, Ellie Lieberman, Jesse Hindman, CD Storiz, and so many others. For those who were with me for one novel or many, for those of you who chatted about plot lines and characters in person or over the phone or in text messages, for those who only made it a little way into a piece before giving me critical feedback about why you chose not to go on, please know that all of you contributed to a better piece of writing. I owe you tremendous debts of gratitude.

To the teachers who have inspired my love of art and writing, this trilogy would never have been possible without you. I stand on the shoulders of your wisdom, caring, and knowledge. Thank you for the time and effort you put into me so that I could pass it on to others.

I would also like to acknowledge the source imagery for some of my illustrations. I started with very specific visions of many of these characters and scenes, but every good artist needs reference material to help that vision stay true to life. So, thank you to Joe Garland (layout guru) and the following photographers on UnSplash.com:

Emmanuel Ikwuegbu, Christopher Campbell, Sophie Grieve-Williams, Sean Foster, Alexander Krivitskiy, Amanda Ware, and Valdemars Magone. Also a posthumous thank you to Dante Gabriel Rossetti, whose work inspired the cover art of both Book 1 and Book 3 in this trilogy.

And finally, to you, my dear reader. Thank you for going on this journey with Gracie, even though she told you from the start that it would end in disaster. It is a peculiar trait of our species, that we can engage in telepathy by writing things on a scrap of paper and handing it to another human, and thereby mourn for people who were never even alive to begin with. Thank you for bringing Gracie to life with each page you turned. Without you, she truly would fade into the nothingness of imaginings, memories, and dreams.

With eternal gratitude,

Abigail Silver